THE
PIRATE'S CURSE

Weight of Souls

Toni Runkle & Steve Webb

Black Rose Writing | Texas

ISBN: 978-1-68513-635-2
PUBLISHED BY BLACK ROSE WRITING
www.blackrosewriting.com

Printed in the United States of America
Suggested Retail Price (SRP) $24.95

The Pirate's Curse: Weight of Souls is printed in Baskerville

*As a planet-friendly publisher, Black Rose Writing does its best to eliminate unnecessary waste to reduce paper usage and energy costs, while never compromising the reading experience. As a result, the final word count vs. page count may not meet common expectations.

Praise for
The Pirate's Curse Series

Book One of the *Pirate's Curse Trilogy, Brigands of the Compass Rose,* was named the 2024 Best Independent Book Award winner for YA/Tween novel and was a 2024 American Writing Awards Finalist in both Fiction Fantasy and Fiction YA categories

"In *Weight of Souls,* the authors deliver a treasure chest's worth of page-turning action and adventure that will keep readers locked in... YA readers will relish this lively fantasy undertaking."

—Booklife

"A thrilling, emotional roller coaster of an adventure. I was hooked from the first page to the last. It's *Treasure Island* meets *The Outsiders* in a grand adventure not to be missed!"

—Haris Orkin, award-winning author of the
James Flynn Escapades

"A non-stop adventure of self-discovery and danger, *The Pirate's Curse* delivers on everything it promises and more. Hop on board and hold on tight!"

—Douglas Green, author of *A Dog of Many Names* and
The Teachings of Shirelle

"A tale of teens training to battle against a menacing supernatural threat? Sign me up! Action, adventure, and heart. *The Pirate's Curse* has it all! This is one boat ride you'll never forget (if you survive, that is)!"

—Kevin D. Ross, ACE. Emmy-nominated editor of
Stranger Things and *Yellowjackets*

THE
PIRATE'S CURSE

Weight of Souls

To my husband Randy,
whose love gave me the faith to become a mother.
And to my daughter Julia,
who every day reveals to me the joy of being one.
— Toni

To my mother Kathy,
who instilled the love of reading in me,
and then didn't recoil in horror
when I told her I wanted to be a writer.
— Steve

Chapter 1
The Dreams Return

Bonnie Hartwright stood in the surf, water up to her knees, basking in the warm rays of the sun. She blinked at the fractured sparkles of sunlight that reflected on the calm waters of the ocean. A soft breeze caressed her cheeks and she felt at peace.

SUDDENLY something broke the glass-smooth surface of the sea and just as quickly disappeared. A fin! A dolphin, perhaps? Bonnie squinted as she scanned the water, looking for it. When it reappeared, her heart jumped. It was huge. No dolphin at all, it was a shark and was coming straight for her!

"Run!" That familiar voice again.

Bonnie turned and slogged through the surf toward the beach. She knew she had to get to the sand before "it" got to her.

Reaching the shore, she kept running, glancing back just in time to see the shark propel itself from the water and then transform as it landed on the beach—into an enormous wolf. Black and snarling, spitting rabid foam from its powerful jaws! Bonnie ran harder. Before her at the edge of a dune, she saw a thicket of trees. She threw herself over the dune and rolled into the woods.

Everything turned STILL and COLD and DARK. As if night had fallen in an instant.

Bonnie's eyes adjusted to the darkness; she stood and found herself amid towering pine trees. She gulped for air—her breath coming out in puffs of white mist as snow fell around her. She was confused. She'd never seen snow before. What was she doing here?

She listened for the wolf, but the forest was silent. She saw a FLICKER of yellow light coming from up ahead and moved toward it, not noticing that as she walked, she left no footprints in the snow.

Ahead in a clearing was a rustic cabin, smoke billowing from its chimney.

She was drawn to the side window from which the light emanated and peered through a crack in the curtains. It was a bedroom, a small fire crackling in the fireplace. In the bed under the window, she saw the figure of an older man with salt-and-pepper hair. She watched with odd fascination as he breathed steadily—a tranquil look on his face.

"The sleep of a light soul." The thought jumped into her head, surprising her with its strangeness.

Then the man shifted, revealing, on the side of his neck, a birthmark! Not just any birthmark, but the Stain of Musangu. Like hers! He was marked for death just as she was!

Fear gripped Bonnie. She wasn't supposed to be here. Wherever here was. This was wrong. She needed to get away.

She turned to run but was stopped by a rustling from the woods. She quickly ducked behind some shrubbery; as she did, a branch SCRAPED hard across her cheek. She stifled a yelp as the wolf moved past her to the front of the cabin. It leapt onto the porch and she watched in shock as it now took the form of a man—tall, wiry, intimidating—though in the darkness Bonnie could not make out his features.

A blinding panic shot through her. Bonnie had to warn the sleeping man! She BANGED on the bedroom window. YELLED for him to wake up! But he only continued his peaceful slumber.

SUDDENLY, a CRASH from the front of the cabin. SHOUTS! Sounds of a scuffle. The man bolted upright as the bedroom door BURST OPEN!

A ponytailed man in a billowy shirt backed into the bedroom, sword held high as he fended off TWO DANGEROUS-LOOKING ATTACKERS. Pirates, from the looks of them.

It was a fierce battle, but the ponytailed man quickly disarmed the marauders and dispatched them both. From the tattoo on his wrist, Bonnie could see this man was a fellow Brigand of the Compass Rose.

A flood of relief washed over Bonnie as the Brigand helped the cowering marked one to his feet. But her relief quickly gave way to horror.

THWUCK! The point of a cutlass appeared through the midsection of the Brigand's abdomen. Blood spread slowly across his shirt. His shocked face mirrored that of the marked man. Then the Brigand collapsed onto the bed revealing...

A fierce-looking man with dark hair and matching goatee. The man from the porch! The calico print of his shirt confirmed what Bonnie already feared: that the shark and the wolf and this man were all the same being. That they were all...

CALICO JACK RACKHAM!

"You have been a difficult one to track down," Rackham growled at the marked man. "Normally, I would revel in your agony, but you've already wasted enough of MY time."

"Nearly all of it!" The old man laughed, surprising the pirate, who could only stare at him, puzzled. "You fool! Look at me!" He held a lamp up to his emaciated face. "Cancer found me long before you did! I've but days left!" He laughed again, his chuckles breaking into deep, heaving coughs.

"AHHH!" Enraged, Calico Jack dragged the man into an adjoining bathroom. Bonnie watched in horror as Jack shoved the man's face into a brass tub still full of water from the night's bath. The man struggled desperately but was no match against the powerful pirate.

Bonnie SCREAMED and SCREAMED and POUNDED and POUNDED. She ran around the house, desperately trying to gain entry, but no door or window would yield.

She returned to the bedroom window in time to witness the marked man fall lifeless to the floor, eyes frozen in death.

Jack bared his wolf-like fangs, foam dripping from his mouth. Rabies-infested spittle fell onto the hourglass ring on his finger as he raised it to admire. Bonnie watched with fascination as a few grains of sand defied gravity, moving upwards into the nearly filled hourglass. She froze as Jack drew a long knife, knelt, and began cutting the birthmark from the man's neck.

"NOOOOO!" Bonnie hit the window with such force that the glass CRACKED.

Calico Jack looked up, surprised. Bonnie jerked away, falling backward into the snow and—

BONNIE AWAKENED with a start, grabbing for her sword, Siobhan. She needed a moment to orient herself, blinking in the deep purple sky broken by rays of golden light. She discovered that she was nowhere near a cabin in the snowy mountains, but lying on the deck of the True North as the schooner bobbed, anchored in the peaceful waters of Cormac's Cove.

SQUAWK! Crossbones, Bonnie's feral parrot friend, fluttered over and perched beside her, cocking his head in concern.

"It's okay, boy. It was just a nightmare," she assured him, realizing she was safe—on the ship that had become her second home.

For months now, Bonnie had insisted on sleeping on the *True North* rather than in the onshore cabins with her fellow Brigands. No one knew what to make of it, really. They just assumed it was a part of her grieving process. She let them think that. After all, losing her father and discovering she was marked for death was enough to change anyone.

The truth was much more unsettling. Since the events of the past summer, something dark had been awakened within her.

Shivering in the January chill, Bonnie wrapped herself more tightly in the heavy quilt from her makeshift bed. But it wasn't the chilly Carolina morning that made her blood run cold. It was the nightmare. The first since...

Since before my father was murdered.

That thought made Bonnie shiver even harder. Crossbones moved to her and nuzzled her neck.

With the bird still on her shoulder, Bonnie got up, re-sheathed her sword, and took a deep, steadying breath, taking in the sunrise over the Atlantic from the pier at the Cove.

Cormac's Cove. The secluded compound had been her home for less than a year, yet it felt like a lifetime. She'd seen plenty in her 16 years—abandonment as a baby, a childhood spent bouncing through foster homes, run-ins with the criminal justice system. Those experiences had led her to believe she was strong enough to handle anything. But they hadn't prepared her for the world she encountered when she stepped through these gates, a world of magic and secret societies. And curses.

After all, it's not every day that this sort of thing happens. How many other girls discover they're descended from not one, but two pirate queens—Anne Bonny and Mary Read? And how many find out that this lineage marks them as human sacrifices in a 300-year-old pirate's quest for immortality?

It's a lot, to be quite honest.

Bonnie's fingertips brushed the raised birthmark on her shoulder blade, hidden beneath the tattoo of the Brigands of the Compass Rose—the secretive group that had plucked her out of juvey and changed her life forever. Though the tattoo masked the mark's appearance, she could still feel its rough texture lurking beneath the ink. A constant reminder of her fate.

The *Stain of Musangu.*

As her generation's bearer of the mark, she was condemned to death at the hands of Calico Jack Rackham. To escape the hangman's noose three centuries earlier, the notorious pirate had made a deal with certain dark forces: he could continue to live, but only by sacrificing his own descendants, drowning each marked one himself to pay the price.

Bonnie didn't know the victim in her dream—likely a marked one from a bygone era. It wouldn't be the first time she'd had such a nightmare. She once dreamed of Jack and Anne Bonny's son Seth, the first in the line to be cursed. That time, she had witnessed Jack viciously drown his own flesh and blood, stealing from him the only thing that mattered to the old pirate: time.

Bonnie wondered, as she often did, how much time she herself had left before Jack caught up to her and ripped the stain from her own flesh, adding the mark to his collection and Bonnie's years to his own life.

Setting her jaw, Bonnie pushed the thought away. She tugged on her boots, tucked her wild curls under a backward Pittsburgh Pirates cap, and vaulted gracefully over the ship's rail onto the pier. Sticking the landing like a gymnast, she set off on her daily ritual: a several-mile run around the perimeter of the Brigands' walled-in compound. As always, Crossbones flew alongside her, swooping through the trees as she covered her familiar route.

It had become an obsession with Bonnie, the running. Up hills, over sand dunes, through the surf, pushing herself to the point of exhaustion. Bonnie didn't know if she was running *from* something, or *to* it. Probably both.

When Bonnie wasn't running, she was practicing with her sword. She still flinched at the memory of being a second too slow to kill the pirate Maks after he murdered her father the previous summer. Her blade had been true, but her will had faltered. So instead of avenging her father's death, she could only watch helplessly as Maks disappeared into the dark waters, letting the ocean do what she should have done. It was a mistake she vowed never to make again.

It all made her feel more in control—the sensation of pushing her body to its limit. Already she was seeing results; her once skinny frame now taut with muscle, her reactions more cat-like by the day. *In preparation for the inevitable.*

Despite the Brigand promises of her protection, Bonnie couldn't shake the doubt that had seeped in. *Probably why I had that dream.* Still, if and when Calico Jack Rackham came for her years, she was determined not to give them up easily.

Bonnie came to the top of the hill, stopped by the little chapel there, and took a big gulp of her water as Crossbones fluttered wonkily onto a nearby rock.

"Tired, boy?" She poured some water into the top of her flask, and the bird drank it thirstily, its exhaustion mirroring her own.

Bonnie looked up at the sky. From the position of the sun, she knew that the others would be up and knew what that meant. She was late for morning training.

Again.

Chapter 2
Morning Routines

WHOOSH! CLANG! Bonnie whipped her sword through the air and came blade to blade with Luz Delgado. With Siobhan humming in harmony, she drove Luz back across the clearing between the cabins. Ever since Reed Ballister had taken control of the Brigands, he had instituted these pre-breakfast training sessions. And after what they had all been through, not one Brigand complained. Bonnie tried a move on Luz, but she parried the blow and drove her back with swing after swing.

"Wassup with you, *chica*?" Luz asked as she swung her sword. "You out of it today."

"Just make sure you keep those knees bent," Bonnie said as she defended the advance.

"You worry about your own butt!" Luz said with a laugh and pulled a move that Bonnie hadn't anticipated. And sure enough, Luz forcefully knocked Siobhan from Bonnie's hand, sending her sprawling to the ground.

Bonnie nodded in appreciation as Luz helped her up and tossed Siobhan back. Fierce, loyal, and streetwise, the former *chola* Luz had become one of the Brigands' best fighters and Bonnie's most ardent defender—a necessity in the fight ahead. Still, Bonnie hated being bested. It wasn't like her. *It's that stupid dream*. It was still niggling her.

The two combatants went over to the old Boreas cabin, where the rest of the crew was watching from the steps. Crossbones flew from the porch rail to perch on Bonnie's shoulder.

"Excellent moves, Delgado," said Zion Campbell, who had recently morphed into the Brigands' de facto trainer. "You're off your game today, Hartwright."

"Yeah, what's up, Hartwright?" Tanner Prescott snarked. "You were looking like a half-assed extra on one of my dad's movies."

Bonnie glared at him. Despite being a skilled sailor, Tanner would forever be the douchey, rich kid who could always get under her skin.

"Hah! Tanner found a way to mention his dad's a big-shot producer BEFORE breakfast today!" Micah Maguire said, scrolling through his phone and putting his hand out. "Yeun, Wendell, Zion. Pay up, losers!"

The boys forked over the loot—two homemade cigarettes, a Kit-Kat bar, and a sample-sized bottle of sunscreen. With no money anywhere on the Cove, the booty from care packages from home had become coin of the realm.

"Hey! You're not supposed to have that phone out during the week," said Barnaby Chisolm. Though he'd grown a bit and ditched his big glasses, the 13-year-old Barnaby remained the rule follower of the group.

"Relax. I've encrypted the data," Micah replied. "'Sides, it's on airplane mode."

"Oh, is *that* why nobody texts you?" Tanner asked. "I thought you were just horribly and tragically unpopular."

"I think you're talking about yourself. When was the last time you heard from your dad?" Micah said.

Tanner scowled. Micah had touched a sore spot.

"Hey, bae! You looked smokin' out there," Daya Cepeda said to Luz, punctuating the statement with an arm around Luz's waist and a quick peck on her cheek.

"Woo! Hot girl-on-girl action!" Tanner said, applauding. "Usually, I'd need an online subscription for that!"

"Eat shit, *pendejo*," Daya said, accentuating her request with a well-placed backhand to Tanner's ribs. Indeed, ever since Luz and Daya had become an item a few weeks earlier, Tanner wasted little opportunity to needle the two about their budding romance, commentary which had exactly zero impact on either of the girls. Tanner doubled over from the jab, which sent the Brigands into fits of laughter.

Bonnie looked around at her crew, touched by their friendship, though the foster girl in her still struggled to accept it. At summer's end, they'd refused to leave her in a show of loyalty. Usually, new Brigands would return home to their families or apprentice with seasoned fighters, but their insistence—a near rebellion—had swayed Reed to let them stay on at the Cove.

It wasn't the normal way, but then things weren't normal. Besides, Reed didn't exactly want to be the one to break up the band that had fended off Calico Jack's men and saved Bonnie from being kidnapped. He knew that she trusted them as much as she could trust anyone.

Arranging for everyone to stay took some doing. Barnaby's dad, a high-ranking Brigand, needed convincing—proud his son had found his "inner macho" but worried about the danger. Tanner's dad, busy filming in Mexico, had given up trying to control his son. The parents of Micah Maguire and his brother Malachi—a hulk of a boy who pinned the needle on the autism meter—agreed to let them stay only after Grandma Winnie promised their studies would continue—which they did, much to everyone's dismay. The rest? A breeze. The overworked, understaffed child welfare system let countless kids fall through the cracks every day, leaving them unnoticed and unclaimed, so what was a half dozen more in the grand scheme of things?

"We have a little time before the breakfast bell," said Zion. "Let's do some sparring."

Zion, despite his imposing muscular frame, was terribly shy. But it had come out that he'd won the Golden Gloves regional boxing championship back in Mississippi and was runner-up in wrestling. He'd started both sports at nine years old as part of a youth diversion program after being caught stealing copper wiring from a construction site. The revelation of his prowess impressed all the Brigands, and after some coaxing, Zion began hosting daily training sessions that quickly became a morning staple.

"I'll go!" Bonnie volunteered.

"You just went," complained Kevin Yeun, the spiky-haired sailing whiz who'd guided his Zephyrus crew to victory in the Triquetra Challenge the previous summer.

"I want to go again." Bonnie was determined to shake herself out of her funk.

"Okay. You and Yeun," Zion said.

Bonnie went back to the center of the clearing near the tall oak tree. Yeun took up a defensive stance a few feet from her.

"Okay. On my—" Zion began.

Suddenly, Bonnie lunged, tackling Yeun to the ground.

"Hey!" Yeun yelled.

"Whoa! Bonnie! Bonnie!" Zion pulled her off. "We wait for my signal! You know the rules. What's with you today?"

Bonnie stopped, suddenly aware of all eyes on her. She knew she was acting nuts but couldn't stop herself.

"I-I'm sorry. I guess I'm just sick of waiting," Bonnie said. "Waiting for the signal, waiting for Reed to let us off this cove, waiting for Jack to make a frickin' move. I just don't think I can sit around anymore and do more nothing!"

"I'm with Bonnie," Luz said. "After a while, even kicking Tanner's ass isn't that much fun anymore."

"Ha! Maybe on Earth 12 in the multiverse, you beat me," Tanner said. "Here on this planet, I like my chances."

To which Luz replied with a subtle, yet effective retort of which only the best debaters are aware. She flipped him off.

Zion avoided both the dispute and Luz's middle finger by turning the conversation back to Bonnie.

"We're with you, girl, for real," Zion said to murmurs of agreement. "But for now, all we can do is just keep beasting it up, so when the time comes, we'll be ready."

"Well, I'm ready now!" Wendell said. "Just say the word, Bonnie, I'm—"

"Locked and Loaded!" They all said in unison, having heard the budding pyromaniac's credo too many times before. "We know, dude!"

Even Bonnie had to smile. Wendell had become the Brigands' unofficial munitions expert and was constantly seeking opportunities to put his expansive demolitions expertise into practice. In other words, he was always eager to blow shit up.

"Okay. Back to positions. On my signal!" Zion shot a warning look at Bonnie, who nodded. "GO!"

The sparring resumed. Yeun fought well, but Bonnie, eager to redeem herself after her mediocre showing earlier, used punches, flips, and some moves Zion had taught her to gain the upper hand. Finally, she was about to pin Yeun, knees on his arms, when—

"Curls!"

The shout interrupted the battle. Yeun took advantage, shoving Bonnie off him and scrambling to his feet. Bonnie followed, brushing dirt off her clothes.

Wilder De Luca stood at the edge of the clearing, fresh from helping Grandma Winnie prepare breakfast, having drawn KP duty for the week.

Wilder had been Bonnie's first friend on the Cove and someone she'd once had feelings for. But that was forever ago. Any thoughts of romance between them had given way to graver concerns. As a result, the chocolate-eyed boy had been exiled to that strange gray area between brother and dear friend that neither of them needed to talk about much. Though it was clear to anyone who had eyes that Wilder still had it bad for her.

"What's up, De Luca?" asked Tanner. "Grandma Winnie send you on another blackberry run?"

"The boy king has summoned Bonnie to the throne room," Wilder announced.

"What's Reed want now?" Bonnie asked.

"How should I know? Maybe he wants to share his latest innovation in knot-tying. Whatever it is, I'm *sure* it's life and death."

"What isn't with him these days?" Bonnie moaned.

Everyone knew what she meant. Since the eighteen-year-old Reed Ballister had taken over leadership from his grandfather, he was constantly working to reinvent the Brigands, determined to return the group to its former glory. His endless ideas, rules, and strategies left no room for anything else—not even casual conversations. This shift grated on the group, especially Bonnie. Since the summer, their relationship had cooled considerably, and the former ease that she'd felt with him was replaced by uncomfortable silences.

"This *better* be important," Bonnie grumbled. "I was about to finish off Yeun."

"Ha!" Yeun said. "I was just playing possum before going in for the kill."

"Rematch!" she yelled as she sprinted toward the main house.

Wilder didn't even bother to follow. He didn't have it in him. And neither did Crossbones.

"C.B.," Wilder said to the bird, stroking its feathers, "we're definitely gonna have to level up our cardio if we want to keep up with her."

The parrot just nodded its head, watching Bonnie disappear into the trees.

Chapter 3
News from Afar

Bonnie sat in Reed's office in the main house. It had been Eleazer Ballister's until the old captain retired, and the scent of his pipe tobacco still lingered in the air. The aroma wasn't the only evidence of the recently retired captain; Reed had preserved the decor out of respect for his grandfather. The old-timey wood paneling, worn leather chairs, and huge mahogany desk all remained. And above the fireplace still hung the portrait of Mary Read, the Brigands' foundress. Beneath it on the mantel was the reliquary holding her mummified hand, both constant reminders of their purpose. Behind the desk, a massive map displayed sightings of Calico Jack's ship, the *Perdition*. Pushpins covered the map, marking every corner of the globe the ship had crossed, a testament to the reach of Jack's floating fortress.

Still, Reed had added some of his own updates to the office. A high-powered Wi-Fi router blinked on the fireplace mantel. With the help of Micah, he had set up an encrypted messaging app so that all the Brigands in the field could be reached at a moment's notice. On the desk, numerous computer monitors emitted an electronic blue glow that contrasted with their rustic surroundings.

To Bonnie, the most out-of-place thing in the room was Reed Ballister himself. It was still weird to see Reed, the lanky boy she'd scuffled with on her first day on the Cove, sitting behind the big desk and in charge of the entire Brigand operation. In the months since her arrival, Reed had gained muscle and a sharpened jawline. And even if he had trouble looking at her directly these days, *he still has those dreamy gray eyes*, she couldn't help thinking.

She would have had trouble taking him seriously if not for the fact that Reed's grandparents were there as well. Captain Ballister stood gravely next to Reed. His kindly wife, known to all as Grandma Winnie, pressed a cup of tea on Bonnie, one she hadn't requested. Bonnie suspected it carried Winnie's "inexplicable discomfiture" potion—a concoction only served when something was seriously amiss.

Reed eyed Bonnie curiously. "What happened to your face?"

"My face—?" Bonnie's hand felt something wet on her cheek. She saw blood on her fingers and suddenly remembered getting scratched on the exact same cheek in her dream. "Oh. Musta got nicked while we were training," she said, rationalizing it in her head.

The Ballisters looked at Reed, but he said nothing for a good long time. Bonnie finally spoke up.

"You know, the last time you brought me in here like this, you guys told me I was cursed. So whatever this is, I'm pretty sure I can handle it."

Ballister put a steadying hand on Reed's shoulder.

"Bonnie. Last night..." Reed started but hesitated. He looked down. "Something happened..."

"What, did Jonesy fall off the dock again?" Bonnie joked, masking her growing unease.

"No. Well, yes, but that's not what this is about," Reed simply said. More silence.

"You're seriously starting to freak me out! What happened?!"

"Calico Jack has claimed another marked one," Captain Ballister finally said.

Bonnie jumped up, her tea spilling onto the floor. "He got my mom?!"

"No, no dear. It wasn't your mother!" Grandma Winnie rushed to comfort Bonnie, but she was having none of it.

"Wait... what—?" Bonnie's mind began racing. Besides her and her mom, she knew of only one other living marked one. Not long after Bonnie's oath of allegiance to the group, all the newly anointed Brigands had been told of his existence, but nothing more. Not a name nor age nor location. Nothing. It was all strictly need-to-know. The secrecy, they said, was to keep the person, and Bonnie for that matter, as safe as possible.

"His name was Ned Masterson," Reed explained. "He'd been under Brigand protection for years. In a secluded location. We're not sure how Jack found him... he shouldn't have been able to, but—"

"But he did," Bonnie said quietly.

Bonnie's words hit Reed hard, guilt etched across his face. But she had no time for his feelings—her own were overwhelming. Slowly, realization struck, and her hand moved back to the blood on her cheek.

"Tell me. Did it happen in a cabin? In the snow?" she asked, dread rising. "Was Ned an old man with cancer?"

The Ballisters stared at her, stunned.

"H-how could you know that, child?" Captain Ballister asked.

"Because I saw it last night. In my dream."

"But I thought the dreams had stopped," Grandma Winnie said, deeply concerned.

"So did I," Bonnie murmured.

The room fell into heavy silence, each waiting for some hidden truth to reveal itself. Reed and his grandparents exchanged grave looks, and a chill ran down Bonnie's spine—not fear, but the sense that something beyond them was stirring once more.

*   *   *   *   *

The day was sunny, brilliant blue skies with puffy white clouds. *A disturbingly beautiful day for a funeral*, Bonnie thought as she made her way to the Field of the Fallen, the cemetery behind the little chapel on the hill where they had buried her father not that long ago. And now, more death. Dozens of Brigands had come from far and wide to attend the burial of Ned Masterson and the three Brigands—Carlos Huayta, Leslie Boswell, and Hart Thorp—who had made the ultimate sacrifice for his protection.

Bonnie had met Hart Thorp. He'd been one of the pallbearers at her father's funeral. She recalled how his hands had trembled slightly, the weight of grief making him stumble with the casket. He'd been so kind to her that day, sharing the stories of his adventures with Bobby as young corsairs in their summer together at the Cove, his boisterous laugh punctuating each of his tales. *A laugh forever silenced.*

"You think this is the first time a stained one has gone to another stained one's funeral?" Bonnie asked Wilder, who walked beside her.

She knew Wilder hated when she called herself "stained"—Jack's term that the Brigands avoided as self-loathing. Maybe it was. Bonnie didn't care. It was how she felt.

"You don't have to do this, you know," Wilder said. "No one would blame you if you sat this one out."

"And give this crowd an excuse not to come to *my* funeral? No way!"

Wilder scowled. Luz, walking nearby, gave him a concerned glance. Around them, the rest of Bonnie's class of Brigands marched solemnly. No one seemed that amused.

Five days earlier, after the news of Ned Masterson's death had broken, Bonnie's crewmates had closed ranks around her. Not just as supportive friends, but as Brigands sworn to protect her.

Despite the Cove being magically impenetrable ground, they insisted Bonnie move back into the cabins. Luz and Daya took up bunks beside her, while others kept watch in shifts. Reed increased sword training, and Zion intensified his hand-to-hand combat sessions. Classes were suspended—no one was going anyway—as the young Brigands ensured Bonnie was never alone.

Even now, at the gravesites, they surrounded her like Secret Service agents. Bonnie thought their efforts naive—Ned had been protected, and now he was gone. But she tolerated it for their peace of mind, just as she tolerated this day filled with loss. She bowed her head as the priest offered a final blessing over the four casket-filled graves.

"Lord, bless these brave souls forever with Your eternal peace. Let the sounds of strife be calmed in Your endless grace, ever mindful that we the living cherish their spirit and continue the fight in their name."

The words of Father Foley washed over Bonnie, but she barely registered them. She focused instead on the familiar headstone of her father nearby. She had taken to visiting Bobby Maynard's grave frequently of late. Not to work through any grief, but because it connected her to the only thing she felt she could count on these days—her rage. Rage at her fate. Rage at the unfairness of it all. Rage at a God who let such horrors happen. And that rage was the one thing that made her feel closer to life than to death. She felt it now, rising in her. Tightening its grip on her.

As the last shovelful of dirt fell upon the graves, Bonnie's rage continued to simmer.

And she embraced it.

Chapter 4
The Conclave

The din of voices filled the Battle Barn to the rafters. The place was packed with the Brigands who had come for the funeral earlier that morning. Reed had ordered them to stay, calling his first official meeting since he had taken over.

At the center of the barn was the replica deck of the *True North* where Bonnie had first learned her fighting skills. For this gathering, the foredeck had been transformed into a makeshift dais. Reed sat there at a table, flanked by Captain Ballister and Wicked Pete Devlin, the brawny Irishman who'd plucked Bonnie out of juvenile detention last spring. The men had their heads together deep in discussion with Wakeman Chisolm, Barnaby's father and a senior member of the Brigands' high council. A magnificent, burly man—Chisolm was such the opposite of his shrimpy son that it was almost as if they were different species.

"Is this a Brigand meeting or an AARP luncheon?" Wilder said, settling in on the floor next to Bonnie.

Bonnie glanced around, noting for the first time how many Brigands were older. Younger faces were scarce—a reflection of the diluted bloodline, waning commitment, or both, something Captain Ballister had mentioned before. Even their crewmate Hashpipe, who'd survived the summer trials and the battle with

Calico Jack, had limped back to his family farm in Texas and disappeared. Bonnie couldn't blame him; he *had* been badly injured in the fight. Still, it did not inspire confidence.

BLEEEEEOOOOO! The sound of the old seadog Jonesy's horn filled the air and cut through the clatter. The same animal horn instrument that had welcomed Bonnie and her crewmates to the Cove so many months ago.

"Let the emergency conclave of the Brigands of the Compass Rose commence!" Jonesy proclaimed, his horribly burned ear and eye patch lending gravity to the announcement. And for once, he looked sober, a true sign of how seriously even he took this recent turn of events.

Reed Ballister nodded to Jonesy and stood up to address the gathering. The grumbles from the crowd made it clear not everyone in attendance embraced their young leader.

"Thank you, Mister Jones," Reed began, ignoring the dissent. "And thank you all for staying. I know this has been a hard day, but we need to discuss what happened and where we go from here."

"I don't need talk. I need payback!" someone shouted.

"Hear hear!" Shouts of agreement and angry calls for retribution filled the air.

"Yaaaas! I'm locked and loaded and ready to rumble!" Wendell chimed in, leaping to his feet. Zion yanked him back down, silencing him with a glare. Growing up in a dysfunctional home, Zion had developed a keen sense of when was a good time to shut the hell up, and now was one such occasion.

"I know revenge feels natural," Reed pressed on, raising his voice over the unrest, "but we must proceed cautiously—"

More shouts! More complaints! Protestations echoed through the rafters.

"SHUT YER CANKER-BLOSSOMED GOBS!" Wicked Pete shouted, slamming his sword into the table, nearly splitting it in half. "Show some respect! Let young Captain Ballister speak!"

The Brigands fell silent, cowed by Pete's imposing presence. Crossbones, who was perched in the rafters, fluttered his wings in response.

Bonnie saw Reed's cheeks flush—a telltale sign of his embarrassment—but he pushed forward. "Most of you know Wakeman Chisolm."

Barnaby sat up straighter, pride evident on his face.

Reed continued, "Mr. Chisolm has been investigating how Calico Jack tracked down our safe house. Mister Chisolm?"

Wakeman Chisolm stepped forward, his deep voice resonating through the barn. "Though this is a sad day, it's good to see so many friends—those among us, and those we buried today." His voice broke, tears glistening in his eyes. The raw emotion moved even the most hardened Brigands.

"As most of you have heard, Ned Masterson had recently been diagnosed with cancer," Chisolm said, his tone steadying. "In his final week, it seems he secretly reached out to an estranged daughter he hadn't spoken to in thirty years. Maybe to settle accounts, maybe to say goodbye. We don't know the details—she has since disappeared." The Brigands murmured; they all knew what "disappeared" likely meant.

Chisolm pressed on. "What we do now know is that Calico Jack had been keeping tabs on this woman all these years. When Ned contacted her, Jack intercepted their communications. That fatal misstep led them to our safe house."

The room grew heavy with the weight of the revelation.

"A reminder that Calico Jack has got eyes everywhere," Reed warned.

"Then it weren't on us!" someone said, and the crowd seemed generally relieved by that information.

"What a relief!" It was Bonnie. She couldn't hold it in anymore. "A marked one is dead, but at least it wasn't our fault! While we're at it, let's celebrate the fact that since Ned was dying anyway, Jack got hardly any time from him!"

"Bonnie, I know you're upset," Reed said. "We all are. But we can't let this shake us. We have to remember we still have a mission here. And that mission is to keep you safe."

"And what about my mother? Brigid Byrne is still out there with a mark on her flesh, too! Why aren't we out there looking? You've been promising for months. Or doesn't she matter?"

"Psshaw! We don't even know she's still alive!" came a call from the group. It was Two-Blades McCallister, one of the oldest (and to Bonnie's way of thinking, most cantankerous) Brigands. He got the nickname Two-Blades from his habit of brandishing swords in both hands when he went into battle. These days, it seemed like the only thing he could brandish was a colostomy bag.

"We *do* know she's alive!" Bonnie said strongly.

"Based on what? The word of some cut-rate swami from Tuscarora?" Two-Blades continued, rising with the help of the Brigand sitting next to him. "We've all heard about your so-called evidence, and I'm sorry, it just strikes a lot of us as pretty weak tea."

Murmurs of agreement rippled through the group. Tales of Bonnie's encounter with the Gullah fortune tellers and their fleeting contact with her mother during a late-night conjuring session were well known by now. But it had been centuries since anyone with any real magic had been part of the Brigands, and skepticism had taken root. Like all things, untended faith, over time, can fade.

"Hey!" Wilder stood up in defense of the fortune tellers. "Fatimata and Ophelia Robinson are the real deal! And good people. They used their sight to help me find my mom!"

Wilder was infuriated by the insult. He had forged a special bond with the two Gullah women, especially Fati, who'd taken an instant liking to the boy. The connection only grew stronger when the two women volunteered to accompany him to New York City and use their abilities to help locate the body of his missing mother. She'd died of a drug overdose beneath a bridge, heartbroken over the death of Wilder's father. Fati had even insisted on paying to give the woman a proper burial next to her husband, a gesture that left Wilder eternally grateful.

"Well, if Brigid Byrne is still alive, why ain't there been a hint of her since she abandoned the Brigands?" asked the Brigand who was propping up Two-Blades. "It ain't like we didn't look for her for years."

"Probably because she knows she still can't trust the Brigands to keep her safe," Bonnie said.

Gasps of offense followed.

"That's not fair, Bonnie, and you know it," Reed said.

"Isn't it?" Bonnie countered, her voice rising. "It's why she left with me. It's why she hid me. My God, we just buried four men today! Your own parents were murdered!" Reed fell silent. Bonnie pressed on. "And now this group, whose sole purpose for existing is an ancient curse, refuses to believe my mother's alive because we found out through *fortune tellers*? What a freaking joke."

That did it! A tremendous uproar filled the barn! Everyone shouting at everyone else. The older Brigands accused the younger ones of disrespecting the revered organization. The younger Brigands accused the older ones of being so stuck in the past they could no longer keep up with Calico Jack, who himself had embraced the future. Accusations and counter-accusations flew until—

"That's enough, all of you!" Captain Ballister bellowed amid the clamor. When everyone was quiet, the captain struggled out of his chair, aided by Wicked Pete. The kidnapping and death of Sheriff Bobby Maynard that summer had taken a toll on everyone, but it was most noticeable in the person of Captain Eleazer Ballister. After he relinquished command of the Brigands and in the wake of the killing, the captain's health had begun to deteriorate. Gone was the virility that once seemed to radiate from his every muscle. In its place, a man bowed, but still not broken. He steadied himself on the back of his chair as he spoke.

"Our foundress Mary Read is turning over in her grave!" he declared. "Have we forgotten we are brothers and sisters, bound by our oaths? This division is shameful!"

A heavy silence followed. Ballister turned his gaze to Bonnie. "Mistress Hartwright, as a marked one, I understand recent events have shaken your confidence. But you are also a blood Brigand. To question the devotion and sacrifice of this group is an insult to all who paid the ultimate price, including the ones we buried today, and I might add, including your father."

Bonnie thought of how her dad and her friends had all fought so valiantly to save her and she did feel some shame. Not at what she had said, because she'd spoken her truth, but at *how* she'd said it.

"I'm sorry, Captain Ballister. I'm just worried about my mother."

"With respect, Mistress Hartwright," finally spoke another of the Brigands. It was Kazumi Kawaguchi, an elegant gray-haired Japanese woman in her 60s. She had a samurai sword strapped to her back, and the look of a woman who wasn't afraid to use it. "Do you not think it valid, if Brigid Byrne is indeed alive as you say, to question why she hasn't at the very least let her own daughter know? As a mother, nothing would stop me from getting to my child."

The woman warrior had asked the very question Bonnie had asked herself many times.

"Maybe she doesn't know I'm here!" Bonnie suggested. "Maybe she's too afraid or hurt or in trouble."

"For sixteen years!? Ha!" Two-Blades scoffed. "Nah. She's dead or don't want to be found."

Bonnie had a few choice retorts in mind involving four-letter words, but this time managed to hold her tongue. Remembering the adage Grandma Winnie once shared about getting more flies with honey, she took a different tack.

"Whatever the reason, speaking as a Brigand," she said with all the earnestness she could muster, "isn't that what we're honor-bound to do? To find marked ones and assure their protection? As a marked one, I hope that's still true." She was shameless in her emotional appeal, but she saw the sea of faces soften. "And if she is dead, shouldn't we know that for sure, too, one way or another?"

"Aye, Mistress Hartwright! 'Tis still true long as I draw breath," Wicked Pete said adamantly. Then he faced the crowd. "Whether ye believe it or not, we got to operate as if her mam is still alive. And we got to do everything in our power to find her. It's our sworn duty!"

The crowd didn't disagree. In fact, many nodded in support. Her crewmates all applauded loudly.

Bonnie shot Reed a look, challenging him.

"All right," Reed finally agreed. "Beginning today, in addition to keeping Bonnie Hartwright safe, we will resume full-scale Brigand efforts to locate Brigid Byrne. If she's out there, I want her found."

Bonnie beamed, excited at the prospect they were finally going to do something.

"However," Reed said, "we will continue to proceed as if Calico Jack is close at hand. Which means Bonnie will remain on the Cove under 24-hour protection—"

"What!? I am a Brigand! I should be out there looking too!"

"This is not up for debate," Reed declared. "This meeting is adjourned."

And just then, any attempt at diplomacy on Bonnie's part vaporized.

"What happened to taking the fight to Jack? We've been sitting here for months! What are you so afraid of? You're supposed to be a leader! Lead already!" she was shouting now.

"For the record!" Reed turned and angrily addressed Bonnie. "I would give anything if my father was here to do this job. But he's not. Because as you were so kind to point out, he's dead. In service to this cause. So, I'm what you got. Like it or not."

⚓   ⚓   ⚓   ⚓   ⚓

Back in the Boreas cabin, Bonnie was practically bouncing off the walls. Her crew around her, trying to calm her.

"This is bullshit!" she said. "Reed expects me to sit around while the senior citizen brigade half-asses it looking for my mom? They may as well kill her themselves!"

"I dunno, Bonnie," Barnaby said. "Reed kind of has a point. It's not safe out there right now."

"It's not ever going to be safe!"

"I hate to say it because, you know, Reed," Wilder said, "but until we get a lead on your mom, it might be better for you to lay low. I mean, where would we even start to look?"

"I don't know. But I know I won't find her sitting around here helping Grandma Winnie make marmalade!"

"Look. If anybody gets even the slightest whiff of your mom, we'll leave the Cove, Reed's okay or not. I'll be the first one on the boat with you," Wilder promised.

"Me, too!" Luz jumped in. The others nodded in solidarity. Even Tanner after a hard nudge from Daya.

"They won't." Everyone jumped. It was Malachi Maguire, who almost never spoke so hearing his voice startled them. Until now, he'd been quietly sketching in his notebook, creating detailed drawings of the herbs in Grandma Winnie's garden from memory.

"What do you mean, Malachi?" Micah asked his brother.

"They won't. Only Bonnie," Malachi said.

"I wish there was a Google Translate for your brother, bro," Yeun said.

Bonnie's eyes lit up. "It's obvious. He's saying I'm the only one who can find her!"

The Brigands exchanged uneasy glances. They knew full well that Malachi rarely spoke without purpose.

"Now if he'd just tell us where to start," Wilder said. "Micah, can you adjust your brother's settings a bit?"

"I'm not my brother's keeper," Micah grumbled.

"You kinda are," Wilder said.

"Hey, Mal," Micah said, sidling next to him. "Anything else you could share, maybe? A hint? Anything?"

But Malachi just went back to drawing as if his brother hadn't said a word. He was deep in his own world again, where he spent most of his time.

"See? He doesn't listen to me anymore."

"Okay. Well," Luz said with a frustrated sigh. "We know it's gotta be Bonnie, at least. The question is, how?"

Suddenly, Wilder whipped his head around. "Bonnie!" he said excitedly. "You have to talk to Fati and Gam Gam again!"

"Why would I do that?" asked Bonnie.

"Because Malachi's right. The Brigands won't find anything on your mom," Wilder explained. "If we find her, it'll be through you."

"I think we all sorta already agreed on that," Bonnie said.

"Right. But the question is, why? And the answer is that you're the one with the connection to her. You *have to* have them do another session."

"And how would this time be any different than the last time? Or the time before that? You want me to beg them for another reading just to hear that they can't break through again? That someone's put up some kind of psychic firewall?"

"That was before. Things are different now."

"How are they different?"

"Because you had that dream."

"What does—aghh! You're not even making sense, De Luca," Bonnie said.

"If there's one thing I learned hanging around the Robinsons, it's that there is a logic to their magic; it's not just a bunch of random hocus pocus.

"Think about it," he continued, words spilling out of him in one breathless burst of energy. "Last time you saw your mom, you were still having the dreams, right? You even dreamed about that first one, what's his name, Seth? Maybe the reason you haven't gotten through to your mom lately is you haven't been dreaming. But now, you *have* dreamed—about Ned Masterson. A marked one! A crazy real dream. Like you were actually there, you said. There must have been some strong connection between the two of you. So maybe that's been the key all along. If there are psychic walls, there have to be some kind of, I dunno, psychic windows or something, and maybe it's opened up again with that dream. Maybe your mom, who's also marked, is on the other side of it. And maybe you ought to see if you can get through that window, before it shuts again!"

Wilder doubled over, gasping for breath.

Everyone stood staring at him.

"Or not," he said with a shrug.

But the chocolate-eyed boy had convinced Bonnie. Regardless of what Reed said about staying on the Cove, Bonnie was definitely going to see the fortune tellers. And that was just going to have to be that.

Chapter 5
The Fortune Teller

What Wilder said about there being logic to magic made a strange sort of sense to Bonnie. And, following that logic, she decided that she should visit Fati and Gam Gam on Tuscarora Island. Over the last few months, Fati had always come to Bonnie to ensure her safety. But looking back, every reading that yielded any results had taken place *away* from Cormac's Cove—at the farmers' market, the fortune-telling shop, or Fati's condo in Highcross. Bonnie wondered if the magic of the Cove itself might be a hindrance, especially since Reed had recently gotten Fati and Gam Gam to strengthen the magic of the perimeter for the first time since Mariama had conjured the protective shield around the place almost 300 years before.

No one knew if the Cove's magic mattered, but they all agreed it was a theory worth testing. The only problem was that with his new emphasis on Bonnie's safety, Reed would never allow it. So, they did what Brigands always did when faced with a problem with the rules—they broke them.

The plan was simple: Bonnie would sail the Brigands' small skiff, the *Solstice Skye*, to Tuscarora Island in the early morning hours, during her daily run so nobody would miss her right away. There, she could see Fati at her shop and cajole her into another reading. Of course, she wouldn't go *alone*. With Calico Jack out there somewhere, she could be daring without being stupid. So, with Wilder as her second, she slipped out of the cabin before sunrise the next morning and the two of them headed for the dock and hopped on the *Solstice Skye*.

"Taking a little detour on your morning run?"

Bonnie's head whipped around to find Reed Ballister standing on the shore.

"Shit! Who ratted me out?" Bonnie asked. "It was Barnaby, wasn't it?"

"You think I don't know you by now, Bonnie Hartwright?"

Bonnie flushed in anger and embarrassment. "If you know me so damn well, you know you're not going to stop me from going," she said, unlashing the boat from its mooring cleat and throwing the rope in Reed's face.

"I do know that. That's why I'm coming along to..." he said, "...where are we going?"

"Tuscarora," Wilder replied. "Fati and Gam Gam."

Reed nodded and got on board.

"Seriously?" Bonnie was stunned. "After that whole speech in the barn? Suddenly you're changing your mind? Why?"

"Because changing *my* mind is a hell of a lot easier than trying to change yours," he said. "I figure if I can't keep you on the Cove, at least I can keep you safe. You can tell me the plan on the way; let's go."

Wilder announced, "All hands. Stand by to raise the jib! We sail this day for Tuscarora Island!"

"Just cleat the line," Reed said with an eyeroll as he pushed off from the dock with a pole.

And with that, the trio was off.

.   .   .   .   .

The *Solstice Skye* cut through the waters of the sound. On board, Bonnie, Reed, and Wilder worked in wordless unison to guide the skiff to their destination. As they worked, Wilder kept on high alert, scanning the horizon for any unusual vessels.

Though the literal sailing was smooth, the mood on the boat... not so much. There was an awkward silence among the three of them. It had been a while since they'd sailed as a team, and even longer since they'd done anything at all together. Once, they had been an inseparable triumvirate—a close-knit trio bonded by friendship and shared loss. But time and circumstances had driven a wedge between them. They were different people now. Bonnie had been overtaken by her brooding thoughts and relentless preparation for the fight to come. Reed was now burdened far too early with leading and reorganizing the Brigands. And Wilder, isolated from them both, had started spending more of his spare time with Fati and Gam Gam. Since their trip to New York, he'd grown closer to the two women, doing odd jobs for them at their condo in Highcross, and helping out at the farmers' market on weekends.

For the three of them to be thrown together again, it felt to Bonnie like coming back to school from summer vacation after weeks apart and not knowing if you and your friends still had anything in common. So far, it didn't seem promising.

.   .   .   .   .

"Ain't this a surprise!" Fati Robinson wrapped Wilder in her ample arms as soon as the trio walked into Fatimata's Potions and Fortune Telling Shop in Tuscarora Island's tourist quarter. Her beads and bangles jingled loudly as she nearly squeezed the breath out of the lanky boy. "Gam Gam! Look who came for a visit!"

With the help of her cane, Fati's frail and blind grandmother Gam Gam arose from behind the counter to greet their visitors. The tiny woman was almost lost amid the riot of products on display at the front of the shop: bottled potions and herb bags called gris-gris, all manner of Afro-Caribbean related trinkets, hoodoo dolls and souvenirs. And, of course, the ever-present giant jar of floating pickles.

"Wilder De Luca!" Gam Gam said with a grin, touching the boy's face.

Bonnie saw the genuine affection that had developed between the women and Wilder and felt a stab of envy.

"Master Reed. Miss Bonnie, I been 'spectin' all y'all," she nodded to each of them despite her cataract-glazed eyes.

There was a time that a visit from these three wouldn't have been greeted so warmly. It wasn't that long ago that the barrel of Fati's shotgun had met Wilder at the door of the Robinsons' condo. But the events of the previous summer had softened their relationship, and Fati and Gam Gam both realized that, like it or not, their fate was now intertwined with that of this cursed teenager who stood before them.

"Gam Gam told me you'd be coming," Fati said. "What can I do you for?"

"Gam Gam didn't tell you already?" Wilder teased.

"Gib' a ole woman a brek. I's blind. Ain't see ebryting!" Gam Gam said with a laugh.

Bonnie quickly explained their situation and why they had come in person.

Fati nodded seriously and pulled back the hanging beads to the adjoining fortune telling room. "You. Out!" She yelled at a tourist seated at the table, tarot cards splayed out in front of her.

"B-but you haven't told me my future yet," the woman objected as Fati yanked her out of her chair.

"Use sunscreen. Get a prenup. Quit smoking and invest in an annuity," Fati said as she hustled the tourist toward the door.

Gam Gam handed the woman a pickle as Fati closed the door on her, locking it and putting the CLOSED sign in the window.

"Well don't just stand there gawking, children. Sit!"

✻ ✻ ✻ ✻ ✻

A diffuse, slanted ray of winter sunlight filtered in through a window, illuminating the curl of smoke rising from the skull-shaped bowl at the center of the fortunetelling table. Gam Gam sat outside the mystic circle, leaving the divination to Fati. She'd once told Bonnie she was too close to the grave to take part in such things anymore. It took way too much out of her.

It was a familiar scene, though the last time they'd gotten a reading from Fati, she hadn't been dressed up in the elaborate headwrap and colorful Ankara African print dress she wore to lure in tourists. The Robinson women may have had "the sight" but to make a living from it, they had to lean into the stereotypes expected by the free-spending white folks who visited the island on vacation. This included the fake pidgin accent Fati used, which she thankfully dropped for this occasion.

"Y'all know the drill," Fati said. "C'mon. Don't be shy."

They all joined hands. Bonnie grasped Wilder's hand on one side and Reed's on the other. The first time she'd touched either of them in a long time. It set off something funny, and not entirely unpleasant, in her stomach.

"Now," Fati said. "I'm gonna say one more time I'm not making no guarantees. I didn't find out anything the last however many times and I ain't holding out hope this time either, dream or no dream."

"I'm not expecting anything," Bonnie assured her.

"Yah mus b'lieve an ain't doubt, 'cause dah one who doubt be like a wave 'pon dah sea, blow an toss by dah wind," Gam Gam said.

"In plain English, woman?" Fati asked.

"Give yahself a little credit, Fatimata. Believe," Gam Gam sighed and turned to Bonnie. "And yah... tink on yah mamma. On what ties dat bind yah!"

Fati closed her eyes. "Okay. Let's see what we see, shall we? Bonnie, focus all your heart on your mother.

"Mmmmwwww," Fati made a low guttural noise and rolled her head. "I call upon the spirits that surround this girl. Venture near. Touch her soul and feel her wanting. The wanting of a child who longs for her mamma. Lead this child to the woman who gave her life. Who nurtured her with her own blood and then spilt that blood delivering her unto the world."

Suddenly, Bonnie felt her head start to spin. She clutched Wilder's and Reed's hands tightly as if they could keep her grounded. But she felt herself being sucked into a vortex.

VISIONS ERUPTED: *The Cave o' the Four Winds. The name Brigid Byrne written on the stone ceiling. A terrible storm at sea. A young woman wails in the throes of childbirth. Then, a different place. Remote. Desolate. A turbulent ocean. Waves smash against towering black, craggy rocks. The waves reach high. Higher. Higher. Lightning! Thunder! More flashes of light. Then BLACKNESS!*

Bonnie was suddenly falling. Falling. Then a CRASH! Snowy woods. A dimly lit cabin. Ned's face under water gasping for breath. Drowning. Blood. The mark being ripped away from his flesh. A knife-wielding hand with an hourglass ring, nearly filled with sand. And then blackness again.

"Breathe! Bonnie, breathe!"

"Huuuuuh!" Bonnie took in a gulp of air and opened her eyes to find herself on the floor, surrounded by the others.

"She's breathing. Thank God. She's breathing!" Wilder said.

*   *   *   *   *

A few minutes later, Bonnie sat at the table, sipping on a cup of herbal tea. Her hands were trembling and the cup clinked when she put it in the saucer. She looked up at the others.

"Did you see?" she asked.

"We saw," Wilder said. Reed nodded.

"For a second, after the cave, I thought I saw something," Bonnie said, "but it was a jumble, some weird island, and then I was in my dream, which I wasn't even focusing on."

"I thought there was something too," Fati concurred, "but then we hit that damn wall again! Whatever it is, it's like nothing I ever felt. Curious. Don't know how we ever got through the first time."

Fati shook her head, recalling the previous divination that revealed Bonnie's mom was still alive. "Maybe they just wasn't expectin' us…"

"Dat's dah old magic we keep knockin' heads 'gainst," Gam Gam announced.

"Old how?" Reed asked.

"Couldn't rightly say," the elderly woman replied. "Older'n our own. Older'n dah Good Book even. And our Saviour hisself. But dat's all's I could say 'bout it. I ain't dat worldly a woman."

Bonnie looked disheartened.

"I'm sorry, Bonnie. I got your hopes up. Guess I was wrong," Wilder said.

"No yah wasn't…" Gam Gam said.

Everyone looked at the old woman expectantly.

"Yah been right 'bout a window been open. But ain't to yah mamma. To dah dream yah had. Dah one we done seen bits of. Ain't jus' a vision, Bonnie. It been a portent."

"A portent?" Wilder asked.

"Like… a warning," Fati explained.

"Well, if that dream was a warning, it was too late," Reed said. "By the time Bonnie dreamt it, our men were already dead."

"Dat weren't dah warnin' she been gittin', boy!" Gam Gam snapped. "It been somethin' way more dire."

They looked at one another; it was hard to imagine anything more dire than four dead men in the middle of a forgotten forest.

"What was it then?" Reed asked.

"Y'ain't see it? None of y'all? Even I seen it, and I weren't in dah circle. Oh, dah blackness of it!" Gam Gam brought her hand up to her face and placed it over her blind eyes as if to shield herself from the truth of what she was about to say. "Dah ring, with dah hourglass. It nearly full."

"So—?" Bonnie asked.

"So, dah end is nigh, chile. Cuz when he collect enough years… Dah dark soul of Jack Rackham gone be immortal."

"Good lord," Fati whispered.

Immortal. Gam Gam's words staggered Bonnie. "Did you know about this?" Bonnie asked Reed.

"No!" Reed was in shock. "It's never what we were taught."

Over the centuries, the Brigands had just assumed that by protecting marked ones from Calico Jack, they could keep him from adding years to his life. At the very least, they could keep him at bay as he burned up the years he'd collected. And if they were successful enough, he'd eventually run out. It turned out that they'd been deluding themselves. Once that hourglass was full, Jack would win. Forever.

Bonnie shuddered, remembering what Captain Ballister had once said about Calico Jack's reign of terror. "Imagine the evil a man could do," he'd said, "when there is no expiration date on his soul."

"Man," Wilder shook his head, stunned. "It's kind of an important little nugget to know. Not exactly fair."

"Dark forces ain't 'bout what fair," Gam Gam said. "Dey out tah win and destroy."

Bonnie felt a pang of guilt. She had seen the ring in countless dreams and visions. Even watched with fascination as the grains of sand defied gravity, moving upward from one globe to another, filling it. Yet it never occurred to her what it meant if it finally filled. How could she be expected to know, if the Brigands hadn't even known!?

"How many?" Bonnie asked with dread. "How many years does he need to—?" She couldn't bring herself to actually say it out loud.

"Dat I couldna see," Gam Gam admitted. "But he very close. Just say, he ain't needin' tah wait 'nother generation."

Bonnie, Reed, and Wilder stood, blindsided and devastated by this new truth.

"Then Jack'll stop at nothing to get to me... or my mom," Bonnie concluded.

Gam Gam nodded. "Always been so, men like dat, in league wid dah darkness."

Reed shook his head, crumpling into a chair. "We've failed. Three hundred years and it's over." He put his head in his hands.

"Ach! Y'all jes ain't know!" Gam Gam said. "'Dah weapon we fight wid ain't dah same dah people o' dah world fight wid.' Dat right dere from Saint Paul hisself."

"Which means what exactly, woman?" Fati asked, exasperated. "These babies don't have time for your riddles."

"Which means," the old woman said with a sly smile, "I know somebody dat might kin help."

Chapter 6
Behind the Sheltering Sky

"Hop to, Brigands! I want to be into deep water before sunrise!!"

Reed stood at the pier's edge, overseeing the flurry of activity as the Brigands readied the *True North* for their journey. The news of Calico Jack's impending immortality had shaken the entire Brigand community. But for Reed Ballister, it had done more than that—it had ignited a fire in him. After the trauma of Bobby Maynard's death, he'd hesitated to leave the safety of the Cove, but he was now determined to go back on the offensive.

Their destination on this winter morning: Hamhock Barony, the Georgia coastal town where Gam Gam had grown up. According to the old woman, it was steeped in powerful magic, much more powerful than what either Fati or Gam Gam could muster on their own. And it was with the help of that magic, she was convinced, that Bonnie would find the answers she needed to finally locate her mother.

The problem was that the folks there "didn't cotton to strangers," as Gam Gam put it. As a result of persecution, those with magical inclinations had long ago gone deep underground. The Brigands would need an entrée into their secret world and the only one who could provide that was Gam Gam herself. Fati was dead set against her grandmother traveling in her frail state but finally relented when reminded of the stakes. And since she'd never consent to the old woman going alone, Fati joined the trip as Gam Gam's caring, if not exactly enthusiastic, travel companion.

Of course, Bonnie's safety was paramount in Reed's mind. However, it was crucial to find Brigid Byrne before Calico Jack did, and everyone knew Bonnie was the key to that. So in the end there was no debate. She was going, too. They would just have to be as safe as possible. With that in mind, Reed decided that in addition to the entire crew of Brigands, Wicked Pete would accompany them for protection.

Once the preparations were complete, Reed and Bonnie were approached by Captain Ballister and Grandma Winnie, who had come out to the pier to see the *True North* off on its new adventure.

"Be ever watchful," Ballister warned his grandson. "Jack tastes the blood in the water now. I wish I could take your place at the helm."

"A Brigand's duty is not to finish the fight," Reed said, quoting from memory, "but to keep the fight alive for another day. You told me that yourself."

"I'd be okay if you *did* finish it," Grandma Winnie said. "I've seen enough young folks off to battle to last me a lifetime."

"Fair winds and following seas, boy," Captain Ballister said. "I love you, Reed. More than anything." He hugged him as if it would be the last time.

"Mistress Hartwright!" Jonesy flagged down Bonnie as she was heading up the dock. "I got somethin' for ya."

The old sea dog shuffled his feet a bit and looked the other way before unceremoniously shoving something into Bonnie's hand.

Bonnie looked down at the heavy metallic object she held.

"The Compass of Moirai?" Bonnie asked.

Sure enough, it was the enchanted compass used for centuries to match corsairs with their crews every summer. That is, until Bonnie had touched it and it had practically imploded in her hand. She remembered the horrible guilt for destroying something so beautiful, so old, and so important. And Jonesy had blamed her, calling both it and her bad omens.

"Why are you giving this to me?"

"The most confused we get is when we try to convince our heads of something our hearts know is a lie," Jonesy said. "Les jus say, I ain't confused no more. Fair winds to ya, Mistress. Come home safe." He moved down the dock, wiping what might have been a tear from his one good eye.

Meanwhile, Grandma Winnie gave Bonnie a huge basket full of sandwiches and an even huger hug. She whispered into her ear. "You take care of yourself, dear. Keep your eyes sharp and your heart open. And heed the signs. Like I taught you."

"I will, Grandma Winnie," Bonnie said. "And I'll bring her back, I promise. I will find my mother."

Reed took his turn hugging his grandmother, then they joined the others on the ship.

"Anchors aweigh!" he yelled, met by a chorus of "Aye, Captains."

The schooner glided out of Cormac's Cove, the wind catching its sails.

Bonnie stood at the bow of the ship, feeling the cool breeze against her skin. Crossbones flew over, alighting on her shoulder. She felt a surge of anticipation mingled with nervousness, and truth be told, a big heaping pile of good old-fashioned fear.

All the Brigands felt it; their usual morning banter was suppressed by an uneasy silence. Yes, this was a new adventure, but more than that, it was a journey into the unknown that would test their mettle in ways they couldn't yet fathom.

.   .   .   .   .

The next day and a half were uneventful. Wilder and Micah alternated in the crow's nest and neither saw any sign of pursuit. Still, all remained vigilant. Only Gam Gam seemed to be relaxed and reveling in the trip. In fact, she seemed completely in her element, more animated than Bonnie could remember. She spoke lovingly of Hamhock Barony, the small island where she made entry into the world over ninety years earlier. Though she hadn't visited in decades, the memories were still vivid.

Barnaby, who always made it a point to know everything about everything, said that Hamhock Barony was one of many seacoast homes of the Gullah-Geechee people, descendants of West African slaves. "The name 'Gullah' comes from Angola, where they came from, and 'Geechee' from the Kissi tribe," he explained.

"Dat so?" Gam Gam remarked with a pleased slap on her knee. "Ain't known dat mahself!"

As the ship glided past one of the small ports along the South Carolina coast, she looked out over the waters. "'Twas mah people's Ellis Island, dis here," Gam Gam said as they passed, "'Ceptin' for the freedom part."

Ripped from their homeland, the enslaved Africans could count among them tribal royalty—high priests, conjurers, and root workers who brought with them the knowledge of their culture and magical ways. Being of an oral tradition, Gullah folk passed down these practices—hoodoo as it was called—from generation to generation in whispers.

Even when they embraced Christianity, many held onto the old ways, incorporating them into their worship in the new Praise Houses built for their Sunday services. They saw no conflict between magic and religion.

"It's alla part of God's great glory and mystery," Gam Gam said.

But they knew the outside world didn't see it that way. Too many root workers were accused of witchcraft and jailed or harassed by the "upstanding" folks outside their enclaves for their magic to be practiced openly. If anyone came seeking its help without the most unimpeachable of references, they'd surely be turned away.

Though the history was fascinating, Bonnie noticed it was when Gam Gam talked about her own youthful memories that she truly came to life. She spoke of towering live oak trees covered in

Spanish moss. White sand beaches with water so blue it was hard to tell where the sea ended and the sky began. And a childhood filled with bare feet and rope swings and running through fields of swaying sweetgrass, catching fireflies in glass jars.

"Man. If I grew up in a place like that I'd never leave." Luz sighed longingly.

"So how come you never went back?" Zion asked.

"That's on me," Fati said quietly.

"Nu-uh baby girl. Mah choice. An' well, more'n a little bit, yah mamma's," Gam Gam assured her. "Yah sees, I married a handsome boy name of Winstead Robinson, and we had us a beautiful baby girl, Litia... dat's Fatimata's mamma."

"My mamma was so beautiful," Fati added wistfully.

"When Litia was but 19, she run off wid a soldier, Chester Simms, who come tah Hamhock Barony on a weekend pass," Gam Gam continued. "Yah see, like me and mah Fati, the second sight shoned bright as dah sun in mah Litia. God's gift she didn't nevah come tah 'preciate." Gam Gam sighed.

"Whether mamma left for love or to escape the burden of her gifts, well that depends on who was telling the story," Fati said. "But for whatever reason, she never told my daddy about her sight."

"Soon aftah, her young man, like so many young Black men o' dah time, he done got his orders tah ship out tah Vietnam. Fight a war haftaway 'cross dah world fah a country didn't give him much mind one way or t'other," Gam Gam shook her head sadly.

With plans to marry upon his return, Litia waited for him in his hometown of Highcross. But he was killed in action, and Fatimata was born a few months later. Litia was determined to raise her daughter away from the low country of the Gullah-Geechee—and the legacy of her gift—and stayed in Highcross in hopes of a "normal" life for her child. She cut off all ties with her family back home.

"Litia's faddah done took it real hard. Died of a broken heart, mah Winston," Gam Gam said mournfully.

When Litia fell ill years later, Gam Gam sensed it and came to care for her. After Litia passed, Fati, who was still a child at the time, begged to stay in Highcross, so Gam Gam stayed to raise her. By the time Fati was grown, it was Gam Gam who needed care.

"So's like I say, 'twas mah choice, and I ain't regretted it one second."

"Well, I'm glad you didn't go back. We would have never met you," Wilder said.

Gam Gam stared sightlessly in the direction of Wilder. "Regret, dat's for folk who don' unnerstan ebryting happen cuz God want it to, bad or good, ebryting got its purpose." She squeezed the boy's hand.

Bonnie wondered what purpose all that had befallen this dear old woman could possibly have served but could come up with nothing. The answer, perhaps like her mother, was yet to be discovered.

Chapter 7
Aboard the Perdition

The cargo ship *Perdition* cruised silently through the Sargasso Sea, hundreds of miles off the Atlantic coast. Above deck, it appeared like any lumbering cargo vessel transporting goods across the globe. But below, deep in the bowels of the ship, lay a hidden nightmare.

Scritch. Scritch. Scritch.

The cringe-inducing scrape of metal against metal emanated from the corner of the darkened hole of a room. The only light within fell from a small porthole encrusted with grime and sea salt that barely allowed the sun's rays to penetrate the gloom.

CLANG!

Just then, the sound of a deadbolt being pulled reverberated loudly. A door opened, and bright light poured in from the hallway revealing a prison cell—dank, claustrophobic, with fetid air that reeked of mildew and despair. Huddled in the corner, a man. Or what was left of him, anyway.

Maksymillian. The pirate who had let Bonnie escape back in the Carolinas. The Brigands had presumed him dead, but here he was, still clinging to the threads of life. His clothes hung from an emaciated frame. His raw, bloody wrists bore the marks of heavy chains, his nails were caked with dried paint, and his right hand was missing a finger—healed into a useless stump, a grotesque reminder of failure.

Most horrifically his lips had been stitched together with string and a sail needle—an ancient pirate punishment. The grotesque crosshatch pattern over his mouth made it impossible for him to speak or eat properly.

"Grub time, Maksy-boy," the muscular armed guard at the door pronounced and slid a metal plate of what could only charitably be called food across the floor to him.

Maks lunged, shoveling the runny porridge through the tiny gaps in his sutures. Most spilled to the floor, where he wrestled a rat for the scraps. The rat lost. Maks tucked its crushed body into a pocket—a snack for later—and finished his meal, the only food he'd likely see that day.

The guard took a step toward him and Maks scurried back, pushing himself into the corner, wild-eyed.

"Relax, mate. Boss just wants to see ya," the guard said, keys jangling. "You might want to freshen up first."

Maks cringed as the guard unshackled him and pulled him to his feet. As he led Maks roughly out the door, the light from the hall fell briefly onto the wall in the corner. Scattered on the floor were piles of rodent bones. Tiny rat pelts tied together in an ever-expanding spiral. And on the wall, a single word scratched hundreds upon hundreds of times into the painted metal:

Several minutes later, Maks's broken frame was deposited in a heap in the dimly lit captain's chamber of the *Perdition*. The walls were lined with plundered treasures, tattered maps, and grisly trophies of conquest. Standing before Maks was the source of his torment: Captain Calico Jack Rackham.

The pirate was a tall and imposing figure—his black hair and goatee framed a face that was strikingly handsome despite three centuries of harsh living and treacherous battles. His long calico coat billowed behind him as he paced the room, and on the middle finger of his left hand, he wore the nearly filled hourglass ring.

Maks, oblivious to his surroundings, rocked back and forth, muttering incoherently. Weeks of isolation and torment had shattered his once sharp mind.

"Maaaa-aaaks," Jack sang, leaning forward, poking a finger on Maks's nose with each syllable. "She... is... on the move!"

Maks's head jerked up. "Hmtmmt?" he garbled through his stitched lips.

Jack laughed. "I thought that might get your attention, mate. Yes. Our friend Bonnie Hartwright. Our spies say she's aboard the *True North*, heading south from Cormac's Cove."

Hearing Bonnie's name, Maks could feel his body tense. He hated her. Every lash, every hunger pang, every hour in shackles— he blamed Bonnie for it all, but most of all for humiliating him in front of Calico Jack—the only being ever to find worth in his worthless soul.

Maks struggled to get to his feet, but the guard shoved him back down to his knees.

"Not so fast," Jack said, cupping Maks's chin in his hand. Ever so gently, he stroked the scar Bonnie Hartwright had made on his cheek. "Am I to understand that certain lessons have been learned? Hmmm?"

Tears welled in Maks's eyes. The tender touch of Calico Jack, the man he had so bitterly disappointed, was almost more than he could bear. He nodded, trembling with gratitude.

Rackham stared back with malevolence and calculation. He sat on the edge of his desk in front of Maks. He reached for his belt and, with a flick of his wrist, produced a long knife, its jagged blade gleaming ominously in the dim light.

Maks flinched. He squeezed his eyes shut and braced himself for the dull sensation of the knife entering his body. Instead, he felt the blade graze his lips. The first suture on his mouth gave way, then another, then another. He slowly opened his eyes.

"I believe you," Calico Jack smiled and handed the dagger to Maks, who made swift work of the remaining stitches, oblivious to the nicks he was inflicting on his lips. Blood welling up in the corners of his mouth, he gasped for breath as soon as he was able.

Maks rasped, "Thank you, Captain, for your mercy."

"Mercy's got nothing to do with it." Jack took the knife from Maks and put it to his throat. "You've mucked up some carefully laid plans, you have. And now it falls to you to make it right again," Calico Jack said harshly.

Maks squirmed against the cold steel of the knife but said nothing.

"Since you are the one most familiar with this girl, this Bonnie Hartwright, I need you to track her," Calico Jack continued. "But you must not attempt to intercept her or harm her in any way. You are simply to report back on her movements. Do you understand?"

"Aye, Captain." His senses already becoming keener, Maks kept his expression neutral. Calico Jack knew nothing of his attempts to murder Bonnie on the *Dark Star*, an act which would have robbed the pirate captain of her years.

"Fail me, even a little, and I'll put you down like the pathetic mongrel you are."

Jack removed the blade from Maks's throat and plunged the knife into his desk, causing Maks to blink.

"I want to know where she's going and why. You'll have men and resources. Now get out of my sight. Don't return until it's done."

The guard yanked Maks to his feet and dragged him from the room.

"You sure about this, Jack Rackham?"

Jack turned to see Salifu, the towering African shaman, standing in the doorway to his bedchamber. Salifu's piercing gaze hadn't dulled since the day Jack met him in 1720.

"Surely there be other men in your command who can perform this task."

"That's the difference twixt you and me, Salifu," Rackham said, yanking the knife from his desk and sitting down. "You may know all about your mumbo jumbo, but me, I know people. Any fool can see how he hates the girl. And there ain't no better motivation in this world than hate."

"Except perhaps love," reminded the shaman.

"Love!" scoffed Jack. "Wouldn't know about that. The only woman I ever loved sent me to the gallows and her little girlfriend started these infernal Brigands of the Compass Rose."

"Some might say that making a pact to kill her descendants might have soured her on you," Salifu suggested.

"Well, that, my magical friend, is coming to an end." He fingered his necklace of leathery trophies—marks ripped from the flesh of each of the stained ones. "The girl will lead me to her mother and this wild goose chase will be over. The Brigands will be powerless, and the true reign of Calico Jack Rackham can finally begin."

He looked at his nearly full ring. He exhaled, the anticipation palpable—but behind his bravado, a flicker of fear shadowed his eyes.

Chapter 8
Hambock Barony

Despite the choppier seas of winter heading to spring, the *North* made good time. And Reed announced they should be arriving at their destination by afternoon.

Bonnie could swear that the closer they got, the more invigorated and youthful Gam Gam appeared. Her hunched back straightened some. Her milky eyes sparkled. Bonnie remembered Winnie telling them about sea turtles that would travel thousands of miles to return to their place of birth to lay their eggs. "Natal homing," the biologists called it. Winnie called it the "native call"— the primal pull of nature beckoning a soul home to where it belonged. Maybe that's what Gam Gam was feeling. It made Bonnie wonder where her own soul belonged.

·   ·   ·   ·   ·

"Land ho!" Wilder shouted from the crow's nest as the *True North* approached a bustling coastal town.

"No shit," replied Tanner Prescott from the forecastle. "We've been following the coast the whole trip."

"I just always wanted to say that," Wilder replied, scaling down the main mast. "It sounds so cool."

"Mister Chisolm, set course inland," Reed ordered Barnaby at the wheel. "We've arrived."

"Aye, aye!" Barnaby replied with his usual enthusiasm and steered the ship westward. Bonnie rushed to the foredeck to take in their destination.

The *True North* was headed for Port Pinckney, the mainland marina for the area known as Hamhock Barony, which not only included this coastal town but also several low-lying islands just offshore. The town was located along what was known as the Gullah Cultural Heritage Corridor between the cities of Charleston and Savannah.

As they approached the marina, it was clear they had arrived on a special day. There were tents and canopies set up everywhere. The area was crowded with tourists. A banner hung high from light poles. It read:

Welcome to
GULLAH-GEECHEE HERITAGE DAYS

"Looks like they started the party without us," Luz said, taking in the lively festival.

"Long as they have food," Micah added.

"Don't think Skittles qualify as Gullah cuisine," Tanner said.

"Hey. I been off the high fructose and red dyes for months," the newly fit Micah proclaimed.

"And the snack food market still hasn't recovered," Yeun laughed.

Wicked Pete lingered on the *North* "just in case," but the rest of the Brigands disembarked to explore the bustling oceanside plaza. Getting Gam Gam ashore required the gangway, but once on land, she moved with surprising speed toward the festival sounds. As they moved away from the pier, Crossbones fluttered onto Bonnie's arm and nuzzled close to her chest.

Atmosphere-wise, it reminded Bonnie of the farmers' market in Highcross, except here, the booths specifically featured arts, crafts, food and customs reflecting over 300 years of West African influence on the community. Musical instruments made of gourds known as shekere. African American quilting. Drum making. Gullah folk art. Conspicuously absent were the cheapo tourist-trap trinkets that seemed to attract so much attention in Highcross.

"Dis jes' how I 'member it," Gam Gam said as she strolled among the booths arm in arm with her granddaughter.

"Gam Gam, I know you got the sight. But I also know you ain't seein' all this," Fati said.

"Chile, I may be blind, but I kin still hear and smell... and feel." Gam Gam shuffled past various booths and took in their aromas. "Dat dere, dats okra soup, and dems fried pork chops, mmmmm and garlic butter blue crab..."

"She's nailed it," Wilder confirmed, trying a sample from one of the booths.

Fati chuckled, "Boy, you might be a slacker, but you can sure sniff out a free meal from 500 yards away!"

"You blame me? This stuff's way better than Nathan's Hot Dogs!" he said, referring to his hometown of Coney Island's most famous export.

"Maybe she could sniff her way to a burger joint," Tanner said. "This ethnic stuff ain't for me."

"Food got a little too much pigmentation for you, white boy?" Daya said, enjoying the scents that weren't so far removed from those in her Dominican *abuela's* kitchen.

"Oh, and dat dere is a double dutch jump if'n I ever heared one." Gam Gam shuffled across the way to where some Gullah girls were teaching visitors the art of jumping rope. The ropes slapped to a beat on the concrete.

"As a young'un, I was champeen of Hamhock when it come tah dah double dutch," Gam Gam said wistfully. "Dem days is gone."

Suddenly Daya jumped in, herself an expert from Bronx summers playing in front of neighborhood stoops. The Brigands applauded and cheered her on. "Woo, Daya!" After an impressive show, she effortlessly jumped back out. The Gullah girls high fived her and she took a bow.

"I didn't know you could do that," Luz said when Daya rejoined them on the sidelines.

"Every relationship needs a little mystery," Daya said, slipping her arm through Luz's.

"Dammit. Where did Gam Gam get to now?" Fati started to panic.

SQUAWK!! Crossbones flew up over the crowd.

"There she is!" said Bonnie, pointing to where the parrot was up ahead.

Gam Gam was pushing through the sea of people, using her cane to part the way. The Brigands trailed her to a large tent, apologizing to the victimized festivalgoers as they went. Inside, they found a group taking part in a traditional Gullah-Geechee performance.

Men in overalls and straw hats pounded sticks into the ground or clapped in unison. Gullah women in colorful printed frocks, aprons, matching headwraps, and black brogans shuffled counterclockwise in a ring to the beat. One man sang out a phrase and the others responded, the women dancing in their circle and moving their arms as they did.

"Gam Gam! Don't run off like that!" Fati scolded.

"But it's Ring Shouters!" Gam Gam exclaimed, clapping along.

"Care to elaborate?" Bonnie asked Fati as Gam Gam moved closer to the center of the ring.

"I'm Gullah in genes only," Fati shrugged. "Ask the know-it-all."

Not surprisingly, Barnaby was ready with an explanation. "It's a Gullah tradition born from enslaved communities. They used it to communicate across language barriers and embed hidden messages their enslavers couldn't decode."

Gam Gam joined the circle, her cane steadying her as she shuffled and chanted with the other performers.

"*Move, Daniel! Move, Daniel. Go the other way, Daniel!*" sang the lead man as the others pounded their sticks and clapped hands.

The women, helped along by the joyous voice of Gam Gam, responded as they shuffle danced in a circle. "*Move, Daniel! Move, Daniel! Oh Lord, pray sinner come! Oh, Lord, sinner gone to Hell!*"

The Brigands watched and clapped along. The smile on Gam Gam's face could have powered the entire island.

"Wow," Wilder said. "Even if we don't get what we came for, seeing her this happy makes this trip worthwhile."

Fati shook her head with a smile. "Don't disagree with you, boy. Just look at that woman, ain't she a clam at high tide!"

Bonnie, however, couldn't quite allow herself to get swept up by the moment. This wasn't a pleasure trip, and while Gam Gam's happiness was heartwarming, they had a mission to attend to.

"We should go," Bonnie urged.

"What's your rush, Hartwright?" Tanner said, turning to her. "The old lady is clearly having the time of her-uh-hellooo!"

Tanner stopped in midsentence, staring over Bonnie's shoulder, his mouth agape. "That is seriously the most beautiful chick I have ever seen," he said.

"Look who's suddenly got an appetite for ethnic treats!" laughed Daya.

Bonnie turned to see what had grabbed Tanner's attention.

The attractive woman stood out among the Gullah dancers because she was the youngest one in the group. The *only* young one in fact. Also, she *was* strikingly beautiful. Maybe 18 or 19 years old. Luminous almond-colored skin and amber eyes. Her hair in dozens of braids encircled her oval face and went down her back.

"Why do you always have to objectify women?" Bonnie said, hoping to garner a little feminist support from her female crewmates.

Instead, it turned out Luz was singing from the same hymnal as Tanner. "He's right, though," she said. "*Chica* is a total smoke show." She turned to Daya. "No offense, bae."

"What am I, a corpse over here?" Daya said in mock annoyance.

"You'd have to be dead not to notice her," Reed commented.

Bonnie noticed Reed watching the girl with an interest that went far beyond cultural appreciation. Wilder was, too. So were all the guys. A pang of jealousy shot through her. She looked back at the girl, sizing her up. Unlike the other dancers with their sturdy, steady movements, the girl's dance was balletic, imbued with elegance and fluidity—a stark contrast to the bored expression on her face.

She was undeniably stunning and clearly knew it, exuding a self-assurance Bonnie felt she could never match. The jealousy flared, quickly followed by annoyance at herself for letting teenage emotions distract her from the mission, even for a moment.

The dance ended and Bonnie watched the girl beat a hasty retreat out of the tent, not even bothering to acknowledge the applause of the onlookers.

"Uh, I'll be back in a bit. I think I've got some okra to shuck," Tanner said and started after the girl.

"You're not going anywhere!" Bonnie snapped, blocking his way. "We need to stay focused on what we came here for." Bonnie hoped her cheeks weren't as red as the heat she was feeling coming off them. She went over to Gam Gam. "Gam Gam, I don't mean to interrupt your nice time, but do you think you can find the person we came to talk to?"

Before the old fortuneteller could answer, a woman's voice pierced through the crowd noise.

"Ophelia? Ophelia Robinson! Dat you?"

Everyone turned at the sound of the voice. It belonged to a woman roughly Gam Gam's age. She had been one of the dancers who'd just performed. Whereas Gam Gam was blind and barely mobile, this woman seemed spry for her years, running up to Gam Gam and throwing her arms around her.

"Rhoda? Rho Munro?!" Gam Gam cried out, just "knowing" in that way she had.

"It *is* me, Ophie!" the woman replied gaily.

"Oh Rho-Rho. It be too long."

"Now who damn fault is dat, woman?"

"I knowed this woman since we was knee high to a goober," Gam Gam said.

The women hugged tightly and cried tears of joy or maybe of sadness at the years missed. Rhoda took a step back and looked at the Brigands that surrounded Gam Gam.

"Uh oh. This ain't no social visit, is it?"

"We got business dat calls fah a little mo', uh, know-how den ring shoutin' and rope skippin'. If'n yah gets mah meaning."

Rhoda lowered her voice, looking around. "Now, we ain't talk 'bout dat much no more. Specially not to no outsiders," she shot a glance at the group. "Folks don't take well to it dese days."

"It's important," Bonnie interjected. Gam Gam touched her arm in a gesture to get her to back down.

"Sho' we unnerstan' what you sayin'. But it don' mean it ain't still about. I feelt it the second I stepped foot on dah ground. Even before. And I need me access. Like dah girl say, it important. Life or death."

Rhoda thought about it hard. Finally, she said. "You gone have tah talk to Queen Zee."

"Who is Queen Zee?" Reed asked.

, , , , ,

Five minutes later, Bonnie and the Brigands stood before the main stage of the festival as Fati and Gam Gam chatted with Rho Munro nearby. A Gullah theater troupe had just finished reenacting the tale of their people's enslavement and liberation to rousing applause. As they left the stage, a handsome middle-aged Black man in a colorful African print shirt took the stage.

"Welcome to the annual Gullah-Geechee Heritage Festival! I'm Martin Grace, though many of y'all know me as Marty, your local plumber," he said, grinning. The crowd cheered, someone hooted, and he laughed. "Thanks, Mom!" Everyone roared with laughter.

"Well, another year, another festival. Our best ever. I don't need to tell y'all who we have to thank for the success of this endeavor.

But lemme introduce her for those visitors among us. Mayor of Hamhock Barony by way of Howard University, none other than my own beautiful wife, Dr. Zenobia Grace!"

An elegant woman, wearing traditional Gullah garb and headdress, walked to the microphone to great applause.

"Thank you, Martin. And Marty is too shy to say it himself, but he wants you to know that Grace Plumbing is running a special this month on rooter work. I can tell you from personal experience, that nobody can clean your pipes like my husband Marty!"

"I'll bet!" yelled a woman from the crowd.

When the audience broke into laughter, Dr. Grace laughed along with them "Y'all are awful, you need to get yourselves to church with those dirty minds of yours!"

After the tumult of laughter subsided, she gathered herself. "Anyway... Welcome all to Hamhock Barony, our little slice of low-country heaven. We're thrilled to share our culture with you. We Gullah-Geechee folk are survivors—our ancestors endured the Middle Passage, slavery, and Jim Crow. Today, we fight to survive climate change, rising waters, and corporate gentrification. But most importantly, as we protect our coastline from the sea, we also preserve our heritage, passing our customs from generation to generation so they're not lost to time.

"So—eat, drink, dance, and ask questions. Just don't ask how we make our sweetgrass baskets; that's a Gullah-Geechee secret! And now, please welcome all the way from Beaufort, the Grammy-winning band, Juke 'n Jelly!"

A combo took the stage and began playing jazz-influenced arrangements of Gullah favorites. Dr. Grace exited the stage and was promptly greeted by Rhoda Munro, with Gam Gam in tow. They hugged and Rho whispered something in Dr. Grace's ear.

From afar, Bonnie watched Dr. Grace's gaze land directly on her, her expression darkening. Bonnie gasped, feeling as though an invisible force were probing her, like an airport security scanner with electric fingers.

A FLASH OF IMAGES: *A crying baby in a pew. A dark-haired girl in shabby clothes being shaken roughly by adult hands. A little older, hiding inside a closet and covering her ears. The same girl, Bonnie, sitting alone with a garbage bag in the waiting area of foster care.*

The visions abruptly stopped. Bonnie blinked and saw Dr. Grace had shifted her focus, briefly talking to Rho Munro and then smiling brightly as she greeted a group of VIPs nearby.

She saw right into me, Bonnie shuddered, reeling from the psychic violation she had just experienced. And she hadn't liked it, not one bit.

Chapter 9
Blue Roots

After Rho reported that Queen Zee had agreed to a sit-down with Bonnie later that evening, the Brigands killed time exploring the festival. They sampled more local cuisine, even picking up some fried oysters and seafood mac to take back to Wicked Pete. All the while, Tanner Prescott scanned the crowd for the beautiful Gullah girl, but she had vanished and Tanner's efforts to ask about her whereabouts came up empty.

Reed and Wilder weren't thrilled with the idea of Bonnie going without them to Queen Zee's house. No one was. But those were the ground rules. Only Bonnie, Fati, and Gam Gam. Take it or leave it.

So, as the tourists thinned out and booths slowly started getting packed away, the three of them went to the marina. Rho introduced them to her grandson, DaBorn, a fortyish man in a graphic tee that read, "*OG—Original Geechee.*" A tall, sturdy man with weathered skin and deep lines etched into his still-young face, he'd been wrangled into transporting the women on his flat-bottomed boat— what the locals called a *bateau*—from the mainland to a nearby low-lying island where the Grace house was located.

"Used tah yah could walk there from here," Gam Gam said.

"Cain't now, less yer the Lord hisself. Welcome to climate change," Rho said.

"I ain't got all day," DaBorn groused. "Them crab traps ain't gonna bring themselves in."

Bonnie stepped onto the bateau when suddenly her heart leapt. She sensed something. Something she hadn't felt since the night of the high seas battle with Calico Jack's pirates.

Death. It smells like death! She quickly scanned the boardwalk and crowd for its source but saw nothing. And just as suddenly as it came, the smell—and the feeling—departed. For a moment, she considered telling the Gullah women what she'd experienced. But she was afraid they would stop her from going to see Queen Zee. And for what, momentary jitters? After all, the pirate she knew as Maks was dead. With her own eyes, she'd seen him fall off the *Dark Star* and drown in the murky waters of the sound. *Hadn't she?*

The bateau made its way through winding waterways of lush green sea grasses beneath a sky filled with soaring ospreys. Returning to the moment, Bonnie caught her breath at the sight of a dolphin breaching in the water alongside the boat, so close that she could almost touch it.

"Dolphins are a sign of peace and harmony," Fati said smiling as the dolphin breached a second time.

"Male dolphins sometimes kill their young," DaBorn said matter-of-factly as he steered the bateau toward its destination.

The idyllic moment was shattered. The three women grew silent.

As the dolphin did a final playful flip and headed out to sea, Bonnie's thoughts drifted to Calico Jack and how he, too, killed his own young simply so he could live as he wished. And how many other parents did wrong by their own children out of their own selfishness. Not a great track record for humanity. Suddenly the dolphins didn't seem so bad.

. . . . .

Once on the island, DaBorn silently led the group along a dirt path lined with swaying sweet grass. They passed the occasional clapboard house, typically up on blocks—protection from flooding. Laundry hung on lines, vegetable gardens filled front yards, and chickens wandered freely. Without fail, every house had blue-painted window frames and doors.

"What's with all the blue?" Bonnie asked DaBorn on one of their many stops to let Gam Gam rest.

DaBorn shot Bonnie a hard look, clearly not one for small talk with strangers.

"Haints is afraid of water," Gam Gam explained.

"Haints?"

"Spirits. We paint dah windows and doors dah color of water. Keep dem out."

"Oh." There was a time Bonnie would have scoffed at such a notion. Those days were long gone.

As they continued on, Bonnie noticed faces that peered suspiciously from windows, through the spaces between curtains. A woman outside taking down laundry quickly bundled her sheets, grabbed her child, and hurried indoors, leaving her chained dog to bark viciously at the strangers. It was a familiar feeling for Bonnie—the Brigands often received the same cold treatment at the Highcross farmers' market. Suspicion of strangers, it seemed, was as universal as folk music.

Near the end of the dirt road stood a small white church, a praise house as they were called around here. It had been built, Gam Gam explained, in antebellum days so that Black folks might find community and worship away from the prying eyes of their enslavers.

"That's really where you were baptized?" Fati asked.

"Yup. It been standin' hunnerd years 'fore I was born and it'll be here long after I give up mah last breath," Gam Gam smiled.

Finally, they arrived at the edge of some woods and DaBorn turned to them. "You're on your own from here."

"Wait. How are we supposed to find the house?" Bonnie asked.

"Just keep on, through them woods ahead," DaBorn said, as if it pained him to do so. "You'll come on the Grace house soon enough. Only folks out this way."

"Tank yah, DaBorn," Gam Gam said. "Tell Rho I be in touch."

DaBorn grunted and turned, heading back the way they'd come, mumbling something under his breath that was incomprehensible but clearly unfriendly.

"What's with him?" Fati asked, continuing in the direction that DaBorn had indicated.

"We way deep in blue roots country now, chile," Gam Gam offered, "don' none of dese folk trust outsiders much."

"I'm from these folks. How am I an outsider?"

"Yah ain't raised up here, girl, then yah don' know, yah jes don' know," Gam Gam said and walked ahead of them, somehow navigating the path without assistance. Fati shook her head and followed behind her grandmother. Now, it was her turn to mutter something under her breath.

Pushing through curtains of moss, they arrived at a house nestled among ancient oaks. Larger than the others they'd seen, it had two stories, a covered porch, and, of course, blue-painted window frames and doors. At the edge of the porch stood a tree with dozens of blue bottles on its bare branches. As the wind blew, the bottles clinked softly, producing an eerie melody.

"Those for haints, too?" asked Bonnie as they approached the porch.

"And the occasional boo hag!"

The group startled at the voice of Zenobia Grace, who was sitting in the shadows, at the end of the porch. She rocked in a rocking chair and sipped on a cup of tea.

"Haints and boo hags get attracted to the sparkling glass and get trapped inside. Can't get up to their dirty doings! Plus, the midday sun burns them to nought."

The woman rose, "I'm sorry if I startled you... I'm Zenobia Grace. You can call me Queen Zee. Come inside."

The group sat in Queen Zee's library. Bonnie was surprised by the eclectic décor. Electric lamps sat next to lit candles. Stacks of scientific books on climatology were intermixed with volumes on herbology, root work, and African rituals. A gris-gris bag rested on the keyboard of an open MacBook Air. Ritual masks hung beside framed college diplomas.

According to Bonnie's quick perusal of the parchment, Zenobia Corrine Grace had a BA in Economics, a master's and PhD in environmental sciences, and a JD in environmental law. The degrees hung over a large potting-style bench covered in various herbs, bottles of potions, and other odd-looking substances. There was a photograph of Dr. Grace with a former first lady and another with a very famous singer who, Bonnie just discovered, had Gullah roots.

"Lot of degrees there," Fati commented. "Impressive."

"I didn't get them to impress," Queen Zee said, pouring tea for her guests. "I got them to fight the enemies of my people."

"What enemies do the Gullah people have?" asked Bonnie.

"Where do I start? We're fighting a war on two fronts 'round here, Miss Hartwright. Coming at us from the west are the mainland corporations that want the land for their resorts. And from the east, here comes the ocean, trying to take back what she gave up a hundred million years ago. So, a long time ago, I decided to arm myself with knowledge. 'If you know your enemies and know yourself, you need not fear a hundred battles.'"

Bonnie nodded. She had seen similar things in Highcross when Charlie Eden and the city council tried to take Cormac's Cove. Though that had turned out to be only partially about corporate greed. *The rest was Calico Jack Rackham trying to acquire the only place I was safe,* she thought. This circled her back to why they were there in the first place.

"Excuse me, Dr. Grace…" Bonnie began.

"Queen Zee when I'm talking with friends. You *are* friends?" she asked suspiciously.

"You can be sure of that," Fati assured her.

"Queen Zee," Bonnie began again, "I don't mean to be pushy or anything, but we're here because my mother is missing. Fati and Gam Gam say you might be able to help us find her."

"You know. I had dreams of you coming," Queen Zee carefully set her teacup down, and it clinked as her hand shook slightly. "Nightmares more like. I was hoping... praying actually, that that's all they were. But deep down I knew... they were far worse than any bad dream."

"If you *have* seen," said Bonnie, "then you know my mother is in real danger."

"Yes. I saw that," Queen Zee sighed. "And, um, other things, too. That's the part that gives me pause."

"Dem other tings are fah dah girl and her folks tah deal wid," Gam Gam said. "Yah don' hafta be worry 'bout dem. All's we need is yah point us in dah right direction and yah part be done."

"These things are seldom cut and dry, Miss Ophelia," Queen Zee said hesitantly. "As I'm sure you know. I put my finger in that blackberry pie, it's bound to come out stained."

"Service to others is our rent here on earth," Fati said. "It's what Gam Gam always says."

"I knowed yah was listenin', mah Fati," Gam Gam smiled.

"So will you? Please, will you help?" Bonnie was close to begging.

Queen Zee leaned back in her chair, squinched her face together and was clearly thinking it over carefully. She seemed to be about to answer when—

"NO WAY!" a young woman's voice shouted and the front door to the Grace house flew open, creating a commotion in the entryway.

The women in the library turned to look toward the fuss.

"I am not doing it again tomorrow! Today was the last time! End of story!"

Bonnie saw that it was the beautiful girl from the circle dance. Only now she was dressed in jeans, sneakers, and a crop top, her traditional costume unceremoniously wadded up under her arm.

"Cordial! It's important to your mamma," Zenobia's husband Martin said, following the girl into the house.

"Then let *her* do it! All this old Gullah stuff's got nothing to do with me! People in this town already think I'm a freak!" She threw her costume to the floor; the dress and headwrap landed in a heap next to the fireplace. She stopped in her tracks the moment she did it as she saw the faces staring at her from the library doorway.

"Zenobia," Martin said, clearing his throat. "We, uh, didn't know you were home. Or that you had company."

"So I see," Queen Zee said, glaring at the girl. "Cordial Grace. Pick those clothes up. Now."

The girl quickly obeyed, clearly fearful of inciting her mother's wrath.

"Generations of your ancestors wore that," Queen Zee continued in a steady voice. "You will respect and honor it, young lady." Dr. Grace turned to the visitors and indicated the young woman. "Behold. The most dangerous enemy of my people yet devised—acculturation."

"Whoa!" The girl froze and looked around the room, suddenly on high alert. "What's going on here? Who are these people? And why am I picking up some seriously bad vibes?"

"These are my guests. Ophelia Robinson, she was born here on the island, friends with Rho Munro. This is her granddaughter, Fatimata. And their friend, Miss Bonnie Hartwright. Ladies, this is my husband Martin and this rude, ungrateful child not living up to her name is my daughter Cordial."

Pleasantries were exchanged until Cordial reached Bonnie. The moment their eyes met, Cordial stiffened.

"Hello, Bonnie Hartwright," she said quietly. Then, her voice turned cold. "You need to get the hell out of our house. Right now!"

Chapter 10
The Conjuring

"I won't do it!" Cordial shook her head. "And if you're picking up half what I'm getting off that girl, mamma, you'd tap out too."

Cordial was speaking about Bonnie as if she wasn't there. Bonnie hated that. She'd had a lifetime of it. But she held her tongue, not wanting to do anything that would derail the reading.

"Don't condescend to me, young lady!" Queen Zee snapped at her daughter. "I've been 'picking up' things off folks since I was half your age!"

The five women were now gathered at a picnic table in the back yard. Night had fallen, and lanterns hanging from the oaks cast eerie shadows on their faces. There were rings of melted wax and ash stains on the table, evidence of past readings.

Following her rude comment to Bonnie, Queen Zee had taken her daughter into the kitchen. After much heated whispering, they both returned—Queen Zee with a plastered smile and apologies, and Cordial with a glowering look and silence. Martin, the lone "muggle" of the family, hastily retreated into the den to watch basketball. It wasn't until Cordial sat at the table across from Bonnie that she decided it was time to reignite the argument.

"But why do I have to be part of it?" Cordial threw Bonnie a disgusted look.

"You refuse to go to college. You hate answering phones for your dad. Time you get your hands dirty, girl, and try the other side of the family business."

"I tried it once, remember?"

"I don't want her here if she doesn't want to be." Bonnie couldn't take it anymore. The idea of Little Miss Perfect poking around in Bonnie's damaged psyche was more than she could stomach.

"Trust me, you want her!" Queen Zee replied. "My daughter may be a supreme pain in the astral realm, but Lord, if she doesn't have the strongest sight in generations! She could be a real battering ram against those walls Miss Fati here bumped into."

"We'll take all the help we can get and appreciate it," Fati said. "Right, Bonnie?"

Bonnie didn't like being used as a life lesson for this brat. But if Cordial *could* actually offer help and Bonnie refused to take it, she'd never forgive herself. Reluctantly, she nodded. "I suppose."

Put in their places by their elders, the two young women shut up and threw side eyes at each other.

"Good. Now don't just stand there. Sit!" Queen Zee commanded. "And let's see what we can see."

*   *   *   *   *

Even with Gam Gam on the sidelines, there was more than enough psychic firepower sitting around the table, and Bonnie joined the mystic circle with great hope. She sat between Queen Zee and Fati. Cordial sat on the other side of her mother.

"Don't we need herbs or some bones or smoke or something?" Bonnie whispered to Fati.

"Someone's been streaming old episodes of *Supernatural*," Cordial snorted.

Bonnie gave Fati a withering look. "Seriously?"

"I add a little theater. So sue me," Fati whispered back.

Bonnie took Fati's hand to close the circle. A powerful electric rush surged through them, stronger than anything Bonnie had felt in Highcross. Blue light shot from their hands, forming a smoky ring above the table.

Cordial gasped aloud, clearly unprepared for the raw power they'd just unleashed.

IMAGES ATTACK IN RAPID SUCCESSION: *Jungle foliage. A mine tunnel. Gunfire! Boots pounding! Explosions. Fires rage. The tunnel collapses. Screams echo. A straw cross. A craggy black rock island lashed by waves. A stag bounds over rugged terrain, morphing into a woman with raven-hair streaked in white. Brigid? She stops at a crumbled wall. Turns, sensing something behind her. Her eyes go wide, as if looking directly at Bonnie, and then the wall EXPLODES!*

The four women were thrown back from the table by the force of the explosion in the vision. The circle of smoke scattered in every direction, leaving eerie blue wisps trailing from their hands.

"Holy shit!" Cordial exclaimed, adrenaline coursing through her body. "That was so cool!"

"My mother!" Bonnie said excitedly. "That was her. Where is she? Did you see?"

"I-I don't know," Queen Zee said, shaken. "There's powerful hoodoo there. Not hoodoo exactly—something else... unfamiliar. I couldn't penetrate it."

"Just like when I tried!" Fati added, relief tinging her voice. "I'd get so close, then BAM—nothing!"

"You ask me, I don't think your mom wants you to find her," Cordial said in that mean-girl-sweet way that Bonnie hated.

"No one asked you! So why don't you just stay out of it!" Bonnie snapped.

"You bring this darkness to our doorstep and then tell me to stay out of it?" Cordial shot back. "I *was* out of it until you showed up!"

"Girls! Hush on up! We're all on the same side here," Fati pleaded.

Cordial glared at Bonnie. Bonnie glared right back. *Were they though?*

"Bonnie," Queen Zee said, "did any of those images mean anything to you?"

"I-I've seen those rocks before. Remember, Fati? During your last conjuring. And that ocean but—everything else..." Bonnie shook her head. What she had seen was like a war zone. "... it didn't make sense."

"May could be, dat's dah problem," Gam Gam spoke up.

"What do you mean, Gam Gam?" Fati asked.

"You lookin' at it from dah wrong way up. Don't none of it mean nothin' tah dah chile. Mebe we needs tah go at it so's it does. Lemme try sumpin." Gam Gam took a place at the table and held out her hands.

"Uh, Gam Gam. Hold up." Fati hesitated. "You haven't been in a circle in a good while."

"Like ridin' my ol' two-wheeler. 'Sides, I feel better'n I been in a long, long time."

"That might be but—"

"We gots tah finish what we started. Yah know dat in yah heart, mah Fatimata. Mebbe I could help. Lemme help." She held out both her hands. Bonnie took one without hesitation. The others stared at her, taken aback by her eagerness.

"She *wants* to help," Bonnie said.

Still grumbling about her grandmother's frail condition, Fati reluctantly took Gam Gam's hand. Cordial and Queen Zee joined in and the circle was complete.

WHOOSH! Bonnie felt the surge of power again, even stronger this time. The others' faces mirrored her shock. Gam Gam's presence seemed to amplify the energy, like a cell tower boosting a weak signal. The blue smoke rose once more, now streaked with lightning crackling in its depths. The table SHOOK as visions came in a flurry:

FLASHES as a GOLD DISC spins swiftly, catching light. Until the gold light becomes... the light of the setting sun.

Bonnie blinks. Eyes adjusting. She is standing on the pier at Cormac's Cove. The True North is docked nearby. Storm clouds brew in the distance and the wind violently whips the Brigand flag on the mast. Captain Ballister and Winnie stand beside her. But they look different. Younger. Winnie's hair is still red, as is most of Ballister's beard.

"Mama? Dada?" A child's voice.

Bonnie looks down, surprised to see she is holding a toddler. The boy gazes up at her, stormy gray eyes, auburn hair... it is Reed! He points.

Bonnie follows his finger to—

Two caskets being unloaded from the ship.

"Oh, my sweet Daniel!" Winnie sobs and Ballister wraps her, Bonnie and his grandson in his arms. Bonnie feels hot tears stream down her face. Ballister shushes her. "There, there, Brigid." He whispers to her.

Brigid?! Bonnie is confused. That's when she catches a glimpse of herself, reflected in the water below the pier. The woman staring back is not her. It's Brigid! Young and very pregnant!

Bonnie realizes she is a passenger in this body. An observer to everything her mother is seeing, hearing, thinking. And feeling because—

Suddenly she grips her abdomen, a SEARING PAIN. Her water breaks.

THE GOLD DISC FLASHES AGAIN! This time its light becomes... the golden glow of a kerosene lamp. Bonnie/Brigid lies on a bed in the throes of labor. Sheets of rain lash a window and lightning flashes outside. The power is out. Bonnie/Brigid CRIES OUT with a final push as Winnie holds up a dark-haired baby girl. A twisted X visible on the baby's shoulder. Bonnie/Brigid SCREAMS!

THE GOLD DISC SPINS and FLASHES! The light becomes... the glow of the full Corn Moon in the sky over the church at the top of the hill. Inside, Bonnie/Brigid holds the marked baby girl over the brass baptismal font, sprinkles holy water over her tiny forehead. The baby coos.

THE GOLD DISC FLASHES and becomes... the light of sunset. A girl on a Greyhound bus looks out the window over a desert landscape. Bonnie once again sees her reflection. Sees a young Brigid peering out from under an oversized hoodie. Dark circles beneath her eyes. Fear on her face. The mewling newborn wrapped tightly against her chest in a makeshift sling made from one of Grandma Winnie's rose print tablecloths. She fingers the hilt of the dagger hidden at her waist.

THE GOLD DISC FLASHES and now becomes... the flames of a hundred votive candles. Bonnie/Brigid stands inside a church holding her baby, who looks innocently up at her.

Bonnie/Brigid is crying, a teardrop falls onto her child's face. The baby blinks. Bonnie/Brigid places the child on the pew. She starts to go, then hesitates. Reconsidering when—

THE SOUND OF A DOOR OPENING at the front of the church. Bonnie/Brigid runs and slips out the front door into the bright daylight.

Peering through a stained-glass window outside the church, Bonnie/Brigid watches as—

A middle-aged priest picks up the baby. As he does, A SMALL GOLD DISC falls from her swaddling. Bonnie/Brigid watches as it spins in SLOW MOTION, over and over, FLASHING in the candlelight. Until it hits the tile floor with a CLINK and—

Bonnie GASPED, her eyes flying open. She found herself in a fetal position on the ground, ten feet from the table. She slowly blinked back to awareness of the commotion around her. Fati wailed. Queen Zee knelt nearby, looking down. She yelled something to Cordial, who sprinted away. Bonnie turned her head to see what they were looking at. On the ground next to her, the prone body of Gam Gam lay unconscious.

"Oh my God. Oh my God!" Bonnie exclaimed, scrambling to her feet.

Bonnie sat shivering on the bottom step of the Grace front porch. It was well after midnight, and she was still reeling from all that had transpired that evening. The vision that had been conjured was more powerful than anything she had encountered in her years of having visions. She actually lived what her mother was living. From the inside. She saw it, felt it, experienced it first-hand. She understood everything her mother had gone through in giving her up and it moved her profoundly. Unfortunately, the power of the vision had nearly killed Gam Gam, and the guilt of that weighed heavily on Bonnie.

After Gam Gam collapsed, the family decided she was too frail to transport to a hospital. And, since road access to the house was dodgy at best, rather than call the EMTs, Mr. Grace had gone to the mainland to fetch the doctor himself.

Meanwhile, Cordial was dispatched to the marina, to tell the Brigands back on the *True North* what had happened. She returned with Reed and Wilder, as they both insisted on seeing Bonnie immediately. Now, they all sat with her, waiting for word.

"I just don't get how you could let Gam Gam do it," Wilder said, frustration evident. "I mean, with what her health's been like lately..."

"She insisted. I tried to stop her! But you know how stubborn she can be," Bonnie replied defensively.

Cordial shot Bonnie an accusatory look over her "interpretation of events." Bonnie glared back, challenging Cordial to contradict her. Cordial kept her mouth shut.

The door creaked open, and Martin stepped onto the porch. Everyone turned expectantly.

"She's conscious," Mr. Grace said. "But Doc Freers says her heart's taken quite a shock. It's touch and go."

A heavy silence fell over the group.

"Can I see her?" Wilder asked.

"She's asking for Bonnie," Martin replied.

Bonnie was startled. Wilder gave Bonnie a wounded look.

"If Wilder wants to go first—" Bonnie started, not sure if she was up to seeing the old woman just then.

"Bonnie," Martin held the screen door open for her. "I don't think you want to make her wait."

Bonnie reluctantly followed him into the house.

*   *   *   *   *

Bonnie stood looking down at Gam Gam, who looked like a small child in the large, overstuffed bed. Queen Zee watched from behind her and at the bedside, Fati wiped a tear.

"Don't be long. She needs her rest," said Doc Freers, a man so elderly himself he still carried an old-style black doctor's bag. "I'll be right outside." He left the room.

Bonnie held Gam Gam's hand and marveled at how tiny and light it felt. As if it were filled with bird bones. Her skin so translucent that every vein was visible. She was more frail-looking than Bonnie had ever seen her. Bonnie thought she seemed as if she was hanging on to the earthly plane by the thinnest of frayed threads.

"Oh, Gam Gam," Bonnie said, tears in her eyes. "I'm so sorry."

"Fah what?" Gam Gam said, removing her oxygen mask with that frail hand. "Bringin' me back to mah home? Cuz dat what yah done chile. I wouldna be here if not fah yah."

"I know but, if I'd stopped you tonight—"

"If'n youda stopped me, we wouldna seen what we seen."

Bonnie was openly weeping now.

"Shush. Ain't no time fah tears." Gam Gam reached up and wiped a tear from Bonnie's cheek. "Time fah listenin'... Yah listenin'?"

"Yes, ma'am."

"Yah gots to go. Yah needs tah leave here and go get yah mamma."

"What? How? We still don't know where she is."

"Dah church," Gam Gam said.

"The church? On the Cove?" Bonnie asked, confused.

"Not dat one... dah one where yah mamma done left yah, in, in..." she struggled to remember.

"In Tucson?"

"Dat dah one..." Gam Gam started but then went into a coughing fit, trying to catch her breath. Fati ran over and replaced the oxygen mask.

"Tell... her," Gam Gam said to Queen Zee through labored breath.

"The church from your vision," Zenobia said. "I can't tell you exactly what it holds, that thing that she dropped before she ran off that day, but I do know it's crucial. Whatever it is, it's your key to her."

"O-okay. As soon as Gam Gam's feeling better and—"

"Now! Do it now! Tonight. 'Fore he comes!" Gam Gam started coughing again and this time couldn't stop. "Danger... is... nigh."

Queen Zee called for the doctor, who came rushing in. He started administering a syringe to Gam Gam.

Bonnie stood immobile, staring at the old woman struggle for breath.

"Don't just stand there. Do what she says, Bonnie!" Fati blurted as she tried to soothe Gam Gam. "This is what you wanted from her. She's given it to you! So go. Now! NOW!"

Shaken, Bonnie stumbled back and then rushed out the door, leaving Gam Gam still struggling for breath behind her.

It would be the last time she'd see the old woman... alive.

Chapter 11
Plans

The high winds and the splashing sea drowned out the buzz of the outboard motor as DaBorn's bateau moved through the early morning blackness. No matter how hard Bonnie stared into that inkiness from the bow of the boat, it was impossible to see where the water ended and the sky began.

To make matters worse, the stretch of shore they traveled along was unpopulated and dark, creating the dizzying sensation of moving through a void. Fortunately, DaBorn knew the coastline by heart, so even with zero visibility and his navigation lights off to avoid detection, he was able to maneuver the crowded vessel safely toward its destination. Bonnie wasn't sure if it was the spatial disorientation or the apprehension at what lay ahead that made her feel so nauseated, but it took all her willpower to keep from throwing up. So she swallowed back the bile, clung to the side of the boat, and stared straight ahead. It was the end of an insane twenty-four hours.

After Gam Gam had given Bonnie her marching orders the day before, everything moved with lightning speed. Reed began plotting a trip to Tucson, but getting there would be a challenge. Sailing to Arizona wasn't an option for obvious reasons, and commercial flights were out—Calico Jack's spy network made that a non-starter. Besides, there were the weapons. No one wanted to risk traveling unarmed, knowing Rackham's men could be lurking along the way. But a band of teenagers brandishing scimitars and cutlasses tends to attract the attention of airport security. So the Brigands were left scrambling for an alternative.

Reed calculated that, if they put the pedal to the metal, they could reach Tucson in 28 hours or so driving straight through. And Wicked Pete, a seasoned field Brigand with 45 years of experience and a contact list to match, knew just who he could call on to get them there. Leveraging Reed's encrypted messaging system, Pete quickly arranged a rendezvous. By early the next morning, Bonnie and a small group of Brigands were set to meet their allies and prepare for the next leg of their journey.

According to Pete, their escorts—the Wayfarers as they were known—were a land-based group of Brigands who knew the backroads of the country inside and out. They would handle the transport, getting the young Brigands safely to their destination. Though Reed and Barnaby knew of them, it was the first Bonnie or anybody else had ever heard of such a group. It had never occurred to Bonnie that a Brigand would be anything but a seafarer. But there was a lot of land between the Atlantic and the Pacific, so she guessed it made sense.

The Brigands disliked the idea of splitting up, but sending everyone just wasn't practical. The Wayfarers could only accommodate five or six people at most, and anything more felt risky. Besides, a separate crew was needed to sail the *True North* back to Cormac's Cove as a diversion, just in case they were under surveillance.

Getting Bonnie to Tucson safely and undetected was the priority, so Reed made his personnel selections accordingly. There were Bonnie and Reed, of course. Wilder made the list because there was no one Bonnie trusted more. Though Zion was their best fighter, Reed decided he'd rather have Luz since she had lately made it her personal mission to keep Bonnie safe. Reed also chose Tanner, figuring he could probably talk his way out of an awkward situation just by leveraging that entitled swagger or dropping his dad's name. Barnaby was added because his knowledge had proven invaluable time and again.

And, since Fati announced she would not be leaving Gam Gam's side, they would just have to go the rest of the way on the information they had. There would be no conjurings performed in roadside diners or motel rooms.

Wicked Pete would only go as far as the meet-up with the Wayfarers—to make the introductions. Simultaneously, the rest of the Brigands would embark on the sail back to the Cove. Yeun would serve as captain and Daya as navigator. The others grumbled a bit about not being "in on the action," but in the end, they knew their vow to the Brigands meant doing whatever their captain saw fit. But it was Micah who was most upset at not being chosen for the trek. Despite Malachi's special talents, they couldn't risk bringing him along. He'd draw too much attention with his hulking size and neurodivergent manner. And since Malachi did not fare well too far from his brother, Micah had to go back, too.

The Brigands said their goodbyes outside the Grace house under cover of night.

Reed and Yeun exchanged a fist bump that quickly morphed into a brotherly hug. "Take care of the *North*," Reed said. "She's the only one we've got."

"I'll make damn sure we sail steady and true."

"Take care out there. Watch out for potholes." Daya said to Reed.

Reed and Daya hugged, which sent her down the row of the traveling party, giving each a goodbye hug. When she came to Luz, she flung herself at her in a big emotional embrace.

"Don't do that, fool," Luz said. "You gonna make me cry. And *chingonas* do *not* cry."

"When you're playing hero, don't forget to watch your own ass out there," Daya implored.

"You think I'm gonna see anything out there that life ain't thrown at me already? I got this."

"C'mon, boy," Bonnie said to Crossbones who was perched on her forearm. "Wanna go on a road trip?"

The parrot SQUAWKED in the affirmative.

Inside the house, Wilder was saying his farewells to Gam Gam, who used every ounce of energy in her body to give him a hug.

"Love yah, sweet boy."

"I love you, Gam Gam."

"Always 'member, belongin' is bein' somewhere yah wants tah be and where dey wants yah. Nothin' else matters..."

Then she closed her eyes and slipped back into unconsciousness, her breathing ragged and shallow. He kissed her forehead and left.

Once they'd made their half-mile trek to the hidden launch, they boarded DaBorn's waiting bateau. He started the engine and was about to cast off when a voice came from the thick woods behind them.

"Hold up!"

They turned around to see Cordial Grace running toward them, a rolling suitcase trailing behind her.

"Um... what are you doing?" Reed asked

"I'm coming with," she announced, loading her case onto the bateau.

"Says who?" Bonnie blocked her path.

"My mom, Fati, and Gam Gam. They decided you're going to need someone with the sight."

Bonnie didn't budge.

"Gam Gam insisted," Cordial said with a smile, tossing Bonnie's earlier words back in her face as if daring her to object. "And you know how stubborn she can be."

Bonnie hated the idea of this girl coming along. Her very presence made Bonnie feel horribly insecure. But Cordial's veiled threat made it clear she'd reveal what truly happened with Gam Gam if she protested.

The rest of the group was in favor of the idea. Reed fought especially hard for her inclusion, which really bugged Bonnie. He even rationalized that since Barnaby was so small, he didn't count as a whole person. So they'd technically only be at five and a half, tops.

"Fine," she finally moved aside. "But she does what she's told or she's out on the side of the road."

Cordial took her seat on the bateau bench and crossed her legs with a smug self-satisfaction that made Bonnie's skin crawl.

And with all passengers finally on board, DaBorn pushed off from the dock and headed into the early morning blackness.

Chapter 12
The Wayfarers

About forty-five minutes into the Brigands' journey to the mainland, DaBorn turned his bateau to the west and came to a stop in shallow waters near an abandoned shipyard. The dark was only just starting to give way to a daybreak laden with heavy clouds. The travelers stepped off onto a boat ramp and thanked their pilot, who only grunted.

"Back in ten minutes," Wicked Pete promised DaBorn. Pete would make the introductions, but his role would end as soon as the Brigands were on their way. And to ensure their safety, Pete explained, no one but the Wayfarers would know the route they were taking. In addition, Pete instructed the Brigands to maintain strict radio silence, keeping all cell phones off for the duration of the trip. They couldn't risk an errant text message being intercepted that might give away their plans or location to Jack Rackham.

Pete led the Brigands to the frontage road that ran along the waterfront and surveyed the empty road in both directions. Crossbones fluttered behind, circling as he followed.

"No sign of 'em," Reed said nervously. "And the sun is almost up."

"They better show," Wilder said. "Cuz it's a long walk to Tucson."

"Never known a more reliable bunch," Wicked Pete assured them.

"So. Who or what exactly are we looking for?" Bonnie asked.

"You'll know when you see them, lass."

In answer, a roar of motorcycle engines filled the silence.

The Brigands looked down the road. From the half-light of the dawn came as odd a procession as ever graced the Eastern Seaboard. An ancient recreational vehicle lumbered toward them with half a dozen motorcycles riding escort. Bonnie and the Brigands were about to make their first contact with "the Wayfarers."

In the annals of the Brigands of the Compass Rose, there have been many tales told, some so many times that they've transformed into legends. Such is the case of the Wayfarers, an unusual branch of the society whose origins remain shrouded in mystery. Some say that with the expansion of the United States over the centuries, it only made sense to have land-based Brigands who could provide marked ones safe transport across the country. Others say that one Brigand abandoned the sea after marveling at the steam engine aboard the Baltimore and Ohio Railroad in 1827. Over time, the Wayfarers' horses had given way to Harleys, and their chuckwagon was replaced by the *Gravel Galleon*, a 1972 Winnebago Chieftain RV.

The procession came to a stop in front of the group and the bikers dismounted. Tanner looked over the RV.

"Holy shit," he said. "Don't you guys own *anything* that's new?"

"Rusty Scofield!" Wicked Pete exclaimed, exchanging a beefy hug with the head biker. "Why, I ain't seen you since—"

"Cape Sable!" finished Rusty, a ponytailed guy who wore his Brigand tattoo on the side of his neck for all the honest world to see. "That scrape with Jack's goons. Showed 'em though, didn't we? I got the nick to prove it." He pulled up his sleeve to reveal a long, ugly scar.

"As do I," Wicked Pete said and pulled up a pant leg, exposing a jagged scar on his calf.

"You boys comparing boo boos?" A woman of about fifty stepped from behind the wheel of the RV. She was petite—barely five feet tall with bleached blonde hair. She hobbled as she made her way over to Wicked Pete, who picked her up. She looked like a doll in his big hands.

"Peg!" Pete said with a smile. "Lookin' as pretty as ever."

As he twirled her, her pant leg rode up, revealing a prosthetic leg coming out of her boot—the source of her limp. All the Brigands took notice, immediately giving one another "get a load of this" gestures and imagining battles that might have cost this woman her leg.

Peg grinned, her eyes lighting up at the familiar face. "And you're still looking like a mountain I'd love to climb."

"There are children present!" Rusty scolded. Peg waved him off.

"You old prude!" she snapped, breaking the embrace.

Peg looked around at the young Brigands. Her eyes fell on Bonnie. "Welcome, all. We may not have the fanciest ride, but we've got character."

"Character?" Wilder said as he eyed the RV suspiciously. "I hope the tires on that thing are younger than its paint job or we won't make it past Atlanta."

Rusty chuckled, a deep, hearty sound that resonated with years of adventure. "Don't you worry. This old gal's got plenty of giddyup left in her. She'll get us where we need to go. Plus, no one'll give her a second look. Which, as I understand, is the goal."

Bonnie approached Rusty. "We can't thank you enough for doing this for us, Mr. Scofield."

"Mr. Scofield is my dad. Call me Rusty."

"Rusty," Bonnie nodded. "We're in your debt."

Rusty waved off the gratitude. "It's what we were born and sworn to," he took her hands in his. "So you must be Bonnie. *The* Bonnie?"

Bonnie shrugged. "I guess my reputation precedes me."

"As well it should," Peg replied.

"Forgive me," Rusty said sheepishly, "but I've never actually met a marked one before. I was wondering if I could see your..."

"This ain't a peep show, Rust!" Peg punched his arm hard. "Let the girl be! Sorry about ol' Rusty. We don't let him out into polite society much."

"It's okay," Bonnie said. She pulled her shirt aside to show them. "There's not much to see. I tattooed the compass rose over it." Crossbones landed on her newly bared shoulder.

"I love it!" Rusty said, inspecting Jonesy's handiwork on the tattoo. "Makes sense, too. You being a Brigand as well."

VROOOM! One of the Wayfarers revved his engine and pointed at the bird. He was a giant of a man with a full gray beard and a black bandana over his bald head.

"Oh, right!" Rusty indicated the parrot. "Bird's gonna have to stay back, I'm afraid. Squirt over there's got a nasty allergy to feathers."

"Oh no! Really?" Bonnie was genuinely disappointed. Crossbones was the only living creature she could tolerate these days.

"Yeah. Sorry," Rusty said, "but ol' Squirt gets within ten feet of a down pillow, and he turns into a puddle of phlegm."

"I think I saw Puddle of Phlegm open up for Arctic Monkeys on their last tour," Wilder joked.

"Aw. Sorry buddy," Bonnie said to Crossbones, scratching under his beak before transferring him to Wicked Pete's arm over the bird's squawked objections.

"Don't fret. I'll see to it he gets extra treats," Wicked Pete assured her.

Then his voice got all babyish and sing-songy. "Would you like some bananas, boy? Or papayas?" Crossbones bobbed his head excitedly at the word. "Oooh, yea! Who loves papayas? Crossbones loves papayas! Yes, he does!" Pete kissed the bird's beak and Bonnie smiled, knowing her bird would indeed be well cared for.

Another roar from the motorcycles.

"Hold your horsepower!" Rusty shook his head. "We Wayfarers aren't known for our manners," he said with a smile. "Besides Squirt, that's Beto, Eladio, Corky, and Doc over there, good Brigands all."

Rusty checked the sky. "Sun'll be up soon. Best we get out of town 'fore it does. Less visibility. Y'all ride with Peg in the cage." He indicated the RV.

Goodbyes were exchanged with Wicked Pete and Crossbones. The crew boarded the *Gravel Galleon*, ready to disappear. The Wayfarers revved their engines and they were off.

The Brigands were headed off the grid and into the unknown. And Bonnie couldn't be more ready.

Chapter 13
On the Road

The journey to Tucson was two thousand miles, a trip Rusty estimated would take six days—nearly four days longer than Reed had originally figured.

The reason for the delay was twofold. First, the bikers just couldn't be expected to stay upright on the road for that many hours without regular breaks; it was simply physically impossible. And second, there was the unorthodox route the Wayfarers had planned. Knowing Calico Jack was aware of Bonnie's existence, Rusty couldn't risk the interstates. Instead, he explained, they'd stick to state and county roads to stay under the radar—a challenging task with six Harleys and a Winnebago roughly the size of an aircraft carrier.

With this route, except for a smattering of backwater towns in the South and Southwest, they'd be able to avoid almost all human contact. The Brigands were under strict orders to stay inside the *Gravel Galleon* for the duration. And if all went as planned, they'd arrive in Tucson unnoticed and in one piece in six days' time.

Six days! Bonnie could feel the anxiety threatening to overtake her. Gam Gam's insistence on reaching Tucson as quickly as possible weighed heavily on her. Adding to her anxiety was an unexpected sense of unease from being far from the ocean. Despite her desert upbringing and former phobia about water, Bonnie had grown attached to the sea, and being away from it left her feeling unsettled.

The moment they boarded the *Gravel Galleon*, the travelers laid claim to the prime spots inside the cabin. With Rusty and the rest of the Wayfarers on their motorcycles, only Peg remained inside the RV as driver, leaving the rest of the space for the Brigands. Which, honestly, wasn't much.

Still, the interior of the refurbished RV was surprisingly nice. Not at all what one would imagine from its rust bucket appearance from the outside. The walls were covered in whitewashed shiplap planks. There was leather banquette seating, and a table made of a gorgeous piece of driftwood sanded to a smooth finish. On the wall was a compass rose fashioned from a retooled boat propeller.

Peg explained that in one of Rusty's many side jobs, he'd worked in a shipyard building yachts, and in the process had become quite handy. So, when the Wayfarers' original camper had given up the ghost thirty years earlier, he'd started to work on his masterpiece.

"Damn. I feel like there should be a velvet rope and a cover charge to get in here!" Wilder said, quickly amending his criticism.

"We leave the outside looking like that so as not to attract attention," Peg explained. "Nobody gives a second look when you pull into a fillin' station late at night looking like this."

"This stained glass is beautiful," Cordial said, watching as the early morning light shone through the multicolored window on the door featuring a mermaid lounging on a rock.

"That's my wink to our seafarin' roots," Peg said. "Gift from an old gentleman friend, a glassworker up in New Brunswick. I was his muse." She posed like the mermaid and let out a raspy laugh.

"You all mind keeping it down?" Tanner yawned and stretched out on the sofa, shoving Wilder and Barnaby off the end.

"Hey!" Barnaby complained, landing with a thud on the RV floor.

"I didn't get my full eight," Tanner said. "Wake me when there's food."

"I know you're a waste of space, bro, but you can't waste *that* much of it." Wilder sat down on top of Tanner to encourage his compliance.

"Okay, Okay," Tanner said, sitting upright again. "But that mini fridge better have Red Bull."

.   .   .   .   .

The fridge, indeed, had energy drinks, along with every other kind of snack food, and the Brigands settled in for the rest of the first leg of the drive. As promised, they saw hardly any other cars on Rusty's route. By noon, they'd hit the Georgia state line and spent the afternoon trekking across Alabama.

At one point, Peg pulled off the road somewhere in the middle of nowhere, and Rusty got off his bike and cooked up some beans, rice, and andouille sausage. It wasn't as tasty as Grandma Winnie's meals, but in a pinch, it did just fine. Rusty said he was pleased with their progress. In fact, it looked like they might even hit Texas before nightfall.

After lunch, Bonnie claimed shotgun in the front passenger captain's chair and planted her feet on the dashboard to ward off any pretenders to her throne. As the RV pulled back on the road with their convoy of Harleys on either side, Bonnie felt the late afternoon sun through the glass of the windshield warming her face and she could almost feel the tension exiting her body. Maybe Gam Gam's warning was wrong. Maybe there was nothing to stress about after all.

.   .   .   .   .

"Nope. She's definitely not with them."

Five miles off the Carolina coast, one of Maks's underlings stood on the deck of a nondescript fishing boat, peering through a pair of long-range binoculars. He was observing the activity at Cormac's Cove, where the *True North* had just docked. They had been trailing the ship for the last 36 hours.

"You sure about that, Kage?" asked another pirate with a man bun. He poked the other in an unsuccessful attempt to commandeer the binoculars to get a peek of his own.

The first pirate yanked the binoculars away from his shipmate. "Yes, Rourke, I'm bloody sure!" snapped Kage, who looked like he was more suited to playing middle linebacker for the Raiders than for a life on the sea. "Looks like half of 'em didn't make the trip back," he muttered as the last of the crew got off. Daya was the only female to disembark, and even at this distance, it was easy to tell the dark-skinned girl walking along the dock was definitely *not* Bonnie Hartwright.

"Dammit!" Maks banged his hand hard on a side scuttle, cracking it. The girl had humiliated him... again. Not only had she given him the slip, but by tricking them into following the ship up the coast, the Brigands now had a day-and-a-half head start on him.

"Calico Jack ain't gonna be happy," clucked Kage, still peering through the binoculars.

"Calico Jack ain't gonna know!" Maks pulled a machete from his belt. "And if anyone says a word, I'll cut your throats while you sleep and feed all of you to the bull sharks."

The crew knew it was no idle threat. Though gaunt from months of near starvation, Maks had a reputation for ruthlessness second only to Calico Jack himself. And now, there was something unhinged about him that made him seem even more dangerous and unpredictable.

When Kage, Rourke, and two other seamen (a slovenly Brit named Graeme and a master sailor of uncertain ancestry by the name of Artemis) had been assigned to Maks's detail for this mission, none considered it an honor. They knew full well the fate of his last crew—all now either dead or in prison. No, this assignment was to be survived, nothing more.

Maks fixed his gaze on the distant cove, a faint outline on the horizon. His mind worked quickly, weighing his options. Without a word, he turned and strode into the pilothouse, boots thudding against the worn deck.

"Artemis!" he barked at the man at the wheel. "Turn this stinkpot around. We go back to Georgia! Now!"

Chapter 14
Gen Zee

Maks's rowboat sliced through the foggy waters near Hamhock Barony, the rhythmic creak of the oars the only sound breaking the silence. Kage and Rourke rowed the boat toward its destination. Maks's eyes, cold and calculating, scanned the shoreline as the small craft approached the quiet sea-island landing. It had been a seven-hour trip back to Georgia, with the throttle down all the way.

Maks sought one man in particular. He had seen him transport the girl on his bateau from the festival to this small island. It had been easy enough to learn his name. Everyone seemed to know everyone in these parts. And though most were tight with their information, they managed to find a chatty sort in the local tavern. Three beers later, they had a name: DaBorn Munro, a local crabber whose family had been in the Barony for generations. *DaBorn*. His name rolled off Maks's tongue with a mix of disdain and anticipation as he envisioned the coming confrontation.

Maks relished these moments, when fear and violence intertwined to yield a result. It was all he knew. How he had been treated all his life. Fear and violence. His own father had taught him that. And he took every chance he could get to dish out what had been so often perpetrated against him.

As Maks climbed out of the rowboat, he moved silently, his boots sinking into the damp sand. His presence was a ghostly shadow in the diminished light of the late afternoon. He spotted DaBorn near the water, bringing in his crab cages, his back to the encroaching danger.

With each step slow and deliberate, Maks approached until he stood just behind DaBorn.

"Afternoon," he said as he hovered over the crabber, his voice already low and menacing.

DaBorn looked up, eyes widening in surprise and then narrowing in wariness. "What you want?" he asked, his voice steady but with an edge of apprehension.

Maks stepped closer. "Information. And yer gonna give it to me."

That's when DaBorn saw the knife.

.   .   .   .   .

Three hours later, Queen Zee stood outside the hospital room where DaBorn lay, beaten and bloodied. His wife and two young children were at his side. Zenobia paced the hallway, her cell phone to her ear

"It's still going straight to voicemail," she said to her husband.

"She hasn't answered since she left," Martin said. "She's not going to now. She's obviously turned it off."

"I pray it's only that," Queen Zee said.

When she first learned that Cordial had gone off with the Brigands, her initial reaction had been anger. Anger that she'd left without a word. Anger that she was being so reckless. But mostly Queen Zee was angry at herself for exposing her daughter to such dangers. She should have known better. She'd seen the look on Cordial's face during the conjuring. Instead of being afraid, she was... fascinated, just as Queen Zee herself had been years earlier when she'd first encountered the dark spirit world.

And if Zenobia knew anything about her daughter, it was that she craved excitement. From a young age, she was always testing the boundaries. It's why she'd had to clamp down on Cordial so hard. To protect her from herself, and from a world that might try to exploit her gifts. And now, she'd introduced her daughter to the greatest peril imaginable. All so she could prove a point about their heritage. The truth of it made her heart ache.

With DaBorn's violent beating, Queen Zee's anger had turned to gripping fear. Before he lost consciousness in the hospital, DaBorn admitted his attackers had broken him. Queen Zee listened in horror from his bedside to the story—he'd given up the fact that the group was heading west in an RV with a bunch of bikers, but not before the fight that had left him in this condition. He'd endured the beating until the men threatened his wife and children. Then he gave in. Queen Zee couldn't blame him. He, too, had been unwillingly dragged into a dangerous situation, one that nearly cost him his life. Only the arrival of a boatful of crabbers had sent his attackers fleeing.

Queen Zee was thankful that DaBorn hadn't known their destination. But she did need to reach out to them. After Cordial's departure, she had sought Fati's help, only to learn the group was incommunicado. Fati assured her that, despite her daughter's disobedience, she was safe and in good hands. But now, after violence had shattered their peaceful community, that reassurance no longer sufficed. Cordial had to be warned—immediately.

*   *   *   *   *

Queen Zee's "prayer room" was a sanctuary in her house, a space adorned with candles, herbs, and sacred symbols. Shelves were lined with jars of roots and powders, and the air was thick with the scent of incense, lavender, and orange peels. To the uninitiated, it looked very much like Grandma Winnie's apothecary back on Cormac's Cove. After Queen Zee had bid her goodbyes to DaBorn's immediate family, she retreated immediately to its refuge.

Queen Zee moved with a purpose, gathering the items she needed for the ritual. This was no "Give-me-the-serenity-to-accept-the-things-I-can't-change" prayer session; she was about to delve into the ancient practice of Hoodoo in a desperate attempt to contact her daughter.

During Cordial's most rebellious years, Zenobia had once tried to intrude on her daughter's psychic space, the way another mother might snoop around in a diary. But Cordial, with abilities that surpassed even her mother's, immediately sensed the intrusion. Furious, she had shut her out and withdrawn even further. Fearing permanent estrangement, Queen Zee had promised never to do it again. Now, however, drastic times called for drastic measures.

She spread a cloth on a table, placing candles at its corners and lighting them one by one. She added a bowl of water at the center, dropping a few sprigs of hyssop into it for purification of any negative energy between her and her daughter that might prevent contact.

She then reached for a small vial of graveyard dirt to help connect her to the spirits. She sprinkled a pinch into the water and took a deep breath, closing her eyes. With a steady voice, she began her invocation.

"Spirits of my ancestors, hear my prayer. I seek my daughter, Cordial Grace. Bring me before her now."

She repeated the chant, her voice growing more intense with each repetition. She held a lock of Cordial's hair procured from her hairbrush over the bowl, letting it drop into the water. She focused all her energy on the lock of hair, willing the connection between mother and daughter to form, to bridge the gap between them.

Miles away, rain pelted the *Gravel Galleon* as it crawled along a muddy back road in western Mississippi. Peg gripped the steering wheel tightly, wrestling against the wind that buffeted the oversized RV. The journey was proving rougher than anticipated. A mudslide had already forced a detour that cost hours, and the downpour ultimately compelled Rusty and his bikers to pull off the road to seek shelter in an abandoned barn. The RV sat nearby.

While they waited for the latest bout of rain to let up, a sullen Bonnie kept glancing into the rearview mirror to the back of the RV. She watched with growing annoyance the little social circle that had formed there.

At its center was Cordial Grace, surrounded by the other Brigands. Cordial seemed to effortlessly fit in, joking and bantering.

"*Verdad?* You can read auras?!" Luz asked.

"I have been known to divine the occasional energy field," Cordial smiled coyly.

"What color's my aura?" asked Tanner, who had a way of uttering every sentence to Cordial to make it sound like a come-on.

"OSHA safety orange," Wilder quickly answered and everyone laughed.

"Yeah. 'Caution, rough road ahead,'" Luz added. More laughter.

"You guys are a riot," Tanner snarled. "You should try your act at Open Mic Night next time you're in juvey."

"So have you always had the power to just *see* things whenever you want?" Reed asked with genuine interest.

Cordial hesitated to answer. She didn't usually talk about her abilities, as typically folks didn't understand. But then, these weren't typical folks.

"Pretty much since I could remember," she finally said. "At first, the visions came whether I wanted them or not."

"That happens to Bonnie!" Barnaby said.

They all turned toward Bonnie, who averted her eyes and feigned disinterest.

"I've gotten better at controlling it over the years," Cordial continued. "It's the same as any other talent you're born with— like perfect pitch or being great at sports. You still gotta learn to hone it."

"Is there a school for that? Like the Brigands have?" Barnaby wondered.

"I wish," Cordial said, wistfully. "Would have been nice to meet others like me."

The Brigands exchanged glances, realizing their good fortune in having each other.

"So how'd you learn?" Wilder asked.

"Mostly my mom."

"That's nice," Luz said. "My *abuela* used to teach me stuff. May she rest in peace." She crossed herself.

"For me, it was a pain. With Queen Zenobia Grace, everything is heritage this, responsibility that. When I was nine, she actually took me to visit people in hospice—those near the end who couldn't communicate. Had me be a conduit—a bridge like for the folks stuck between the here and the there, as mama calls 'em. To deliver last messages. Love, regrets, confessions. Some of that shit was pretty dark."

"Sounds like child abuse to me," Bonnie muttered under her breath. But everyone heard.

"Her heart was in the right place!" Cordial found herself defending her mom, which she never did. "Anyway, I don't do that anymore. I stick to the fun stuff. Like tarot cards."

"And reading auras!" Barnaby said. "Do mine next."

"Yours is easy," Tanner said. "Your aura has a peanut allergy and a pocket protector." Once again, the RV filled with howls of laughter.

But Cordial's laughter abruptly faded. A strange sensation tugged at the edges of her consciousness. It was familiar—it was her mother, reaching out psychically. Anger flared. Zenobia had promised never to invade her thoughts again.

Yet, beneath the anger, Cordial sensed something else: fear. Her mother's energy radiated concern, bordering on panic. For a moment, Cordial considered answering, if only to reassure her that she was okay. But she quickly dismissed the thought.

It was exactly why she'd left behind her phone, shut down and tucked under the mattress of her bed. If she had brought it along, she'd surely have been tracked down by now. The same was true of her mom's attempts to invade her mind space. If she let Zenobia in, even for a second, she'd be back in Hamhock Barony the next morning before her breakfast bacon had a chance to cool.

So no, there would be no "picking up" her mother's calls, psychic or otherwise. She closed her eyes and used all her strength to push her mother away.

Back in the prayer room, Queen Zee nearly toppled over from her daughter's forceful resistance.

"Cordial, please," Queen Zee whispered on her knees. "Talk to me, baby girl."

But the connection dissolved, Cordial's image slipping from her grasp like water through her fingers. The spirits were silent.

Queen Zee's heart ached with the weight of it. She aborted the ritual, extinguishing the candles one by one with slow, heavy movements. She had done all she could, but the outcome was uncertain.

In the *Gravel Galleon*, Cordial opened her eyes to find Bonnie watching her through the rearview mirror, suspicion written all over her face. Cordial quickly turned back to the group, pretending nothing had happened.

"—and it's probably the color of rotten avocados!" Wilder said, finishing a joke that clearly landed with the others.

Cordial laughed, pretending she'd heard what he said, but she felt a sense of unease settle over her. She pushed it aside, focusing on the road ahead. The Brigands had welcomed her into their fold, well, most of them anyway, and offered her a glimpse of a new life, one that was filled with high drama and adventure.

It was a life she was determined to embrace, no matter what her mother thought.

"Not now, Mama," she said to herself in her head. "I need to do this on my own."

Chapter 15
The Roadhouse

"You all stay inside. It won't take long," Peg said as she pulled the RV into a small gas station somewhere near the Mississippi-Louisiana state line.

The rain had ended, and they were back to driving at full speed, but the RV needed to stop yet again for gas. The 1972 Winnebago Chieftain was good for many things, but at about eight miles to the gallon, it wouldn't be winning any awards for its service to the ozone layer. Peg had radioed the other Wayfarers and as was the protocol, the bikers hung back at the edge of town to avoid any curiosity.

Peg hopped out and started fueling. Bonnie stayed inside the motorhome and walked back to the kitchen area. She opened the mini fridge and grabbed a soda.

"Hey, Curls!" Wilder was all smiles. "Thanks for joining us commoners in the back!"

Bonnie gave the line a perfunctory eyeroll and addressed all the Brigands.

"When you guys have time, there's important stuff we need to discuss before we get to Arizona. Privately." The last word was directed at Cordial.

"Of course," Reed said. "Just say when."

Bonnie nodded. She wasn't really thirsty; and to be honest, there wasn't really that much to discuss, but she just wanted to reassert her primacy. After all, what's the point of being marked for death by an ancient curse if you can't use it to your advantage from time to time? Cordial most definitely took note of the snub.

"*Dios Mio!*" Luz said, standing in the doorway of the small bathroom.

"What's wrong?" Bonnie asked.

"Which one of you *pendejos* plugged up the shitter?" Luz turned on the boys.

"Why do you assume it's a guy?" Wilder asked, genuinely offended on behalf of possessors of the Y chromosome everywhere.

"Cuz while it's not all guys, it's always *a* guy!" Bonnie chimed in, having had plenty of foster brothers.

"Also, none of you dudes has spent less than a half an hour each in there since we started this road trip," Luz said. Bonnie and Cordial nodded in agreement.

"What are you, the toilet police?" Tanner asked.

"Hard not to notice in this tin can of a camper," Luz said.

"I can't help it if I have an active metabolism," Wilder protested. "That, and Rusty's beans at every meal don't help."

Barnaby and Tanner nodded in agreement. Dude had a point.

"You idiots are disgusting," Luz said. "Seriously."

She hopped out of the RV and went to where Peg was refueling near the rear of the vehicle.

"What are you doing out here?" Peg asked, a cigarette dangling from her lips despite the "No Smoking" signs plastered on every pump. "You know the deal. Only Wayfarers on the outside 'til we hit Arizona."

"Toilet's backed up. I really need to go."

"Gosh dammit!" Peg said. "I should have warned y'all not to use too much paper. And to double flush. That thing is touchy. We'll have to get Beto to fix it once we're out of town."

"I can't wait," Luz said, looking over at the gas station. "Gotta a Code Red situation." She pulled a tampon from her jeans pocket, showed it to Peg.

"Gotcha," Peg said with a knowing nod, and then scanned the area. "Fine. But be fast."

Luz saluted Peg and walked toward the gas station mini store, taking in the entire scene. The place looked like something straight out of a forgotten era. The station's sign, barely hanging on by a rusted chain, flickered feebly, missing half its letters:

G S
SN CKS
C LD BEER

Luz opened the rickety screen door that led inside.

"Restroom?" Luz asked the obese man in overalls behind the counter.

The man looked up over his magazine and eyed Luz suspiciously. "Through the bar," he growled with a voice stained by years of cigarettes and disinterest. He pointed a beefy finger toward a side door and returned to what seemed to be a fascinating photo spread on the hobbies of Miss January.

Luz's eyes narrowed as she entered what was an adjoining bar. Almost instantly, she was assaulted by the stench of stale beer and cigarette smoke. If the gas station was rundown, the bar was worse—a true dive. The sticky floors were a mix of grime and spilled drinks. The wooden bar itself, chipped and splintering, was covered in water rings from countless mugs of cheap beer.

The clientele matched the ambiance. A handful of truckers and locals slouched around, nursing drinks or shooting pool at a worn table in the back. The patrons turned as Luz entered, their eyes lingering on her in ways that made her skin crawl—her shaved head, piercings, and don't-mess-with-me demeanor standing out in a place like this. But she kept her head down, used to the stares, and made her way toward the far wall, where two doors marked

"Bitches" and "Bros" were painted with crude outlines of a mudflap girl and a bulging bicep.

Luz pushed on the mudflap girl and started to go into the ladies' room, but one barfly decided to assert his perceived authority.

"Excuse me, *sir*," said a big-gutted trucker in a Lynyrd Skynyrd T-shirt, mockery in his voice. "The men's room is over there." Others in the bar snickered and watched with curiosity.

Luz just glared at him and went inside the women's room anyway. A few minutes later when she emerged, two other truckers had joined Big Gut, arms folded threateningly across their chests, blocking her way.

"Look, I don't want no trouble," Luz said, using all the restraint she could muster. "If you'll just let me pass, I'll be on my way."

They wouldn't.

"This state, we got laws against you tranny pedos using the ladies' room," Big Gut said.

"Is that so?" Luz snarled. She couldn't help herself. "What you boys hauling tonight, Tubby? A truckload of ignorance with a few pallets of homophobia thrown in?"

The trucker grabbed Luz by the wrist with his oversized paw. "Yah know, my momma taught me never to strike a woman, but I don't think she had a freak like you in mind when she said that."

"Let go of me now," Luz said quietly. "Or you will regret it."

"Will I now?" The trucker nodded to the others, who grabbed Luz roughly. "Get her inside!" he yelled, forcing her toward the men's room.

"Let's just see for ourselves where this one belongs!" cackled one of the men.

"Get off of me!" Luz screamed, struggling and spitting like a wild badger as the truckers dragged her toward the men's room. She knew that if they succeeded in cornering her in there, it wouldn't be an outcome she'd be likely to enjoy.

Suddenly, she got a leg free and with all her might, she managed a well-placed kick to the crotch of the big-gutted guy. He YOWLED and reeled in pain, allowing her to break free.

Luz grabbed a nearby pool cue. She whirled around to face the oncoming assailants, twirling the cue skillfully in her hands. Thinking they may have underestimated her, the truckers hesitated a moment before lunging back towards her.

SMACK! Luz smacked Big Gut with the end of the pool cue and barrel-rolled across the barroom to put the pool table between her and her attackers. She popped up and pointed the cue threateningly at them. Her Brigand cunning was taking over; she smashed the tip of the cue on the pool table, breaking it off and transforming it into a lethal spear.

"You wanna mess with me?" she challenged them, brandishing the cue over her head.

It turned out that they did, in fact, want to mess with her. All three of them approached her simultaneously, hate in their eyes. She grabbed pool balls and began throwing them. Several hit the men. But a couple missed, flying wildly over their heads.

At that very instant, back in the RV, Bonnie had downed the last bit of her soda and was about to put the can in the recycling when she saw a pool ball SMASH through the window of the bar, leaving shards of jagged glass in its wake.

"Shit!" Bonnie shouted. "Luz is in trouble!" Without hesitation, she jumped out of the RV and barreled toward the entrance.

Bonnie was already inside when the other Brigands piled out to rush after her. Peg stepped in front of the RV door to stop the others, but they pushed right past her.

"Hey!" she yelled after them, but with her bad leg, she knew she couldn't stop them now.

Inside, Bonnie rushed to Luz's side.

"I'm supposed to be the one rescuing you!" Luz yelled, tossing Bonnie a pool cue from the rack.

"I can't take you anywhere!" Bonnie snatched the cue out of the air and in one fluid movement smashed an oncoming trucker in the forehead, causing him to slip on the peanut shells littering the barroom floor.

Suddenly, the two remaining locals who'd been on the sidelines jumped up, ready to defend their home turf as if it were Windsor Castle.

Just then, the rest of the Brigands stormed in. The four Brigand boys dove into the melee, defending their own with a mix of agility and brute strength. Or in Barnaby's case, ingenuity. He smashed the old jukebox and started whipping the 45 records through the air like they were ninja throwing stars, cracking into the heads of the opponents and putting them off balance while the others battled close up. Pool balls collided with a resounding crack, chairs were sent flying, and the bar descended into chaos as the clash intensified.

Bonnie and Luz wielded their pool cues like swords, skillfully parrying blows and delivering precise strikes. Now getting a taste of the Brigand fierceness, the truckers and locals fought back with desperation. But it was too late. One by one, they were disabled by the Brigands until the bar fell silent, except for the occasional groan from one of the vanquished.

The Brigands stood catching their collective breaths, but no one noticed Big Gut crawling behind the bar to retrieve a pistol the bartender kept there. He rose and took aim at Luz. He went to pull the trigger when—

Peg, who had finally made it to the barroom, stepped in front of Luz, grabbed a metal tray from a nearby table, and used it as a shield, deflecting the bullet as if she were some kind of peg-legged, chain-smoking Wonder Woman.

Big Gut took aim again, but he froze when he felt the cold steel of the blade.

"Don't even think about it." Bonnie had pulled a long dagger from her boot and held it against Fat Gut's throat. He slowly raised his arms in surrender.

To which Luz responded by picking up a brass spittoon from the end of the bar and dumping the chaw and spit onto his head. The brown goo dripped down his face.

"You bi—"

WHAM! She hit him across the head with the spittoon, and he fell to the ground, unconscious.

"We better get out of here before the cops show up!" Peg declared, tossing a wad of cash on the bar to cover the damages.

The Brigands beat a hasty retreat from the bar. They tore across the parking lot and jumped aboard the RV, whose door was being held open by Cordial. The last Brigand had just boarded when Obese Overall Guy from the mini-mart appeared out of nowhere and started to push his way into the RV, apparently none too pleased to have been taken away from his reading.

"What the hell are you—"

SMACK! Cordial kicked him hard in the face. He fell backwards onto the asphalt, and she slammed the door, locking it the second the latch engaged.

With Peg back behind the wheel, the RV roared to life, tires screeching as they sped away, leaving the chaos behind.

"Shit!" screamed Luz, putting a towel to her bloody forehead. "Bastards! Every day of my frickin' life this shit! Dammit!"

"Screw them, Luz. They're assholes," Bonnie said.

As Bonnie and Cordial tended to the injured Luz, Bonnie could see the trauma on her face. It hadn't occurred to Bonnie before now that she wasn't the only one who was a target because of how they were born. The difference was, Luz bore it with strength. But being strong didn't mean it didn't hurt.

With the distant wail of sirens echoing behind them, Peg steered the RV westward, leaving that hole of a place far in the rearview mirror as they sped toward safe haven.

Somewhere, anywhere but here...

Chapter 16
Around the Campfire

In the wake of the bar fight, dead silence filled the RV as the *Gravel Galleon* rumbled along a dirt backroad. They'd all gotten a very loud earful from Rusty about the actual definition of the term "lying low," which apparently did *not* include getting involved in brawls with the local populace, no matter how backward and bigoted they might be.

Worried that all of Mississippi law enforcement would be looking for a vehicle matching their description, the Wayfarers decided to leave that state pronto. Following Rusty's instructions, Peg took Highway 18 to Port Gibson, and then switched to the 61, which they took all the way to Natchez, where they crossed over the Mississippi River into Louisiana.

"We have a hidey hole not too far from here where we can lay low," Peg said, lighting up another cigarette. She hit the gas, and the RV sped up as the sun began to set.

As it turned out, over the course of decades, the resourceful Wayfarers had secured dozens of out-of-sight places around the country—"hidey holes" they called them—for situations just like this.

The sun had already set when they reached Terrebonne Parish, just outside the city of Houma, in the area Cajun folk called "Down the Bayou." Peg navigated the winding roads, expertly maneuvering the massive RV through the thick darkness of the swampland. With the help of the moon, trees draped in Spanish moss cast eerie shadows on the road, as the sounds of bullfrogs and insects filled the air.

As they descended deeper into the bayou, the road eventually dead-ended at the water's edge. Rusty and the other Wayfarers were waiting for them, their motorcycles parked on the muddy bank.

"Wasn't sure you'd make it," Rusty greeted them, his scruffy face illuminated by the headlights of the RV. "Lotta overgrowth since the last time we was here."

"What's the plan here exactly?" Bonnie asked, peering at the dark waters before them. "I know you guys got a cool RV and all, but I don't think she's all that seaworthy."

"Ain't she though?" Rusty smiled, giving a nod to the other bikers, who proceeded to remove brush from the shore's edge to reveal a giant customized pontoon boat.

"Another one of my creations, thank you very much," Rusty beamed. "We're taking the RV onto that. Float her deep into the swamp, lay low for the night. By morning, the cops will have better things to worry about than some bar fight back in Mississippi."

"This is awesome!" Wilder said, running onto the deck of the pontoon. "And we thought we weren't going to be doing any sailing!"

"Take it easy, Huck Finn," Rusty chuckled. "Help us get the bikes covered up first."

They all pitched in, using the brush to hide the motorcycles until nothing was visible but what appeared to be a deadfall.

"Don't these swamps have alligators?" Barnaby wondered, his feet in a couple of inches of water.

"Yeah, and I heard they have a taste for shrimp!" Tanner laughed as Barnaby jumped quickly back onshore.

"Take a side," Rusty ordered, and everyone helped pull out the retractable gangway and rested it on the ground. "Ready when you are, Peg!"

Peg expertly guided the RV onto the pontoon while the Wayfarers secured it with chains and blocks under each wheel. With everyone boarded and the gangway retracted, they set adrift into the murky bayou waters. The pontoon was rigged with an outboard motor, but they couldn't risk the noise, so Reed and Wilder were deputized as polemen. At Rusty's direction, they took long bamboo poles and pushed against the muddy bottom of the swamp, sending the boat deeper and deeper into the bayou.

The Brigands floated in silence—their only light source, a single battery-operated lantern. Bonnie shuddered against the cold dampness of the night. Though she could see nothing, she was surrounded by strange sounds. Besides the lapping water, there were chirring insects, frog concerts that would crescendo then go silent as they passed, and once even a hooting owl. But most disturbing was the occasional splash of some enormous something moving in the water alongside them. Barnaby scooched close to Bonnie on the deck and she to him.

Once the fear of being caught receded, the Brigands did what they'd done since their inception—they made do with whatever the situation presented them. The Wayfarer that everyone called Beto got out his toolbox and went to work on the toilet. Doc, the oldest among them, and Squirt, the huge guy with the bird allergy and the ironic name, dug around in the RV, eventually emerging with a collapsible fire pit and an armful of logs. Soon, the deck was alive with a roaring fire, just the thing on this chilly evening. Rusty then instructed the boys to push out into the middle of the bayou to avoid the possibility of a stray spark igniting the moss that hung from the canopy of cypress trees overhead.

"We'll be fine to wait out the night right here. No one comes out this far," he announced. "Mister Prescott, drop the anchor."

Tanner obeyed. The pontoon's anchors weren't like the *North 's* iron one—just weighted grappling hooks that sank into the murky bayou until they found the bottom.

"That oughta hold us for the night," declared Rusty. "Anybody hungry?"

"Only if it's beans," Wilder joked.

"NO!" Beto shouted from under the RV. And everyone laughed for a long, long time.

As the pontoon bobbed silently on the bayou, Rusty went in the RV to prepare dinner while Peg and the others gathered around the fire pit. Soon enough, the clang of spoon against metal pot merged with the chorus of bullfrogs and crickets that filled the air. The warm glow of flames danced on the surface of the tranquil water as the travelers could finally feel what generations of sailors had felt during quiet nights at sea: peace.

*   *   *   *   *

"I can't believe you and my grandpa were on the Cove together!?" Reed said excitedly.

After they'd eaten their fill of Rusty's offerings for the night, they all sat back around the fire pit, doing their best to digest their chow. They were all too amped up to go to sleep so the conversation, as it inevitably does around campfires, had turned to the telling of old tales.

"What do you young'uns say? He was my ride or die," said Doc, the 70-something bald biker with a white beard who had helped set up the fire pit. He was still wearing his biker goggles because, as he explained, they were prescription, and he'd misplaced his glasses. His body was covered in a lifetime of tattoos all faded and saggy from the years of sun and loose skin, including one that said "Born and Sworn"—the same thing Rusty said when he'd met Bonnie, apparently a credo of the Wayfarers.

"The captain and I trained together near on sixty years ago," Doc recounted. "Man, we had us a helluva time, we two hooligans.

Some I could tell you about. Most I couldn't in mixed company. Eleazer Ballister—Eazy we used to call him, cuz the ladies thought he was easy on the eyes. Get it?

"Eazy?" Wilder said, "Makes the captain sound like a rapper."

"Except when he got into a battle, they settled it with a blade, not a microphone," Rusty said.

"Eazy could fight plenty, but he was a charmer, too," Doc continued. "It's no wonder Winnie fell for him so hard. Then again, he fell hard right back at her."

"What were they like, as a couple?" Bonnie wondered. Like most kids her age, Bonnie had trouble imagining that folks the Ballisters' age were *ever* young, much less young and in love.

"The captain and Winifred were quite the pair, practically hippies back in the day," Doc chuckled.

"Like peace signs and tie dye?" Reed asked in disbelief.

"Yup. Honest-to-goodness flower children."

"Grandma Winnie, maybe," kicked in Tanner, "but picturing Captain Ballister in tie-dye makes my brain hurt."

"Don't believe me?" Doc said. "Peg! Peg, you got them pictures?"

"Already on it," she said, having retreated into the RV.

The Brigands all laughed and made jokes, excited by the prospect of seeing younger versions of the old captain and his wife.

"Can you imagine, old Eleazer, uh, Eazy, in the Cave o' the Four Winds rolling a doobie?" Wilder said.

Reed couldn't imagine. Then again, he'd never seen photos of his grandparents young. He'd always remembered them as old. The people they were after they lost their son.

"I knew it was in there somewhere!" Finally, Peg came out of the RV. She had a shoebox in her hand tied with string. She sat and took off the lid, sorting through what seemed from the looks of them to be pictures dating back decades.

"Peg's the keeper of the history," Beto said.

"Such as it is," Peg said. "I'm not very organized, but if I didn't hold on to these, there'd be no record of most of us. Not being family types or the kind to settle down. And that'd be sad, nothing marking you'd ever been here. Oh, here you go!" She handed Reed what was originally a color photo, now faded and mostly in shades of magenta.

Reed's eyes widened in astonishment. "Those are NOT my grandparents!"

In the photo, Eleazer had a full auburn beard and shoulder-length hair. He wore gold-framed sunglasses, leather pants and a fringed vest over, yep, a tie-dyed T-shirt. Winnie was wearing cut-off shorts and a bikini top that left little to the imagination. A daisy behind her ear held back waist-length hair. Both were mid-laugh, radiating joy.

"Now that is one gorgeous couple!" Bonnie marveled, showing the photo to Luz and Cordial.

"Holy shit," said Wilder, peering over the girls' shoulders. "I can't tell if he's fighting evil or scalping tickets to Woodstock!"

"What's Woodstock?" Barnaby asked earnestly, his encyclopedic knowledge obviously having its limits.

"Ballister! Dude. Your grandma was hot!" Tanner wolf whistled.

Reed punched his arm really hard.

"Ow!? I can't help it if she used to be a babe!" Tanner yelped as Reed grabbed him in a headlock. They wrestled until they nearly tumbled overboard. Rusty had to grab them before they could tip into the bayou.

"Settle you two!!" Rusty said. "You'll wake the gators!"

They suddenly stopped, Tanner's head out over the side of the boat. A loud splash echoed beside the pontoon. Everyone peered over just in time to see something large slither beneath the surface. They all scooted closer to the center of the boat.

"Well, I think they're adorable," offered Cordial, staring at the picture. "Your grandpa was very handsome, Reed. You look a lot like him."

Bonnie didn't care for the way Cordial smiled at Reed. Or, to be quite honest, how he smiled back.

"He seems so cool and together," Cordial said, looking back at the photo.

"That ain't how *his* dad saw it," Doc recalled. "The elder Ballister, Cap'n Elijah, was running the Brigands back then, and he was as old school as they come. The two of them would go back and forth like tomcats about anything and everything. I swear if his dad said he didn't like the color green, Eazy would have dyed his beard with pickle juice just to get a rise out of the guy."

"I can't imagine my grandfather ever being rebellious," Reed said.

"Real hellraiser. Till the birth of your own dad," Doc said. "The moment he held little Daniel in his arms, he was a changed man. Showed up on the deck of the *North* the next day with his hair cut, his beard trimmed, handing out cigars. Said having a kid does something to you. Not long after, he took over the reins of the whole outfit. And then it was goodbye, Eazy. Hello Cap'n Eleazer Ballister."

"Responsibility'll do that to a fella," Rusty mused.

Bonnie looked at Reed. He'd changed too since he took over the Brigands and had the responsibility of saving her and the world thrust on him.

Bonnie looked away, thinking of the change that came over her own mother when she was born. And the courage it took for her to run off. During the vision, she had felt how devastated Brigid was at losing Daniel and Catriona. And how scared she had been for Bonnie. It took so much strength to leave her in that church in Tucson when every maternal instinct was telling her to hold the baby close and never let go.

As Bonnie stared into the crackling fire, she felt admiration and love for her mother welling up in her heart. Which made her feel even more desperate to find her before it was too late.

"There wouldn't happen to be any photos of my mom in there?" Bonnie asked.

The Wayfarers looked at each other.

"She was, um, after our time," Peg said.

"So you never met her?"

"Just heard stories," Rusty said after a certain amount of throat clearing. "You know, her being marked of course, raised on the Cove like a Brigand and so forth. Then..." he cleared his throat, "well, her leavin' like she did. You know..." His voice trailed off.

Bonnie frowned. She did know. Like the Brigands at the conclave, the Wayfarers were supremely offended by Brigid's abrupt departure.

Sensing the conversation veering too close to uncomfortable territory, Wilder blurted, "So... Peg... Do they call you that because of your fake leg?"

There was a mix of laughter and shocked gasps.

"Wilder!" Cordial said. "That's none of our business!"

"Oh. Like you weren't wondering the same thing!" Wilder said.

Peg laughed heartily. "My peg leg, you mean? Haha... Never thought of that. Makes sense. But no, my name's Margaret. Folks have called me Peggy or Peg since I was little."

"So did you lose it in battle?" Barnaby asked, hungry for another scrap of Brigand lore.

Peg's expression darkened. "It happened one night. A night much like this." Her voice dropped to a whisper, forcing everyone to lean closer. The flames flickered against her face.

"We were tracking a couple of Jack's men through Bayou Lafourche. Fog thick as pipe smoke. We had 'em, or so we thought. Then, outta nowhere, the water turned against us." Her fingers curled, mimicking a crashing wave. "A rogue surge flipped our boat like a child's toy in a bathtub. We hit the swamp hard, the current ripping us apart. And that's when I felt it."

A heavy pause.

"Teeth. Sharp. Enormous. Teeth."

Barnaby swallowed hard.

"Something huge clamped onto my leg—yanked me clean under!" She mimed the pull of an unseen force. "Darkness! Mud! The water churned around me. I fought, kicked, and clawed at its snout, but the leviathan wouldn't let go! It was dragging me down, down, down into the black."

The fire crackled, sending embers into the night. The Brigands held their breath.

"Then, just as I saw my life flashing before my eyes—I did the only thing I could." Peg tapped the side of her head with a nicotine-stained finger.

Her voice dropped even lower. "I took out my knife and cut my own leg clean off!"

GASPS! Barnaby's face drained of color.

"Doc and Rusty dragged me to safety. But that gator... it just floated there. My leg in its mouth. Watching. Waiting. Eyes like lanterns, teeth like razors. It wanted me to know—I got away once." She leaned in, her voice barely a breath.

"But next time... I won't be so... LUCKY!"

SPLASH! A sound echoed off the side of the boat and the entire group jumped. Someone swore under their breath.

"Gotcha!" Peg burst out laughing, which turned into a phlegmatic cough. "You should see the looks on your faces!"

The Wayfarers howled and Doc emerged from behind the RV, having just chucked a log into the water to punctuate the story.

The Brigands groaned, shaking their heads as they realized they'd been had. Barnaby clutched his chest. "How old do you have to be to have a heart attack?!"

Peg wiped a tear from her eye. "I wish the story was that exciting," she said, "but no. Lost the leg a few years back up in the Black Hills of South Dakota. Took a curve too fast and ended up under the tire of an oncoming SUV. That was the end of my biking days."

"Youch!" winced Wilder.

"But I got me a free handicapped parking placard out of the deal! Lose some. Win some!" She laughed.

The other Wayfarers HOWLED along with her. The Brigands did, too.

As the campfire crackled and evening wore on, they all shared tales of their adventures. Rusty spoke of his early days with the group, weaving narratives of a time when the world seemed less complicated, but just as dangerous. Doc chimed in with chronicles of harrowing encounters and narrow escapes, each more improbable than the last. And though it took a little coaxing, Squirt finally recounted the incident years ago when he'd saved Ned Masterson by stuffing him into the luggage compartment of a Greyhound bus bound for Des Moines to evade Jack's men. The young Brigands listened intently to the stories, which they found every bit as bracing as those told by Captain Ballister during Celestial Navigation class back on the Cove.

As the Wayfarers spun their tales, the camaraderie among the travelers deepened. They weren't just fugitives seeking refuge from the law; they were a family of misfits bound by a vow and the unspoken code of the road.

Though they couldn't compete with the Wayfarers in sheer volume, the younger Brigands threw in a few of their own stories as well. They told of the squall and the high-seas battle with Calico Jack's men, earning them a measure of respect from the older travelers. The waning fire, the bayou water lapping against the pontoons, and the occasional wail of a loon created a surreal backdrop for each narrative.

Eventually, the appetite for stories waned, and a hush settled over the deck. But not for long. In their fellowship, the Wayfarers began to sing a haunting song of the sea, one Bonnie recognized from her Lore & Shanties class. "Leave her, Johnny" told of a crew nearing the end of a journey and of how difficult the voyage had been. As the Wayfarer men sang harmony, Peg's warm, alto voice led the lament to a life of hardship on the seas:

> *Oh, the times were hard and the wages low*
> *Leave her, Johnny, leave her*
> *I think it's time for us to go*
> *And it's time for us to leave her*

Leave her, Johnny, leave her.
Oh, leave her, Johnny, leave her
For the voyage is long and the winds don't blow
And it's time for us to leave her

The melody drifted through the swamp like a lullaby. Yet, as the Wayfarers sang of a journey's end, Bonnie knew hers had only begun. What would she find when they got to Tucson? Would they really discover a clue that would lead to her mom? Or, would it turn out to be a colossal waste of time? The questions created an uneasiness in her heart that even the most beautiful song could not soothe.

Chapter 17
Mad Maks

Straddling a motorcycle, Maks squinted down from his perch at the swamp preserve's edge, desperately hoping he hadn't missed the girl. After his "questioning" of the crabber DaBorn, Maks knew Hartwright and her band of delinquents were being shepherded across the country by the Wayfarers, the infamous land Brigands. But Hartwright's deception back in Georgia had given them a head start, and the trail had gone cold.

With no choice, Maks had to call upon Calico Jack's sprawling spy network for sightings. Word traveled fast—and back to the *Perdition*. Rackham was incensed that Maks had lost the girl yet again. A flurry of calls followed, which Maks summarily ignored, each voicemail dripping with more venom than the last. Jack tore into him with insults—Maks was an idiot, a failure, a liability. Each word sliced deep, but the sting only fueled his obsession with finding Hartwright.

The leads trickled in. Then, a hit—a truck stop in Mississippi. A police scanner crackled with reports of a bar fight—victims nursing bruises, claiming they'd been jumped by crazed meth cookers traveling in a beat-up RV. Maks recognized the vehicle's description. The stained-glass window. It had to be the Brigands.

But the victims' lie made sense. No one wants to admit to getting their butts kicked by a bunch of teenagers.

When a trapper outside Houma reported the same RV veering off into the swamp, Maks knew what they were up to. The bayou was the perfect place for someone trying to disappear to take refuge. Hadn't he done so himself many times as a child? He had been raised near here, in Terrebonne Parish—he knew this country intimately. And he knew eventually the Brigands had to emerge. So, he and his men took positions here and waited.

Being back in Louisiana stirred painful memories. Maks was born the son of a Cajun farmer and a young Polish woman who'd stowed away to New Orleans seeking adventure. His mother died giving birth to him, leaving his father alone and bitter. When he wasn't drowning his grief in whiskey, Maurice Broussard was taking a leather strap to his son, brought on because he "looked too much like his mother," or he "should have died instead of her," or just out of the general orneriness of the day.

For 14 years, that was Maks's life. Until the night he fought back.

After a particularly vicious beating, with his father passed out in another drunken stupor, Maks seized his opportunity. Gathering his things and taking what money the old man had, he savagely beat his tormentor, whipping his father with the leather strap as he flailed in bed begging for mercy. Then, Maks ran and never looked back, not caring if his father lived or died.

Like his mother, he craved escape. Adventure. The ocean.

New Orleans gave him all three. A stranger offered him work on a ship—work that turned out to be on Calico Jack's crew. It was quickly apparent that Rackham's operation was pretty shady, but by then Maks's conscience had been dulled by years of abuse. He energetically threw himself into his new vocation.

He wasn't book smart but knew how to survive, so he quickly climbed the ranks, earning a reputation for ruthlessness along the way. Calico Jack took notice, and soon Maks found in him the father he'd always longed for. Rackham's morsels of validation became everything to him—a twisted loyalty he couldn't see was nothing more than yet another abusive relationship.

He emulated Calico Jack in every way, eventually even adopting the speech and mannerisms of his beloved captain. And, being put in charge of the operation around Cormac's Cove the previous summer had been his ultimate reward. But because of the Hartwright girl, that approval had evaporated. The thought of it made every muscle in his body tighten in rage.

"Boss! BOSS!"

Maks was shaken from his dark thoughts by a voice coming through the headset inside the motorcycle helmet in his lap. He put on the helmet.

"It's them!" the voice exclaimed. "We found 'em! What's the order?"

RUMBLE!

Maks heard the Wayfarers' cycles before he saw them. Then they appeared, flanking the RV like some bizarre motorcade. A surge of elation hit him. This wasn't chance—it was destiny. He felt it as surely as he felt the weight of his obsession. His fingers tightened around the handlebars of his motorcycle. Fate had put the girl in his path and he was ready. Maks grinned, wiping the drool from his scarred lips.

"Move out!" he commanded into his headset and then took off down the road.

This was the moment he'd waited for—the moment he'd clung to life for in that dark hole. The moment that he'd finally exact his revenge on Bonnie Hartwright.

.   .   .   .   .

Now out of the dense swamp, the Brigands were back on the road, unaware of the war party now headed their way.

As usual, Bonnie was perched in the front passenger seat. Rusty had given them the all-clear, and she should have been feeling relieved. But her gaze kept shifting back in the rearview mirror to the banquette, where Cordial was yet again holding court, this time doling out palm readings.

"This is your life line," she heard Cordial coo, her meticulously manicured fingertip lingering on Reed's hand. "It's nice and long. Looks like you'll be sticking around a while."

"I'll be sure to alert Calico Jack."

Cordial let out a feminine laugh and tossed her head back in a way that irked Bonnie. She glanced down at her own ragged nails, chewed to the quick.

"Best not to do that," Peg said from behind the wheel.

"Do what?" Bonnie quickly stuffed her hands into the pockets of her hoodie.

"Best not judge the inside of your life against the outside of others," Peg said, eyes flicking to Cordial.

"How about the *outside* of my life against the outside of others?" Bonnie sighed, looking at the perfectly coiffed Cordial and then at her own unruly hair in the enormous side-view mirror.

"Don't go down that rabbit hole. Gotta let folks love you for who you are. Self-acceptance is a hard place to get to sometimes, but when you arrive, it's a whole new ride."

"How long did it take *you* to get there?"

"Any day now," Peg winked. Bonnie smiled, leaning back, finally relaxing a bit when—

STATIC! The walkie on the dashboard crackled to life.

"Heads up, all!" Rusty's voice broke through. "We might have ourselves a tail."

"Talk to me, Rust," Peg said as the Brigands crowded forward.

"I had Corky hang back to watch our six. Looks like we picked up some company near Marsh Vista—a pack of hogs and a pickup. Might be nothin', but let's put some distance between us."

"I'm on it," she said, gunning the engine.

"And Peg. Anything goes down, you get that girl outta here. Understand?"

"Roger that," she replied, taking a curve at high speed.

Bonnie held on tight, dread flooding her veins.

From a high point in the road, the pirate Rourke observed the caravan speeding up as two bikers peeled off, ducking into the trees.

"They're onto us!" he growled into his headset, fists clenched on the handlebars.

"Dammit. Musta had a lookout," Maks replied as he raced down the road. "Take care of it, Rourke!"

Rourke swung his bike around, burning rubber as he sped in the opposite direction.

Just then, the pickup, a huge tricked-out F-150, pulled up alongside Maks. "Yo. We're only supposed to be keeping tabs on them." It was Kage at the wheel, speaking into his own headset. "We fall back now, they maybe think we're just some randos and we keep our cover, get closer to 'em later."

Maks just snarled at Kage and then revved his engine, signaling for the others to follow as he took off toward the caravan.

Moments later, Corky, the Wayfarers' lookout at the rear, watched in surprise as Rourke crested a hill and roared right for him.

Corky put a hand on his sword, not certain what to make of the situation. Then he saw it. A broadsword strapped to the oncoming cycle.

"Pirates! It's—" he yelled, drawing his blade an instant too late.

Rourke swung a heavy chain from his lap, striking Corky's chest. The Wayfarer flew from his bike, skidding across the asphalt before slamming into a boulder—motionless.

Inside the RV, silence fell as Corky's words sank in.

"Cork! Come back!" Peg pleaded, with only static in reply. Peg's hand grabbed the sawed-off shotgun strapped under the dashboard.

"Hang tight," she called, flooring the gas pedal.

The Brigands all looked at each other and without having to be told, drew their own weapons. As the RV hurtled around curves, Cordial clung to the table while Tanner protectively shielded her with his body.

"They're coming up fast!" Barnaby yelled, watching through the rear window as the pirates' motorcycles approached the convoy with the truck not far behind.

An all-out road war erupted between the Wayfarers and the pirates. Sword strikes clanged, metal meeting metal, as they fought with primal ferocity, all the while keeping their motorcycles speeding down the road.

Rourke roared up and joined the fray, his motorcycle overtaking Squirt and Eladio. With a savage kick, he sent Eladio sprawling into the ditch, his bike flipping end over end and landing with a sickening crunch.

Further back, Rusty was in a bitter fight with Maks. He fought hard, but the older Wayfarer was struggling against the younger, more vicious pirate, even one who had recently been tortured to the brink of death.

"They're in trouble. We gotta help 'em!" shouted Bonnie, adrenaline thrumming.

"What can we do from in here?" Wilder asked.

"From in here? Nothing," Reed replied and flung open the RV door.

"The hell you doing, Ballister?" Peg shouted.

"Doc! Over here!" Reed cried out. He waved to Doc, and the Wayfarer pulled up next to the RV. Reed leapt, landing perfectly on the back of Doc's motorcycle facing backwards.

"That was a thing of beauty!" marveled Cordial.

Bonnie watched as Reed, his sword in one hand and Doc's in the other, immediately took out two approaching pirates, knocking them off their bikes with blows to the chest.

Wilder then lunged out the RV door, tackling a pirate biker and wrestling him off his motorcycle with a few moves he'd picked up from Zion. The pirate hit the asphalt hard while Wilder barely managed to keep the Harley upright. Stunned that he'd pulled off the maneuver, he steadied the bike and sped toward Reed, who was locked in combat with another pirate. The two young Brigands fought side by side.

PEW! PEW! PEW!

As Reed and Wilder battled, Rourke closed in on the RV, aiming a handgun at its rear tire.

Peg swerved, trying to shake him off. Several shots went wild, one smashing through the window.

"Get down!" Bonnie shouted, shoving Cordial under the table just as a bullet struck where she'd stood.

The road curved sharply. Peg had no choice but to follow, white-knuckling the wheel as she went.

"Hang on!" she yelled.

The *Gravel Galleon* lurched left, its right wheels lifting off the pavement. Everyone inside tumbled like rag dolls. Peg yanked the wheel back, barely keeping the RV from going off a steep hill.

"That was a close one!" Peg exhaled but then suddenly slammed hard on the brakes. They had reached a winding patch of road that left no room for error. "This isn't ideal!"

"Tanner, give me your belt!" Bonnie shouted, rising to her feet.

"What for?"

"Just give it!" She yanked it off him in one swift motion.

"Does this mean we're going steady?!"

"In your dreams, frat boy."

Bonnie secured one end of the belt to the handrail by the open door and wrapped the other around her wrist.

"Are you nuts?!" Tanner yelled as Bonnie looked out over the open road, the asphalt blurring beneath her.

"They won't hurt me! They want me alive!"

"And they can't hurt you if you kill yourself first, either!" Tanner yelled.

Seizing the moment, Bonnie swung out of the camper toward Rourke.

At the sight of her, Rourke briefly stopped shooting—just as she'd counted on. She raised Siobhan and brought it down hard, slicing through his outstretched arm. The gun flew from his grip. He yowled, his arm hanging at a freakish angle, blood gushing from the wound.

He slowed for a moment as he struggled to pull out a sword of his own from a scabbard on his belt. But just then Bonnie swung out even further to kick him square in the face. His SCREAMS could be heard as he flew off his bike, over the side of the ravine and disappeared.

Bonnie swung back into the RV.

But Peg hit a bump and Bonnie lost her grip on the belt. She started to tumble out of the RV, but Tanner grabbed her and pulled her back to safety.

"Thanks," she said shakily.

"For what? I just wanted my belt back," he said with a sly grin. "It's Gucci."

Bonnie smiled, returning the belt. She had to hand it to Tanner. There were moments, few and far between mind you but moments nevertheless, that he wasn't a *total* douchebag.

"Dammit girl!" Peg screamed, bringing them back to their present peril. "Do that again and I'll have ya hogtied the rest of the trip!" Then she grumbled under her breath, "How'm I supposed to protect a fool?"

"Uh-oh! We've got more trouble." It was Cordial. She'd come out from under the table and was peering out the back window with Barnaby. The truck driven by Kage was catching up to them. The others rushed to the rear of the RV. Sure enough, the F-150 was closing hard.

A violent screech of tires echoed as Maks approached the truck from behind.

"Hold her steady!" he yelled into his headset.

Kage slowed and came up even with Maks's motorcycle. Maks kicked off from his bike and landed in the bed of the truck, steadying himself as he banged on the roof.

"Go! Get me up there!" he barked, brandishing his sword. Kage sped up, weaving through the chaos until they were inches away from the RV.

BANG!! Inside, the Brigands felt the camper shudder.

"Holy heck! They're boarding us!" Barnaby shouted.

"Oh my God!" Bonnie's stomach dropped the moment she saw the gaunt and haunted eyes in the rear window.

"Bonnie!" Barnaby said, sharing her horror and disbelief. "It's—"

"Maks!" she said.

"It can't be!"

But it was. He was alive! Her intuition about his presence at the Gullah festival had been right! Bonnie locked eyes with her father's killer—now more beast than man, eyes burning with madness. Then, his face suddenly vanished as he continued his ascent up the side of the RV.

Bonnie moved to go after him, but Luz stepped in front of her.

"NO! Stay inside! You hear me? I got this," Luz growled. "Tanner. Gimme a boost!" On his shoulders, Luz popped open the ceiling air vent and then disappeared onto the roof.

On top of the speeding RV, Luz positioned herself defiantly as Maks appeared before her.

"If it ain't the freak from the beach," he scowled, his sword at the ready. "You cost me a coupla good men. Lemme see if I can repay ya. Man to *man*."

"*Pinche cabron!*" Luz brandished her blade. "Maybe you won't talk so tough once I slice off your *verga* and feed it to the coyotes!"

Maks viciously swung his sword.

Luz met his blade with hers—CLANG! She held him off, but he got in close. She barely dodged his next strike but lost her footing. She tumbled over the side of the roof, grabbing onto a long metal antenna.

"Luz!" Bonnie yelled. Luz's feet dangled wildly outside the side window. Barnaby and Cordial rushed to open it, punching out the screen and bearhugging her legs to keep her from falling.

Bonnie scrambled to climb through the roof opening, but Tanner yanked her down hard.

"Don't be stupid!" he snapped, then surprised her by pulling himself up instead.

Tanner was halfway onto the roof when he saw Maks about to bring his sword down on Luz's fingers. Instinctively, he drove his blade deep into Maks's calf.

Maks HOWLED and turned on him. He lunged, tackling Tanner as soon as he was fully out of the RV. They rolled across the roof, punching and grappling. Only the luggage rails kept them from tumbling off onto the hard pavement below. Weak from his time in the hole, Maks fought with sheer madness. He clamped his teeth onto Tanner's ear and yanked—nearly tearing it off. Tanner YELPED, blood cascading down his face.

Behind them on the road, Wilder had caught up to Kage in his truck. Wilder jumped from his cycle onto the truck's bed and with the hilt of his sword, smashed out the back window of the cab.

Kage fought him off with one hand while trying to steer with the other, but Wilder jammed his sword into the dashboard through the steering wheel, locking it in place. The truck hit a curve—too late for Kage to correct. He slammed the brakes, but the truck skidded and crashed into a slope.

Wilder leapt off just in time, rolling across the ground, bruised but alive. He limped to the wreck, where a bloodied Kage lay slumped over at the wheel. Wilder reached in and pulled his sword from the dashboard.

"I'm gonna need that for later," he said and started back for the road.

Up ahead, Doc pulled his motorcycle alongside the RV's rear ladder. Reed leapt off the back, barely catching a rung. His feet scraped the asphalt, his sword clattering away behind him. Weaponless, he climbed to the top.

Just in time.

Maks was straddling Tanner, trying to bring his dagger down into Tanner's neck. Tanner was using all his remaining strength to hold him off.

Hearing Reed's approach, Maks turned his head—just for a second—but it was enough.

Recognition coursed through Reed's body. He was face to face again with the assassin of his own parents. And here this villain had yet another Brigand under the knife. The rage and revulsion staggered him as he struggled to maintain his balance.

Reed lunged and grabbed Maks around the waist, tackling him to the roof. He felt his pure hatred for this man begging for release, and he punched Maks hard in the face. Once. Twice. Three times.

"Why don't... you just... die!" He struck again.

Maks tumbled over the side of the camper and disappeared.

Reed stepped to the edge to ascertain Maks's fate when—

"Get down!" Peg screamed out the window.

A tunnel loomed ahead. She slammed the brakes, tires screeching.

Reed dove belly-first onto the roof, barely missing decapitation. Darkness swallowed them as they entered the tunnel. Then, just as suddenly, they burst back into daylight.

Peg fought the wheel, finally slowing and stopping the RV. Black smoke billowed behind them.

Reed pulled Tanner to his feet, then helped Luz up onto the roof. They all turned to stare at the mouth of the tunnel, waiting... After what felt like an eternity, four motorcycles emerged.

The Wayfarers!

The battered group approached the camper. Beto, Squirt, Doc, Rusty—and Wilder, now riding along on Rusty's bike. He held Reed's sword, which he'd retrieved from the pavement.

No sign of the pirates anywhere.

"Oh my God... I-Is it over?" Cordial asked, voice shaking.

For now, Bonnie thought, for she knew better.

Back before the tunnel, water rippled in an irrigation canal. Maks emerged from it, limping. Blood ran from his mouth. He licked it, savoring it as if it gave him strength. He walked to the edge of the road and heard the sound of a struggling motor.

The F-150! It was battered, its windshield cracked, airbags deployed—but somehow, Kage had gotten it running and back on the road. He pulled up, seething.

"You're a dead man, Maks," Kage said, blood streaking his face. "You really bollocksed it up this time. When Jack finds out—"

His words cut off in a wet gurgle.

Maks stepped back, his dagger buried deep in Kage's throat.

"Shut up," Maks pulled Kage from the cab and threw his body to the asphalt. "Shut up shut up shut up!" He kicked Kage repeatedly.

As Maks stood over Kage's lifeless body, his phone buzzed again. Again, the private number. And again, Maks didn't answer. Instead, he dismantled the phone—snapped the SIM card, tossed the battery, and flung the remains into the irrigation ditch.

He got up into the truck and put it into gear, his unblinking eyes set and determined. The wounded truck lurched forward, toward the west. Knowing Hartwright as he did, having studied her background, Maks knew where they were headed. Knew as surely as he knew what he needed to do when he got there.

Chapter 18
Counting the Cost

"No survivors," Doc said to the group, he and his bike covered in dust and blood.

Sitting in the long shadow of a rocky outcropping, the RV was surrounded by what was left of the motorcycles. At the center were the travelers—battered and worn from what would become known in Brigand lore as the "Road War." Young and old listened with heavy hearts to Doc's report.

After the encounter with Maks and his men, Rusty had dispatched Doc and Squirt to double back and tend to Corky and Eladio, who had fallen during the fight. Sadly, they both lay dead on the roadside, two more noble sacrifices for the cause. In addition, Doc reported Maks had somehow escaped the scene.

Again, Bonnie thought and shuddered. *Like a villain from a shitty horror movie.*

The rest of the group had limped along a county road until Rusty deemed it safe to stop. They wound up in the middle of an abandoned hog farm somewhere in Texas. The Brigands needed to regroup. And they needed to look over the RV, bikes and themselves for damage. While Beto checked over the camper, Peg got out the first aid kit and tended to the wounded with the help of Cordial, who was surprisingly adept under pressure.

"I got ahold of Pete," Rusty informed Doc and Squirt through jagged breath. "He's got a clean-up party en route outta Lafayette."

The two Wayfarers nodded solemnly. Bonnie swore she saw a tear mingle with the dried and crusted blood on Rusty's cheek. Peg was openly weeping even as she stitched up Tanner's ripped ear. Even Tanner was in such shock he didn't complain about the lack of anesthesia or a board-certified plastic surgeon.

During their encrypted call, Rusty learned that a distraught Queen Zee had reached out to Wicked Pete. She'd told him everything—about Cordial not having permission for the trip. About the attack on DaBorn and Maks learning of their plans. And finally, about Cordial's refusing her mother's repeated attempts to warn her.

"So you lied to us!" Reed was livid. Though he wasn't a yeller, he was on the verge of it with Cordial. "You lied about Gam Gam wanting you with us! Why?"

"I-I didn't think you'd let me come otherwise," Cordial stammered. For the first time, her usual confidence evaporated. She could only stare at her sneakers as Reed laid into her.

"Damn right we wouldn't!" Bonnie said, piling on with perhaps more venom than was absolutely necessary.

"I don't get it, Cordial. Why didn't you answer your mom?" Luz asked.

"I just thought she was pissed and wanted me to come back."

"So what, you left her on read?" a bloodied Wilder wondered.

"I actually kind of blocked her," Cordial replied sheepishly.

"So, hey, I got an idea," Wilder said. "Next time you get an urgent telepathic message from an all-powerful psychic, YOU PICK UP THE FREAKIN' CALL!"

"Not cool!" Barnaby chimed in.

"I'm so sorry," Cordial shook her head. "I just wanted to get out of Hamhock Barony and have an adventure."

"This ain't no adventure to us," Luz snarled. "This is life and death!"

"I guess I just didn't think—"

"That's right, you didn't think," Reed interrupted, "and because you didn't, Brigands died! We could have lost Bonnie! Do you know what THAT would mean?" He was unleashing all his anger and grief on Cordial, blaming her for everything.

"Come on, Reed. That's unfair," Tanner spoke up. "Even if Cordial didn't come with us, Maks would have found out from that DaBorn guy. It would've been the same exact shitshow!"

Bonnie wanted to dismiss Tanner's argument as just his slimy way of mashing on Cordial. Which it probably was. But he was actually right. What happened wasn't all on Cordial, not even close.

In fact, as long as blame was being divvied up, Bonnie knew that she could be doled out a share as well. She could have spoken up about her "sensing" Maks at the festival. But she didn't. Instead, she'd rationalized it away as her imagination. After all, she thought she'd seen Maks drown. Seen it with her own eyes. Still, she should have said something. But she kept her mouth shut because she was afraid they'd abort the mission. Or at the very least, send her back to the safety of the Cove and carry on without her.

"You're going back," Reed announced to Cordial. "I want you gone as soon as possible."

Cordial nodded through tears. "I can get a flight from Dallas."

"We don't have time for a side trip," Bonnie objected. "We gotta get to Tucson ASAP. Especially with Maks still out there!"

"Okay," Reed said. "We wait. The mission takes priority. But once we hit Tucson, she's on the first plane back."

Everyone murmured in agreement. Even Cordial, who nodded in acceptance of her fate.

Her adventure was over.

*　*　*　*　*

Bonnie lay staring out the small window of the RV, curled up on the loft cot while the other Brigands sat silently below. The *Gravel Galleon* sped along the main highways now, having given up on getting to Tucson unseen and settling for getting there fast.

The moon had already set, so Bonnie could see the stars all the way to the horizon along the Texas landscape. It reminded her of being on the deck of the *North*, far away from all the troubles of the world. How she wished she could be there now. Maybe then she could escape the thoughts that were suffocating her and keeping her from sleep.

They were like a fever dream, these thoughts. How she hadn't stopped Gam Gam from doing the divination. That she hadn't spoken up about sensing Maks. That she had let Cordial take the whole blame for the attack. It wasn't like her to be so selfish, so vindictive. But something had shifted in her since Bobby Maynard's death. Something dark that she was having more and more trouble suppressing.

Mixed up in the jumble was *Maks*. She kept seeing him in her mind's eye. The twisted look of madness on his face. The scarring on his mouth. An old pirate's punishment, according to Barnaby, reserved for sailors who crossed their captains. Had Maks been punished because of her? Was it behind the viciousness of his attack? The body count? Was that on her too?

"Stop it!" she silently commanded. *"None of this is your fault. You're the victim here. You're the one Jack wants dead! You didn't ask for any of this!"*

She rolled over on her back. She knew she wouldn't sleep, but at least she was determined not to focus any more on the guilt.

Instead, she decided to focus on what was important above all else—finding her mother.

Nothing else mattered.

Chapter 19

If You Want Something Done Right

The image of the badly wounded Rourke filled a large monitor in the *Perdition's* control room, the bustling center of operations for Calico Jack's empire.

He was calling from a rundown motel outside Lubbock—his arm bloody and lying at a grotesque angle, his nose swollen and broken.

"They're all dead," he reported to his boss. "'cept me, whom he *left* for dead. Most was kilt by Brigands. But Kage. That was Maks. I saw the body myself... his throat cut... the truck gone."

Standing in the midst of his most trusted subordinates, Jack Rackham stared at the screen, showing no emotion as he listened to the litany of ways that Maks had betrayed him. He only bit on his lower lip, the sole indication of the storm brewing inside his chest.

"Where is Maks now?" he asked, still in unnervingly even tones.

"Gone after the girl, I reckon, so hellbent to kill her, he was. West most likely, which is where they was heading when we come up on them. But that's just my figurin'. Maks, he kept his plans to hisself. We just done what it was he said."

"So, you attacked on his orders? Despite *my* orders that the girl be discreetly followed and NOT HARMED?!"

As Jack raged, Rourke shuddered in fear. He had slipped up. As the only survivor, he could have said anything. But he wasn't smart enough to figure that out ahead of time. *Idiot*, he thought to himself. Rourke knew his life was over. Jack would see to it the moment he caught up to him, and catch up to him he surely would. He hung his head, waiting for the volcano to erupt.

"BLOOOOODY HELLLLLL!" Jack threw a metal stool at the monitor—it shattered and sparked before going black, ending the transmission.

All eyes locked on him. No one dared move or say a word. They had certainly seen their temperamental captain in a fury before. But they'd never seen him so shaken. And they had never, ever known anyone to defy Calico Jack as Maks had just done. Not during their lives or, according to lore, the lives of anyone before them.

The fact that someone had dared to deprive Calico Jack of the years that were rightly his, and in such an insolent way, well, it shook the pirates' confidence in their captain's dominion over them. Rackham could see the doubt in their eyes and he was *not* happy.

"Find the girl!" he bellowed. "And Maksymilian! I want him alive so I can look him in the eye when I choke the life out of his traitorous body!"

He stormed from the control room, his furor lingering in the air long after he left.

⸳　⸳　⸳　⸳　⸳

Writhing bodies in pain. Faces twisted in agony. Demonic figures with animal incisors tearing into the flesh of the damned. Images from paintings, mosaics, and ancient vessels. The styles varied—Egyptian, Medieval, Renaissance—but the theme remained the same: depictions of the eternal agonies of Hell.

Surrounded by the grotesque visions, Calico Jack sat in a centuries-old leather chair inside a windowless cargo container turned museum of the macabre. Veins bulged at his temples as he studied the art. Some pieces were stolen masterpieces—Botticelli's *Chart of Hell*, Van Eyck's *The Last Judgment*, Beutler's *Torments of Hell*. Others were flawless reproductions he'd commissioned. One painting stood unfinished on an easel—his own creation, more vile and terrifying than all the rest. His own eyewitness account.

"Here you are... yet again," Salifu emerged from the shadows of the doorway.

"This was supposed to be easy," Calico Jack growled. "Our bargain should have been consummated by now!" He slammed his fist on the armrest of the chair.

"We could not foresee the... complications these last few centuries."

"You mean Mary Read and her infernal band of merry idiots!"

"It's not idiocy that's kept sands in the bottom of your hourglass, Jack Rackham. The Brigands have been a formidable adversary. Not to mention—"

"They've been lucky!" he cut the shaman off, nervously playing with the ring on his finger.

"As you say," Salifu said, but he knew better. So did Jack.

Rackham rose, gesturing at the paintings. "Do you recall when I started this collection?"

"My memory is infinite."

"January 23, 1767. The first time that Read woman denied me my years. Took me nearly twenty years more to collect on that one."

Jack examined one of the paintings closely, focusing on a particularly gruesome scene of torment. "This gallery was begun as a reminder of what I would face if I let it happen again," he continued, eyes still fixed on the painting. "Yet, here I am, three hundred years later, still scratching and clawing for the years that are due me!" He examined the hourglass ring, now nearly full. "Finally, I am on the cusp of immortality! And I will not permit that pissant to pull it from my grasp!"

"I tried to warn you about Maks," Salifu calmly reminded him.

"You didn't try hard enough!" Jack railed "You're good for nothing! You couldn't find the girl. It took the Brigands to do that. You haven't been able to find her mother all these years. I don't even know why I still keep you around."

"Terms of your deal, you know as well as I."

Jack lunged at Salifu. He grabbed the beads around the African's neck and pulled them tight.

"It's a shite deal! And your boss is shite! And you're shite! I ought to send you back to the bowels of the earth where you belong!"

Salifu did not flinch. He did not waver. Instead, a slow smile crept across his face. He took great pleasure in watching yet another "client" unravel. Jack Rackham was far from the first to regret a deal with the netherworld. In his many incarnations as an emissary of darkness on earth, Salifu had witnessed it countless times. The familiar spectacle never failed to amuse him—watching the strong crumble, the bold turn to cowards, the proud sink into despair.

"Unless you get there first," Salifu said, his smile broadening.

The words shot through Jack like lightning. So unnerved was he by the shaman's comment and malevolent gaze that he let go of the beads and staggered backwards.

"I won't go back there! Never!" His voice was filled with fear. Jack had first sought immortality for the power and riches it would allow him to amass. But after his glimpse of Hell, those forty days after his hanging and before Salifu finally released him from the grave—something more primal motivated him. Absolute terror at the prospect of an eternity in that dark place. "And I will not wait another generation before I am assured of it!"

"What will you do, Jack Rackham?" Salifu asked, genuinely curious.

"I'm going to find the girl myself."

"What is the saying? Patience is a virtue?"

"Well, I'm not virtuous, and I'm certainly done being patient," Jack said. "If Maks kills Hartwright, I may never find the mother.

She's evaded me too long. And I've already lost too much because of it."

Salifu tilted his head, giving Jack a quizzical look. It wasn't like him to be this reckless, to leave the safety of the *Perdition* for a foray into the unknown. Sensing the shaman's doubt, Jack eyed him directly.

"We have another saying I've picked up over the years," he said. "'If you want something done right, do it yourself.'" He whirled and stormed out of the gallery, leaving Salifu in his wake.

All lines were about to converge, with Tucson as their intersection.

Chapter 20
Home Again

It took hours of nonstop driving to do it, but by late the next day the Brigands had rolled into Tucson without further incident. Upon arriving, they decided they needed to ditch the RV and switch to a lower-profile vehicle for the next part of the mission. The motorcycles had peeled off to a prearranged rendezvous point in the desert while the RV headed into town. Now, it sat idling in a strip mall parking lot, awaiting word that Bonnie, Luz, and Wilder had successfully boosted a more suitable ride.

"Keep your eye out for a Kia or Hyundai," Bonnie said in a whisper as she moved through the darkened streets not far from her old house.

Wearing hoodies to obscure their faces, the trio kept to the shadows as they looked for their target.

Bonnie had picked the ironically named Flowing Springs neighborhood near South Tucson because it was filled with middle-income families who'd not only be in for the night but would likely drive the kind of car she was looking for.

"Why? Those cars are lame, man," Luz complained. "Why don't we just take that one?" She indicated a sporty-looking Mazda parked in a driveway. "Lights are out in the houses up and down this street. It's just asking to get jacked."

"We're not jacking. We're borrowing. Besides, those cars have beaucoup anti-theft features," Bonnie said. "All we got is a screwdriver and a USB cable we took from the RV. No way we're getting one of those. But..."

Bonnie stopped at a Kia Soul parked on the street. She looked around to make sure the coast was clear. "Kias and Hyundais, they're a cinch to break into..." she explained. As she said it, she made quick business of getting the door open and slid into the driver's seat. "They have crap for a steering column. To keep costs down, they used cheap plastic and an ignition switch that happens to be just the size of a USB port."

Bonnie's hands worked with a familiarity born of countless repo missions. Fueled by muscle memory and the thrill of the moment, she barely had to look below the dashboard. It took her only a few seconds to pry the plastic casing away from the steering column with the screwdriver and a couple seconds more to hit pay dirt. *The ignition switch!*

"Once you breach the switch, all you have to do is—" She put the end of a USB cable into what used to be the keyhole and...

VROOOOM!

"Dayum, *chica*!" Luz was impressed. "Not bad for a *gringa*!"

"I have never been more turned on in all my life," Wilder said.

Bonnie laughed. "You're such a dork," she said. "Everybody in!"

"I got shotgun!" Wilder declared.

They all jumped in and Bonnie hit the gas.

.   .   .   .   .

Moments later, they arrived back at the RV to gather up the others. First though, Barnaby quickly switched out the license plates with some Montana plates that Peg had in her stash for just such a situation.

The Brigands all piled into the Kia. It was a tight fit and Barnaby had to cram himself into the cargo area in the back to make it work. There had been discussion about whether or not to bring Cordial along, but in the end Reed decided that since the next flight to Georgia wasn't until morning, they may as well put her to use. After all, they didn't know exactly what they'd be looking for once they got to the church. Even Bonnie couldn't disagree with that. A remorseful Cordial was eager to help, hoping to make up for what she'd done before she went home. Bonnie put the Kia into drive, and they were off in the direction of St. Brigid's parish church.

As she drove, Bonnie stared out at the familiar bland tan houses with the rock-filled front yards that lined the pot-holed streets. Here and there were occasional strings of leftover Christmas lights clinging for dear life to the eaves of the homes. And of course, it wouldn't be Arizona without the obligatory saguaro cactus planted smack dab in the middle of those seas of decorative pebbles. During the oppressive heat of summer, these saguaros stood sentry, the only sign of life in the entire neighborhood.

As Bonnie took in her old stomping grounds, a strange sensation moved through her—one she couldn't quite name. Nostalgia? Not exactly. Nostalgia implied fond memories, and in sixteen long, hard years, she didn't have many of those. No, this was more like stepping into a foreign country she'd only read about in books. Everything looked familiar, yet it felt like she'd never truly been here.

Because, in a way, she hadn't.

The Bonnie who'd lived here was a different girl, from a different time.

"Can't believe you actually grew up in this hole," said Tanner, who could no more imagine living here than he could on the planet Tadmor, 45 light years from Earth. "No wonder you're so f'd up."

"And you had all the advantages. So, what's your excuse?" Bonnie shot back with such venom, it shut Tanner up.

The church was located not far from where Bonnie had lived with the Krokels, her last foster parents, before the crazy chain of events that landed her on Cormac's Cove. And despite there being many routes to St. Brigid's, Bonnie found herself going the way that took them right through her old neighborhood.

There was the Safeway where Bonnie went to shoplift necessities for her and the other fosters whenever the Krokels blew their state check on booze and lotto tickets. There was the Brass Rail, the seedy little dive that the Krokels were supposed to have gone to on the night that Bonnie got arrested for torching the clothes of those horrible high school girls who threw her in the pool. And then—she slowed—there was the Krokel house.

It looked different. No junk-strewn yard, no rusted car parts. The place was dark, abandoned. A "FOR SALE" sign stood out front.

Satisfaction surged through her. Maybe Clint's repo business had soured once he lost his free labor. Maybe they'd packed up and slunk back to Jackie's nowhere Texas hometown. Whatever the reason, their absence cut the last tie to her old life.

Good riddance, she thought.

"You know that place?" Wilder asked.

"Just the house of someone I used to know a long time ago."

As she turned the corner, suddenly, she slammed on the brakes.

"What the heck, Bonnie?" Reed asked.

"There!" she pointed.

Up ahead, a billboard towered over a taco shop. It was faded, but the image was unmistakable. A blonde teenage girl. Her age, height, and weight.

HAVE YOU SEEN ME?
Mandy Brooks

"That's her!" Bonnie said. "That's Mandy!"

"Mandy as in flaming underwear Mandy?" Wilder asked. "The bitchy girl who got you thrown into juvey?"

Bonnie nodded.

"Wow. What do you think happened?" Tanner asked.

"Karma probably," Bonnie surmised.

"That's a horrible thing to say," Cordial spat. "I don't know what she did, but no one deserves to just disappear!"

"Says the runaway in the backseat," Bonnie said.

"Wonder if they ever found her," Luz said.

"No," answered Barnaby, having scanned the QR code on the billboard. "Says here she went missing on the way to school last May. Vanished without a trace."

"Last May?" Wilder exchanged glances with Bonnie. "That's when you got to Cormac's Cove."

"Damn," Luz said. Everyone else was silent.

"That's... weird," Bonnie said distantly, still staring at Mandy's photo on the billboard.

"The timing sure is," Reed said. "That was when she posted the picture of your mark on social media... the one that led us to you."

"Yeah," Bonnie said, hands tightening on the wheel. "And a few days later, she's gone."

The Brigands exchanged looks, each imagining what might have happened to Mandy. And every scenario led back to the same unsettling possibility.

*   *   *   *   *

With Bonnie at the wheel, the Kia navigated through the flow of traffic as they approached the parish church. Finally, after all that had happened, they were about to reach their objective, the one place that might hold the key to finding her mother. But nothing could have prepared them for what they encountered when they arrived.

"What's that smell?" Reed asked.

"Sorry if I reek, bro," Wilder said. "Italians are naturally sweaty."

"No, not that," Reed said. "Something's burning."

Indeed, the air hung heavy with the scent of burning wood, mingling with the sharp tang of scorched plaster. As they pulled up to the church, they saw it. St. Brigid's stood engulfed in a tempest of flames!

"NO!" Bonnie stumbled out of the car.

"Holy shit..." marveled Wilder as rest of the Brigands piled out of the car after her.

They all stared from the sidewalk as all around them embers pirouetted in the air. The fire's radiant glow painted the landscape in a hellish palette, casting shadows that danced on the ground before them.

A solitary figure emerged. It was a nun in full habit, singed and distraught. She stumbled out of the church. The Brigands ran to her.

"*Por favor!*" the nun implored, her voice strained and desperate. "*El padre Hartwright todavía está dentro. ¡Debes ayudar!*"

"She says the priest is still inside!" Luz translated.

"Father Hartwright!" Bonnie gasped and started toward the entrance, but Reed held her back.

"No!" Reed implored. "That thing is a blast furnace!"

"He's right!" Tanner said in agreement. "Let's just wait for the fire department!"

"You hear any sirens?!" Bonnie yelled over the roar of the flames. Bonnie broke free from Reed, shoving him away. She ran toward the church, eager to save the man who had saved her so many years ago. But more than that, she was determined that they hadn't come all this way in vain. She heard her name being called somewhere behind her, but it seemed far away and unimportant.

Entering the church through the charred front door, Bonnie was immediately accosted by thick, choking plumes of smoke, a swirling onslaught that clung to everything about her—clothing, hair, and even her taste buds. She struggled to make her way through the mission's interior, now a maelstrom of chaos.

"There!" She heard Reed's voice next to her and saw that both he and Wilder had entered the inferno. Blinking through stinging, watery eyes, she looked to where Reed was pointing at the front of the church.

Near the altar was Father Hartwright, sprawled on the floor, his hands still cradling a monstrance containing the sacred host. They all rushed to him. The elderly priest was badly burned.

"Father Hartwright!" Bonnie said as she knelt next to him, gripped with fear that he might be dead.

"Is he—?" Wilder asked.

Suddenly, the priest opened his eyes and met Bonnie's gaze. Something flickered there. Recognition? But how could that be? He hadn't seen her since she was an infant.

BOOM! A stained-glass window exploded from the heat. Glass rained down all around them. Bonnie instinctively covered the priest with her body. She could feel the shards bounce off her back as she shielded him from harm.

"We gotta get him out of here!" Reed shouted.

He helped Bonnie to her feet, and the three of them struggled to carry the priest toward the entrance. As they moved through the nave of the church, the flames gnawed at their backs, the heat intensifying with every step. The pews, the altar behind them, the tabernacle, the sacred artifacts—everything was being consumed by the appetite of the unrelenting blaze.

They emerged gasping and coughing and desperately sucking in the cool night air. The other Brigands rushed to help. Tanner, Luz, and Barnaby brought the priest over to a grassy area and laid him down. Cordial immediately knelt over him and put her ear to his mouth.

"I don't think he's breathing!" she said and started compressions.

By now, onlookers had gathered and fire engines had pulled up. Firefighters ran to the church, hoses in hand, and began dousing the blaze.

As the water flew, Luz crouched next to the sister, comforting her in her native language. *"Todo estará bien, Hermana. Ayudarán al padre Hartwright. Todo va a estar bien..."* As she spoke, Luz gently stroked the nun's cheek, exhibiting a kindness and compassion that the Brigands hadn't seen from her before.

"Over here!" Bonnie shouted toward one fire engine. "We need help!"

A firefighter and an EMT ran over with a gurney.

"Stand back!" The EMT pushed through the Brigands and immediately went to work, taking over compressions from Cordial. "You kids go over to the rig. Have them check you out!"

Bonnie just stood there, watching in shock as Father Hartwright was rushed to a waiting ambulance. Suddenly, she felt herself being tugged at. It was Wilder, yanking her away from the scene. The others were already in the car. Luz was behind the wheel, pulling away from the curb.

"We better make ourselves scarce!" Wilder insisted, pushing Bonnie into the back seat of the moving car.

Just then, the ambulance carrying Father Hartwright sped off, lights flashing and sirens blaring. Bonnie looked out the back window. The once serene St. Brigid's Church was succumbing to the flames that, to Bonnie, seemed to dance with malevolence.

Bonnie turned around and the Brigands looked at one another. No one had to speak. They were all thinking the same thought.

This was no coincidence.

Chapter 21
Between the Here and the There

CLICK. HISS. CLICK. HISS. The rhythm of the ventilator punctuated the silence in the ICU room where Father Hartwright lay in a coma.

The Brigands had followed the ambulance to a hospital, just blocks from the church. After waiting outside until it seemed safe, Reed sent Tanner in to do recon. First, because he wasn't covered with ash and soot like the others, but also because it didn't hurt, according to Luz, that he was white, rich, and entitled.

"You people can pretty much go wherever you want, no questions asked," she said.

"'You people'?" Tanner said. "What do you mean 'you people'?"

"Calm down, Rosa Parks," Wilder said. "We'll hold a candlelight vigil for you once we're inside. Now, git!"

Luz was right, of course. Tanner sailed past the security guard parked in front of the nurses' station. Then, he flashed his toothy smile and name-dropped his producer father to a young ICU nurse who happened to be a huge fan of Gordon Prescott's *Blood of the Buccaneers* movie franchise. After putting his name in the visitor's log "so the girls on the day shift would be jealous" and promising her a signed photo of the film's star, Cade Collins, Tanner was in. He got a room number and an assurance from the nurse that she'd conveniently leave her post when the Brigands entered through a propped open exit door.

Now in Father Hartwright's room, Bonnie looked down at the priest. He was battling for his life, burns all over his body, his lungs badly damaged by smoke.

"Heck of a reunion, huh?" Wilder said, leaning against the wall, exhausted.

"I should have thanked him when I had the chance," Bonnie said.

Reed frowned. "What do you mean?"

She let out a slow breath. "A few years ago, after I found out where I came from, I went back to St. Brigid's. I don't even know why—maybe I thought I'd ask him about that night, about my mother. Maybe I just wanted to see it for myself."

Wilder tilted his head. "And?"

Bonnie shook her head. "It was a Sunday morning. He was giving a mass. I sat in the back and listened to his voice, and all I could think about was how I had been just dumped there." Her voice dropped to almost a whisper.

Reed's expression softened. "Did you talk to him?"

A bitter laugh slipped from Bonnie's lips. "No. I freaked out. Ran out the side door before he even knew I was there. Never even said hello. Never thanked him for saving me. Now I'll never get the chance."

A heavy silence settled between them. Bonnie's fingers curled into fists at her sides. "Another life wrecked because of me. Because of this goddamn mark and whatever curse runs through my veins."

"This is not on you," Reed said firmly. "You didn't do this."

Bonnie's eyes flicked to his. She didn't argue, but she didn't agree, either.

"Well, it wasn't no accident," Luz offered. "The place reeked of gasoline."

"I think we know who did it," Wilder pushed off the wall, rolling his shoulders. "The question is why."

"We'll never find out now. Unless toast can talk," Tanner said. Everyone looked at him in disbelief. "Sorry, that was—I-I didn't mean it."

"You never mean it!" Bonnie burst out. "But you end up being an asshole just the same!"

"What's going on here!?" A sharp voice broke through the tension. An older nurse, stern-faced and clearly unreceptive to Tanner's charms, had appeared in the doorway. The young nurse who'd let Tanner in hovered nervously in the background.

"Who are you kids?" the senior nurse demanded. "You're not supposed to be in here. Family only."

"She *is* family," Wilder jumped in. "She's his, um, granddaughter. Bonnie, show your ID."

Bonnie produced the only ID she had, an expired Arizona learner's permit she'd gotten for her scooter. It wasn't much, but the last name "Hartwright" matched the priest's medical chart.

The nurse eyed her skeptically. "Granddaughter? I thought the guy was a priest."

"A youthful indiscretion," Wilder offered. "It got straightened out with a few Hail Marys."

The nurse frowned but relented. "She can stay," she said, handing the ID card back to Bonnie. "The rest of you, out!"

The group exited. Bonnie remained, though unsure why. There was nothing she could do. All was lost.

"Bonnie." It was Cordial. She'd slipped back in.

"Go away—"

"Listen. I might be able to communicate with him," Cordial said.

Bonnie suddenly turned to her. "Can you?"

"Sometimes, I can make contact. You know, when people are on the verge."

"I thought you didn't do that sort of thing anymore?"

"So you *were* listening."

"Can you do it or not?"

"I can try. Do you want me to try?"

As much as she didn't care for this girl, she wasn't about to look a gift psychic in the mouth.

Bonnie stepped aside and Cordial moved to the bed. She winced at the badly burned face of the priest.

"Father Hartwright?" She tentatively took his hand in hers. The moment they touched—

A WHITE-HOT LIGHT. THEN PITCH BLACKNESS.

Cordial was plunged into a dark netherworld, black with nothingness. Whispers filled the void around her. She cringed.

"F-Father?" she whispered uncertainly. "Are you here?"

The whispers grew louder, closing in on her, but Cordial resisted panicking. Something swirled in the darkness. Many somethings in fact, though she couldn't make out exactly what. But she knew—they were souls. Restless, desperate souls, all at that moment crossing over to the other side. She shuddered.

"I have a message from Bonnie," she said into the blackness. And SUDDENLY he was standing there next to her, his badly burned hand on her shoulder.

Startled, she YELPED!

Back in the ICU, Bonnie watched Cordial seemingly staring into nothingness. But she could hear every word she was saying. Frightened, Bonnie stepped toward her. Cordial looked at her; her eyes turned blue and rheumy, like the priest's. Not her brown eyes at all.

"Bonnie?" the voice coming out of Cordial was otherworldly, masculine and elderly. "Bonnie, is that you now?" she said in a lilting Irish accent. "I haven't seen you since you were but a wee lass."

"F-Father Hartwright?" Bonnie said hesitantly.

"Ah child. I'd wondered what'd become of you," he said. "And here, look how you've grown into a fine young woman. I'm so very sorry for what has befallen you."

"You know?"

"Only now, because I am between planes, is it known to me."

"Hurry!" Cordial's voice burst forth this time, her eyes flashing from blue to brown and back again.

In the void, the shadows thickened. Grasping hands clawed at Cordial. She was running out of time.

Back in the hospital, Father Hartwright's voice returned. "Your friend is right. Time is short. What is it you seek?"

"The night you found me," Bonnie said. "Something fell from my blanket, something small..."

"Ah. I thought it might have some significance, though I knew not what. I kept it in case you would return."

"Where is it?"

"Hidden. I will show your friend."

"Thank you, Father. For this and... for everything you did for me. I'm so sorry what's happened–"

"No need to worry for me," he said. "I have almost finished the race. As for you... Just stop him. Stop him!"

"Ahhhh!" Cordial's own screams tangled with the priest's in a plaintive wail.

Back in the in-between, the shadows surged, tearing at Cordial's hair and clothes, screeching, beseeching, begging for her help! Her arms flailed, fighting them off as Father Hartwright was pulled into the blackness.

"Cordial! Cordial!" Bonnie shook her.

Cordial was curled on the floor, arms over her head, swiping at unseen hands.

"It's me!"

"Bonnie?" Cordial stopped struggling. She blinked, breathing hard. She was back. But her hair was disheveled. Her dress ripped in places. There were scratches all over her arms and face.

"I got it!" Cordial smiled. Pleased.

,　　.　　,　　,　　,

"So you gonna tell us what the hell happened in there?" Tanner asked Cordial as the Brigands headed out to the Kia in the parking lot.

"Let's just say there are souls who are not exactly stoked to be leaving the life plane."

The Brigands exchanged glances, imagining what horrors Cordial must have encountered. And though she'd never admit it, even Bonnie felt a flicker of admiration for the Gullah girl's courage.

Cordial pushed back her ruined hair.

"So," she said. "Are we going after this supposedly 'important' clue or not? I've got a plane to catch."

Chapter 22
All that Glitters

The Brigands stood in a dark alleyway across from the smoldering church. St. Brigid's mission-style architecture had succumbed to the fire, leaving only an empty husk of a building in its wake. With the fire long extinguished, the only illumination came from the sodium streetlights casting a sickening yellow pinkish glow that Bonnie remembered only too well. She had spent many a night under these lights, roaming the streets and suffocating in the heat of the Arizona desert.

A single fire engine remained, standing sentry in front of the church in case of flare-ups. The lone firefighter in the cab scrolled through his phone, ironically chain-smoking and flicking ashes out the window.

"Whatever it is, it's in the rectory, under a brick in the fireplace hearth," Cordial said.

"We'll have to go in from the back," Reed said, eyeing the fire truck. "Tanner, you're with me. Wilder, you and the others stay with Bonnie. Get her back to the Wayfarers if things get messy." He turned to Cordial. "Ready?"

She nodded, and the trio disappeared down the street, then circled back around behind the church.

Though the priest's residence had suffered significant damage, the fireplace in the rectory was still standing, untouched by the flames. A pristine University of Mary Marauders plaque hung above the mantel, as well as a clock stopped at precisely one minute to midnight.

"Where exactly?" Reed asked, surveying the room.

Cordial held up a finger indicating for him to hold on, then closed her eyes.

FLASH! A vision. *A man's hands putting a box under a brick.*

She stepped forward, confidently brushing away dust and soot from the brick she saw in her vision. It was loose. She pried at it; it jiggled but wouldn't budge. Reed slipped his dagger in and worked it free, uncovering an old, battered strongbox, locked tight. He and Cordial exchanged a triumphant glance.

"Someone's coming!" hissed Tanner, arriving from his lookout post at the front of the house. Reed scooped the strongbox out of the hole, and the trio bolted out the back, barely escaping the detection of the entering firefighter, the lit cigarette still dangling absurdly from his lips.

But they were out. And they had it—whatever "it" was.

. . . . .

Bonnie carefully opened the strongbox. She had used her pocketknife to pop the rusted hinge off the lid as soon as they'd arrived at the Wayfarers' desert encampment. Dawn was approaching, but it was still dark out. The group huddled next to the RV, surrounded by the towering saguaros, their faces illuminated by a roaring campfire.

Bonnie scanned the expectant faces—Brigands, Wayfarers, even Cordial. This is what they had come all this way for. What they had lost some of their own for. Bonnie hesitated, worried that whatever was inside would be a dead end, or, in some ways, that it wouldn't be.

"Open it already!" Barnaby said impatiently.

"Give it!" Tanner snatched the box and unceremoniously dumped its contents onto the ground.

"Tanner, be careful!" Reed barked, but only half-heartedly, for he was just as eager as anyone to see what was inside.

Papers spilled out of the box. A passport unused since the 90s. A yellowed, heartfelt love letter from "K" that lamented Father Hartwright's decision to choose the church over her. Some scattered old photos of what must have been his family back in Ireland. But nothing metallic or shiny.

"What the hell?" Bonnie said, sifting through the pile. "What the actual hell! It's not here!"

"Hold on!" Wilder picked up the box and shook it. Something inside clinked against the metal sides. "There's still something in here." He stuck in his hand and removed the velvet lining from the bottom.

"Aha!" He produced a small metallic object that glinted in the firelight.

"What is it?" Luz moved in for a closer look.

Wilder handed it to Bonnie, who held it out in her open palm for all to see:

"It's a pin... with a compass rose," Bonnie said.

"Not like any compass rose I've ever seen," Barnaby said.

"Definitely not the Brigand compass rose anyways," Reed added.

They were right. This was no Brigand insignia. Instead of the familiar points of a star, interlocking swords indicated the directions. And rather than the roses weaving around its center, serpents slithered between the blades. It radiated menace, a mark of something far darker.

"Lordy. Is that—?" Doc whispered.

"It is," Rusty said grimly.

"The FF," Peg concurred. "Haven't seen that symbol in years."

Bonnie was almost too afraid to ask. Almost. "What the hell is the FF?"

It was Reed who answered. "The Féth Fíada," he said, exchanging looks with the Wayfarers.

"Wait. You know what this is?" Bonnie asked.

"Only very generally. I've never seen that symbol. But I've heard of the FF. They were a splinter group of Brigands back in the day," Reed said. "Grandfather didn't say a lot about them, except they didn't last very long."

"I've heard of the FF, too," Barnaby said. "Overheard anyway. My dad didn't seem to want to talk about them much."

"Good reason," Rusty said. "They were a radical bunch. Started by an ex-Brigand the name of Johnny Keane."

"Irish guy," Doc said. "His granddad fought 'longside Michael Collins and the IRA back in the War of Independence. Had fightin' in his blood."

"Real good lookin' but intense," Peg said, "in a brooding bad boy way that had all the gals swoonin'."

"Present company NOT excluded." Rusty gave her a side glance.

"Hey! A girl's gotta have a hobby!" She winked. "Hold on a sec." Peg disappeared inside the RV and returned with her box of photos.

"This is him right here." Peg handed over a photo. A younger version of herself stood beside an intensely handsome man—black hair, piercing gray eyes, sharp features.

"Looks more like an Instagram pretty boy than a Brigand," Wilder snorted.

"Hell yeah. I'd hit that, and I don't even like guys," Luz added, passing the snapshot to Tanner.

"What does 'Féth Fíada' mean?" Bonnie asked.

"Some Celtic thing," Doc answered with a shrug. "Keane was really into that pagan shit."

"So why'd this *pendejo* break off from our group?" Luz asked.

"He didn't like how the Brigands was being run," Rusty said. "Felt they needed to be more on the offense. Take the fight to Jack."

"He wasn't wrong," Reed said. The young Brigands agreed.

"Yeah, but it's *how* he thought they ought to go about it. Keane was a believer in fighting fire with fire. Real scorched earth kind of stuff."

Rusty looked at Doc. "Remember when he took out Jack's whole drug operation on Andros by poisoning the local drinking water?

"Yup," Doc said. "He got Jack's men all right but took out a couple hundred villagers while he was at it. Didn't blink an eye."

"Seriously?" This was news to Reed.

"Oh, yeah. He was extreme!" Peg said.

"What does some old group that isn't even around anymore have to do with my mother?"

The Wayfarers exchanged uneasy glances. Bonnie could tell there was something more to the story.

"I could think of one thing," Peg said.

"Margaret. It ain't our story to tell," Rusty warned.

"Rust, I think we all seen what comes of keeping secrets," Peg said. Everyone avoided looking at Cordial, who looked down, ashamed. "The girl's got a right to know."

"Know what?" Bonnie asked.

Interlude
The Adoption

Just outside Rockport, Massachusetts
Thirty-three years earlier

The night sky was a sprawling canvas of glittering stars, so close they seemed almost within reach. Snowflakes drifted gently, adding to the thick, white blanket covering the ground. A narrow, winding road cut through the winter landscape, bordered by towering pines. A Ford Escort made its way along the icy path, a fresh Christmas tree tied to the roof. Inside, warmth and laughter filled the car as a cheerful holiday song played on the radio.

"Sing with us!" a woman called over her shoulder from the passenger seat, her eyes sparkling with joy.

A three-year-old girl with dark curly hair giggled from her car seat in the back, clapping her mittened hands to the beat. In the driver's seat, her father kept his eyes on the road but couldn't resist joining in, his voice blending with his wife's. The car felt like a bubble of happiness, insulated from the cold and darkness outside.

SUDDENLY, headlights appeared behind them. The man's brow furrowed with concern as he glanced in the rearview mirror.

"What is it?" the woman asked.

"That car behind us is coming up awfully fast."

The lights grew brighter, dangerously close. At the last second, the vehicle braked but stayed tight on their bumper.

BEEEEEEP! The tailgater laid on his horn. The loud noise startled the child, and she began to cry.

BEEP! BEEP! BEEP! BEEP!

"He's probably drunk," the father said. "Lot of holiday parties this weekend."

"It's okay, sweetie," the mother said, unlatching her seatbelt so she could turn to soothe the child. "Jeff! Slow down and let him pass."

The man tapped the brakes, signaling for the other car to pass. But it kept aggressively riding their tail, its horn BLARING.

Suddenly, another car sped out from a side road and pulled up alongside Jeff. A third vehicle emerged on the passenger side. They were boxed in. Jeff's heart pounded as he glanced at the driver on his left. The unknown man made a gesture to pull over.

Instead, Jeff floored the gas pedal. The Escort surged forward, trying to break free. But as they reached a curve, the tires hit a patch of ice. The car fishtailed wildly.

"Hold on, Emily!" Jeff tried to keep the car on the road, but it was too late. The car spun around, tires screeching on the ice, and it careened off the road, down a steep snow-covered embankment, then slammed violently into a tree.

The front of the car crumpled against the tree trunk, steam billowing from the hood. Emily's screams had been cut short—her head slumped against the shattered windshield. Jeff groaned, barely conscious, his bloody forehead resting against the steering wheel.

From the back seat came a small, trembling voice. "Mama?"

Outside, a man made his way down the embankment, his breath visible in the frigid night air. He reached the wreckage and peered inside. Seeing the child still whimpering in the backseat, he called up the slope, "Keane! You're gonna want to see this!"

Another figure arrived at the bloody scene. He blew on his hands for warmth and pulled down the hood of his parka. He was striking—black hair, piercing gray eyes. He surveyed the wrecked car before leaning into the driver's side window. Jeff stirred, his eyelids fluttering.

"You should have listened," Keane said, leaning in close.

He grabbed Jeff's head and slammed it brutally against the dashboard. His body went limp. Keane unfastened the seatbelt, making it look as though the driver had been thrown forward in the crash.

Then, Keane moved to the other side of the car, where Emily was pinned from the chest down by the dashboard. She groaned, eyes opened wide in fright but unable to move or speak. Keane put his gloved hand firmly over the woman's mouth and nose.

As the woman fought desperately for breath, Keane looked over the seat to the child sitting there.

"It's okay, little one. It's okay," he said in a soothing tone that belied the violence he was committing.

Finally, the woman stopped struggling.

Keane went to the child and took her from her car seat, cradling her small, trembling form in his arms. She gazed up at him, too afraid to cry. He cooed quietly to the child and then pushed up the girl's coat sleeve. There, clearly visible on the forearm in the glow of the taillights, was what he sought:

The Stain of Musangu. The mark that set her apart from the rest of humanity, and to Keane's way of thinking, the key to its salvation.

"I got you, Brigid," he said, looking into the girl's frightened eyes. "I got you."

With steady steps, he carried the child back up the slope toward the waiting cars, his boots crunching in the snow. As if guided by fate, the wind picked up, turning the snowfall into a blizzard. Before long, their tracks would be gone, the storm erasing any trace of their passage.

The girl was safe now, and he vowed to keep her that way. No matter the cost.

Chapter 23
The Féth Fíada

"I don't understand." Bonnie was stunned by the story she'd just heard. "I thought my mom's parents died in a car accident."

"They did," Reed insisted. "That's how my grandparents told it anyway."

"How I heard it too," Barnaby agreed.

"In a car *crash*, yeah," Doc said. "But it wasn't no accident."

"But why would he do that?" Wilder asked.

"Brigid's folks, they didn't want to hear nothing about the curse or the mark or any of it," Doc explained. "Told the Brigands to get lost. Thought the whole thing was nuts."

"Weren't the first," Peg muttered.

Rusty jumped in. "And Captain Ballister said there was nothing to be done 'cept keep an eye on Brigid from afar, like the Brigands always done in the past with nonbelievers. But Keane? He didn't think marked ones should have a say in the matter. Believed the stain—er, mark—took that right from them when they was born."

"That's bullshit," Bonnie said, bristling.

"Just saying how he saw things. Any case, he didn't think he could just leave Brigid out there for Jack to get. But Ballister gave him the 'it's how it's been done for centuries' speech and that was that. Or so we thought."

Doc picked up the story. "After the crash, Brigid came to live on the Cove. Keane and his lot were on protection duty that night. Claimed Jack ran them off the road and that he fought to rescue Brigid."

"Did my grandfather buy it?"

"You tell me. How many Brigands get into a tussle with Jack Rackham's boys and come out of it without a scratch? The captain couldn't prove anything, but he knew in his heart that he couldn't trust Keane no more no how. Next thing, Keane's gone—took some Brigands with him, including everyone who was there that night. Not long after, we hear they started the Féth Fíada."

Reed shook his head. "My grandfather never said a word about this."

"Well, I'm not surprised he wanted to keep a lid on it," Rusty said. "It being a black mark on the Brigands and all."

"What about Brigid's family? Grandparents, aunts, uncles?" Barnaby asked.

Rusty shrugged. "Maybe they filed a missing persons report in Massachusetts, but by then, Brigid was on the Cove. Who'd think to look there?"

"What happened to the FF?" Bonnie asked.

"They lasted a few years, really disrupted Jack's operation for a bit. But like every Icarus, Keane got cocky, got himself killed during an attack on one of Jack's ships. Maybe ten years back now. After that, the FF went silent. Ain't no one heard from 'em since."

"This is all very fascinating, finding out more about my dumpster fire of a past," Bonnie said. "But none of it explains what this pin was doing on me at the church the day I was left there. Or how it's supposed to help me find my mother. Unless there's something I'm missing."

Everyone sat silent.

"Yeah. That's what I thought."

Bonnie looked down at the pin in her hand, glinting in the firelight. All they'd been through and yet another dead end.

. . . . .

Bonnie yawned and slowly opened her eyes. She blinked to orient herself. She was lying on the cold desert ground, the fire dying. The first rays of morning light were coloring up the horizon. *Strange.* She didn't remember doing it, but somehow she had dozed off and from the looks of it, so had everyone else. But it had been a long and emotional night. Careful not to disturb the others, she rose to her feet, wrapping a blanket around her shoulders to ward off the cold.

She walked to the edge of the encampment to watch the sunrise. As she did, she heard a strange humming coming from a nearby cluster of saguaros. Bonnie's hand went to the hilt of Siobhan and she carefully moved toward the sound, the humming growing clearer with each step. Soon it transformed into a discernable song. A woman's voice, soft and hymn-like:

> *Sails groan 'gainst dah force o' winds,*
> *Mah soul set free, g'bye*
> *'Lectricity splits horizon lights*
> *From shore tah sea tah sky*
>
> *O compass rose guide me*
> *Mah journey's next road*
> *Travel o travel shall I*
> *Shall I-Oh-*Well! Hullo, Miss Bonnie Hartwright!"

Bonnie stopped in her tracks. Sitting before her in a rocker in the middle of the desert was Gam Gam.

"I been waitin' fuh yah," she said.

"Gam Gam? W-what are you doing out here?"

"I come tah see yah, chile, o'course." Gam Gam arose and spryly approached. She touched Bonnie's face. "And look at yah. Jes' as beautiful and strong as I 'magined."

Gam Gam looked directly at Bonnie. Her eyes were as clear as the day she was born. The old woman's cataracts were gone!

"You can see?!"

"Course I kin see!"

"And you don't need your cane!"

"Dats how it is when yah ain't bound no mo' by dah frailties of dah flesh."

Bonnie's breath hitched. "You mean you're—"

"Yup. Done gone tah glory."

And with that, Bonnie dissolved into tears.

"Shush, no need fuh dat. I lived me a long and happy life. No regrets—dat's dah bes' journey anyone kin walk on dis here earth."

"I'm sorry," Bonnie sobbed. "It's just. Everything's awful. This whole trip was a failure and we're not any closer to finding my mom. And now this."

"Dat's what I's here fuh. I come wid mo' tidings 'bout yah mamma."

Bonnie sniffled. "I don't understand."

"Whenst I was making mah, er, transition, I took me a little detour," she said, "and was able tah break through dah veil what yah mamma's been hiding undah. Well, whatevah strange magic dey playin' at, wasn't 'spectin' an ol' soul from beyond. Didn't feel me 'til it was too late. Not 'fore I seen dis anyways." Gam Gam pointed her bony finger over Bonnie's shoulder toward the sunrise.

Bonnie turned and there, in the middle of the desert, was a stone monastery! Nothing like the mission-style churches of Arizona, it looked ancient, but somehow new at the same time. Ivy-covered walls, green flowy grass, a cool ocean mist swirling above the rocky steps that led to the entrance. Seagulls called and circled above. Bonnie sensed that this was not just far from Tucson—it was far removed from this place and time altogether.

Gam Gam took Bonnie's hand and led her into the monastery— through an archway and down a long corridor. There, in an alcove, they stopped before a mosaic set into the stone. Intricate and beautiful in its design. Thousands of tiny stones arranged to form an elaborate image:

Dominating the mosaic was a fierce angel holding a balance scale in its hand. The angel's eyes burned with cold judgment as two human figures, one on each of the pans, were being weighed. One looked toward the heavens, hands clasped in prayer. The other's face was twisted in fear, his side weighed down closer to the flames of Hell that raged below, eager to claim his soul.

"What is this place?" Bonnie asked, shuddering at the apparition of stone and mist before them.

"Dis be where yah need tah get yahself tah," Gam Gam said cryptically.

"Which is where exactly—?"

A deafening BOOM shook the earth. Electricity CRACKLED through the sky.

"Do I gots tah do ebryting for yah?" Gam Gam said to Bonnie. "Jes' seek and ye shall find. Knock, and dat door be open. And all dem sayin's."

ANOTHER BOOM of LIGHTNING!

"Comin' already!" Gam Gam shouted to no one Bonnie could see. "So impatient!

"G'bye chile." She turned to go.

"Gam Gam, wait!" Bonnie ran to her, wrapping her arms around the small woman. "Thank you for everything. I-I—" Bonnie still struggled with the words; though she felt them, they tasted strange in her mouth, having been denied them so long. But Gam Gam understood.

"I know," she said with a nod. "I loves yah too, chile."

Bonnie started to let go, but Gam Gam held tight, whispering in her ear, "Jes' member tho. Things ain't always come out what dey seem. Look to dah scales, chile. And watch dah weight o' yah own soul."

Gam Gam stepped back and Bonnie realized the monastery was gone, vanished into the desert air.

Then, with confident strides, the old woman walked straight toward the brilliant sunrise, her figure becoming a silhouette against its blazing red-orange glory. She got smaller and smaller and fainter and fainter as she went. The smaller she grew, the fainter her voice became, resuming the song she had started:

O compass rose guide me
Mah journey's next road
A throne tah dah heaven's most high

O compass rose guide me
And lighten mah load
Travel o travel shall I, shall I
Travel o travel shall I

Bonnie blinked and Gam Gam was gone. Tears streamed down her face. The pain was so exquisite that it made her long for the days when she cared for no one.

Then the world around her began to dissolve. The earth, the sky, even the sun, all evaporated into mist until she stood alone in a dark, formless void.

She turned back—the mosaic! It still floated before her. The stones pulsed, their colors oversaturated, like one of those old Technicolor films that Bonnie sometimes landed on when scrolling through videos. Then, as if the scene had come to life, she saw the image moving.

The lower side of the scale suddenly plunged into the fire. Into the abyss. Toward one man's eternal damnation—

GASP! Bonnie gulped for air and her eyes flew open, tears streaming down her face. She was lying on the ground, still in front of the dying fire, the first rays of morning lighting the sky. The others were all awake, looking down at her with concern. Bonnie opened her hand; she still clutched the FF pin.

She felt a gentle hand touch her back. She turned to see Cordial kneeling next to her. Their eyes met and Bonnie saw that the Gullah girl's face was also streaked with tears.

Cordial knew. She knew Gam Gam was gone.

"Bonnie," Wilder said, helping her to her feet. "It's okay... you were having a dream. It was just a dream."

Bonnie looked back to Cordial. They both knew that for Bonnie, "just a dream" did not exist.

Chapter 24

Next Steps

Bonnie saw it on Cordial's face before she'd even spoken a word. Though she had known the truth in her own heart, Bonnie needed the confirmation.

"It's true, Bonnie. Miss Ophelia passed away late last night," Cordial confirmed, having just gotten off the phone with her mother. "Fati and my mom were with her."

Wilder sank onto the RV steps, his legs unsteady. His friends closed in around him.

"I'm sorry, man," Reed said, a comforting arm on Wilder's shoulder. "I know what she meant to you. She meant a lot to all of us."

"Wilder, if you need to go back..." Bonnie started.

"Yeah, I can see if there are still seats on Cordial's flight," Barnaby said, already on his phone.

"No," Wilder shook his head. "My place is here. Gam Gam would understand."

Reed and Bonnie both nodded.

"Then let's honor Gam Gam and do what she asked," Reed said.

*   *   *   *   *

Hundreds of images flew by on Peg's laptop screen. All similar to the mosaic from Bonnie's dream, though none exactly like it: a figure holding scales, measuring human lives. Whether from ancient Egypt, pagan times, or the Renaissance, the theme remained constant—the Weight of Souls.

"It's about judging souls after death," Barnaby explained. "Determining who goes to Heaven or Hell."

"The same dude's in a lot of the pictures," Tanner observed as Reed scrolled through the images.

"That's the archangel Michael," Barnaby said. "He is supposed to lead the armies of Heaven in a battle against Satan in the End Times. After which, everybody's going to get judged."

"Hope this dude grades on a curve," Wilder said.

Luz recited from memory, "*Saint Michael the Archangel, defend us in battle. Be our protection against the wickedness and snares of the devil. May God rebuke him, we humbly pray; and something, something, cast into Hell Satan and all the evil spirits who prowl about the world seeking the ruin of souls. Amen.*"

Everyone looked at her as if she'd just swallowed her own sword. She shrugged. "My *abuela* took me to the gringo mass every Sunday to practice her English. We said that prayer every week at the end of the service. Guess it stuck with me cuz it's some pretty trippy shit."

Wilder shook his head with an astonished smile. "Just when you think you know a lesbian gangbanger..."

"This is going to take forever," said Reed, scrolling through the images. "There's just so many."

"Keep looking," Bonnie said, eyes glued to the screen. "I know I'd recognize it if I saw it again. It was beautiful... and creepy at the same time."

Reed shook his head. "I'm just going to need something more specific to go off of..."

"Then let's get something more specific," Wilder said, a spark of an idea forming.

, , , , ,

Within moments, they were on an encrypted video call with Cormac's Cove. Micah sat at his computer while Malachi sketched in his drawing book, translating Bonnie's description.

"It was like a painting, but made of little tiles," she explained. "What's that called again?"

"A mosaic," Barnaby supplied.

"Yes! A mosaic, Malachi!" Bonnie said excitedly.

Micah glanced at his brother, who remained focused on his drawing. "You hear that, Malachi?" No response. "He's got it."

"How's it looking?" Bonnie asked impatiently.

"Give him a minute, Bonnie," Micah sighed. "He's not AI."

"How do we even know this place is real?" asked Zion, who was sitting arms folded in the back of the Boreas cabin with Daya, Wendell, and Yeun.

"That's what I said!" Tanner jumped in. "I mean, I dreamed I made out with this hot actress once, but I then saw her at a premiere a couple of weeks later and she acted like she'd never met me."

"In her defense," Wilder said, "who would admit to making out with you?"

"This what you saw?" Micah held the drawing up to the camera.

Bonnie stared at the screen in awe. Malachi's sketch was perfect—the archangel's stance, the clouds, the scales, the desperate look of the condemned man. It wasn't just similar. It was the exact same image!

, , , , ,

Despite the million questions from the Cove about the journey, there wasn't time for a long conversation. Condolences over the loss of Wayfarers and Gam Gam were exchanged and the call ended.

Reed immediately took his screenshot of Malachi's drawing and uploaded it to a reverse image search site online. Within seconds, they got a hit of the drawing that Malachi had just done.

The image was on a website that looked like it had been created back when everybody was using dial-up modems. According to the site, called "churchlore.com," the drawing was from the fifth century. It was a monk's rendering of a proposed mosaic for "the new monastery," complete with an admonishment (translated from old Gaelic) on the bottom of the page that the artist not overcharge for materials as he'd done on the last project.

"It says here," Reed said, reading aloud, "that 'the exact location in question remains shrouded in mystery, but likely it was from one of the monasteries that popped up on the islands off the coast of Ireland as Christianity took hold in that country.'"

"Ireland?" Luz said. "Isn't Anne Bonny from Ireland?"

"Yep," Barnaby said. "She grew up in County Cork before coming to the New World."

"The website doesn't say anything about Cork," Reed said. "It says it's probably from one of the islands right off the coast near a placed called Dungarry. Though the exact location is lost to time."

"Never heard of it." It was so small even Barnaby didn't know about it.

They all looked at each other excitedly. Whether or not the proximity to Anne Bonny's birthplace held meaning, they took it as such.

"So. How do we get there?" Wilder asked.

A knock at the RV door interrupted them. It was Rusty. "Miss Cordial, we best get going if you're gonna make your flight."

The Brigands had all been so absorbed they had completely forgotten that Cordial was leaving. And now that the moment was at hand, it hung heavy over them.

"Well. That's my cue," Cordial finally said as she picked up her packed bag. "Don't want to give my mom another reason to kill me."

Cordial hugged everyone. "For what it's worth, I think you guys are so amazing and brave. Calico Jack better watch his back." Then she turned to Bonnie. "I hope you find your mom."

Cordial opened the camper door and stepped down out of the RV. Rusty took her bag as she got on the back of his Harley. He started the engine.

"Wait!" The word escaped Bonnie before she knew why. "You don't have to go."

Reed and Wilder shared a surprised look. In fact, they all did, knowing Cordial wasn't exactly on Bonnie's list of favorite people.

"Bonnie, I thought we decided—" Reed began.

"That was before she helped with Father Hartwright. And the pin. Sure. She screwed up. But she might come in handy," she said, not looking at Cordial.

The words felt like sand in Bonnie's mouth, but Reed considered them carefully. Then he nodded. "Up to Cordial, I guess."

"Are you sure?" she asked Bonnie directly.

"I'm not gonna beg," Bonnie said, suddenly irritated. She spun and disappeared into the RV, the screen door slamming behind her.

Cordial jumped off the bike. "What the hell. Not like Zenobia can kill me any deader."

Reed clapped his hands together. "Well then," he said. "Anybody have any bright ideas how we're getting to Ireland?"

Chapter 25
A Plan is Hatched

Reed's question was met with a foot-shuffling silence the likes of which hadn't been seen in a good long time. After the difficulty of the trip to Tucson, a journey halfway across the world with this group seemed fraught with unimaginable challenges.

Finally, it was Tanner who spoke up. "How far are we from Mexico?"

"I know you probably got some hottie stashed away in Cabo, Tanner," Wilder objected, "but this is hardly the time—"

"No, idiot," Tanner explained. "My dad is shooting *Blood of the Buccaneers IV* around Puerto Peñasco. And where my father is, his private plane is, too."

"The father who sent you to Cormac's Cove for totaling his Ferrari, who hasn't returned your texts since you joined the Brigands, is gonna let us use his plane?" Bonnie asked skeptically.

"You totaled a Ferrari?" Cordial asked.

"Okay, he might not be thrilled about it, but trust me," Tanner said. "All I need to do is make a scene with the press around, and I'll get what I want. Always have."

"This ain't a trip to Disneyland, Spray Tan," Luz huffed.

"Four hours!" Barnaby announced after checking his phone. "It's only four hours to Puerto Peñasco from here!"

Bonnie looked to Reed. "With that plane, we'd get to Ireland in hours instead of days."

Reed considered the plan, his brows furrowed in thought. "Let's pretend your dad *will* say yes," he said. "We still have to get over the border. We don't have passports. Most of us don't even have legal IDs."

Luz laughed at the conversation and said to Cordial. "These white boys kill me." Cordial smiled and nodded and pretended she knew what Luz was talking about.

Reed turned to Luz. "If you have an idea, just say it."

"You think your homegirl can't get us into Mexico?" she said with a sly smile. Luz leaned back against the RV, her eyes gleaming with confidence. "I come from a long line of the documentally challenged. If you know what I mean."

The others, in fact, did not. But Luz was more than happy to show them.

*   *   *   *   *

Twenty minutes later, the Brigands piled out of their Kia in the parking lot of a local home improvement store. With Luz leading the way, they moved through the lot toward a group of day laborers near the entrance. While the others hung back, Luz stepped forward and addressed them in fluent Spanish.

"*Disculpen,*" she began. "*Estamos buscando a alguien que pueda ayudarnos a cruzar la frontera hacia México.*"

"*¿Hacia México?*" one snorted, and a couple others actually burst out laughing at the request, which more than a little annoyed Luz.

"*Lo digo en serio,*" she said.

The laborers exchanged nervous glances. They were wary of gringos, especially those that didn't look like they needed their lawn mowed.

"Dry wall, tree trimming, painting, odd jobs *solamente.*"

"Hey Reed," Luz said. "We got any cash?"

Reed produced a handful of bills. "Just what Wicked Pete gave me when we left."

Luz held up the wad of bills.

That did the trick. One laborer gave them a name: Diego Maldonado.

And just like that, they had found their connection.

*   *   *   *   *

With Maldonado's name and address in hand, the Brigands bid farewell to the Wayfarer bikers who'd accompanied them back into town. Rusty kept it brief.

"With Brigands, it's never 'goodbye'—just 'see you later.'"

Peg saluted Bonnie from the driver's side window of the Winnebago. "If I had grandchildren, I'd tell 'em about the time I had the great honor of protecting the marked Brigand, Bonnie Hartwright. Stay true."

Bonnie saluted back. The other Brigands followed suit. Peg began to sing as she put the behemoth into gear and pulled away.

> *For the voyage is long and the winds won't blow*
> *and it's time for us to leave her!*
> *Leave her Johnny leave her!*

The remaining Wayfarers on motorcycles fell in one by one behind her, all joining in the song as they did.

> *Leave her Johnny leave her!*
> *But now we're through, so we'll go on shore*
> *and it's time for us to leave her!*
> *Leave her Johnny leave her!*

Their voices faded with distance and the roar of engines until they disappeared over the horizon and were gone.

*   *   *   *   *

Navigating through South Tucson's roughest streets, the Kia arrived at a secluded warehouse marked "AgMex USA." They ditched the stolen car outside the gate, but not before they'd filled the tank, locked all the doors, and left a thank-you note on the dashboard. Arriving at the entrance to the warehouse, Luz knocked firmly on the rickety wooden door.

The door swung open, revealing a rugged-looking man with a grizzled beard and sharp eyes. He eyed the Brigands with suspicion, his gaze lingering on Luz.

"*¿Te llamas Diego Maldonado?*" Luz asked the man.

"I speak English plenty," he grunted. "What do you want?"

"We need to cross into Mexico," she said.

"*Into* Mexico?" Diego frowned. "I usually bring people out. Why don't you just cross at the checkpoint at Nogales like the U of A frat boys do on the weekends?"

"Let's just say we're a special case and leave it at that," she said matter-of-factly.

The coyote eyed them warily, sizing them up with a mixture of suspicion and curiosity.

"Special costs extra," he said at last.

Luz produced a huge wad of cash that Rusty had given her for the transaction. "I think this ought to cover it."

Diego took the cash, counting it quickly. He nodded.

·   ·   ·   ·   ·

Maldonado led them behind the warehouse, where an 18-wheeler labeled *Gallegos Grains* waited. Its rail-thin driver, Edison, wore a ball cap barely containing his wild black hair.

"You'll hide under the tarps," Edison explained. "We're hauling soybeans. If we get inspected, you bury yourselves in the beans."

Wilder grinned. "*Soy*beans? I'm more of a baked beans guy."

"Believe me, we know," said Barnaby, eliciting the laughter that every well-crafted fart joke was bound to get from a teenage audience.

With one last glance at Edison and Diego, Bonnie and the Brigands settled beneath the tarps as the truck roared to life and began to roll south down the road.

.   .   .   .   .

While the semi trundled along the freeway, the young Brigands talked about anything and everything as they lay on the pile of soybeans.

"Luz Marisol Delgado. You are a woman of many talents!" Reed said.

"Yeah. Thanks Luz," Bonnie said. "You rock."

"Thank my *abuela*. She took me and my brother Alejandrino back and forth plenty of times, you know, for birthdays and weddings and funerals and stuff. On the down low."

"She sounds cool," Barnaby said.

"She was a queen. There for us after our mami died. My dad, he was never worth nothing. And after he went to jail for manslaughter, my abuela took me in. Only person who ever believed in me."

"I'm sure that's not true," Cordial said. "What about your brother?"

"I told you. My old man went away for manslaughter." She looked at Cordial as if she were dense.

"Oh. Oh! I'm sorry, I didn't know, I..." Cordial's voice faded as the meaning sunk in.

Bonnie wasn't shocked. None of the Brigands were. They knew Luz's backstory. In fact, they all knew it was what was behind Luz's fierce protection of Bonnie. A makeup for what she perceived was her failure to protect her brother.

"Anyhow. I'm glad my *abuela* wasn't around to see the shit I got into after she passed," Luz continued. "She would be so ashamed."

"Well," Bonnie said, "I bet she'd be pretty proud if she saw you now."

"Yeah, ass-deep in tofu."

TAP TAP TAP! That was the signal from Edison. They were arriving at the border. The truck downshifted as it slowed and stopped, engine idling.

Bonnie went over Edison's instructions in her head. If they got stopped, they needed to get invisible real quick. The Brigands looked at one another. The air was thick with tension, each passing moment stretching on agonizingly as the agents circled the truck.

"Abrelo," came a voice from outside the truck.

Bonnie's first year Spanish was good enough to know what that meant. The guy wanted Edison to take the tarps off so that the load could be inspected.

"Dive!" Bonnie whispered.

One by one the Brigands' heads vanished into the soybeans.

The tarp flew open, and a beam of light pierced the darkness.

Time seemed to stand still as Bonnie held her breath, every muscle tense in anticipation.

SPOOSH! Bonnie heard the sound of something probing the load.

SPOOSH! SPOOSH! Edison had mentioned that sometimes the agents took long poles and dug around to make sure there wasn't any contraband among the loads.

Bonnie felt the soybeans shift around her as she fought to control her rising panic. The lack of oxygen reminded her of the drowning dream. With every moment and every SPOOSH of the border agents' poles, the walls of the trailer seemed to close in around her.

Just when it felt like she couldn't hold her breath another moment, SHOUTS could be heard from outside the truck. A dog barked.

"¡Por aquí! ¡Encontré algo!"

Suddenly, the poles receded from the soy beans and the border agents could be heard running from the truck toward whatever had caught their attention.

Bonnie felt the rumble of Edison's engine as it sprang to life and pulled back out onto the road.

She burst into the cool night air, gasping for breath as she collapsed onto the top of the bean pile in a heap. Around her, the other Brigands and Cordial emerged from their hiding places, all sucking in air.

Luz peeked outside from under the tarp. She smiled. *"Bienvenidos a México, bandidos!"*

Chapter 26

Jack in Tucson

Calico Jack Rackham, the shaman Salifu at his side, stood in front of the burned-out church, the embers of the fire having gone cold. In the time since the blaze, the police tape that surrounded the scene had come loose and now fluttered in the night wind.

Once Rackham had given the order, it didn't take long for his sophisticated computer algorithm to flag the fire at St. Brigid's—a church bearing Bonnie's mother's first name and run by a priest with the last name of Hartwright. No believer in coincidences, Jack immediately set out to investigate. Salifu's warnings not to act rashly were met with disdain and a declaration that he was done taking advice from "one who stands in silent hope of my ruin."

Jack moved toward the church while Salifu hung back—careful not to get too close to consecrated ground.

Inside the church, Jack walked past the charred pews and blackened statuary, stopping right in front of the marble altar, the only thing not destroyed by the blaze. He looked back at the bronze and gold inlaid tabernacle behind the altar, now just a twisted hunk of melted metal. Above it, a scorched crucifix hung precariously from the wall, the corpus barely recognizable from the soot that covered its body.

Rackham reached up to the remains of the cross and gave it a nudge. That was all it took. The crucifix plummeted from its perch and shattered on the floor at his feet. He took pleasure in this act, like a cruel child pulling the wings off an insect.

Jack continued down the aisle past the burned-out baptismal font. He noticed something on the floor amidst the ashes of the pews. He leaned down and picked it up. His lifeless black eyes narrowed at the sight. It was a piece of charred glass, the shattered remains of a mason jar.

The pirate lifted the fragment to his nose. The faint aroma of gasoline still clung to the glass. Jack clenched his fist around the shard, squeezing it so tightly that it pierced his skin, causing his hand to bleed.

"Maks..." he growled in barely contained fury.

The fragment fell from his hand and he stormed down the aisle, drops of blood mingling with the debris and ashes as he exited what was left of the church.

*   *   *   *   *

"Pathetic, isn't it?" Calico Jack said as he circled the priest's hospital bed. "You live a life, and this is what it comes to, lying in some bed, wallowing in your own waste, being fed through a tube."

"Death comes for all eventually," replied Salifu.

"Not if I have anything to say about it," Jack said, licking a drop of blood from his still bleeding hand.

After they left St. Brigid's, Rackham and Salifu went immediately to St. Joseph's hospital. A quick perusal of local news items had confirmed that the fire's only victim, Father Seamus Hartwright, was being treated there for burn injuries over 80 percent of his body.

Visiting hours were long over, and the burn ward was eerily quiet. In the private room, the father clung to life, still hooked to a number of life-sustaining devices.

The steady BEEP BEEP BEEP of the machinery tried Rackham's patience. "Wake him up!" Jack commanded.

"He now lies between the here and hereafter," Salifu said. "Few can reach travelers in that undiscovered country."

"Don't lie to me, you fiend. There's always a way!"

The corners of Salifu mouth betrayed a faint smile. After 300 years, he still took pleasure in tormenting Calico Jack Rackham.

"Well, perhaps there is one thing..." He then produced a small vial from the folds of his robes. The murky liquid inside seemed to swirl on its own.

"Here," he said, handing the vial to Jack. "This potion will awaken him, but in a trance-like state, more susceptible to your inquiries."

Jack grabbed the vial impatiently. He then ripped the breathing tube from the priest's throat. Father Hartwright struggled for air as the alarm on the vent sounded, but Rackham yanked the plug from the wall. With one hand he forced the priest's mouth open and with the other he poured the liquid down his throat.

Salifu then spit on his hands and clapped them together three times. He leaned over the bed and rubbed his fingers over the pastor's ears and mouth. Taking a step back, he watched in silence.

Father Hartwright stirred, his eyes clouded with confusion. "Jesus, Mary, and Joseph," he rasped. "Will no one give me peace?" Seeing Salifu at the bedside, the priest's eyes widened in recognition. "You! You're one of them. An emissary of Lucifer himself!"

"The good padre here seems to be on a first name basis with your boss," Jack said to Salifu. "Prayers won't save you now, Father, only answers. The children who visited you—what were they after? And where are they now?"

The priest's lips moved silently for a moment before he spoke, his voice trembling with resolve. "For... we... battle... against... not flesh and blood... but principalities... and powers..."

"What?" Jack asked in frustration. "What the hell is he on about?"

"He is quoting from the *Bibeli Mimo*," replied Salifu. "None other than your Christian holy book."

"Well, forgive me, but my aptitude for citing scripture has waned a bit."

"Ephesians Chapter 6, Verse 12," explained the shaman. "'For we battle against not flesh and blood, but principalities and powers, against the rulers of darkness in this world, against wickedness in high places.'"

"Is that so?" Jack leaned down over the bed, his face inches from the priest. "Father, you have no idea..."

Father Hartwright turned slightly and faced Jack directly. Mustering all his fading strength, he spoke again. "You're... afraid. Desperate. A filthy coward... I can smell it on you."

The rebuke caused Jack to back away, consumed by dread. "Shut up!" he screamed.

The old man sat bolt upright as if possessed by a surge of otherworldly strength. He grabbed Jack by the collar and spoke his next words as if he knew they'd be his last. "Depart from me, ye accursed ones!" he hissed, quoting scripture again. "Into everlasting fire..."

"Shut your goddamn mouth!" Rackham struck the priest. Then he grabbed the pillow from the bed and pressed it over Father Hartwright's face.

The priest struggled weakly beneath Calico Jack's weight, but it was futile. Within moments, he let go of the pirate's collar. His movements grew still, the room falling silent once more. Jack withdrew the pillow, his chest heaving with exertion, fear still wild in his eyes.

"Next time, answer a bloody question!" he snarled. Gathering his composure, he turned to Salifu. "Let's go. It's time for us to pay a visit to an old friend."

Jack and Salifu left the room and walked briskly past the nurses' station. On the desk, the visitors' log had been splayed open. On the floor nearby lay the lifeless bodies of the two night nurses, their necks snapped by Jack's powerful hands.

"Terrible security 'round here," Jack casually remarked, glancing at his handiwork as he moved down the hallway to the elevator and pushed the button. It opened, and he and Salifu stepped in. Just as the elevator doors slid closed—

The pirate Maks slipped out from the nurse's lounge where he'd been lurking. He walked over to the desk, stepping over the bodies to get a look at the open visitors' log.

Maks followed the trail of Jack's bloody fingerprints down the list until they stopped on one specific name: TANNER PRESCOTT.

The boy from the Cove, the one who'd witnessed his killing of Deputy Wayne.

Gordon Prescott's son.

Maks licked his lips.

Chapter 27
Pirate on the Set!

Two hours after crossing the border, Edison's truck rolled into Playa Inmaculada, a seaside town just south of Puerto Peñasco—or, as Tanner put it, "where the magic happens."

Once a quiet fishing village, the town had been transformed into a massive movie set, home to all of Gordon Prescott's *Blood of the Buccaneers* movies. Honey wagons, makeup stations, and lighting trucks lined the streets. Cobblestone roads were ripped up by heavy equipment, and facades of "pirate town" buildings stood in front of modern trailers. Some palm trees had been burned as part of a recent scene. And the beach was littered with half-empty water bottles.

Cables ran everywhere. Crew members were running here and there. And those who weren't were sunning themselves on top of the trailers. Even the locals had succumbed to the Hollywood way, wearing T-shirts that advertised the latest installment of the movie as they served *helados* and grilled shrimp from their carts for jacked-up prices.

"Welcome to Port Royal, Jamaica," Tanner said, climbing out of the truck. "Or at least as close as we can get on a 130-million-dollar budget."

"Now we just have to find Tanner's dad," Wilder said, surveying the chaos. "Easy as flan, right?"

"It is if you practically grew up here." Tanner motioned for them to follow.

As they wove through the set, the Brigands took it all in. Towering ships, their sails artificially billowing with the help of wind machines, stood against the azure sea. Actors in extravagant costumes wielded prop swords, looking more like frat bros at a Halloween party than hardened pirates.

"Pirates didn't use arming swords! Did nobody do any historical research?" Barnaby scoffed.

"Other than watching every version of *Treasure Island* ever made?" Wilder said.

Bonnie, proud of her corsair heritage, folded her arms. "I thought your dad was a Brigand for a while. You'd think some authenticity would've rubbed off."

Tanner shrugged. "Authenticity probably wasn't in the budget."

His dad, Gordon Prescott, had spent time at the Cove in his youth but, like many before him, found the Brigand life too risky. Instead, he capitalized on his heritage, producing the fourth most successful pirate franchise in movie history.

A frazzled crew member suddenly appeared, clipboard in hand. "Are you extras? Get a meal voucher and head to Wardrobe. We're already an hour behind."

Tanner grinned. "Sheila, you don't recognize me?"

She squinted. "Tanner? Haven't seen you since *BOB II!*"

"Who's Bob?" Cordial asked.

"And why are there two of him?" Wilder added.

"*Blood of the Buccaneers,*" Tanner explained. "That's what they call the movies round here."

Sheila chuckled. "You've grown up to be a handsome devil like your dad. Breaking hearts back home?"

"I don't know about that," Tanner said and actually blushed. "Speaking of my dad. Know where I can find him?"

Sheila sighed. "Not a great day for a family visit, Tanner. Cade's got his diva pants on. But if you must, he's over by the alehouse set. Just look for the biggest crowd and the yelling."

They found Gordon Prescott at the heart of the set, barking orders amidst a staged sword fight. And he looked, well, like you'd kind of expect Tanner's dad *would* look: impossibly tan, with frosted gray hair, an age-defying neck, and draped in carefully curated linen and cashmere. A commanding presence, he gestured sharply as cameras rolled.

"Cade! Just do what the stunt coordinator showed you," Gordon snapped. "We're burning daylight here!"

Cade Collins, the film's lead, scowled. A pretty boy with perfect hair, he barely looked like he could wield a steak knife, let alone a broadsword. "But it looks lame," he complained. "Can't we make it cooler, like the last scene in *Yojimbo*?"

"He's not wrong," Luz muttered. "Does look pretty weak."

Gordon groaned and whispered to his assistant, "Disconnect his Netflix." Then, he called to the director, a harried young man barely out of film school, "Connor, do we have a problem?"

The director threw up his hands. "Gordon, PLEASE tell him *Yojimbo* was set in 19th-century Japan. This is the 18th-century Caribbean!"

"Seventeenth century!" Barnaby shouted.

Silence. All eyes turned to him.

"It looks 17th century, at best," he clarified. "Though, judging by your sets and costumes, that's not even a given."

Gordon's eyes narrowed. "Who the hell is this kid and how did he get on my set!?"

"He's with me." Tanner stepped forward.

"Tanner?"

"Hey, Dad. Surprise." Tanner's usual bravado was nowhere to be found.

Gordon's jaw tightened. "What the hell are you doing here?! And who are these kids?"

"These are my... friends," Tanner said, though he didn't sound entirely sure.

"Gordon!" Cade called. "Are we going again or what?"

"Kind-of-in-the-MIDDLE-of-something-here, Cade!" Gordon bellowed. Then, low and close to Tanner. "Go wait in my trailer."

"I need to talk to you now," Tanner said, voice rising. "It's an emergency. Life and death!"

The set fell silent, all eyes on the father and son. Several smartphones could be seen recording video.

Gordon forced a tight smile. "Of course, son." He turned sharply. "Sheila! I'll be in my trailer."

Sheila clapped her hands. "Okay, folks, take ten! And somebody hose down the bar wenches again!"

As Bonnie and Reed followed the Prescotts, the rest of the Brigands stayed behind, watching Tanner disappear into the lion's den.

⋅ ⋅ ⋅ ⋅ ⋅

Inside Gordon's lavish trailer, Tanner's dad paced around like a man double parked. Tanner entered, followed by Reed and Bonnie.

"They can wait outside," Gordon said.

"No. They're staying. This involves them."

"How does it involve them, Tanner? What's this little floorshow all about?" Gordon demanded.

"It's about the Brigands," Tanner started.

Gordon's expression darkened. "Not a great start."

"You know I'm one of them now. My name's on the wall in the cave and everything," Tanner said proudly.

"Oh, I'm quite aware," his father said coldly, completely unimpressed. "I got your texts."

"I wasn't sure. You never replied."

"And you never came home at the end of summer like you were told."

"I was still in training and—"

"Training? You were never meant to take this Brigand nonsense seriously. You were supposed to be miserable for a summer as punishment. Then come home and enroll at USC like we discussed!"

"What for? It's not like you would have been there or anything!"

"Just like your mother. Everything's my fault! Excuse me for working so I could provide you with everything you could ever want!"

"How do you know what I want? You never asked."

Bonnie and Reed stood awkwardly, watching the scene.

"Fine. Tell me what you want, Tanner. I'll have Sheila Venmo you. But make it fast because I've got more important things to do than get involved in whatever little melodrama is going on in your life."

Bonnie saw Tanner's heart sink. He'd hoped for something—anything—from his father besides disappointment.

"Tanner, maybe we could just ask for what we came for," Bonnie stepped in.

"The Gulfstream," Tanner said matter-of-factly. "I need to borrow it."

"You disrupt my work just so you can take your friends on some joyride with my plane? The answer is no."

"It's not a joyride! We need to go to Ireland. This is important Brigand business!"

"I don't believe that for one minute."

"It's true, Mr. Prescott," Reed said. He hesitated for a moment, but then went for the kill shot. "It has to do with Calico Jack."

At the mention of Calico Jack, the color drained from Gordon Prescott's face.

"Are you kids insane? Absolutely not!" he said in a whisper, as if afraid someone was listening.

"Just hear us out." Desperate, Bonnie spoke up, something she had never told a stranger. "I'm marked, sir. I don't have to tell you what that means. And there's something in Ireland we really need to find. It could save lives. Access to the plane would really help us in our fight against Calico Jack."

"Nothing can help you with that, young lady." Gordon turned back to Tanner. "I'm finished financing your lifestyle, Tanner. You want to defy me? Do it on your own dime. No more trust fund. No more credit cards. And definitely no more jet. Not now. Not ever."

KNOCK! KNOCK! The trailer door opened. Sheila stuck her head in.

"Gordon, we need you back on set pronto! Those kids are re-choreographing the fight scene and Connor's losing his mind!"

"Goddammit!" Gordon banged on the wall of his trailer and turned to go. "Why did you have to come? No one wants you here."

He stormed out of the trailer.

"So," Tanner said, holding back tears, "you've met dear old Dad."

"Man," Bonnie said. "And I thought being a foster sucked."

"Sorry, man," Reed said. "I know that didn't go the way you wanted it to."

"Screw him," Tanner said and stormed out of the trailer.

*   *   *   *   *

Back on the set, Luz and Wilder were giving sword fighting lessons to Cade. Connor was slumped in his director's chair, his face in his hands. Dripping wet barmaids stood irritated and shivering in the background.

"That move is dope! What's it called?" Cade asked.

"The Diluvian Whirl," Wilder said.

"Hey you, stunt coordinator guy! How come you don't have me do stuff like that?"

"Come on, we're leaving," Reed announced to the other Brigands as he marched passed, trying to keep up with Tanner. Wilder shrugged and handed the blade back to Cade, and he and Luz joined the group.

"Hey, where you going?" Cade yelled after them.

"You got this, bro!" Luz shouted back at him. She turned back to the Brigands. "He doesn't got this."

Wilder concurred, "Never will."

As they followed Tanner, Reed quickly filled in the group on what happened in the trailer.

"So now what?" Barnaby asked. "Edison isn't around anymore to take us back."

"I said I'd get you there. And I'll get you there," Tanner whirled on them.

"How exactly?" Bonnie asked with more than a hint of frustration in her voice.

"Just follow me," Tanner said as he commandeered a six-seater golf cart from the lighting department. Everyone hopped on.

Moments later, they drove toward a dusty airstrip, a private jet parked in the distance. As they approached the plane, Bonnie could see a man in a baseball cap in the cockpit. Tanner waved at the man, who smiled from ear to ear and opened the boarding door.

"Well looky what the cat drug in," the pilot said, standing at the stop of the stairs.

"It's good to see you, C.J.," Tanner replied.

"Thought you were back East at some fancy sailing school," C.J. said.

"That what the old man is telling people?" Tanner asked and casually started up the steps.

"Hold on." C.J. stepped in front of the door. "What's going on?"

"Didn't anybody tell you?"

"Tell me what?"

Tanner feigned exasperation. "That is so Sheila. My dad wants you to fly us to Ireland. There's some prop or something that he needs picked up for BOB IV."

"Tanner Prescott, you don't think my bullshit detector still works?" the pilot answered with a knowing smile. "I've known you since you were scamming the housekeeper for extra pudding pops."

"C'mon. One quick flight to Ireland. You'll be back before anybody misses you."

"Tanner! It's five thousand miles!"

"C'mon, man. Do me a Sarah."

"You're seriously calling a Sarah on this? Must be desperate."

"Uh, what's a Sarah?" Reed asked.

"Sarah's my wife," C.J. answered. "Couple years back, I was gonna miss our anniversary because Gordon sent me to Napa last minute to buy a bottle of wine. So Tanner here arranges for a limo for my wife, a yacht, roses, string quartet, private chef, the whole deal. Then he helicoptered me in just in time to meet her at the dock. Made it look like I set the whole thing up. And now, whenever he gets in deep shit..."

"He asks you for a Sarah!" They nodded in unison.

"Why, Tin Man, you do have a heart!" Wilder teased.

"Shut your yap," Tanner shot back.

C.J. looked at them, considering.

"So... what's this prop we're picking up?" he finally said with a wink.

After the passengers had entered, Tanner followed C.J. into the cabin of the jet and took a seat in his dad's favorite recliner, allowing its plush leather to encase him in luxury one last time.

If he was indeed cut off from the family money, he intended to go out in style.

Chapter 28
A Farewell

It took four hours before Gordon Prescott got wind of Tanner's commandeering of his airplane. It did not go over well. Within minutes of the discovery, he was on the phone to C.J., who at that moment had the Gulfstream somewhere over eastern Alabama.

"Crap! How'd he find out?" Tanner asked as he looked at his cellphone, which was blowing up with angry text messages from his dad.

"Seems Connor fired the stunt team, and they needed the plane to fly in some katana expert from Japan," said C.J., who had the plane on autopilot and was now in the cabin speaking to his unauthorized passengers.

Luz and Wilder looked guiltily at each other.

"Yeah, that one might be on us," Wilder said.

"Hope I haven't gotten you in too much trouble, C.J.," Tanner said.

"Nah. After 12 years, I know where all the bodies are buried. He is pretty pissed at you, though. I'd stay out of his way for a while. Like the next five years."

"Or the rest of my life," Tanner said and pocketed his phone without responding.

C.J. headed back into the cockpit. "Looks like it's gonna be enchiladas for dinner tonight."

Bonnie exchanged glances with Reed and Wilder, unsure of how to navigate the situation. Then Bonnie was hit with an inspiration.

"Wait! How far are we from the East Coast?" asked Bonnie.

Barnaby checked the flight tracker. "We're about 45 minutes out of Savannah."

Bonnie turned to Reed. "How long would it take the *True North* to get back to Georgia?"

"Hold the phone. You're not seriously suggesting we sail that old tub to Ireland, are you?" Tanner asked.

"That'll take forever!" Luz objected.

"You got any better ideas?" Bonnie snapped.

"I don't know," Reed said. "The *North* hasn't crossed the ocean in a while."

"1857, to be exact," Barnaby said.

"Yep. That qualifies as 'a while,'" Tanner nodded.

"I may have pirate blood," said Luz shaking her head, "but that seems dangerous even to me."

"The *North* is more than seaworthy," Bonnie said, defending the honor of the ship she'd come to love. "She's like the day she was built. Plus, you can't track her; there isn't a microchip anywhere on board."

Reed nodded. "That's a good point."

"Don't know about you all, but I could use some fresh sea air after all that desert dust," Wilder said. Everyone concurred. They looked to Tanner.

Tanner went to the cockpit. "C.J., did my dad say he wanted *us* back in Mexico, or *the plane* back?"

C.J. chuckled. "I swear, kid, there ain't a loophole invented that you couldn't drive a tank through. What are you thinking?"

What they were thinking was that C.J. would touch down in Savannah under the guise of refueling. From there, the Brigands would disembark and find their way back to Hamhock Barony, aided by a few of Cordial's family connections.

Sure enough, once they landed, it didn't take long for them to secure transport. Gullah-Geechee folk lived up and down the Georgia coast, so Cordial made a couple of phone calls, and soon they were on their way back to the island in the back of an appliance delivery van. The van was driven by a guy named Vandi, who just happened to be Cordial's second cousin once removed. All through the trip back to Port Pinckney, Vandi kept shaking his head and reminding Cordial that her mother would not exactly be rolling out the red carpet for her when she arrived.

"Queen Zee's not gonna be happy," he said for the third time. "My mamma says she's been heated something awful almost since the moment you ran off."

"I get the picture, Cousin Vandi," Cordial said.

"I hope you do. Soon enough you'll be seeing that picture in 3D."

Though it wasn't the boldest prediction anybody had ever made, Vandi's prognostication turned out to be pretty much on the money. Upon their return to the island, they found Queen Zee waiting on her porch, arms crossed and loaded for bear.

"I foresee this getting ugly," Cordial said, viewing her mother's stern expression. "You all might wanna make yourselves scarce for a bit."

Not that eager to get swept up in Queen Zee's wrath, the Brigands decided that just about then would be a good time to pay their respects to Gam Gam at the cemetery.

"Good idea," Luz said. "A cemetery will be a lot more peaceful than this place."

"I bet Times Square on New Year's Eve would be more peaceful," Wilder surmised. And with that, they left one very disobedient girl on Zenobia's doorstep.

,   ,   ,   ,   ,

Bonnie and the other Brigands stood at the foot of Gam Gam's grave. It was in a cemetery not far from the Grace family homestead and less than a quarter mile from where Gam Gam had made her entrance into the world over 90 years before. The grave was fresh, the earth still dark and damp.

"I wish you could have been here," said Fati, who had joined them. Having rented a small house in town during Gam Gam's illness, she'd been visiting the grave daily. "The whole community came out for her burial. Hundreds of folks. She woulda loved it. She was so happy to be back home."

Bonnie couldn't bring herself to meet Fati's eyes. Her cheeks flushed in shame, remembering the part she played in Gam Gam's collapse. So instead, she focused on the items on the grave, many of which she recognized. As was Gullah tradition, they were articles used by the dearly departed—things that bore a strong spiritual imprint. In this case, the nylon hairnet Gam Gam wore to bed nightly, three different bags of gris-gris that she always carried, and the favorite kerchief she kept tucked inside her sleeve for her hay fever. Next to the kerchief was a necklace of silver links given to her by her beloved husband, Winstead. Last was her driftwood cane, as twisted and worn as the old woman's body had been at the end.

Bonnie associated that walking stick the most with the woman who'd guided her to the truth about her own life. She took some solace knowing that Gam Gam was finally free of it—spry and clear-eyed like the powerful young woman she had been once. And now would forever be.

One by one, the Brigands moved to the grave to say a final goodbye. Wilder lingered there. Bonnie placed a hand on Wilder's shoulder. "You alright?"

Wilder nodded, wiping his eyes. "I loved her, you know. She was like the nonna I never had."

"She loved you too, boy," Fati said and wrapped him in a big hug.

Bonnie couldn't bear the grief or the guilt. She turned away and faced the cemetery that stretched behind her. Centuries' worth of headstones as far as the eye could see, some so old they were covered in moss, ivy and even mold from the damp. It reminded her of the Field of the Fallen back on Cormac's Cove. This cemetery, too, was a place where members of a society could be revered for centuries by those who followed in their footsteps.

But to Bonnie, it mostly looked like... peace.

*   *   *   *   *

Once they'd paid their respects at the graveside, they accompanied Fati to the Grace house. Upon setting foot inside, they could clearly see that Cordial's prediction had come to pass. Cordial leaned against a wall, her arms crossed and a nasty scowl on her pretty face. Queen Zee sat on a chair, her arms crossed and jaw set in a genetically identical fashion to her daughter.

"My daughter informs me she's been invited to accompany you further on this little quest of yours," Queen Zee said.

Reed nodded. "If that's alright with you."

"Oh, so I *do* have a say?"

"Mother. We discussed this."

"No, Cordial. We most certainly did not. First you run off with these *pirates* without telling me—"

"Mama!"

"—we didn't know about that," Reed interjected.

"— and now you inform me you are going off again, across the ocean no less! No discussion. Not so much as an 'if you please'."

"Think of it as my semester abroad," Cordial joked. But Queen Zee wasn't having it. "You have been on me to embrace my Gullah heritage for my whole life—"

"You embrace our heritage through respect, not by running headlong into danger."

"Maybe I'm finally doing something that matters—more than basket weaving or giving tours at the cultural center. They actually *need* me."

"They could take Fati!"

"Oh no. I can't," Fati said, shaking her head. "I'm afraid I got no adventure left in me."

For the first time, Bonnie took a good look at the fortune teller. Fati looked haggard, thinner, deep dark circles under her eyes. Gam Gam's death, the whole situation in fact, had taken a serious toll on her.

"Anyway," Fati continued, "this mess is way higher than my paygrade. That's why we came to you in the first place."

"I wish you hadn't," Queen Zee said bitterly. "Getting our family mixed up in this nasty business."

"It was you who made me do the divination, mom!"

"That was a mistake! This whole damn thing is a mistake! I take it all back!"

"You sound like a crazy woman!"

"Cordial Grace! Do not speak to your mother that way!" Mr. Grace, who had up to now hung in the background, cautioned in the sort of half-hearted response that only comes from years of futility. "Let's just discuss this like adults."

"Adults? Hah!" Queen Zee scoffed. "I still pay for her food, her phone, the clothes on her back, a place for her to lay her head at night!"

"Guess what?" Cordial slammed her freshly retrieved phone onto the counter. "Now you won't have to! You are hereby absolved of any further care of me! I officially declare myself emancipated!" Cordial stormed out of the house.

Everyone stood awkwardly, unsure what to do.

"Well, that could have gone better," Wilder said.

"Dr. Grace," Reed said. "We don't want to come between you and your daughter—"

"A little late for that..."

"—but Cordial's right," Reed continued. "The truth is, I don't think we can do this without her. We sure couldn't have done what we've done so far."

Queen Zee looked away, as if an answer to the dilemma might be hidden under the sofa cushions.

"Ma'am, you know what's at stake," Bonnie said. "You've seen what could happen if we don't succeed."

"Yes. And what could happen even if you do," Zenobia said ominously.

Chapter 29
A Visit from Calico Jack

Whenever Prescott Pictures (a division of Black Flag Holdings, LLC) was in Playa Inmaculada, the entire town seemed to move at the same pace as whatever iteration of *Blood of the Buccaneers* happened to be filming that year. On this night, the shooting had gone three hours later than planned, so most of the cast and crew had foregone their usual after-hours margaritas in favor of sleep. While there were a few die-hard grips and soundmen still out on the town, most were nestled in their beds at the Villa Alameda Hotel, just down the beach from the set.

Executive producer Gordon Prescott was among them, but sleep eluded him on that night. He lay in his suite on the eighth floor, stewing over his son Tanner and the stunt he'd pulled. Defying his orders by staying at Cormac's Cove with those so-called Brigands of the Compass Rose had been bad enough—it was supposed to be a punishment, after all. But to show up unannounced and demand the Prescott private jet? For Brigand business?! It was a little much, even for him.

He tried to pinpoint where the kid had picked up such an unapologetic streak of rebellion, but quickly the answer was obvious—a child mirrors his surroundings. And it was no mystery whose reflection the boy was seeing. The thought might have amused him under different circumstances. But not now. Not when it involved *him*.

Calico Jack Rackham. The very name made his body shudder in fear.

As if summoned by his thoughts, a gloved hand clamped down hard over his mouth.

Prescott's eyes opened wide. Calico Jack towered over him!

"Ahoy there, Gordo!" The pirate lifted his hand off. "Permission to come aboard? Oh, wait. I don't need permission." He laughed.

Gordon sat up, his voice unsteady. "Jack! To what do I owe this... surprise visit?"

Rackham's smile was anything but friendly. "Really, Gordon. Coyness doesn't become you."

Jack poured himself a drink from the bar, his icy gaze still locked on Prescott. "Walked by the set on my way here. Those ships look ridiculous. I do hope you're spending my money wisely."

Gordon's eyes flicked nervously to Calico Jack's companion—a muscular African man with an artfully scarred face. He'd heard about Salifu, the conjurer, but this was the first time he'd laid eyes on the man—if that's what he was. In fact, this was only the second time he'd met Rackham face-to-face. The first was when he was just starting out in Hollywood and having trouble getting financing for his movie idea about pirates, not such an easy sell back in those days. Gordon had been "escorted" to the *Perdition* for the meeting. After that, all their dealings had been handled through intermediaries. Jack was famous for never leaving his ship. That he was there now made Gordon very, very afraid.

Jack downed the drink. "Your boy," he said. "Where is he? And don't play dumb. I know the stained one is with him."

Gordon's face tightened, his eyes narrowing. "I don't know."

Jack was on him in a flash, a hand around his throat, his voice now a menacing whisper. "Don't lie to me, Gordon. You know what's at stake."

Prescott spoke hoarsely. "T-They *were* here. I don't know where they are now. I swear."

Jack released his grip and his smile returned, cold and devoid of humor. "Perhaps a little motivation is in order," he said. "How about I pull the funding for your little cash cow, Gordon? What would you say to that? All of it. Gone."

He snapped his fingers in Gordon's face to accentuate the point.

"And after a forensic audit triggered by a carefully placed tip? You'd probably be looking at serious jail time, boyo. So you'd be gone, too. And what a shame that would be..."

Gordon's heart pounded in his chest. He'd always known Jack was using his movies and their "creative accounting" to launder money from his other operations. It was, after all, the implied deal they had struck when Jack had financed Prescott's "big break."

"Or," Jack said, his eyes boring into Gordon. "You could permanently disappear."

Gordon's shoulders slumped, the fight draining out of him. "Alright," he said softly. "I'll tell you what I know. But you have to promise not to hurt Tanner."

Jack's expression softened slightly, but his eyes remained cold. "It's only the girl I'm after."

Gordon took a deep breath. "They're headed for somewhere in Ireland. They didn't tell me why. 'Brigand business' was all they said. They stole my plane but only made it as far as Georgia before I had my pilot turn back. Whether or not they get to Ireland is anybody's guess."

"I need you to find out," Rackham said, tossing Gordon's smartphone to him.

"He won't answer. I've tried texting him. See? We're not exactly on speaking terms at the moment."

Jack studied him for a moment, then nodded. "A pity. But then, all families are filled with snares and pitfalls, are they not? Your son won't talk to you. I had to kill mine. These things happen.

"If you do happen to repair relations with that prodigal of yours, I am the first call you make. And don't even think about warning him," Jack cautioned. "It'll be bad. For both of you." He went to the door. "By the way—your films are an embarrassment."

Without another word, Jack turned and strode out, Salifu at his heels.

As their footsteps receded down the hallway, Gordon sprang from his bed, fear and anger churning in his gut. He rushed to the bar and poured himself a glass of scotch. The ice cubes rattled against the sides of the tumbler as he tried to steady his shaking hands long enough to bring the glass to his lips.

He practically inhaled the drink and quickly poured another. He stood at the window and looked out at the lights of the seaside town. His thoughts kept drifting back to his son. He looked at his phone, started to text Tanner to warn him, but ultimately couldn't bring himself to do it.

He could only hope the Brigands would stay one step ahead of Calico Jack, whatever their mission in Ireland was. If he were a praying man, he might have actually prayed for the safety of his boy. But he wasn't. So instead, he just hoped. Hoped, and downed a second glass of whiskey.

*   *   *   *   *

From 1000 feet over the Sea of Cortez, Calico Jack looked out over Playa Inmaculada from his private helicopter, now en route to an airstrip owned by some of his associates in the trafficking business. From there, he and Salifu would fly to Cuba, where a boat would ferry them to rendezvous with the *Perdition*, which upon his orders was now heading toward Ireland.

His mind raced. *Ireland.* It made sense; his descendants' lineage had ties to that land. His own wife, the betrayer Anne Bonny, had been born there. *But what was Hartwright's business there? Could she somehow have stumbled on the trail of her mother?* Time would tell, he was sure of it.

And time was one thing that Calico Jack Rackham had in abundance.

Chapter 30
The Fog Shroud

With the *True North* en route from Cormac's Cove, the Brigands set about planning for their trip to Ireland. Without engines, the trip would take weeks. But it was the safest way. Despite his push to move into the future, Reed had to remind himself there were definitely some advantages to the ways of old.

The *North* was already laden with food and supplies when it arrived in Georgia. It was a bittersweet reunion. Hugs were shared and tears shed over the loss of the Wayfarers and of their dear Gam Gam. Despite the grief, there was a great sense of relief to be together once more. No one had to say it. They just knew. Together they were less vulnerable... stronger.

Bonnie would have opted to set sail immediately, but Barnaby pointed out that waiting until nightfall would provide the best cover under the new moon. Everyone agreed, and the day was spent prepping the *North* for its first transatlantic voyage in over a century.

It was well past sunset when the crew finally had the *North* squared away. Without a moon, the island and the sea beyond were cloaked in darkness. The only lights were the handful of lanterns that the crew and those who came to see them off—Fati and Mr. Grace—were using to guide their way.

Cordial went up to her father and looked past him into the dark woods for any sign of her mother. "She's not coming, is she?"

"You know your mama. She can hold on to her pride like no one I've ever known," her father said. "'Cept maybe you."

Cordial smiled and hugged him hard.

"I'm proud of you," Martin said. "And if your mama could bring herself to say it, she'd tell you she's proud of you too."

"I love you, Papa."

"I love you too, baby girl. Stay safe."

Cordial walked up the gangplank onto the ship past Bonnie. They exchanged a quick look and Bonnie could see the hurt in the girl's eyes.

"Okay, all electronic devices off and in the box!" Micah called out and began making the rounds with a small wooden lock box to collect anything that could lead to them being traced.

Tanner moved to a far corner of the ship to do a final check of his phone before handing it over and saw a series of new texts from his father:

Dad: *Sorry about before*
Worried about you
Where are you?
LMK you're safe
Please

Tanner was stunned and maybe even a little suspicious at this sudden show of concern after the fury his father had unleashed. But then, he reasoned, Gordon's son had never before faced a ruthless undead pirate on the verge of world domination. So there was that. Tanner wrestled with the urge to continue ignoring the texts out of spite, but he didn't know when or if he would be able to talk to his father again. And his heart ached for the connection he'd always craved.

"Cough 'em up!" Micah said as he got closer. "Your twelve Instagram followers will just have to live without you for a while."

Tanner made his decision and quickly texted.

Tanner: *Can't talk rn*
Sailing for dungarry
Will call when I can
TTYL
And... thanks

He turned off his phone just as Micah arrived and dropped it in the box.

"Welcome to the Dark Ages," Micah smiled and locked the box. "All stowed, Cap'n!" he shouted to the helm.

Reed nodded. "Then let us prepare—"

"Wait!" a voice cried from the darkness.

Heads turned and saw Zenobia Grace stepping onto the sandy spit of shoreline.

Bonnie saw Cordial light up as she rushed to her mother. Cordial hesitated a moment before Zenobia enveloped her in a big hug.

This must be what it's like to have a mother who cares, Bonnie thought, *even if she didn't always agree with her headstrong child.* She imagined the same kind of reunion with her own mother.

Queen Zee carried a bag over her shoulder as she walked up the gangplank with Cordial. Once on board, she plopped down her bag and announced, "Before you leave, there's something we got to do first."

It turned out that once it became obvious Cordial could not be dissuaded, Zenobia decided to ensure the group set sail under the safest circumstances possible. And that, she said, could only be achieved one way...

"Magic," she whispered solemnly.

⦁   ⦁   ⦁   ⦁   ⦁

Soon, all were gathered on the deck around Queen Zee, who had removed bags of gris-gris, potions, bones, and an ancient book filled with handwritten scribbles of spells and incantations. She flipped through the yellowed pages, stopping at one titled "FOG SHROUD."

Queen Zee explained that there was a story of a group of captives during the Middle Passage who were set to land not far from where they now stood. Their ship had crashed into some rocks in a dense fog. In the ensuing chaos, the Africans managed to overwhelm their English captors. But rather than come ashore, they leapt into the ocean, still bound in chains. They began to swim, back towards their home in Africa. While they were ultimately lost to the waters, to these proud people, it was preferable to a life of slavery. The sea was freedom from bondage for their souls at least.

"That's why folks round here still say 'the water brought us here, the water will take us away,'" Queen Zee said reverentially. "Their souls still linger here, returning when called upon to provide safe passage under a veil of fog for those who need it."

The Brigands were moved by the story and watched wide-eyed as Queen Zee performed her ritual before a candle flame that burned solidly, blocked from the wind by the huddled bodies of the travelers. A guttural hum escaped her throat as she spoke words in a language Bonnie didn't recognize.

"*Bịa ebe a! Bịa ebe a!* I call upon the spirits of my ancestors. Protect these young ones. See them out to sea, away from the eyes of those who mean them harm. I call upon the shroud of fog! *Wetuo anwụrụ ọkụ!*"

Lightning flashed across the sky, and a sudden gust of icy wind whipped over the deck. Everyone jumped. Then nothing. Stillness.

They waited in silence. Still nothing.

"Is that it?" Wendell murmured. "I got better protection in the hold in the form of gunpowder." Yeun nudged him hard.

"Uh, what's supposed to happen?" Bonnie whispered to Cordial.

"No idea. This shit's new to me, too."

"They're coming." It was Malachi's voice, so forceful and unexpected it startled them. They all turned to see him staring at the horizon.

"There!" Micah shouted and pointed out to sea.

And sure enough, in the distance, a tsunami-sized wall of fog, eerie blue with flashes of lightning within, was rolling toward them.

Bonnie felt the little hairs on her arm stand on end even before the fog hit them. Soon, the wall of fog was upon the ship, first swirling tendrils like fingers around their feet, then slowly engulfing their bodies until they could barely see each other through the thick mist.

"They are here," Malachi announced.

Initially, the others weren't sure who "they" were. But Bonnie could hear them. Whispers. Voices. Unintelligible, at first, then in some kind of foreign tongue. Murmurs all around them.

And there was something in the fog. Movement. Shapes. People.

"*Dios mio*," Luz said and crossed herself, kissing the crucifix she wore around her neck.

Bonnie shuddered, recalling a Thanksgiving when she was about seven. Stuck indoors with one of her worst foster families, she was miserable. The day was filled with drinking and fighting and too many so-called "uncles" who gave her the creeps. Unable to take it any longer, she slipped out and found her way to a playground. A rare fog had settled over Tucson, its white blanket eerily close as she lay across the monkey bars, staring into the void. Trying to empty her mind, she focused on the fog but began seeing unsettling shapes, her nightmares come alive. Heart racing, she ran back to the foster house, preferring real-life monsters to those conjured by her imagination.

This night, this bluish fog, was like that. Only worse. Because she knew it was not her imagination. She *was* seeing the forms of people, in chains, speaking unintelligible words that comforted and troubled her in equal measure.

"They will accompany you until you are safely away," Queen Zee pronounced as she packed up her things.

"Thank you, mama," Cordial said.

Zenobia put her bag over her shoulder. "If you die, I'll kill you," she said giving her daughter another quick hug then rushed down the gangplank.

Cordial watched her disappear into the fog. "Some moms bake cookies. Mine casts protection spells."

"Let us away, Mister Yeun!" Reed called.

"Aye, Captain!" Yeun answered, and they were off, the blanket of fog keeping pace as they moved out into the open water.

As the *True North* pulled away from the coastline and the sails strained against the winds, Bonnie was overcome by a foreboding feeling. She looked back toward the mist-covered shoreline but couldn't make out a thing. She looked forward over the bow of the ship and saw more nothingness. No past, no future. Only an eternal present for as far as the eye could see.

It was terrifying.

,　　,　　,　　,　　,

Had Tanner trusted his instincts, he would have known better than to respond to his father's texts. For at that very moment, Gordon Prescott sat slumped in the Medical Support trailer on the set of *Blood of the Buccaneers*. His face was a patchwork of bruises. The mugging had been swift and brutal—a blur of movement as he walked from his hotel to the set. He didn't get a good look at his attacker. His wallet and cell phone were gone in an instant.

The production manager Sheila stood nearby, her arms crossed in frustration. "We need to call the authorities," she pressed.

Already spooked by the visit from Calico Jack, Gordon shook his head. "No cops. We're already behind schedule as it is. I'm not adding some Mickey Mouse police investigation to the mix."

Instead, he instructed Sheila to cancel his credit cards and phone service, and to procure replacements. No distractions. No delays. Most especially, no outside scrutiny. He had neither the time nor the desire to dwell on the incident or the unease creeping into the corners of his mind.

.   .   .   .   .

Miles away, Maks leaned against the railing of a small fishing boat, the faint hum of its engine blending with the rhythmic slap of waves against the hull. In his hand was Gordon Prescott's cell phone, a trophy from the mugging. A sharp smile curled his lips as he scrolled through the messages on the screen—Tanner's reply.

"Dungarry," Maks muttered under his breath.

Maks had his own father to thank for the success of his strategy. After all, the man taught him all about false remorse. He'd delivered enough of it after drunken beatings. And Maks knew what it meant to be a child who desperately wanted to believe his dad cared. Even against all evidence to the contrary.

He wasted no time deleting the thread of messages between father and son. The weight of the phone felt lighter now, its purpose fulfilled. Maks hurled it overboard and watched it vanish into the churning depths.

The coastline of Playa Inmaculada grew smaller on the horizon, its bustling set now little more than a dot, punctuated by the silhouette of a pirate ship flying Calico Jack's infamous Jolly Roger, the flag Rackham had personally designed centuries before. Maks chuckled to himself, a laugh that echoed long after the phone was swallowed by the sea.

Chapter 31
The Doldrums

The doldrums. Until she came to the Cove, Bonnie had only heard the word used in the context of her emotions. "You're in the doldrums," her state-appointed psychologist Dr. Ellen would say whenever Bonnie's depression flared up. It annoyed her to have her pain framed in such a lame way, but she never had it in her to object. Now, she understood the true meaning of the word—and it was just as lame.

The actual doldrums, a windless region near the equator, were far from their current course. But that didn't mean the *North* was safe from dead calm conditions. After tacking against headwinds for over a week, they'd sailed straight into the clutches of the Azores High, a sprawling system of weak, shifting breezes that could stall a ship for days. The crew had worked hard to make steady progress, but now they were drifting, the sails slack, the ocean stretching out in every direction without a hint of movement. And there was nothing to do but wait—wait and watch the sky, feel the air, and hope the wind would return.

And while they might have been miles from the literal doldrums, psychologically speaking they were smack dab in the middle of them. The five straight days of no movement already felt like an eternity—especially to Bonnie, who was desperate to reach her mother. A gray haze loomed over them, blotting out the sky. The sun, a dim orange dot, struggled in vain to pierce the gloom.

Yeun initially thought it might be the lingering effects of the fog shroud and wondered if Cordial could do anything to help. But she assured them the spirits had departed days ago—once they'd reached open water. Not that she would have known what to do anyway. She found herself wishing she'd paid more attention to her mother's cultural lessons, an admission you couldn't have pried out of her with a pair of pliers just a few weeks before.

As the days without wind piled one on top of the other, the delay frayed everyone's nerves. The Brigands snapped at each other over the littlest things. A three-hour debate broke out between Micah and Barnaby over the proper installation of a roll of toilet paper on the holder. Yeun and Zion constantly bickered about the true origin of Korean fried chicken. And Tanner just lay around, not doing much of anything. He did his chores only when prodded and even then whined about it the whole time. Which was normal for him, but in this environment, it just pissed everybody off.

Being the only couple on board, Luz and Daya spent most of their time together at first. But the reunion soon turned sour, and by day three they'd staked out positions on opposite ends of the ship because the relationship "needed space."

Wilder did what he could to keep spirits up, making jokes that initially got laughs. But being stuck in the middle of the ocean presents particular challenges to sustained comedic excellence, and eventually he only managed to irritate everyone. After all, there are only so many cracks one can make about a dwindling supply of potable water before it stops being funny. Ultimately, he just shut up lest he risk being thrown overboard.

As for Bonnie, she found herself slowly pulled back into the dark thoughts she'd fought so hard to escape—the hopelessness of finding her mother, the nightmares that somehow always ended in her death. She kept her fears hidden from the others; she'd gotten good at that by now, burying her face in her pillow and keeping quiet about the dreams that left her doubting herself, doubting their mission, and wondering why she'd ever set fire to that basketful of clothes in the first place.

Only Malachi appeared unaffected. He had taken to fishing. But even the fish seemed to lack energy as they just drifted insouciantly past his hook without a hint of interest. It didn't seem to bother him, however. He was content to sit for hours on end, his line in the water, staring into the gray that surrounded them.

The way Bonnie saw it, the only good thing about their plight was that it kept Reed too focused on their predicament to notice Cordial fawning over him. Bonnie hated how Cordial, now out of the doghouse with the Brigands, used her flirty questions to stroke Reed's ego. And though she'd never admit it, she was more than a little jealous.

Tanner also felt jealous of Cordial and Reed's budding little whatever-it-was and took every opportunity to needle Bonnie about her "boyfriend" and his new squeeze. But that only earned him a swift nut-thwack and a sulky retreat below deck, muttering about the lack of ice.

Bonnie bristled at the comments. Reed had never *been* her boyfriend in the first place. Any feelings they might've had for each other were now buried under the weight of the Stain of Musangu, or so she told herself. It was easier than admitting she'd pushed him away—as she had done to everyone.

By the eighth day without wind, the crew's spirits had dulled into a languid haze. They lounged on the deck, drained and silent, until Cordial broke the monotony with a sudden outburst.

"Aaauuugh!" she shouted so suddenly it caused everyone to jump. "Never have I ever been so supremely bored in my whole entire life!"

Daya rolled her eyes. "Girl. This ain't nothin'."

Like every comment coming out of Daya's mouth lately, the remark irked Luz, who snapped, "Ay! What could be more boring than this?"

"You don't remember the Farmers' Market in Highcross?" Daya replied. "Spending an afternoon with rich people and their essential oils and artisan zucchinis? I wanted to pull my nails out just to feel something."

A few chuckles rippled through the group, breaking the gloom.

"Yo ho ho! Fellow Brigands, I just struck paydirt!" Tanner said, emerging from below deck carrying a dusty bottle of rum. "Found it in back on the bottom shelf of the pantry."

"Bet Jonesy stowed it there," Barnaby surmised.

Reed quickly shut it down. "Uh-uh. No drinking. We're on a mission, remember?"

"A mission that's currently stalled in the middle of the Atlantic Ocean," Tanner said just as he was about to take his first swig. Reed snatched the bottle and dumped its contents overboard.

"I said no!" Reed's firm tone silenced the group as the last of the rum fell into the water.

"Bro, you used to be more fun," Tanner sulked, flopping down to join the group. "No, wait. That was me. God. Look at me now. Pathetic."

The silence lingered until Wilder spoke up. "I know how to kill some time. Have you ever played 'Never Have I Ever'? Cordial said she's never been this bored, so somebody else say what they've never done."

"That's a drinking game, dude," Tanner objected. "And Mr. Straight Edge over here just fed all our alcohol to Malachi's fish."

"No booze," Wilder said. "Just use our hands instead. If you *have* done something, you have to raise your hand. It'll still be fun."

"Ooo! It could help us get to know each other better," Cordial said excitedly.

"Or get dirt on each other," Luz teased.

"I'll start," Wilder said, and paused like he was about to reveal a big secret. "Never have I ever... eaten pineapple on my pizza." The admission elicited a disappointed groan from those who were hoping for something a little more salacious to get the game started.

Luz's arm shot up. "Dude, that's like the national cuisine of East L.A."

One by one, everyone else's hands went up, too.

Wilder shook his head. "And I thought you people were my friends."

"Okay, who's next?" Yeun asked. "Bonnie, what about you?"

"This game's for kids," Bonnie said, memories of playing it back on the playgrounds of Tucson flashing in her head. Mandy Brooks and her catty friends used to use that game to make other girls feel bad about themselves. Plus, Bonnie wasn't exactly thrilled about revealing secrets to anyone, especially with an outsider like Cordial Grace around. "I'm out," she declared.

"Never have I ever been such a wet blanket," Cordial said, clearly intended for Bonnie. There were a few titters, but Bonnie's glare shut everyone up pretty quickly.

With Bonnie pouting in the background, the game continued, the unresolved tension between her and Cordial simmering beneath the surface. Confessions started to trickle out—harmless ones at first, even silly ones—Yeun admitted he'd never learned to speak Korean. Tanner revealed he'd never set foot in a Walmart. When Micah was 11, he purposely "lost" Malachi in a grocery store because he was tired of him tagging along. Wendell confessed that he'd never *actually* burned down his parents' barn (his cousin did) but since he got the blame, he decided to embrace the reputation.

After Barnaby said that he'd never, ever in his whole wide life cheated on anything, everyone else raised their hands. Even Cordial, who admitted to once buying an essay online for her AP Environmental Science class when she was crunched for time, prompting Bonnie to snicker under her breath.

"What's so funny?" Cordial challenged.

"Oooo. Miss Perfect cheated on a test," Bonnie said, her voice dripping with sarcasm. "Alert the authorities and cancel her Brandy Melville credit card!"

"Hey!" Cordial retorted. "I may not be a juvenile delinquent like y'all, but that doesn't make me a goody-goody."

Bonnie's voice sharpened. "Compared to us? Yeah, it kinda does."

Cordial bristled. "Just because I don't make a habit of shoplifting candy bars from 7-Elevens doesn't mean I'm uncool."

"It was Children's Tylenol from Walgreens, actually," Bonnie shot back, her tone defensive. "When your foster mom spends the last of her state check on gin instead of medicine for a baby with a fever, you don't have much choice."

The group went quiet. Bonnie immediately regretted sharing. The pitying looks she was getting pissed her off.

It was Luz who spoke up to break the uncomfortable silence and change the mood.

"I got a juicy one. Never have I ever hooked up with a member of the *opposite* sex," Luz said and it certainly changed the mood.

Tanner immediately raised his hand. Luz was shocked when Daya also raised hers.

"What?" Daya shrugged. "It was an experimental phase, and that boy was fine."

Soon, everybody put a hand in the air. Except Bonnie, who still wasn't playing.

"Oh, come on," Tanner said. "I know for a fact this ship is full of virgins. Get your hand down, Owl Eyes. You too, Maguire."

Reluctantly, hands fell—Barnaby, Micah, Wendell, and then Reed. Yeun and Zion held firm. And Cordial didn't drop hers either, which earned her pats on the back from Luz and approving laughter from the others.

"What can I say? I'm a liberated woman in touch with my sexuality," Cordial said casually.

"I'm Tanner Prescott, and I approve this message!"

Bonnie flushed with embarrassment, suddenly painfully self-conscious of her own lack of experience and worldliness. God, she loathed this girl.

"Never have I ever used feminism as an excuse for being loose." Even as the words came out of her mouth, Bonnie knew she shouldn't have said them.

The laughter died instantly. The group looked between Bonnie and Cordial.

"Well," Cordial said evenly, her voice cutting like a blade. "Never have I ever slut-shamed another girl to cover up for being a frigid bitch."

"Never have I ever gotten handed everything in life and then run off because I didn't get my way with Mommy and Daddy," Bonnie snapped back.

"Never have I ever hidden behind frumpy clothes and bad hair because I was ashamed of who I am and where I came from."

"I have NEVER been ashamed of where I come from!"

Cordial's eyes blazed. "Liar! I've seen inside you. You're full of shame—just like you're too ashamed to admit you have feelings for Reed. And you hate me because you can't be the center of attention anymore!"

Bonnie was mortified. This girl had seen into her and laid her open for all to see. And they were looking. All eyes were on her. Bonnie couldn't take any more.

"You're such an entitled little bitch!"

She bolted across the deck and disappeared into the crew cabin. Wilder looked around, then got up to chase after her.

The silence that followed was deafening.

"Well, um, that was fun," Tanner said uncomfortably. "Should we do charades next?"

⁊   ⁊   ⁊   ⁊   ⁊

Bonnie lay in her bunk, staring at the ceiling. She could only imagine what they were saying up on deck. The regret over her lashing out at Cordial gnawed at her. She covered her face with her pillow. How could she ever face them again?

CLOP. CLOP. CLOP.

The sound of boots on the wooden cabin stairs broke through her thoughts.

"You okay, Curls?" Wilder's familiar voice broke the silence.

"Do I seem okay?"

He sighed. "Why don't you come back on deck? We don't have to keep playing the game. Wendell said he knows some card tricks."

"No thanks."

"Then... I'll stay down here with you, if that's okay?"

"I'd rather be alone." She rolled over to face the wall.

"Curls." His tone softened. "I'm sorry if I've been kind of preoccupied lately. After the funeral for my mom and then Gam Gam... I just kinda been wrapped up in myself. But I want you to know that I'm here for you. No matter what. You can always talk to me. Even if it's about Reed."

Reed. Wilder's kindness only made her feel worse. He was taking the blame for the distance between them when they both knew it was really her. He didn't deserve to be sidelined just because she'd been distracted since Cordial started sniffing around Reed. She turned to face him.

"I'm sorry, Wilder. It's not on you. I don't know what's going on with me—"

"Look, Bonnie... I know you got a lot on your mind, but maybe— I dunno—maybe you don't have to shut us all out of what you're going through."

Bonnie studied his face, the way his dark eyes searched hers. There was something different in his expression—something raw.

"I mean, I know I joke around a lot, but I'm not just trying to be funny." His voice had dropped lower, rough with something that wasn't quite uncertainty. "I see you, Curls. I see how much you carry, and I'd do anything to take some of it off your back. Just let me." He took her hand.

She swallowed hard. "Wilder..."

TAP. TAP.

They both looked up to see Reed standing there. Bonnie quickly pulled her hand away from Wilder's.

Wilder's jaw clenched, and for a split second, something flickered behind his eyes—a jealousy that ultimately turned to resignation.

"Hey, man. Can I talk to Bonnie for a minute? Privately?"

Wilder looked to Bonnie. She knew he wouldn't leave without her okay. She gave him a nod. "I'll be topside if you need me," he said and disappeared up the stairs.

Bonnie sat up and looked at Reed, who sat uncomfortably across from her on a wooden crate.

"There's nothing going on between me and Cordial," he started.

"It's none of my business even if there was," Bonnie interrupted quickly. "It's not like there's anything going on with us, anyway."

Reed hesitated. "Right. And there can never be."

Bonnie felt the words hit harder than she expected. Reed saw it.

"Bonnie, I won't lie—I've had feelings for you. I think you're amazing. You're not like any girl I've ever met. But I'm a Brigand, and you're a marked one. It's forbidden."

"So much for breaking away from old traditions?" she said, feeling tears welling up in her eyes.

"Sometimes, there are reasons for traditions, Bonnie. The last few months have made that clear. It's not just about the rules. It's bigger than that. If we got involved, I'm not sure I could make the decisions I'd need to for the Brigands. For you. Not with Calico Jack and everything else hanging over us."

Bonnie's stomach sank, anger bubbling up again. "So what, we can't even be friends now?"

"No, we can be friends," Reed said gently. "But the vow comes first. Always. You know that, don't you?"

She did. But it didn't make it any easier to hear.

"Just go."

"Bonnie—"

She turned away from him. "I said go."

Reed stood up but hesitated, torn between staying and leaving.

Suddenly, the ship lurched violently, sending him sprawling forward—right onto Bonnie's bed. Right on top of Bonnie.

For a moment, their eyes locked, faces inches apart. The longing between them was undeniable. Slowly, they began to lean in toward each other—

"WIND!" Voices from above shattered the moment. Cheers erupted from the deck. "We got wind!"

Chapter 32
Éire

Once the wind arrived, it never relented. The sails swelled, the masts groaned, and the *North* heeled under the force. Despite the vigilance needed to stay on course, no one complained. Bonnie found the rest of the journey exhilarating. And, on the plus side, everyone was so occupied with sailing, nobody even brought up the unpleasantness that had erupted during "Never Have I Ever." Still, Bonnie and Cordial kept a safe distance from one another for the rest of the voyage.

Nothing prepared them for the sight of Ireland's coast. Soaring cliffs, coral beaches, and rolling dunes edged with grass stretched endlessly. Raised in the desert, Bonnie had thought the lushness of North Carolina was something to behold. But it barely compared to Ireland, where the island's ancient beauty stirred something deep within her.

Per Wicked Pete's instructions, they anchored the *True North* in a secluded cove, well-known to the Brigands but hidden from cargo ships, fishing boats, and, most importantly, Calico Jack's spies. Navigating in was tricky—the cove was rocky, the waves brutal. Lesser sailors would have wrecked their vessels. But their seafaring bloodline and a centuries-old Brigand map helped them avoid the most dangerous shoals. Yeun stayed with the ship as the rest of the travelers went into town to investigate.

At sunset, they took dinghies down the River Lynch, landing on a remote beach near Dungarry. Freezing rain pelted them as they made shore. To stay low-key, no one carried swords, but small blades were hidden among them—just in case.

When the landing party reached Dungarry, they were taken aback by the old-world-ness of the tiny hamlet—buildings made of stone, sod or clay, traditional Irish shopfronts with leaded glass windows, a couple of pubs, and not a chain store in sight. It reminded Bonnie a little of Highcross if Highcross were authentic. If it weren't for the parked cars, lorries, and electric streetlights, Bonnie would have sworn they'd stepped back in time. The group looked around the empty cobblestone streets. From the looks of the golden light emanating from the windows, most of the folk had taken shelter inside.

"I miss California," Tanner grumbled, pulling his collar up. "Even Mexico was better than this."

"The hell you mean 'even Mexico'?" Luz demanded.

"This place isn't exactly a hotbed of activity... or anything hot for that matter," Cordial said, shivering.

"Yeah. The only thing we're gonna find out here is a case of pneumonia," Wilder agreed.

"You guys are wimps," Barnaby said. "This is springtime in Chicago!"

"Any ideas where we start?" Micah asked. "We can't just wander the streets and hope we bump into a monk."

"Let's just ask somebody," Bonnie said, seeing an elderly man emerge from a nearby pub, wobbling slightly. Bonnie intercepted him, nearly causing him to fall.

"Excuse me, sir! Have you seen this?" She showed him Malachi's drawing of the mosaic, careful to shield it from the rain with her coat.

The old man scowled and rattled off something in an accent that was as impenetrable as it was surly before disappearing into an alley.

"What did he say?" Daya asked. "And what language did he say it in?"

"That was English... I think," Reed replied.

"Well, it should come with subtitles," Daya said.

"I thought the Irish were supposed to be friendly," Cordial complained.

"I have a thought," said Wilder, shivering. "Let's get in out of the cold. Get a hot chocolate and make a plan."

"Hot chocolate?!" Tanner rolled his eyes. "Oh my God. This isn't a pirate crew; it's a freakin' girl scout troop!"

Bonnie sighed. "Fine. This pub looks like a locals' hangout. Someone's got to know something," she said, pulling open the door.

"Malachi!" cried Micah. Everyone turned to see Malachi crossing the street.

"Where the hell's your brother going?" Zion asked.

"Ask Cordial; *she's* the mind reader," Micah grumbled, chasing after him. "Malachi! Get back here!"

The others followed as Malachi disappeared around a corner. When they caught up, they found him standing at the bottom of a basement stairwell beneath a red neon sign:

NECROPOLIS

Frenetic music boomed from within.

"Looks like Malachi found the portal to hell," Wilder said.

"Is it dry and warm?" Luz asked. "That's all I care about."

"Malachi, do not go in—" Micah started. But it was too late.

Malachi disappeared through the doorway.

Everyone looked at Micah, irritated, as if he could have somehow prevented it.

"Hey. I'd put him on a leash, but he'd drag me."

No choice, the group grudgingly followed.

Inside, the bar lived up to its ominous name. Neon red lights made the place look like a hellscape. The walls were plastered with strange, demonic-type symbols, band posters, and macabre decorations like headless baby dolls. A suit of armor held a chalkboard advertising drink specials with names like the Napalm and Kitten's Death shots.

"Remember, no drinking," Reed warned, which was promptly followed by the group heading to the bar en masse to order their favorite cocktails.

"We might need more piercings to fit in here," Wilder said, hoisting the pint a tatted-up barmaid had just thunked down in front of him.

"Speak for yourself," Bonnie added, proudly flashing her hardware.

On the tiny stage, three stringy-haired young men pummeled their instruments into submission. They all wore white face paint and black "corpse" makeup to match the look of the teenagers in the crowd. The audience thrashed wildly in front of them as the lead "singer" screamed lyrics at an ear-splitting volume:

Bruised flesh! Lacerations!
Ready for obliteration!!
If I go down, you're going with me!
Choke on the annihilation!

Wilder looked at Bonnie and smiled. "A little ditty from their Christmas album, I suppose..."

Malachi was at the front of the stage, bobbing his head to the aggressive beat as the throng flailed around him. Bonnie looked at the other Brigands—loud noises usually had Malachi cowering like a dog in a thunderstorm.

"You never know someone, I guess," Bonnie said.

Scotch in hand, Tanner sidled up next to Cordial, who was at the bar with Luz. "So what do you think?" he shouted over the music.

"You white folk come up with a lotta crazy-ass shit is what I think," she shouted back.

"Not so crazy if you think about it," Luz said, leaning back. "These kids are pissed off. Half of this town is stuck in the past; the other half is boarded-up storefronts. It's not that different from the *barrio*, or your little *pueblo* in Georgia. What's the future for them here? So they get together with their friends and come here, just to deaden the pain a bit."

"You sound pissed off, too," Cordial said.

"At one time, maybe," Luz said, looking across the bar to where Bonnie stood with Daya. "But now I got purpose. Among other things."

Daya caught Luz's eye and just smiled the purest smile that seemed as out of place in this pit of despair as a bouquet on a dung heap.

Just then the band launched into another head-banger.

Luz knocked back her drink. "Screw it," she said. "I'm gonna dance."

She walked over to Daya and took her hand. The two disappeared into the thrashing crowd.

Bonnie walked over to the bar and ordered an ale, pointedly ignoring Cordial right next to her.

Cordial glanced over. Tipsy and therefore brave, she said, "Not that it's any of your business, but I've only ever had one boyfriend."

Bonnie blinked. They hadn't spoken since the scene on the *North.* "What?"

"Three years in high school. He dumped me after I told him about my 'gift.' Said he couldn't be with a freak. I thought he loved me."

Bonnie hesitated. She had no idea what to say—or what Cordial expected her to.

"What the hell, as long as I have the reputation..." Cordial downed her drink and walked over to Reed and Tanner, grabbing both by the hands. "C'mon boys, let's deaden the pain together."

She led them out onto the dance floor, shooting Bonnie a defiant look as she did.

In retaliation, Bonnie grabbed Wilder's hand and followed. Soon, all the Brigands were dancing. Wilder flailed around as if he'd just swallowed plutonium. Bonnie laughed. She swayed hesitantly until a local boy bumped into her. She bumped back—hard. Again. And again.

She got it.

The music. The chaos. The anger.

She threw back her head and screamed at the top of her lungs. It felt good. No—it felt amazing. It felt *liberating.*

*   *   *   *   *

Later, during a break in the music, the sweaty and exhausted Brigands enjoyed a hot meal—stew, chowder, and fish and chips. Micah tried to coax Malachi into joining them, but his brother stood resolute in line at a table where the band was selling its merch.

"He doesn't even listen to me anymore," Micah said as he rejoined the others.

"Why don't I try?" Bonnie offered.

She approached Malachi, gently touching his arm. "Come eat something with us."

Malachi didn't respond. When it was his turn, he stepped up to the table displaying three home-burned CDs and T-shirts with *Blighted Omen* plastered across the front in a jagged, bloodthirsty font.

"Come on, buddy. You don't want any of this junk," Bonnie said.

"Oi! Let the lad decide for himself!" growled the group's lead singer, Aidan.

"No offense," Bonnie said quickly. "It's just—he doesn't even have any money."

"He's got good taste though, don't he?" the singer replied as Malachi showed the CD to Bonnie. "That's *Devil Inside Me*, our biggest seller. Sold nine copies last month alone!"

The CD cover art stopped Bonnie cold. She took it from Malachi, looked at it closely in the dim light. It was exactly the image they were searching for: a drawing of the angel, the scales, tortured souls, Heaven and Hell. All of it. It was *the* mosaic, the one Gam Gam had shown her. The same image, only weathered, missing tiles— like it would look today.

"W-where did you get this? The picture! WHERE?"

The singer yanked it back, grinning. "Ah-ah-ah... What's it worth to you?"

.   .   .   .   .

The Brigands sat at the back of the club with the band members— Aidan, as well as his buddies Kieran and Shane—while the crowd milled about between sets. All the Brigands wore newly purchased band T-shirts, clearly the price for ten minutes of Blighted Omen's precious time.

Up close and with the lights up, they looked less like rebellious rockers and more like acne-pocked teens playing at being dangerous. Especially as they devoured their fish and chips.

Shane, the bass player with long hair as greasy as his fingers, leaned close to Bonnie. "Nice piercings, doll. Got any others you could show me?" He licked his fingers.

Bonnie blushed. She wasn't used to getting hit on.

"No, she does not!" Wilder said definitively. Everyone looked at him. "T-that I know of."

Flattering as the attention was, Bonnie was determined to get to the bottom of the mystery. "The picture on the CD cover. Where is it from?"

"I wouldn't know," Aidan said casually. "That was our ex-drummer, Fionn. He drew it."

"Great skins man, Fionn," Kieran said.

"Also a great artist. Real gift with a pencil—since primary school! Remember that koala he drew in the jacks?" Aidan added.

They all nodded nostalgically.

"Shame he had to quit the band," Shane lamented.

"Real shame, it was," Kieran agreed.

"So this Fionn knows where the original is?" Bonnie pressed.

"He did the drawing, didn't he? Seen it somewheres 'round here, I reckon. Where was that then, boys?"

"Somewheres. 'Round here. For sure," Shane and Kieran echoed.

"Well, can you call and ask him about it?" Reed asked.

"Nah. When his da made him quit the band, he wouldn't let him see us no more and took his mobile."

"And the good amp!"

Bonnie's patience was wearing thin. "Okay. How CAN we get ahold of him?"

"He works at his family's butcher shop over on Bridge Road," Aidan said. "Nasty business, butchery, him being vegan and all."

"You know, they say pigs is smarter than most toddlers," Shane said.

"They're certainly smarter than you, ya tosser," Kieran replied, earning him a flurry of punches on the arm.

"Aiiighhhh!" Bonnie slammed her hand on the table, startling everyone. "The address. For the love of God, just give us the address!"

*　　*　　*　　*　　*

O'Doherty & Sons
Family Butchers
Est. 1873

Early the next morning, Fionn O'Doherty held up the CD as he leaned against the brick wall outside his family's shop, his apron smeared with blood, vaping an e-cigarette. He was surrounded by Brigands.

"Yeah. That's one of mine. What's it to ya?"

He was a lanky kid with a buzz cut in the awkward growing-out stage. Like his former bandmates, he still had acne, though his was buried beneath dark-metal tattoos on his face.

"Where'd you see this?" Bonnie asked, perhaps a little too intensely.

Fionn stiffened up. "Didn't steal it, if that's what yer implyin'."

"Not at all." Reed stepped in. "Actually, we think it's incredible."

"Yeah?" Fionn perked up. "I-I got others if ya wanna see." He beamed, glancing around before pulling a phone from his apron.

Bonnie was about to object, but Reed signaled her to hold back. Fionn scrolled through photos of his artwork and Reed leaned in.

"Wow," Reed said, genuinely impressed. The drawings were exquisite—delicate and detailed, a sharp contrast to the tough image Fionn projected. "Guys, check this out."

"Damn, dude. You got a gift," Wilder said.

"No cap," Luz added. "Serious talent."

Malachi patted the boy's back, appreciating a fellow artist.

The boy turned bright red. "I, well, it's a hobby now, but if I can get me enough money, I was thinkin' art school. Maybe a graphic novel."

"That's great," Bonnie interrupted, "but can you just tell us where you saw the original? We know it's a real mosaic, and we need to find it. It's important."

Fionn hesitated. "Uh... I dunno. No one's really supposed to go there." He took a step toward the door. Tanner smoothly blocked his path.

"You know," he said, arm around the boy, "my dad's a film producer in Hollywood. "Always looking for talented artists to do storyboards."

"Yeah?" Fionn lit up.

"Sure. I could put in a word. But, y'know, quid pro quo."

"I ran across it, over on Crag Inish," he said.

"Crag Inish," Reed repeated.

"That's just what us locals call it. Less an island than a bunch of rocks juttin' outta the water. Wretched place. There's some religious ruins out there from the olden days. Like where blokes in long robes would go to pray and whip on theirselves and such."

"A monastery?"

"That's it!" Fionn said. "Monastery or something."

They exchanged excited glances.

"We go out there sometimes," he continued. "You know, drink, get high. Waters are pretty rough out that way, so no one else bothers."

"Where's it at?" Reed asked. "Can you show me on your phone?"

"Oh, ya won't find it on any app," Fionn said.

"What in the BLOODY HELL is this about?!" An angry voice cut through the moment.

A burly middle-aged man, also wearing a blood-smeared apron, stormed over and ripped the phone from Fionn's hand.

"What'd ya, go into me press and snake back the phone?" he said angrily. "And what's this?" He saw the pictures on the phone. "I thought we threw all this rubbish in the turf fire. You got pictures of it still?!"

"S-sorry, Da!" Fionn cringed.

"I tole you to forget this molly-assed tripe!" His father hurled the phone to the ground, smashing its screen.

"Noo!" Fionn reached for it, but his father shoved him hard against the wall.

The boy flinched, tears in his eyes.

"Hey!" Bonnie said. "Get off him!!"

The man whirled around and lifted his hand to Bonnie. "You want a taste?"

Malachi, Luz, and Barnaby stepped forward. The other Brigands tensed, hands drifting toward their knives. Seeing the size of Malachi, the butcher backed down. He turned to Fionn and grabbed him roughly by the arm.

"Get yer arse back behind the counter where you belong!" As he shoved the boy back inside, Fionn called over his shoulder.

"South-Southwest off Tammany Point. Look for the black rocks!"

The butcher slapped his son on the back of his head, leaving a bloody handprint from his glove. And they disappeared inside the shop.

The Brigands took a last look through the shop window at the red-faced young man behind the counter, still being berated by his overbearing father.

"What a dick," Daya remarked.

"Now I get the music," Barnaby said.

"Guess soul-crushing adults are a universal thing," Wilder added.

Bonnie clenched her fists. If this were three hundred years ago, she wouldn't have hesitated to run that bastard through.

Chapter 33
Crag Inish

Crag Inish looked as unwelcoming as Fionn had warned. As the dinghy neared the rocky shore, Bonnie's pulse quickened—she'd seen this place before. During the conjuring with Fati, then again in the vision on Hamhock Barony. Back then, she hadn't known what it meant, but now she was sure—they were on the right path to finding her mother.

Because of the dinghy's size and the need to leave Brigands behind to defend the *True North*, Reed split the group. He, Bonnie, Wilder, Luz, Tanner, Zion, and Malachi would go to the island as a landing party. Again, Yeun would stay back and command the ship, with Barnaby, Daya, Micah, and Cordial as a makeshift crew. Though Barnaby insisted Bonnie would be safer if he were there, ultimately, he was ever the good soldier. As was Daya, who had great respect for Reed's leadership. Micah wasn't so understanding.

"So I have to babysit Malachi while you guys are in Tucson, but he gets to go without me now?" Micah scoffed. "Pick a lane, man."

Reed reasoned that Malachi had to come. He had recreated the mosaic flawlessly, as if he'd seen it before. Given his abilities, he might be able to steer them to the real thing.

As the Brigands approached the island, the waters were so treacherous that finding a place to set ashore was challenging even for blood-born pirates, leaving Bonnie to wonder how Fionn and his pals had managed it. Then again, they *had* grown up in this harsh environment, and there wasn't much that could stop teenage boys in search of thrills.

"Why would anybody want to build a monastery here?" Zion wondered.

"I guess some people will do nearly anything to be left alone," Wilder said.

"I get that," Bonnie said, having often longed for the days when she was anonymous. *Before the curse. Before everything.*

When they finally arrived, Reed and Zion managed to maneuver the boat to the single spit of sand that was visible on the leeward side of the island. It was narrow, but just enough land for them to pull the boat onto. The other Brigands hopped out and joined the two boys on the sand.

"Looks like we found the place where Seamus McMetalhead and the gang come to party," Tanner said, pointing to some discarded bottles, cigarette butts, and a broken bong floating in a nearby tidepool.

"What pigs," Luz said. "Disgusting!"

"Yeah, it's hard to believe nihilistic death rockers wouldn't be eco-friendly," Wilder remarked.

"We better set to," Reed said. "This far north, we'll lose the light pretty quick. Especially with those dark clouds moving in." He indicated a storm brewing on the horizon.

"Okay, Malachi," Bonnie said, holding up the drawing. "Remember this?"

Malachi stared at the drawing, unresponsive.

"Mal, pal, think," Wilder urged, tapping the paper. "Where is it?"

Still nothing.

"Maybe we should've brought Cordial," Zion muttered.

"She'd be better company than this walking billboard for Adderall," Tanner huffed.

"Give him a minute!" Bonnie snapped. "He's not a fortune-telling machine." She turned back to Malachi. "See the angel with the scales? Heaven, Hell? You saw this in your head. It's somewhere on this island. Can you show us where it is?"

Malachi looked up at Bonnie and met her with his piercing eyes, but still no response.

"We're gonna have to split up," Reed finally said. "This place has too many 'hidey holes' as Peg would say. Okay. Luz you're with Bonnie. Wilder—"

"Wait! Look!" Bonnie pointed.

Malachi was heading south, just beyond where they had landed. The group exchanged glances, then followed.

At first, Malachi led them along the jagged shoreline, their boots crunching over seashells and the occasional piece of driftwood. Bonnie's mind was racing. The vision, the mosaic—it all felt real now. Real and close. Amid the calls of the gulls, blood thrummed through her veins as she trudged against the strong winds.

"Feels like we're at the end of the world," Wilder murmured.

"Or the beginning," Bonnie said.

Suddenly, Malachi veered up a rock-strewn hill, forcing the others to follow. The climb was brutal—no clear path, just volcanic rock and dwarf shrubs. More than once, someone stumbled, catching themselves before tumbling onto the jagged terrain. Only Malachi moved with certainty, as if he knew exactly where to step. Maybe he did.

"Oof!" Bonnie ran into the back of Malachi, who'd come to an abrupt stop.

They'd arrived at a high point on the island, where they emerged onto a small clearing of limestone. Eons of water had cut grooves into the rock to create individual blocks of stone, as if the whole thing had been constructed by a mason.

"Wow. Nature's patio..." Wilder said. "All we need is a barbecue grill and some deck chairs."

Weeds sprouted everywhere and moss covered the stones which, along with the constant spray from the ocean, made the surface very slippery. On one side of the clearing, sheer cliffs dropped into the ocean and on the other, the towering rocks they'd seen coming in.

"Malachi? What is it?" Bonnie asked cautiously.

"Here," he said simply. Then he sat down, pulled out his notebook, and started sketching a tiny yellow burnet rose growing stubbornly between the cracks.

"Okay," Reed sighed. "Let's split up, but nobody stray too far. Holler if you find something."

Bonnie and Luz headed left. Pouring over every crevice, kicking at moss, and pushing aside shrubs, they searched for any sign of the mosaic or even a path that might take them there.

Then Bonnie spotted something. At first glance, it looked like an accidental smattering of limestones overgrown with weed and moss leading up a slope. But on closer inspection, she thought they seemed too regularly spaced. Bonnie pulled away the overgrowth to reveal crude steps, cut into the limestone. Next to it, under a shrub, was a discarded vape pen.

"This way," she said and started up the steps. Her heart pounded with anticipation as she and Luz began their ascent. As she moved higher up the stone staircase, the sound of the ocean faded, drowned out by the howling wind.

They passed through two massive rock formations that kept the path hidden from below. On the other side, they reached the top. There, hidden amidst the towering black rocks that surrounded her, were ruins—stone structures half-standing and covered in moss and brine. The scent of damp earth and decaying vegetation hung heavy in the air.

"Holy shit!"

"Is this it?" Luz asked.

Bonnie nodded, looking around her in wonder. "The exact monastery. Give or take a thousand years."

"I-I'll go get the others!" Luz started back down the stairs, shouting as she ran. "Hey! Everybody! Up here!"

Bonnie could hear Luz's voice fade in the distance as she continued on. Siobhan in hand, she made her way through the ruins, her footsteps echoing on the stone floor. The monastery had an otherworldly beauty, the gloomy light filtering through gaps in the roof, illuminating the way through the shadows. The wind moaned through the chambers.

Bonnie came upon a large rectangular room lined with crumbling columns—what once had been the cloister. Now, it was littered with debris; shattered pieces of stone and plaster made walking difficult. Whatever brought this place to ruin had happened a long, long time ago.

Bonnie's boots crunched as she made her way through the building. She ran her flashlight over the darker corners to uncover remnants of ancient images. A serpent. A deer. A cross. A bird maybe. They were all so faded it was hard to tell. But nothing even close to the mosaic.

Then she stopped in her tracks. She'd almost missed it; it was so strewn with debris. But at the end of the room was an alcove. The ceiling had collapsed, allowing light and the elements in. It was drizzling now, and Bonnie felt the moisture on her face. She clambered over a large fallen column, slippery with moss and grime, turned the corner, and her breath caught.

The mosaic!

It towered over her. What was left of it, anyway. The lower part of the angel's body was chipped away, its tiny tiles long missing, as was the top of one wing, and the entire image was encrusted with salt and mildew. But there was no mistaking it.

Bonnie marveled at the mosaic's chilling detail—Heaven above, an angel holding scales, weighing the fate of two souls—one uplifted in prayer, the other writhing as demons surely waited in Hell below. Though faded and broken, the angel's fierce gaze bore into her, heavy with judgment. A wave of guilt surged through her, permeating every pore. She felt a shiver move down her spine.

Suddenly, a hand grasped her shoulder. She swung Siobhan around and barely missed relieving Reed of his entrails. The rest of the Brigands were behind him, staring transfixed at the mosaic.

"Shit! Give a girl a warning, Ballister. I could have gutted you!" Bonnie was shaken.

"I called your name like three times," Reed defended himself. "But you were in a trance or something."

"Where's Malachi?" Bonnie asked, noticing he was the only one not there.

"He stayed down below to stand guard," Reed explained.

"Or to look at the flowers," Zion added. "Hard to tell which, to be honest."

Wilder took it all in. He shifted back and forth. "That's freaky. No matter where I move, I feel like that angel's eyes are following me."

"It's making me feel like I gotta say an Our Father or two..." Luz said.

"Hell, throw in the whole Rosary," agreed Wilder.

Bonnie was glad she wasn't the only one who felt it—the powerful guilt the image provoked.

"Okay. We're here. It's there. So where's your mom?" asked Tanner.

They all stood in silence, not having contemplated the possibility that finding the mosaic wouldn't be the end of their quest.

"Keep looking," Wilder announced. "There's gotta be something here. Gam Gam would not steer us wrong."

They started scouring the ruins. Sifting through debris. Tapping walls for secret passages. Bonnie stayed in the alcove, focused on the room with the mosaic. She felt certain whatever clue they might find would be nearby.

She was running her fingers against the damp tiles of the mosaic when she felt a hand grab her shoulder roughly.

"Ow, Reed!" she began and turned to find herself face to face with two masked strangers. They were dressed in black, from their heavy leather boots to the ski masks over their faces. In their hands, gleaming steel blades promised menace.

"Look out!!" Bonnie screamed to warn the others, her sword already in motion.

Steel clashed against steel as Bonnie swung Siobhan, deflecting a brutal strike. Sparks burst as blades met, the force jarring her arm. Siobhan hummed gloriously when she found her mark.

The air crackled with the energy of the fight. The rhythmic *shing* of swords and grunts of the combatants filled the chamber. Bonnie's muscles burned as she parried a relentless onslaught of heavy blows, her steps quick and deliberate as she tried to outmaneuver her opponents.

Her adversaries' every swing was precise and deadly. Bonnie ducked under a wide arc of one strike, a sword whistling over her head. She retaliated with a quick thrust. One masked stranger twisted away at the last second, Bonnie's blade scraping harmlessly against his leather armor.

"Bonnie!" Reed's voice cut through the chaos.

Through the archway she glimpsed the other Brigands, all engaged in a similar battle with at least a dozen assailants. They were horribly outnumbered.

A blade whistled past her ear. She ducked, countering with a sharp swing. Siobhan found flesh—a grunt, a stagger—but another attacker took his place coming from—where, she wasn't sure—some opening in the darkened corner?

Bonnie found herself surrounded by three fighters, their swords flashing ominously. She blocked a strike from the left, only to be caught off guard from the right. Pain exploded in her shoulder as a blade grazed her. She cried out, Siobhan slipping from her grasp. An arm went to her neck and closed tightly around it. She fought fiercely to escape, but the air to her lungs constricted, the world around her going gray before finally going BLACK.

*   *   *   *   *

Malachi Maguire ran. Just ran.

While standing guard at the base of the staircase, he had been overcome with a sense of danger and rushed up to join the others. When he got there, the Brigands were in the thick of the sword battle with the masked attackers. And Bonnie was nowhere to be seen.

Malachi tried valiantly to save them and even took out a couple of assailants himself, but in the end, there were just too many of them.

"Malachi!! Go! Go!" Reed had commanded as the Brigands were being overwhelmed. "You know what to do!"

Malachi gave his attacker a vicious headbutt that sent him collapsing to the ground like a bag of gravel. He felt the crunch of bone against his forehead, the warm trickle of blood down his face. Then he turned and ran.

Malachi knew what Reed expected. He had to go back to the *North* and warn the others. The rain was coming down in torrents now, so it took nearly an hour to reach the shoreline in the dinghy. Then, he passed through the secret inlet until he could see where the *True North* was anchored. He rowed for another twenty minutes before arriving at the ship.

As Malachi approached, Barnaby called from the crow's nest to all on board. "Boat ahoy!" he yelled. "It's Malachi! And he's alone!"

*   *   *   *   *

Malachi sat curled up in a corner of the ship's galley, gasping for air and rocking back and forth in an effort at self-soothing. Micah crouched next to him, trying in vain to calm his brother.

"I knew we all should have gone!" Micah said. "I'm getting sick of getting left behind."

"You don't suppose Jack got them?" Wendell asked. The galley fell silent at the thought.

"This is bad, man. This is really bad," Barnaby said, double-timing his pacing.

"Calm down!" Yeun said, trying to maintain a level head. "We don't know anything yet. Cordial, What's your sense?"

"This is bad, man. This is really bad," she concurred.

"Malachi. Was it Jack?" Yeun asked.

"Them," was all he said.

"Yes. You said that. But who is them?" Yeun asked, frustration creeping into his voice.

Malachi sprang to his feet. "Them! Them!"

The ship's cabin door burst open with a deafening crack. Ten armed figures stormed in, clad in black leather, faces masked, guns trained on the Brigands.

"I'm pretty sure he means them," Micah said, slowly raising his hands in surrender. One by one, the others followed suit.

⸎   ⸎   ⸎   ⸎   ⸎

Within minutes, the young Brigands and Cordial were bound and herded onto a waiting speedboat. The sea spray and the engine's roar made conversation impossible, but the captives' fearful eyes spoke volumes. The wind whipped at their faces and the cold bit into their bones as the boat sped toward Crag Inish.

What they didn't see was that at that moment, a small rowboat had drawn alongside the *North*, and a nine-fingered man was climbing the ratlines. He dropped silently onto the deck and raised a pair of binoculars. He watched with bloodshot eyes as the speedboat headed toward the towering black rocks in the distance. Eyes hollow from hunger and exhaustion. But more than anything else, eyes fevered with madness.

Chapter 34
Inside the Compound

BEEP! BEEP! BEEP! BEEP! Somewhere between conscious and unconscious, Bonnie became vaguely aware of strange electronic noises, like buttons being pushed.

WHOOSH!

Was that a door sliding open? Then a blast of cold air jarred her awake.

Bonnie blinked, struggling to focus.

The room she was in now was nothing like the ruins of the monastery. Sleek, climate-controlled, and ultra-modern, with polished concrete walls and floors and LED lighting. The hum of electrical equipment surrounded her.

Bonnie found herself zip-tied to a large leather chair, making escape impossible. She sat at the end of a long conference table surrounded by two dozen empty chairs. She noticed her injury was already bandaged. *How long had she been out? And what had become of the others?*

A mounted security camera stared down at her from one wall. She had been told that Calico Jack had embraced the modern world. They weren't kidding. *But how could Gam Gam's message have delivered them directly into his hands?* None of this made sense.

She addressed the camera, her voice raspy and sore from being choked out during her capture. "Where am I?"

There was no answer.

"Where are my friends?!" she demanded.

Bonnie heard a shuffling noise. It came from the dark corner across the table from her—someone was standing there.

"Who's there?" Her mind flashed to the dream she'd once had of Calico Jack hiding in the dark corner of a church, his sharp wolf teeth visible in a slash of light. She swallowed her fear. "Show your face, you goddamn coward!"

"Bold words for someone tied to a chair."

The figure slowly stepped into the light. The man now in front of her was nothing like the Calico Jack Rackham she'd seen in paintings or dreams. It wasn't even his underling Maks. This man was ruddy-faced, in his 40s, with asymmetrical, unattractive features. Muscles pulsed beneath a black leather uniform that marked him as higher-ranking than her captors. His expression was relentlessly humorless and unforgiving.

Though this man wasn't Calico Jack, he frightened her just the same.

"How did you find this place?" he finally asked, his tone calm but laced with anger.

"Where are my friends?"

The man slammed his hands on the table. "I'm asking the questions!"

Despite her best efforts to appear unfazed, Bonnie flinched. Which she hated herself for—it betrayed weakness.

"I'll tell you how we found the place," she offered, "if you tell me where my friends are."

The man lunged, grabbing Bonnie's face with a crushing grip. Pain shot through her jaw, tears stinging her eyes, but she refused to cry out. Instead, she bared her teeth.

"Tell your boss he'll never get my years!"

Bonnie saw the man's eyes flick over her shoulder, reacting to some unseen person behind her. Then, just as suddenly as he'd grabbed her, the man let go, his jaw clenched in frustration.

Bonnie moved her face, waiting for the feeling to return. She tried to turn, but her bindings held her in place.

A huge video monitor flickered to life on the wall in front of her. On-screen, her fellow Brigands—Reed, Wilder, Luz, Tanner, and Zion—sat bound in a concrete cell.

Malachi! He was missing from the group. Was he still free? Or was the reason for his absence far worse? Bonnie held her tongue, wary not to tip them off in case Malachi had escaped.

"Tell Jack to let them go," Bonnie bargained with the man. "It's me he wants."

A woman's sharp laugh cut through the room. Bonnie strained against the zip-ties.

"Who's there?! Who are you?"

"You've grown into a devoted young woman. I'll give you that. Spectacularly stupid, but devoted," said the woman as she stepped in front of her captive. At the sight of her, Bonnie's heart leapt.

She was beautiful, though hard living and a disregard for grooming made her look older than her thirty-some years. Her black, curly hair was disrupted by a thick streak of gray-white that framed one side of her face. Beneath the same leather uniform as the others, she was slim but muscular. Bonnie knew at once who this woman was.

"Brigid?"

"I think you know who I am. The question is... why didn't you just STAY. THE. BLOODY HELL. AWAY!?"

,　　,　　,　　,　　,

Snakes and Swords.

Now untied, Bonnie stood in the conference room, alongside the other captives from the landing party. Shocked, she was staring at the ceiling. She hadn't thought to look up at first, just as she hadn't when she first entered the Cave o' the Four Winds back on the Cove. She had failed to see then the compass rose symbol of the Brigands.

Here, too, a compass rose adorned the ceiling, but this one was inlaid with gold and silver. Copper snakes coiled through its intricate design, their fanged heads pointing outward alongside swords marking directions. It was identical to the pin they'd recovered beneath the hearthstone in Father Hartwright's rectory.

The realization swept over her and swallowed her whole. They hadn't been caught by Calico Jack's men at all. They were captives of the Féth Fíada! The group still existed, and her mother Brigid Byrne was somehow part of it!

"So. All these years?" Bonnie's voice wavered. "Y-you've been hiding out with the FF?"

"Hardly hiding. I *am* the FF," Brigid replied. "Everything it is, I have built. Isn't that right, Donovan?"

"Yes, ma'am," Bonnie's interrogator answered.

"It was my understanding the FF wasn't around anymore," Reed said.

"Exactly! How do you find something that doesn't exist?" Brigid explained. "The very words *Féth Fíada* mean magical mist. It used to be summoned to protect the warriors of this land. Behind it, they became invisible, like a ghost or a forgotten memory."

"A fog shroud..." Bonnie murmured.

"Precisely. We've survived by remaining hidden."

"But *someone* must know about you by now," Reed said. "The CIA, MI6, Mossad..."

Brigid smirked. "Who do you think takes credit for our handiwork? They know we're here. It simply isn't in their interests to expose us."

"Well, you sure picked a great hiding spot," Wilder muttered. "No one would think to look here in a million years."

"Yet here you are, at my doorstep," Brigid said, a sharp edge to her tone. Reaching into her pocket, she pulled out the FF pin recovered during Bonnie's capture. She tossed it onto the table, watching it spin before it settled.

"I take it this had something to do with it," Brigid said. "I should have burned down that church long ago."

Bonnie was horrified. "*You* burned the church?"

"We thought it was Calico Jack," Reed said in disbelief.

"He's responsible for a great many things. That is not one of them," Brigid said.

"How did you even know we were going to Tucson?" Luz asked.

"Jack isn't the only one who has spies," Brigid said dismissively.

It dawned on Bonnie. Her mother had known she'd been found and known she was on the Cove. She'd known and done nothing.

"Father Hartwright was badly burned in that fire," Bonnie said.

"He wasn't supposed to be there," Brigid replied flatly, then fixed her gaze on Bonnie. "So Bonnie. Why have you come all this way?"

Bonnie hesitated, the words she truly wanted to say caught in her throat. Instead, she said, "Calico Jack... his ring is almost full. When it is, he'll be immortal."

"What are you talking about?" Brigid laughed. "That's impossible."

"It's the truth," Reed assured her.

"We only just found out ourselves," Bonnie added.

"Aglain!" Brigid screamed. "Get me Aglain! Now!"

Soldiers scrambled to heed her command.

WHOOSH! The door slid open, and an odd-looking man entered the room. He looked out of place in his high-tech surroundings, as though he'd just stepped through a time portal. His long face was heavily lined, framed by stringy hair and a beard streaked in various shades of gray. His lanky body was draped in floor-length, earthy robes, cinched at the waist with rope, and his head was wrapped in a twisted crown of twigs. His spindly fingers clutched a blackthorn staff.

"This is Aglain," Brigid said through gritted teeth. "My *supposed* advisor in all things—beyond the ordinary. Aglain, as you can see, the guests that you foretold have arrived."

He nodded to the group.

"These young people inform me that somehow our mutual enemy approaches immortality," Brigid continued, glaring at him. "I told them that it couldn't be; you surely would have told me such a thing."

Aglain closed his eyes, then after a moment, opened them again, clearly shaken. "They speak the truth."

Brigid was reeling. From the look on her face, Bonnie could see that the news was as devastating to her as it was to them.

"It might have been nice if YOU had told me that," she snarled at Aglain, then turned to Bonnie. "So... despite knowing this fact about Rackham, you left the Cove and exposed yourself and the world to such danger. Why would you do something so utterly reckless?"

"I... we came to save you," Bonnie stammered. The words felt foolish even as they left her mouth.

Brigid looked at Bonnie with a mix of contempt and disbelief.

Just then, a phone on the table buzzed. Brigid picked it up.

"Bring them in." She slammed down the phone, turned to Aglain, furious. "You. You're useless. Out of my sight." She waved him away.

As Aglain reached the door, it opened. Cordial and the remaining Brigands from the ship were led in past him, wet, bound, and at gunpoint.

"Now..." Brigid said, circling the new group of captives. "Who exactly needs saving?"

Chapter 35
The Grand Tour

After their hostile encounter, it was clear to the Brigands that Brigid was upset not only by their very presence, but also by the news they'd brought about Jack. She didn't quite shoot the messenger, but she had the entire group thrown into cells under armed guard before storming off to her private chambers with Donovan in tow.

It was hardly the reunion Bonnie had imagined. You don't exactly dream of meeting your long-lost mother while you're tied to a chair. She only had herself to blame, she thought as she sat on a hard bunk. She'd allowed herself to do the one thing life had taught her never to do—hope. She should have known better. The rejection was almost too much to bear. Though her crewmates sensed her pain, they dared not try to comfort her. Instead, she was left to brood in silence.

After two days of no contact, the Brigands' minds went to all manner of worst-case scenarios and started to plot a possible way to escape. But then, everything shifted.

"Oh-six-hundred! All hands turn to!"

LED lights flickered to life and the cell doors clanged loudly open. The Brigands groaned as they were rudely awakened from their uncomfortable slumber.

Brigid reappeared—almost cheerful. As much as someone like her could be, anyway. And in an instant, they were free.

Bonnie didn't know what had changed, but she didn't care. She was just relieved that Brigid was now treating them like "honored guests" rather than prisoners. She set them up in proper barracks, promised three hearty meals a day, and, most shockingly, decided to open up her entire operation to them as long as they had "come all this way," she explained.

"What I'm about to show you," Brigid said, "no outsider has ever been privy to."

And what an operation it was! The next few days were a whirlwind of excitement for Bonnie and her crew as they discovered that Crag Inish didn't just hide the ruins of an ancient monastery. It housed a state-of-the-art underground paramilitary facility beyond any imagining. And there seemed to be something there to enchant and seduce every Brigand. Well, except Reed, who was highly skeptical of Brigid's motives and her radical change of heart. Not to mention the ever-present armed escorts she'd assigned to them. Still, he agreed to go along to "assess the FF for Brigand purposes going forward."

The first day, Brigid led them into a large freight elevator and pressed a button for one of the lower floors.

"Everything you're about to see is cutting-edge. Sophisticated and unparalleled. You should count yourselves very lucky."

Tanner whispered, "Why do I feel like she's about to offer me a deal on a timeshare?"

Not having been raised with "timeshare money," Bonnie couldn't quite relate. Still she got the gist. But *what* was Brigid trying to sell exactly?

The elevator opened. Brigid walked ahead to a door and input a password into a code box.

As the lock disengaged and the steel doors slid open, a collective "WHOA!" filled the air, with a "*Dios mio!*" thrown in—courtesy of Luz, naturally.

Inside stretched an armory straight out of a Marvel movie—endless rows of shelves stocked with high-tech weapons. Machine guns, grenades, flamethrowers, anti-tank missiles, mortars, recoilless rifles...

"You won't find many governments with the organization, scope and firepower of the FF," Brigid bragged.

"Oh mama! Mama mama mama! Come to papa!" Wendell swooned, stroking an underslung grenade launcher.

Micah rolled his eyes. "Careful, bro, or it'll slap a restraining order on you."

"Is this a Heckler and Koch?" Wendell asked, entranced.

"You have a good eye," Brigid replied. "That's the M320. It can ruin a drug smuggler's birthday party from 350 meters away. Bonnie, you didn't mention you had an armaments expert in your midst."

Wendell beamed at the compliment. Bonnie swelled up at being singled out.

"We've got plenty of experts," Bonnie blurted. She winced at how eager she sounded.

"I look forward to getting to know them all," Brigid said.

As the tour continued, Bonnie spotted their confiscated swords locked inside a cabinet. She glanced at Reed. He had noticed too, his jaw tight with frustration. Bonnie silently pleaded with him not to make a scene.

"So, if you got all this gear, why are you still toting swords around?" Reed wondered to nods of agreement. Bonnie was relieved—it was a benign enough question.

"A reminder of where we came from," Brigid explained. "We're still Brigands at heart."

"Wait," Reed said. "Everyone in the FF is a blood Brigand?"

"Some more than others," came a voice from behind them.

They all turned to see Donovan, who'd suddenly materialized. "You didn't tell me you decided to show them around," he growled, looking at Brigid.

"An oversight." The two locked eyes, tension thick between them.

"How many are under your command?" Reed pressed, ignoring the interchange.

"Fifty-three here on Crag Inish, more in the field," Brigid continued.

"Where did they come from?" Barnaby asked.

"Some we found on our own. Others didn't make the cut at the Cove."

"You recruit from our rejects?" Wilder asked.

"We don't take everyone. But qualities that may have been disqualifying from the Brigands can often be... repurposed."

"I always wondered what happened to those dudes," Tanner mused.

"Us also being Brigands at heart and all... any chance we get *our* swords back?" Reed asked.

"I'm sorry. All visitors stow their weapons here. Protocol."

"Excuse Reed. He feels naked without his weapon," Bonnie tried to make a joke of it.

"I understand, Bonnie," Brigid said. "You'll get your weapons back when you leave."

"And when will that be exactly?" Reed pushed.

Brigid met Reed's gaze. She smiled. "Reed Ballister... I know you. I used to change your diapers. You were always a wee fussy one."

Everyone SNICKERED and Reed turned beet red.

"You're free to go whenever you like, Mr. Ballister. No one's keeping you here."

Despite the armed guards shadowing their every move, she said it as if the Brigands had a choice in the matter. Then, dismissing the whole conversation, Brigid turned to the group. "Now. Who wants to see the ground-to-air missiles?"

To Reed's dismay, Brigand hands shot into the air. If indeed, they could leave anytime they wanted, nobody seemed that eager to do so.

. . . . .

So it went. Each morning after breakfast, Brigid gathered her "guests" for an in-depth look at the various components of the FF operation. With every revelation, the Brigands seemed more and more won over by the FF. Especially Bonnie, who basked in Brigid's particular attention. Brigid wasn't warm and squishy like Grandma Winnie, but her deference to Bonnie—directing questions to her, watching her reactions—made her feel important.

Donovan made a point to follow along every day, albeit with the enthusiasm of someone enduring the Bataan Death March. And, after his tense exchange with Brigid on the first day, Reed had decided to disengage and simply observe everything in silence. Which was just fine with Bonnie; as long as he kept his mouth shut, he couldn't do any damage. The way she saw it, the FF was awesome, and she was amazed at what her mother had built.

Among Brigid's most impressive achievements was an entire floor dedicated to tactical combat training: a vast facility that featured a fully functional weight room, ruck packs for weighted ruck training, VR battle simulation areas, and pads for hand-to-hand combat. It was a far cry, the Brigands mused, from the ship deck replica, sawdust floor, and antique weaponry back on Cormac's Cove.

"Sounds like things haven't changed much," Brigid said. "Not that I expected them to."

Particularly impressed with the setup were Luz and Zion.

"Shondra here would be happy to show you some moves if you'd like," Brigid offered. "She's specially trained in Krav Maga."

"Hell yeah!" Luz replied, stepping forward. Zion held her back.

"Uh. If it's okay. Reed?" he said, glancing to Reed for permission.

Bonnie nervously looked from Reed to Brigid, who was registering the exchange.

"We Brigands are always open to improvement," Reed nodded, and Bonnie exhaled.

Luz and Zion peeled off from the group as Shondra, a fierce-looking young woman with a fade, started showing Luz the ropes. Feeling a little territorial, Daya decided she too *absolutely* had to learn some moves and joined in. They didn't reappear until dinner.

On another day, the group lost Tanner and Yeun to the flight simulation bays.

"Flight sims with custom avionics!" Yeun said, strapping into a sim seat.

Tanner took a seat next to him. "I always wanted to learn to fly, but my dad never let me!"

"Maybe cuz last time you flew, it was his Ferrari into a light pole," Wilder said.

"You total one vintage sports car, and suddenly you're grounded for life," Tanner muttered.

Brigid stepped in. "FF members have the opportunity to become pilots. In fact, we encourage it. You wouldn't believe how often it comes in handy in our line of... work."

They believed it plenty. After all, they'd just spent weeks on the Atlantic. Brigid was both shocked and impressed that they had crossed on the *True North*—the very vessel on which she'd learned to sail.

"That's so old school," she said after hearing the story. "And so Eleazer Ballister."

Bonnie saw Reed bristle at the comment.

"Captain Ballister taught us everything we know," Yeun jumped in to defend the captain. "Going old school kept us safe under the radar."

"I'm sure it was useful in the past. But now we have a thing called cloaking technology," Brigid said. "Let's bring you into the future."

And just like that, Tanner and Yeun were paired with instructors.

As the days passed, the rest of the compound proved equally impressive. AI intel centers that had Barnaby salivating. At the push of a button, he could analyze any database in the world. Micah fawned over systems that had the capability to hack into high security servers yet remain undetectable themselves. The first thing he searched for was Area 51. His eyes went wide.

"I wonder if Tanner's dad ever thought of making a pirates vs. aliens movie. Cuz, uh, he should get on that pronto."

"Could you get into the Fed Crime Database?" Wilder asked. "There's a few items there I wouldn't mind deleting."

"Let's give it a shot," Micah rubbed his hands together eagerly. And like the others, he was given free rein to become familiar with their operations.

Even Malachi found his place in the compound—at the Controlled Environment Agricultural Center, the underground farm where all the food for the facility was grown and harvested. He spent hours there among the crops, drawing in his sketchbook.

Each corner they turned in the complex, each innovation, each gadget, each self-propelled thingamabob was greeted with wide-eyed appreciation by the Brigands—even Reed occasionally admitted it was impressive.

Bonnie was gratified to see her mother and the Brigands getting along. It felt like bringing a boyfriend home and having your family love him—if she'd ever had a boyfriend, or an actual family.

Throughout their tour, they would sometimes catch sight of the robed figure, Aglain. His enigmatic presence seemed to drift through the compound like a shadow, occasionally whispering something in Brigid's ear or watching the newcomers with curiosity. Bonnie noticed his cool gaze sometimes lock onto Cordial, the air between them crackling with unspoken tension.

"What's the deal with that dude?" Daya asked in a hushed tone one night as they all lay in their bunks. "All decked out in those sheets and shit. Gives me the creeps."

"I know, right?" Tanner said. "Like bro, the Renaissance fair isn't 'til fall."

"I think he's a mystic of some kind," Barnaby said.

"For sure he is," Cordial agreed. "I recognized his magic the minute we were in the same room. I'm pretty sure he's the one that blocked us from seeing your mom when we did the divination back at Hamhock, Bonnie. Remember?"

"Yeah." The powerful memories still haunted her.

"What kind of magic is it, Cordial?" Wilder asked, propping up on one elbow.

"Definitely not Gullah. Something older. But it's not like I'm some expert on magics of the world."

"I bet he's a druid priest," Barnaby offered.

"Not like any priest I ever took communion from," Luz remarked.

"Not a Catholic priest, Luz. Druids are pagans," Barnaby explained.

"Yeah. Their religion goes way back," Micah jumped in. "Before Christianity. They believe spiritual truth is found in nature." They all looked at him, surprised at his knowledge.

"Video game?" Tanner asked.

"*Runestone II: Scroll of Elowen,*" he explained.

"That game is awesome!" Wendell said. "Much better than *Baldur's Crossing*! Man, I miss video games."

Tanner shook his head. "You nerds are gonna save a lot of money on condoms."

"Druid priest," Zion nodded. "That makes sense. All the animal horns and branches and that robe."

"Bro, don't tell me *you're* a gamer, too?" Tanner said.

"No. But I have a library card. You should look into it sometime."

"So this Aglain's basically the firewall to this place," Reed observed.

"He may be more than that," Barnaby interjected, not to be outdone by mere gamers. "Druid priests have always been high-ranking in Celtic culture—as keepers of lore, medical experts and even political advisors."

"Whatever he is," Cordial continued, "I'm pretty sure I pissed him off."

"How? You've never even talked to him!" Bonnie asked.

"Didn't have to. When we first got here, he tried to penetrate my magic. But I wasn't having it. Like, buy me a drink first, dude. I just blocked him, like I did my mom. Got the sense he wasn't used to someone being stronger than him, mystically speaking."

"Wouldn't be the first old white dude who underestimated a woman of color," Daya said, high-fiving Cordial.

"We just better be sure we don't underestimate *him*," Reed warned.

For once, Bonnie agreed with Reed. She wasn't about to let some old-world mystic stand between her and what she came here for—to connect with her mother.

Chapter 36
Mothers, Fathers, & Daughters

Her stomach in knots, Bonnie walked in lockstep with her armed escort through the corridors on the way to Brigid's office. Since their arrival on Crag Inish, every encounter with her mother had been carefully choreographed and strictly focused on FF business. There had been no private moments, no space to speak freely. Finally, Bonnie had taken matters into her own hands and requested this meeting. She didn't even mention it to the others because it was, well, something personal.

She wasn't sure how Brigid would react to the news she carried—that her father Bobby Maynard was dead. But she felt strongly that she should know.

Or maybe, if she admitted it to herself, she was using the news as an excuse for some alone time with Brigid. Still, though she was starting to tire of the formality of their interactions, Bonnie savored every moment of them.

She marveled at their similarities—not just the dark hair and eyes, but little things, like how their left eyebrows arched when considering something or how their index fingers matched the length of their middles. Meeting her mother was like solving for X in an equation. With both parents now known to her, who she was finally made sense. At least on the surface.

But it wasn't just the physical. There was something primal in her draw to Brigid—a woman she'd never known yet felt innately connected to. It reminded her of the pull she'd felt toward Bobby Maynard, but even that was complicated by walls of resentment. This was different. This felt immediate, as if tied to something deeper than logic. She'd read once that mothers carry their children's DNA even after birth. Maybe that explained it.

She hoped Brigid felt it too, though the cold distance her mother maintained between them left her uncertain.

A part of her thought that if she waited long enough, proved herself enough, she could make it happen. Because, like all abused and abandoned children, she had convinced herself that her mother would eventually come around and admit that she wanted Bonnie, that she had never stopped loving her, which was probably what Bonnie longed most in the world to hear. But for now, that would have to wait. She had other business.

*   *   *   *   *

Bonnie sat alone in Brigid's office, nervously awaiting her mother's arrival. She found the space to be like the woman herself. Cold and professional. The only inkling of humanity, the only personal thing in the room, was a handful of photos on a credenza. They all featured Johnny Keane, the founder of the FF. Bonnie recognized him from the snapshot Peg had shown them. Here in color, his wolf-gray eyes and jet-black hair made him look even more dashing, the faint stubble on his face adding an air of careless danger. Though she suspected there was nothing careless about this man.

Most photos captured him dressed in FF gear, ready to lead some anti-Rackham operation. But one was unusual—him in robes, strung with animal bones, standing at a stone altar with the old mystic Aglain.

There was one other photo that sat in an obviously revered position at the center of the others. Bonnie picked it up to get a closer look. In it, a young Brigid (not much older than Bonnie was now) with Keane, their arms entwined, their eyes locked in an unmistakable lovers' gaze. The intimacy of the moment struck Bonnie hard. She couldn't help but feel a pang of hurt on behalf of her late father, knowing that her mother, after abandoning him on the Cove, had fallen in love with someone as magnetic as Keane.

Bonnie's thoughts were interrupted by the WHOOSH of a sliding door. Brigid entered, her movements calm and deliberate. As she walked in, she noticed what Bonnie was holding.

"That's Keane," Brigid said. "He founded the FF."

"I've heard stories. Looks like you were... close."

"He was a force of nature," she said wistfully as she gently took the photo from Bonnie, looked at it a lingering moment, and then put it back with care. She sat behind her desk and her tone turned businesslike. "Now, what is it you needed to discuss in private?"

Bonnie's throat tightened, and she said, "Bobby Maynard's dead."

Brigid sat, unmoving.

Bonnie searched her mother's face for a clue to her emotions. There was none.

"Anyway. I thought you should know," Bonnie pressed on, "since, you know, he was my dad and the two of you—"

"I knew he died," Brigid interrupted, her tone clipped. "I just didn't know he'd told you about... us—but then Bobby could never keep a secret. He was always too sentimental. Never capable of doing what needed to be done for the greater good."

Bonnie tensed. "He died saving me from Calico Jack's men."

"Well," Brigid said, "he died a true Brigand then."

"He didn't do it out of some Brigand duty. He did it because I was his daughter." Bonnie paused, hoping she'd struck some dormant maternal chord in Brigid.

"I'm sorry your father's dead. But he was ruled by his heart. Noble as it was, that softness left him vulnerable. Especially against someone like Jack."

"You know, he never stopped looking for you. For us. Never."

"A lifetime chasing shadows, looking for someone who shouldn't be found and someone who didn't want to be. Such a pity. Bobby Maynard could have been so much more."

Bonnie stared in disbelief, unsure if Brigid's pragmatism was masking her grief, or there was no grief there to begin with.

"I don't know if I should bother to tell you this," Bonnie said. "If it even matters to you at all. But he wanted you to know that he still loved you."

There! There it was—a flicker of something in Brigid's eyes. Brigid's fingers tightened on the desk for a moment. She did care! Somewhere deep inside, the Brigid from the vision still existed. But as quickly as it came, it was gone.

"What did he know of love?" she asked, her voice quieter now, bitter even. "What did either of us? We were children. Stupid, impulsive children. Bonnie. Please tell me that isn't the real reason you traveled all this way! To tell me that?"

The disgusted stare she aimed at Bonnie stung like a rebuke.

"No! I-I told you. I came to protect you from Calico Jack. You're my..." She hesitated, the word "mother" sticking in her throat. "You're marked. And I'm a Brigand. It's my duty." The words felt clumsy and inadequate, given all that she now understood.

"Well, it's a relief to know your reasons were at least more substantive. But as you have been shown, I don't need saving."

And then, it spilled out of her. She wasn't expecting it and certainly hadn't planned it. But Bonnie couldn't stop it.

"Why didn't you save *me*? Why didn't you come back and get me and bring me here?" she asked, her voice pleading and weak, almost as if she were begging. And she hated herself for sounding so desperate.

Brigid sighed. "I knew this question would come up eventually. Look. You were safe. And I couldn't afford distractions. Especially after Keane died."

"Safe? I was in foster care!"

"And look how you turned out. Do you think you'd be who you are without those trying experiences? Neither of us would."

"*Trying* experiences?" Bonnie laughed ironically, staring down at her hands in her lap, at the remnants of a cigarette burn inflicted by one of her foster parents. She blinked, determined to hold in the tears. One escaped and rolled down her cheek anyway.

At first, Brigid sat in silence, unsure what to do. Finally, she got up and came around the desk. Crouching to Bonnie's level, she took her hands in a way that seemed forced—like an actor trying to recall a bit of blocking.

"I can't imagine what you went through," she said. "None of this excuses what happened. You didn't choose to be marked. Neither of us did. But here we are just the same. And we must embrace our destinies. We must fight because no one else has more at stake than us. Because I believe that's what we marked ones are born to do. It's our responsibility."

Bonnie looked into her mother's eyes. They were shiny with righteousness. But there was also pain there. Deep, deep pain. This was the moment Bonnie finally understood the connection that existed between them—not as mother and daughter as she had longed for, but as kindred souls united against evil. Caught between forces of Heaven and Hell, bound by fate and the misfortune of their birth.

"You're a strong girl, Bonnie, I can see that about you. I can also see that the hatred for Calico Jack burns inside you, just as it does within me. The question you must ask yourself is, what are you willing to do to stop him? Because if you don't figure that out and fast, you'll end up like your father."

As Bonnie pondered this, she looked at her mother—at this enigmatic woman who had given her life to the cause, the curse— and she couldn't help but wonder what sort of things *she* had been willing to do to stop Calico Jack Rackham.

Interlude

Lough Derg

County Donegal, Ireland
Ten Years Earlier

Brigid stood on the ferry's deck, staring at the murky waters of Lough Derg. Her face gaunt, dark circles around her eyes, she looked like a shell of a person. The wind tugged at her hair, whipping it into a frenzy that mirrored the turmoil inside her. The island loomed ahead, an ancient place of penitence and prayer shrouded in the Irish mist. She clutched the small Féth Fíada pin in her pocket that Keane had given her to replace the one she'd lost in the church. It was the only thing she had left of him.

Keane. His name was a blade that twisted in her heart every time she thought of him. Though she fought desperately against it, her mind kept replaying the chaos of that night, the explosions on the ship, the rushing to the getaway boat. She could still see the look in his eyes as she cut the escape rope after herself, leaving him trapped. How he mouthed her name as he stared over the rail at her, her betrayal dawning on him just before the giant blast that consumed the tanker... and him with it. How she CRIED OUT in anguish, gutted by her own act!

The ferry docked, and Brigid jolted back to the present. The island was bleak and barren, a fitting reflection, Brigid thought, of her soul.

She fell in with the stream of disembarking pilgrims. They were a ragged group, all suffering psychic pain. All seeking absolution, a release from their sins. Penitents had been making this journey to this little island in a remote lake in County Donegal for centuries.

The pilgrims moved slowly, some shuffling, towards the basilica where they would begin their rituals. Most of them removed their shoes at the dock, allowing the sharp rocks of the island to dig into their feet, allowing the pain they felt to fuel their repentance. Shortly, they would be greeted by priests who saw to it that none of them slept during the three-day rite.

Brigid moved through the crowd, entering the basilica. The confessional booth stood at the far end, a small wooden structure that seemed out of place amidst the ancient stone walls. She entered, the door creaking shut behind her, sealing her in darkness. The screen separating her from the priest was thin, a flimsy barrier between her and the man who would hear her sins.

"Bless me, Father, for I have sinned," she began, her voice steady, though her hands shook. "It has been... a long time since my last confession." In fact, Brigid couldn't remember when, if ever, she had been to confession. So far had she removed herself from religion. But she was desperate now. And it was that desperation that brought her here.

The priest's voice was gentle, soothing. "Take your time, my child. Tell me what weighs on your soul."

"I was part of something," she said slowly, carefully. "Something that cost a man his life. A man I loved. He died because of me."

The priest was silent for a moment, then he spoke, his tone compassionate. "Guilt is a heavy burden, to be sure. But through repentance and God's mercy, you can find peace and lighten your soul."

She had to stifle a laugh. His words were so simplistic they struck her as trite. She wondered if he would still believe that if she told him the truth. How she and Keane had been part of an epic battle against evil, how they were fighting for a great cause, only for Keane to waver in his conviction. Softened by his religion and the influence of the *druid priest who guided him straight into doubt about their purpose. How she had to kill Keane because of it, for the greater good. Or the whole world would have paid the price. She started to tell him, but instead—*

"Peace? Oh Father. There is no peace for me. Only a burning hate and need for revenge. For, you see, I am cursed."

The priest sighed, a sound full of sorrow. "It may feel that way, but I'm sure that is not true, lass. Every life comes into this world blessed. Made sinless through the waters of baptism."

This time Brigid did laugh. The priest was confused.

"If you truly believe that, then you are a fool and know less of your God than I do."

She stood abruptly, a cold resentment filling her, suddenly realizing all this had been a mistake. She would not find redemption here. The wooden confessional shook as she shoved the door open.

The priest called after her, "My child! Whatever troubles you, know that hatred and vengeance will only lead to more pain, and in the end cost you your eternal soul."

Brigid whirled around and pulled up her sleeve, exposing her mark.

"Too late, Father! My soul has already been bought and paid for!"

She rushed from the church, leaving the priest puzzled and even frightened at the sight of the mark, though he didn't know why.

Outside, the frigid wind was biting, but Brigid welcomed the cold. It matched the icy resolve in her heart. She had come here seeking something, but as it turned out, it wasn't forgiveness. It was clarity. Who needed forgiveness when one had righteousness on their side? Why should she beg for absolution for something that had to be done? As for her soul, well, she couldn't fret over something that had never been hers to begin with.

As Brigid made her way toward the ferry, she passed by the well of Saint Brigid, her namesake. Its stone edges were worn smooth by centuries of pilgrim hands. The well was surrounded by a multitude of trinkets left by previous penitents: rosaries, faded photographs, handwritten notes, and small, tarnished medals. Each item was a testament to someone's pain, a symbol of their hopes for forgiveness. Brigid's gaze swept over the collection.

All these sinners, leaving tokens of their guilt and sorrow. To her, it suddenly seemed pathetic. How could they believe that a few whispered prayers and simple offerings could wash away their sins? Brigid knew better. It had started with the abandonment of her daughter and had come full circle with the murder of the man she loved.

There was no cleansing the stain of what she had done, no absolution for the role she had played. The well and its trinkets were nothing more than a monument to frailty, a reminder that she could never again allow herself to fall into the same trap of remorse and regret.

She dumped the FF pin onto the heap with the rest of the garbage and strode away.

Brigid's path was set, her purpose clear. No more doubt, no more weakness. She would find Calico Jack Rackham. And she would destroy him. And she would never let her emotions betray her again.

Chapter 37
The Offer

"Brace yourselves, Brigands," Brigid said, her tone full of dire warning.

By the end of the first week, the Brigands had grown pretty accustomed to the impressive architecture and technology of the FF Headquarters. As a grand finale, Brigid introduced them to the FF's central command—"CenCom." Deep inside the compound, it was the nerve center of the entire operation—a vast circular command center, its walls lined with giant high-definition monitors displaying live feeds from every corner of the globe.

Bonnie was shaken—they all were—by the overwhelming scope of scenes unfolding on the screens. Whether from hidden cameras, CCTV, or drones, the live feeds uncovered the gamut of the world's underbelly. A heroin operation in Colombia. Blood diamond mines in Sierra Leone. A warlord encampment in the Congo. A Peruvian counterfeiting hub. Drug and organ trafficking across borders. Even illegal logging in a remote rainforest.

"Holy global criminal empire, Batman," Wilder said what everyone was thinking.

"T-this is all Calico Jack?" Bonnie was staggered. She knew his enterprise was massive, but seeing it splayed out in front of her was overwhelming.

"All of it," Brigid said. "There isn't an evil in the world today that cannot in some way be traced back to Rackham. But then he's had three hundred years to do as he pleases." Her accusatory tone did not escape Reed's notice.

Wilder looked over at Reed. He could see him visually comparing this vast data center with his meager bookshelf full of news clippings, his face sunken by the harsh truth.

"There's no way you could have known about all this, bro," Wilder said to him.

"Why would you?" Brigid asked. "From what I recall of my time with the Brigands, your job is mainly to babysit marked ones."

"From what *I* recall, the Brigands did a pretty decent job of keeping you alive," Reed shot back, finally breaking his silence with anger.

"And for that I'm grateful, Mr. Ballister." Brigid's tone was placating, even condescending. "If you hadn't, I wouldn't be here to fight for the soul of humanity. And as you can see, we are engaged in a world war."

Brigid reached across a console and with the push of a few buttons, the monitors switched to even more disturbing visuals— the forced laborers in sweatshops, addicts in drug dens, victims of human trafficking.

Everyone stared at the horrors displayed there, revolted by what they saw, but unable to look away. The destruction wrought by Calico Jack overwhelmed Bonnie with a feeling of panic. For the first time, she felt the cracks in the foundation of her Brigand training. She felt small and utterly powerless. And her own life seemed insignificant in the face of it all.

"How do you do that?" Bonnie asked. "Fight for the soul of humanity?"

The Brigands all looked to Brigid. They, too, desperately wanted to know.

Brigid's eyes glittered with passion that bordered on zealotry. "We watch. We plan. And when the time is right—we strike."

As the Brigands returned to their quarters, the atmosphere was thick with unspoken thoughts. Whatever Brigid was selling, it was starting to look less like propaganda and more like salvation.

*   *   *   *   *

The room deep within the compound glowed from the light of dozens of candles. The massive stone table stretched nearly the length of the chamber, adorned with a blend of rustic and refined— silver goblets sat beside earthenware plates, merging elegance with tradition. The whole place clearly dated back to an ancient time. The mood was subdued, the Brigands still processing all they had seen.

Their first week on Crag Inish was at an end, and tonight, rather than eating in the mess hall as usual, the Brigands were summoned to dine with Brigid in a private dining hall. As the Brigands took their seats around the table, they whispered among themselves, dying to learn what this audience was about.

Brigid sat at the head of the table, her commanding presence filling the room. The druid priest Aglain sat to Brigid's left—the "heart side" according to Barnaby, which signified the emotional and spiritual realms. To her right sat Bonnie. The significance wasn't lost on anyone—especially Bonnie, who was secretly pleased. Donovan, however, now displaced from his position of honor, sat sullenly on Bonnie's other side.

Contrary to the typical austerity and practicality of the FF, this dinner was a display of abundance the likes of which the Brigands hadn't seen in months. Platters of roasted meats mingled with bowls of root vegetables, crusty loaves of bread, and exotic fruits. The air was heavy with the aroma of spiced stews and freshly baked pies.

To top it off, everyone was given wine. Brigid declared that if the Brigands were old enough to die for a cause, they were surely old enough to partake of life's spirits as well. As he savored his glass of alcohol, Tanner shot Reed a triumphant look. As for Bonnie, the wine and her new position left her feeling a little giddy.

Brigid was surrounded by members of the FF who doubled as servants, ready to swap out a salad fork or draw a sword at a moment's notice.

As one server, a pudgy young man, poured a glass of wine for Reed, they shared a look of recognition. The young man finished his task and hurried away.

"Hey, wasn't that...?" Wilder started.

"Brice," Reed nodded. It was the young corsair who had been devastated when he didn't make the cut the previous summer.

TING! TING! TING! Brigid tapped the edge of her glass with her fork. And the clatter of dining subsided.

"So, now that you've seen it all, I'm curious to know your thoughts," Brigid said, leaning onto her elbows and surveying the Brigands.

"Amazing." "Pretty unbelievable." "I can't believe the scope of it."

"Yeah. I can't imagine how this all came to be," agreed Wilder.

"Mr. De Luca, things never just 'come to be.' They are created by force of will. In this case, it started with Johnny Keane," Brigid began, "with whom I understand you are somewhat familiar." She glanced at Bonnie.

The Brigands nodded, recalling the stories of the Wayfarers.

"One of the best warriors ever descended from Mary Read," Brigid said. "Keane taught me everything I know about fighting Calico Jack."

"Except what the Brigands taught you," Reed said pointedly.

"I would say, *in spite* of what the Brigands taught me, Mr. Ballister," Brigid countered. "After he left the Cove, Keane was lost, aimless, nursing a grudge. But instead of wallowing, he sought out his roots."

"But I thought the Brigands were his roots," Barnaby said.

"We carry many bloodlines within us, as I'm sure you know. Keane also had ancestors here in Ireland who followed older ways, older than even the Brigands. The ways of the Tuatha Dé Danann and the ancient druids. Keane embraced that heritage and, through it, found Aglain here."

All eyes went to the priest. Aglain nodded to the table.

"He taught Keane the wisdom and power of the old ways. Became his spiritual guide and confessor. Mine too, eventually," Brigid smiled.

"John Keane was a truly devout man," Aglain said, making no mention whatsoever of Brigid.

"It was Aglain who led Keane to this island," Brigid continued. "This place had been known to druids for centuries before a handful of monks tried to gussy it up with crucifixes and incense for their own religious triflings."

"Christianity," Luz said pointedly. "It's called Christianity."

"Whatever label this island has worn," Aglain interjected, "the enchantment here is old as time itself. Though its worshippers may have dwindled, the power remains."

"Hey! Kinda like back in my community!" Cordial said, a little buzzed herself from the wine. "But then, there isn't much use for it anymore."

The priest eyed Cordial. "Magic is only as useful as those who wield it. And only as relevant as the purposes for which it is wielded." He lifted his glass to her. Cordial seemed to be struck by his words. They both drank.

Brigid cast a sharp glance between them. She didn't seem to much care for this camaraderie.

"In any case, Keane laid the FF's foundation," Brigid said. "When he died, he left behind the dream but little in the way of structure."

"What happened to him?" Wilder asked. "We've only heard rumors."

Brigid's expression darkened. "What have you heard?"

"That he died fighting Calico Jack," Micah said.

"Just so, sadly," Brigid nodded. "A noble death, but one that left the Féth Fíada vulnerable. That's when I stepped up."

"And they let you? Even though you aren't a Brigand?" Reed asked skeptically.

"You forget that I was raised as a Brigand. Regardless, it was Keane's mandate," Brigid answered flatly.

Donovan coughed. "Excuse me." He took a huge swig of wine.

"Keane knew what was at stake," Brigid explained. "And how I was uniquely situated to lead. He knew what we were fighting for."

"We fight for each other. For the vow," Reed said, his anger seeping through.

"I respect the vow. But it is not enough. Not anymore. Not against *him*. It was your own father who taught me that."

Reed was shocked. "What would you know about what my father thought?"

"Daniel was like my brother," she explained, "and your mother Catriona was my best friend. The three of us were all worried about the future of our children. We discussed it endlessly when I was pregnant with Bonnie—about whether there was a better way."

"My father would never betray the Brigands," Reed said, angry and offended.

"He would and he did," Brigid interrupted. "Before he and Catriona left for their last mission, he reached out to Keane. There were discussions. They were killed before they could act on them. But when Bonnie was born with the mark, well, that's when I made my decision."

"Even though Keane murdered your parents?" Reed said in a retaliatory tone.

"Reed!" Bonnie said, touching his arm to calm him.

"If you think you're going to shock me with that information, you're quite mistaken," Brigid said casually, sipping her wine. "I've known about it for years. Keane told me himself."

"And you were okay with it?" Bonnie asked, surprised by the admission.

Brigid sighed. "I never knew my parents, Bonnie. Not in any real sense. And from what Keane told me, I wouldn't have lasted long in their care. Just as you wouldn't have if we'd stayed on the Cove."

Brigid's eyes softened as she looked at her daughter. "That night I left you in that church. That was the hardest thing that I've ever done in my life. But I knew I'd saved you from Calico Jack. And that made it the right thing to do."

Bonnie was deeply moved.

"I never expected you to find us," Brigid continued. "But now that you have, I can see I've been wrong in trying to keep you away for so long. Having you here, all of you, fills me with regret that our two organizations have had this schism between us. After all, we share the same goals, even if we may differ in tactics. And, in light of the news you've brought about Jack's immortality, perhaps the time has come for some... collaboration between the Féth Fíada and the Brigands of the Compass Rose. And so, a toast!"

She lifted her glass. "To new beginnings!"

There it was, hanging in the air. What Brigid had been selling them all along.

Chapter 38
What Lies Beneath

Brigid's idea for the first-ever collaboration between the Brigands and the Féth Fíada was to bring them along on a local mission. It was a minor operation—one Brigid normally wouldn't oversee—but she decided to lead it so she could personally show them the ropes. Reed didn't like the idea at all but refused to let Bonnie, who was determined to go, join the mission without him. With limited space, Brigid let Bonnie choose who would round out the Brigand contingent. She chose Wilder. The others would monitor the operation from the command center via body cams.

"You guys watch your backs," Yeun said firmly, his voice edged with concern.

"Remember those new moves I showed you," Zion added. "Case things go south."

"I'm putting her in your hands, paisano," Luz said to Wilder, not thrilled he was going instead of her.

"You mean that, like figuratively, right?" Wilder asked. "Cuz otherwise..."

Luz rolled her eyes. "Dork. Just keep her safe, okay?"

"Or else!" Barnaby threw in, adding the most menacing look he could muster.

Bonnie adjusted her pack, taking in the room. The Brigands' camaraderie lifted her spirits, but her gaze fixed on Reed. He stood in a corner with Cordial, deep in hushed conversation. There was something in their body language that struck Bonnie as odd.

Noticing the pair, Wilder yelled across the room. "Hey! Ballister! Hate to cut your little prom-posal short, but we got shit to do."

Reed shot Cordial a quick glance before hurrying over. The look between them seemed to hold more meaning than Bonnie cared for, but she pushed the thought aside—there were bigger things to focus on.

They stepped into the hallway, where Donovan was waiting. Falling in behind him, they made their way through the compound to a water cave that housed their fleet of boats. A speedboat was tied to the dock, Brigid already on board. Bonnie hurried over to join her mother, with Wilder close behind.

"You don't look too happy about this, Mr. Donovan," Reed said as they watched Bonnie boarding the boat.

Donovan shot him a look. "What I think about this... has no bearing on the matter."

"That makes two of us," Reed said, and he double-timed it to catch up to the others as the boat's outboard engine revved to life, piercing the early morning silence.

*   *   *   *   *

As the sun dipped behind the rolling Irish hills, a fog settled over the valleys, fracturing the light into a thousand golden rays. But the beauty of her surroundings was lost on Bonnie. Hidden near the train tracks, she was hyperfocused on the freight train that emerged from the mist, its rhythmic clattering echoing through the twilight. She was about to join the FF on an actual train heist, like something out of a Western movie. The train seemed ordinary enough—hauling sand, construction materials, and other industrial supplies—but it held a secret cargo that they were here to intercept. Bonnie couldn't shake the weight of the moment. This wasn't just another mission; it was Bonnie's first direct action against Calico Jack Rackham and her first chance to prove herself—not just as a fighter, but as Brigid Byrne's daughter.

The rest of the team was already in position. The three Arenado brothers, Mikael, David, and Brayan, were the best fighters in the FF and were on hand in case of any trouble. Finn, an enthusiastic Irishman, and Marcus, a munitions expert from British Columbia, managed logistics. And Donovan, who would have normally run the operation, served as Brigid's second-in-command.

Clad in black leather with her hair tied back in a practical ponytail, Brigid blended seamlessly with the shadows as she assumed command of the strike force. She peered through binoculars and surveyed the countryside from a hidden vantage point near the tracks. She lowered the binoculars and handed them to Bonnie.

Bonnie took the field glasses from Brigid. Her heart raced with anticipation; her mind filled with the stories she'd already heard of her mother's past exploits. This was her first real taste of the life her mother led, and it was exhilarating. She peered through the binoculars and replayed Brigid's instructions in her mind.

When the train passed under the bridge upon which they now stood, they were to jump into the third freight car. According to Brigid's intelligence, it would be an open-topped hopper container hauling a shipment of sand. The sand would cushion their fall and muffle the sound of bodies hitting a train speeding at 50 miles an hour.

Once aboard, they would crawl across the tops of the rail carriages to the eighth freight car—the actual target. That car contained crates of military-grade weapons, all purchased legally by Calico Jack through a shell corporation cheekily named Black Flag Holdings, LLC. The guns were smuggled into Ireland under the cover of night, bypassing direct routes that might attract attention.

From there, it only took a couple of well-placed bribes to get the crates moved by rail to the port town of Waterford, where they would be readied for transport and sale to the highest bidder. This stopover in Ireland was just enough misdirection to buy the weapons safe passage, and very few questions.

As the train approached, the team sprang into action. Timing was critical. Brigid gave the signal, and they moved into position swiftly.

"Jump the moment the coupler between the second and third car reaches the bridge," Donovan said, his voice clipped. "One second too early or late, and you're done."

The train was in full view now as it rattled across the dusky landscape.

"We go on my signal," Brigid whispered.

Bonnie took a breath. With her eyes still on the approaching train and the task before them, Brigid said, "You've got this. It's in your blood."

"How 'bout you?" Reed asked Wilder. "You ready for this?"

"Why wouldn't I be?" Wilder answered. "Let's go—it's pillaging time!"

"Now!" Brigid hoarsely whispered and disappeared over the side of the bridge, followed quickly by Finn, Marcus, and the three Arenados.

"Hurry!" Brigid yelled at her unseen companions.

Bonnie stepped off the bridge.

PLOP!

She felt her body knifing through the loose sand until she was buried to the waist. To her left, she spotted Reed, already upright, having barrel rolled on impact.

But where was Wilder?

Bonnie scrambled out of the sand, her eyes darting around in panic. That's when she saw him—dangling off the back edge of the railcar, fingers slipping. Donovan was dangling there as well, leaning out dangerously, trying to shove Wilder back up into the hopper. Bonnie and Reed lunged, grabbing Wilder's arms and hauling him aboard. Donovan followed, breathing hard.

Wilder sat atop the sand, panting. "Thanks for the shove, man. I don't know what happened."

"You almost got us killed is what happened!" Donovan growled before storming past them toward the end of the car.

The young Brigands exchanged a look, realizing how close Wilder had come to oblivion.

At that very moment on Crag Inish, Cordial Grace stood nervously at the base of an ancient spiral staircase. The steps, hidden in an out-of-the way alcove within the druid priest Aglain's private chambers, looked as though they'd been carved into the rock millennia ago. The drafty space was cold, the damp air wrapping around her like a burial shroud. She craned her neck, staring up at the stone steps that twisted into darkness, vanishing into the open air. A sliver of moonlight shone far above. With every step, she was trying to muster the courage to continue to the top.

The plan Reed had shared with her prior to leaving on the mission was simple—at least in theory. They'd agreed that Brigid's confidante Aglain was the key to discovering whatever secrets the FF might still be withholding. Once Brigid was off the island, Cordial would mentally "tag along" with him, keeping her psychic presence just far enough behind his conscious mind to avoid detection.

She was confident in her part of the plan, having already blocked Aglain's magic during their first encounter, shielding her mind from his probing. She would just flip the script, slipping into his consciousness instead.

And it had worked—mostly. Aglain sensed something, an itch at the edge of his awareness, but it was too vague to pinpoint. Cordial delighted in the power play, smiling to herself as she wove through the corners of his mind while standing at the back of the command center, feigning interest in watching the video feed of the mission. The rush of control was both unsettling and exhilarating.

In her probing, she uncovered the location of his chambers and caught glimpses of his faith—an altar and what appeared to be animal sacrifices. As a Christian and vegan, she found the whole thing repugnant. Everything about this man's ancient faith felt vile to her. Cordial would have completed her mission remotely, but to her surprise the old guy had a pretty good psychic firewall going himself. She should have known, given that their previous divinations at the Barony had been thwarted. To gain anything meaningful, she realized she'd have to do what she dreaded most—put herself in proximity to the pole star of his power. And that meant *physically* trespassing onto his own personal turf.

So, Cordial had waited until she was certain Aglain was asleep. With the remaining Brigands still glued to the mission feed, no one noticed her slip away. Moving silently, she had made her way to the priest's chambers.

Entering the room, she came face to face with the ancient world. Animal horns, herbs, and strange vessels filled the space, lit only by flickering candles. It reminded Cordial of her mother's prayer room, lacking anything modern. The place was old beyond reckoning, and she felt a shiver of unease.

Loud snoring confirmed Aglain's location in an adjoining chamber. Steeling herself, she tiptoed past the noise and moved toward an archway in the rock, drawn by a pull of immense energy coming from there. She had no love for this strange religion, but she could not deny its power.

Now, here she was, standing at the base of the stairs. Cordial forced herself to focus on the halo surrounding the moon at the top—a shimmering ring of light. She had been taught by her mother that this ring symbolized feminine energy and good luck. A few months ago, she would've scoffed—as she did at most of what Zenobia said—but now she clung to the omen, letting it fill her with the courage she needed.

Sister Moon, see me through, she thought.

Cordial's chest tightened as she placed one foot on the first step. The ancient rock was cold and slick beneath her fingers as she steadied herself against the wall. She climbed slowly, her breath coming in shallow gasps that fogged in the frigid air. The steps were worn and uneven.

She hadn't expected to feel this much responsibility. Back at Hamhock Barony, her life had revolved around petty arguments and minor rebellions—tantrums born out of pure petulance. Compared to this, it all felt so small. The Brigands had shown her what it meant to fight for something greater than herself. And now, she was on a mission that could tip the scales of the entire conflict. She cringed, embarrassed by her past behavior. But there was no time to wallow. Cordial's pulse thrummed in her ears as she climbed toward the sky.

Meanwhile, the railway mission was on to the next phase of its operation. On Brigid's signal, the group leapt from car to car until they reached their target—the eighth freight car. Finn and Marcus quickly pried open the car's ventilation hatch with a crowbar. One by one, the team dropped through the open hatch, landing silently on the floor below. Inside, they found the payload. Stacks of wooden crates! Donovan pried one crate open to reveal a stash of DSR-1 precision sniper rifles. Donovan nodded to Brigid.

A strip of frontage road just beyond the next town ran parallel to the train tracks for about three miles. That bought the FF enough time to offload the crates onto a sideboard truck running along that patch of road. The driver of the truck, a tough-looking young Argentinian named Delfina, would have to match the speed of the train as those on board got to work—a feat requiring precision and coordination.

Marcus slid open the freight car door and gave Delfina a thumbs-up. Two FF on the truck bed sprang up, ready to accept the crates. Back on the train, Bonnie could feel the wind whipping through her hair as Brigid signaled her team to form a human chain.

The crew had to work in pairs to move the heavy crates. Reed and Donovan were at the start of the chain. They would pick up the crates and hand them off to Finn and Wilder, who would then pass them forward. For the final link in the chain, Brigid had insisted that Bonnie work directly beside her at the door.

With the Arenados standing guard, Bonnie positioned herself near the door, and the chain started to move. Even with Brigid strong and confident on the other side of the box, Bonnie could feel the weight of the first crate straining her muscles as she took her end from Wilder. But soon Bonnie's Cove training kicked in, and she managed the box into the outstretched hands of the FF on the truck.

And so it went, crate after crate. Each successful handoff felt like a small victory. And with a dash of adrenaline, the boxes were soon flowing onto the truck.

The truck bed quickly filled, the heavy crates jostling slightly as they were stacked. Delfina maintained a steady pace, her focus unwavering. They were making good time, but they knew they couldn't afford any mistakes.

When the last crate was handed over, the truck peeled off the frontage road and disappeared into the darkness with the stolen cargo.

But before anyone could celebrate, the train jolted violently, throwing Bonnie into the side of the car. A deafening metallic groan echoed as the brakes screeched, and for a moment, panic surged.

"What was that?" Wilder whispered.

Brigid held up a hand for silence, unholstering her pistol.

Bonnie looked nervously at Reed and Wilder. Had they been discovered?

Brigid motioned for the team to stay alert and stared into the darkness beyond the open door. But after a tense moment, the train shuddered back to life and continued down the tracks—oblivious to the audacious robbery that had just taken place.

Brigid signaled for the team to disembark. As the train slowed around a bend, they jumped one by one out the open door, rolling as they hit the ground. Bonnie landed beside Brigid in the wet grass, a wide grin spreading across her face. Even in the darkness, Bonnie could make out the subtle nod of approval from her mother.

They had done it.

Back on Crag Inish, Cordial neared the top of the spiral staircase, her precarious ascent nearly complete. She could feel the waves of magic strengthen the higher she got, brushing over her like an invisible tide. Palms slick with sweat and legs aching, she took another step. Her foot slipped and she let out a small sound—then froze.

Footsteps!

Cordial pressed herself into a shadowy recess as the sound echoed below. Daring to peer down, she saw a face lit by candlelight—it was Aglain.

The priest held up his lantern, but its light fell far short of where she'd plastered herself against the wall. Aglain stood very still, as if contemplating something. Cordial held her breath. Then, just as suddenly as he appeared, the priest turned and left. She was safe!

It took her several minutes and the sound of steady snoring before she regained the nerve to continue. When she finally reached the top, she hurried through the opening and stumbled onto a spongy bed of moss. She looked up in wonder.

The wind hit her first, a sharp gust that carried the tang of salt and the scent of damp earth. Around her, towering black rocks jutted into the sky. She had seen these towering rocks when the FF brought them in; they were the highest spot on the island. She would never have guessed that hidden in their midst was a large stone altar. Cordial recognized it immediately—the very place she'd seen during her earlier probe of the priest's psyche. This place radiated magic. Old magic. Older than Gullah magic. Maybe even older than time itself.

As Cordial approached the altar, her skin felt electrified—like negative ions during a thunderstorm. The stone altar top was stained from years of use. Her stomach twisted as she considered the source of the stains, but she forced herself forward—a high-pitched whistling sound rising in her ears as she did. The items atop the altar seemed to pulse with energy. Runes, a chalice, a stone box containing a symbol book of shadows, several sticks carved into wand-like shapes, a stone dagger. Bones—animal, she prayed—were strewn about on the altar and at her feet. Her fingers hovered over the artifacts, the air around them alive with the static charge.

Yes. This was the place. This was Aglain's pole star.

Before she could second-guess herself, she closed her eyes and gripped the altar with both hands.

And the world shifted!

Everything began to spin, and Cordial felt like she was falling. It was all she could do not to heave up her dinner.

Then came FLASHES OF IMAGES. Completely unfettered. Thousands, hurtling at her in rapid succession. Like a history of Celtic magic:

Herbs. Potions. Bare feet running through thick woods. A circle of people in white robes holding candles. Runes thrown across a wooden surface. A woman's hand plunges a dagger into a rabbit's still beating heart. Blood dripping onto stone, pooling into ancient grooves. A giant wicker effigy engulfed in flames, the screams of its occupant piercing the night.

Then, the images changed—now visions from the divination back in Hamhock. This time, they were clearer, more revealing:

Jungle foliage ignited by a blowtorch in Brigid's hands! A mine echoing with gunfire as Brigid sprays a barrage of bullets into the darkness! A tunnel collapsing, silencing the screams of the innocent! Finally, a handsome, gray-eyed man—Keane—running across the deck of a ship. Brigid on a waiting speedboat. Keane gets to the edge, starts to go over, but Brigid cuts the rope free before he reaches it! They lock eyes, the look of betrayal when he realizes what she has done. As she speeds away, the ship explodes. Then from the flames, Aglain appears, standing over Cordial. Peering into her face.

"Ahh!" Cordial gasped, ripped back to the present. She blinked, realizing she was now lying on the slab, body prone to the heavens, as if she were the next sacrificial offering. She snatched the stone dagger and leapt from the altar, ready to fight.

But Aglain was not there. She was alone, except for the haloed moon still watching over her. She gave it a nod of gratitude before she carefully returned the dagger to the altar and headed back down the staircase.

This time, Cordial descended quickly, fear overriding caution. As she crept past the priest's bedchamber, she saw him through the door crack, lying on his bed—his back to her, his breathing steady and slow.

The others need to know, she thought as she rushed from the room.

Behind her, Aglain's eyes opened, glinting in the darkness.

Chapter 39
The Debate

The mission team regrouped at its predetermined location: a secluded farm owned by an FF sympathizer. When those from the train arrived, the others were already hard at work in the barn, loading the crates of guns onto large trucks labeled "Emerald Appliances."

As the loading neared completion, the cold bit at their faces. Bonnie stood with Reed and Wilder, the thrill of the heist still buzzing in her veins. The operation had been seamless—well, except for Wilder nearly getting killed—and she'd played a vital part. A big grin tugged at her lips.

Brigid's eyes sparkled with exhilaration as she approached them. "So?" she asked. "What did you think?"

Bonnie let her grin widen. "It felt... important!"

"You did well tonight, Bonnie. You all did. I'm proud of you. You've got the makings of great FF soldiers."

Bonnie felt warmth swell in her chest. She eyed her mother, her voice steady and proud. "Thank you."

"Well, you know, I hate to brag, but we *were* kind of born into it," Wilder joked.

Brigid turned her attention to the captain of the Brigands. "Reed? You're rather quiet."

"What happens with the guns?" Reed asked, arms folded.

Brigid's expression shifted. "We'll keep some. Sell the rest to some mercenaries in Yemen."

The barn fell into a heavy silence. Bonnie looked at Reed, then back at her mother, unsure if she'd heard correctly. But she didn't want to question her. Not after the inroads they'd made today.

"Wasn't that basically what Jack was going to do with them?" Reed asked.

Brigid's tone cooled. "Except now it's us who make the profit off them."

"I thought the point was that we were stopping them from reaching like terrorists and such," Wilder said.

Brigid sighed impatiently, her tone measured as if speaking to a small child. "No. The point is stopping *Jack* from profiting. We sell the guns, then use the money to fund our fight against him. It's called strategy."

"So you're just another group profiting from trafficking weapons," Reed said.

"It's not about profit. It's about survival. We can't fight Jack empty-handed. Where do you think the money comes from to finance that operation you saw back on Crag Inish?"

"Brigid! Need your okay on this!" it was Donovan.

Brigid's eyes flitted to the delivery trucks where Donovan stood with the other FF, then she returned her gaze to Bonnie.

"It's time you all grew up and see the world for what it is," she said. "And part of that is getting your hands dirty once in a while. I can't tell you what to do, Bonnie, but if you're interested, we've got another mission coming up—one that will cripple Jack's operations. I'd love for you to be there with me. Or you could go home and wait to die." She shot Reed a withering look and walked away.

Wilder sidled up beside Bonnie, his usual grin replaced by a rare seriousness. "Welcome to the FF, Curls. Gray's your new favorite color."

*   *   *   *   *

As the *Perdition* continued its long trip across the Atlantic, Calico Jack Rackham stewed in his private chamber. He had just received the news of the weapons heist in Ireland. And in his anger, he gave the order to "permanently punish" those who'd let it happen.

"And send the surveillance video!" he commanded.

"The Féth Fíada yet again?" Salifu asked. He hovered behind Calico Jack as the pirate contemplated the latest loss at the hands of the FF.

"And yet again, you failed to warn me," Jack said, still squeezing the phone tightly.

Salifu's eyes darkened, something ancient flickering in their depths. "My powers are not on a leash, Jack Rackham. You want clarity? You must stop stumbling in shadows."

"I don't even know what that means!" Rackham objected. "Stop speaking in riddles!"

BEEP!

Jack looked down at his phone. A video file had arrived as an encrypted message—security footage from a hidden camera inside the freight car. He pushed the play button. Jack's chest tightened as the figures emerged on the screen.

"It's her!" Jack said in shock.

The edges of the video flickered, but there was no mistaking who it was—Brigid Byrne. She'd been a thorn in his side for a decade, and now here she was. A low growl rumbled in his throat.

"What's drawn her into the open?" he murmured.

"There's your answer." Salifu pointed to the video. "It appears you have a mutual draw."

Another figure crossed in front of the camera. Rackham stopped the video, jumped it back five seconds, and then played it again, freezing on the image of a second woman.

Bonnie Hartwright! Jack felt a surge of excitement. The two stained ones together! Just as he had hoped. *Planned.* The girl had rooted out her mother.

"Stupid sow," Jack laughed.

"The tides of emotion, if not carefully navigated, can capsize the ship," Salifu observed.

"I'll have that embroidered on a throw pillow," Jack scoffed at the shaman's veiled warning. Jack stared at the screen, the corner of his mouth twitching. He sensed a vibration on his hand and looked down to see the sands in his hourglass ring swirl in excitement. Jack felt the ring pulse hotly against his skin, a steady rhythm, alive and demanding.

He pushed the intercom button on his desk that connected him to the bridge.

"Redouble security on all operations!" he commanded, not even listening to the response that crackled over the speakers.

He hit PLAY again to rewatch the video. Jack leaned back, the leather of the armrest on his chair creaking under his grip.

"Turns out to be a glorious day after all," he murmured.

*　*　*　*　*

Bonnie's head was still buzzing when they returned to Crag Inish. Not only had she successfully worked her first mission with her mother, she had done so well that Brigid had asked her to join on another, even bigger one. Yes, there was the somewhat morally murky matter of what would become of the purloined guns, but by the time Bonnie got back to the island, she'd managed to rationalize that into oblivion. In fact, by the time they returned, Bonnie was feeling downright euphoric. She'd connected with her mom in a way that Reed and Wilder could never understand or appreciate. And if a few rifles had to go to terrorists in Yemen for that to happen, well, so be it.

It all came crashing down when she found out what Cordial had been up to while they were gone. And on Reed's instructions! Every inroad she'd made with her mother was suddenly at risk of collapsing.

"I cannot believe you had her spying for you!" Bonnie confronted Reed as everyone else silently watched.

"For us," Reed corrected.

"Us?" Bonnie spit the word back at him like it was poison in her mouth. "This could ruin everything. Brigid was finally starting to trust us."

"You mean you. Trust you. That's what you really care about."

"Bonnie, I'm telling you," Cordial interrupted, "all that violence we saw during the conjuring back home—that we couldn't make sense of at the time? It's this group. And your mom's behind it."

"What'd you think all that hardware in the armory is for?? Jesus! You don't think Anne Bonny and Mary Read did some bad shit back in the day? Maybe you're forgetting we're goddamn pirates!"

"But guerilla attacks? Bombings?" Reed was horrified by what Cordial had reported.

"What do you want her to do, take Calico Jack to court? Give him due process? You're forgetting who the bad guy is here. The FF, Brigid, may have to resort to some radical stuff every once in a while, but they're doing a public service—trying to prevent the apocalypse!"

"I don't think trafficking weapons is a public service," Daya said. "Just sayin'."

"Yeah. It *would* have been nice to have been given a heads up," Wilder offered. "I'm not sure gun running is something I was planning to put on my resume."

"Bonnie. There's something else." Cordial took a breath. "I think she killed that guy Keane... so she could take over."

"T-that's insane!" Bonnie stammered. "Brigid loved Keane—I don't know what you think you saw, but you are wrong!"

"I know you really wanted this with your mom to work out. But, Bonnie, this kind of stuff—it's not who we are," Reed said, shaking his head.

"Stop saying that! I'm sick of you saying that! You don't know who I am! Hell, I didn't even know until recently!"

Bonnie was raging now. "For 16 years, I've tried to play the game, and what has it ever gotten me? Kicked in the teeth, that's what! And now that I know what this goddam mark means, the rules have changed. And I have the right to change with them! To do what I have to do to survive!"

Bonnie got quiet for a second, then said. "Maybe I'm just finally who I was always meant to be."

"So. What?" Reed asked. "You gonna leave the Brigands? Throw in with the FF?"

"Yes. I am. And you all should, too. We can do something here. I don't want to hide out my whole life, like Ned. And I don't want to chase phantoms. That got your parents killed. And for what?"

"To keep you safe!" Reed said angrily.

"Well, honestly I feel safer here than the Brigands ever made me feel."

Hurt looks all around. Bonnie had said the one thing that cut deep.

"Shit, Bonnie," Tanner muttered. "That's harsh. We *all* sacrificed for you."

Murmurs of agreement.

"You're making a mistake."

Everyone turned. It was Barnaby Chisolm.

"I've kept my mouth shut this whole time cuz I know I'm not the leader, or even *a* leader. But I've been around the Brigands my whole life. Like Reed. And he's right. It's not what this group was created for. And it's not what we were sworn to do. I'll lay my life down for you, Bonnie. Cuz I believe in the cause. And, cuz you're my friend. But this other stuff... I won't do it. And you shouldn't do it either. It's wrong."

Bonnie saw the hurt in Barnaby's eyes. They had been close once. But, as with everyone else, she had driven a wedge between them. Pushed him away. It almost made her pause. Almost.

"I'm sorry, Barnaby," she said. "But this is my life. I gotta start doing what's right for me."

"Well, I won't allow it," Reed said.

"Excuse me?"

"You're a Brigand, as you've constantly reminded us. You swore an oath that puts you under my command. And I command you not to do it."

"Are you actually trying to pull rank on me, Reed Ballister? Well, I'm a marked one too. And marked trumps Brigand."

"I'll stop you."

"You can't."

"Try me. I'll do whatever I have to do to see that this does not happen."

A stunned silence fell over the room. The Brigands exchanged uneasy glances.

Bonnie's glare was ice cold. Then, without another word, she turned on her heels and stormed out.

Chapter 40
(Be) Longing

Reed Ballister paced behind bars, caged in the brig of the compound. In the cell next to his sat Cordial Grace, unmoving.

"Brigid says it's just till the mission is over," Bonnie, on the other side of the bars, tried to assure them. "We just want to make sure you don't try to interfere."

"Wow." Reed shook his head. "I never thought you'd stab me in the back like this."

"I know you don't see it now, but this is for your own good," she said.

"Don't pretend you're thinking of anyone but yourself right now."

Bonnie didn't try to deny it. She knew it would sound hollow if she did, even to her.

"It didn't have to be this way," was all she said.

"No. It didn't."

They just stared into each other's eyes, both full of regret and loss and anger.

"We'll talk about it when we get back." And she walked out.

"There's nothing left to talk about!" he shouted after her and slammed his hand against the bars. "Goddammit! I cannot believe she screwed us over like this!"

Cordial approached him. "You know, Reed, the first time I met you I felt a really strong connection to you—'the pull', my mama calls it. I guess it's cuz I sensed the pressure you felt from your family, from your whole heritage thing, cuz I feel it too. I know what it's like not wanting to disappoint your family, but at the same time resenting the hell out of them for their expectations. I knew you got that about me."

Reed was still fuming. "And that is relevant how exactly?"

"Don't you think maybe Bonnie's feeling that same pressure with her mom?"

"Are you making excuses for her? After the way she's treated you?"

"Not even close," Cordial said. "She's lucky these bars are here, or I'd have slapped her upside the head myself. But it's complicated. She's only starting to get what it's like to be crushed by expectations—by a legacy she didn't choose. The difference is that you and me, we know, no matter how much we screw up, our families will still love us. She doesn't have that. For her, Brigid's little scraps of approval might be the closest thing to love she's ever had."

Reed stared at her, his anger dimming slightly. "That's... surprisingly wise."

Cordial grinned. "Don't get used to it. This wisdom thing is brand-new—like," she checked an imaginary watch on her wrist, "thirty seconds ago."

"So I have to be okay with Bonnie joining her mom?"

"Oh, hell no. Her moms is batshit crazy and this place is about a thousand kinds of wrong. You just need to be a little more understanding while we figure out a way to stop her. Fast."

.   .   .   .   .

The next few days were some of the hardest of Bonnie's life—and that was saying a lot. Her blowout with Reed had left her feeling raw, and the fact that she'd turned him in had driven a wedge between her and the other Brigands. Most, like Micah, Yeun, and Zion, just avoided her, refusing to speak with her and shooting her looks that could wound a rhino. Tanner was more open with his anger, returning to the habit of hurling nasty insults. Even Malachi, to whom emotion did not come easily, showed his disapproval by glaring at her. Which was quite something for a guy who wasn't much on eye contact.

But Barnaby's reaction was the hardest to bear. He just went around looking hurt. Like she had personally betrayed him. And when she tried to speak to him. He behaved as if she didn't exist. Maybe she didn't anymore. Not the Bonnie she used to be, anyway. And yet, she resented him for it, resented all of them. Why was she the one being treated like the villain? They were the ones asking her to choose between loyalty and safety. Between passivity and resistance. Between them and her mother. How could they not see how selfish that was?

Only Luz and Wilder stood by Bonnie and agreed to accompany her on the new mission. Bonnie knew it wasn't because they sided with the FF. In fact, she was pretty sure they didn't. But Luz, still haunted by her failure to keep her younger brother safe, was motivated by her protective instinct, her need to shield Bonnie from harm. And Wilder, well, he was Wilder. He would follow her into a fire. He literally had.

Deep down, Bonnie knew she should let them both off the hook. That she should go on the mission alone. In fact, Daya begged her to tell Luz not to go. But she wouldn't do it. It felt like a victory that they were sticking by her—something she could rub in Reed Ballister's face. The fact that she was now foraging around for things to rub in Reed's face just a few weeks after they'd nearly kissed was proof that the earth had indeed shifted beneath their feet.

But Bonnie didn't have time to dwell on the rift within the Brigands. For the next few days, she, Luz, and Wilder were occupied with morning-to-night training sessions. Donovan and his team laid out the mission: the *Malthus*, a medium-sized cargo ship allied with Calico Jack, was heading across the Atlantic en route to Morocco. Aboard the ship were containers of illegal cargo—pure cocaine, coming from Rackham's operations in South America. Tons of the stuff, hidden in the false bottoms of freezer containers bearing tuna and branzino. It would come ashore in Morocco, be divvied up into smaller portions, and then smuggled into Europe on pleasure craft. Bonnie was relieved to learn that the plan would *not* be for the FF to sell the drugs themselves. Instead, they would board the ship and sink it, sending half a billion dollars' worth of cocaine to the bottom of the ocean.

As Bonnie listened to the briefing, she stared at Wilder and Luz in disbelief. Brigid hadn't been joking when she said they had a chance to strike a serious blow to Rackham's empire. This was big. Enormous. And Bonnie was along for the ride.

*   *   *   *   *

Bonnie stopped short when she saw it lying on her bunk—the black leather uniform of the FF. Her mother must have left it there while she was on her final day of training. Overcome with emotion, she picked it up. It wasn't the airy white dress Grandma Winnie had made for her the previous summer. No. This was something completely different. This was proof she had demonstrated her worth to her mother.

She wanted to see herself, but there was no mirror in the bunk room. So she walked over to the stainless-steel door that led to the hallway and took in her blurry reflection. What she saw looking

RUNKLE & WEBB 291

back at her was a fierce warrior. An honest to goodness member of the FF. For the first time since Bobby Maynard's death, she felt empowered.

Eyeing her image steadily, Bonnie felt a sense of pride, belonging, and most of all... destiny.

*   *   *   *   *

The gathered members of the Féth Fíada stood in tense silence as they waited for Brigid to step onto the stage of the underground amphitheater on the lowest level of the compound. A giant FF emblem—the familiar snakes and swords—hung on the wall at the center of the stage. The air was heavy with the scent of sweat, ammonium nitrate, and anticipation. Everyone knew the stakes—most especially Bonnie, who took her place among the strike team assembled for the mission. She was flanked by Wilder and Luz, who were also dressed in sleek FF uniforms.

The Brigands who hadn't volunteered to go sat glumly on their cots back in their barracks, waiting for Brigid's message to be broadcast over loudspeakers throughout the compound. They had sided with Reed and now that their captain was behind bars, they were confined to quarters.

Aglain stepped forward and led the assembly in a prayer for the mission's success.

Grant, O Spirit Thy Protection;
And in protection, strength;
And in strength, understanding;
And in understanding, knowledge;
And in knowledge...

Watching in the wings, just out of view of the gathering, was Brigid. As Aglain continued the prayer, she betrayed no emotion.

"It's not too late." It was the voice of Donovan, standing next to her.

"Don't start," she said, not taking her eyes off the crowd.

Donovan didn't listen. "I've got three trained men briefed and ready to take the place of those children. Brigid. They're just not ready."

"If I say they are ready, they are ready," Brigid said with purpose. "Besides. When have you ever known me not to show good judgment?"

"You've never had a daughter around to cloud it."

Donovan's words hung in the air like a challenge. Brigid's eyes flashed in anger at her perceived "softness."

"This has nothing to do with her being my daughter and everything to do with making sure that filthy pirate never gets her years. As long as I have her in my control, he doesn't. That, Mr. Donovan, is my priority!"

Brigid's tone brooked no argument, but Donovan plowed on. "I just think we're moving too quickly. There's simply too much at stake—"

Brigid's eyes locked on Donovan, her gaze sharp enough to cut leather. "You confuse me with someone who seeks your validation or approval," she said pointedly. "I require neither. Don't make that mistake again."

She turned away from Donovan and strode with confidence onto the stage, leaving her second-in-command to watch from the wings.

Silence filled the space as Brigid walked to the center of the platform and stepped forward to a microphone stand. She took a breath, letting the moment stretch just long enough to build the anticipation.

"Look around you," she began, her voice clear and commanding. "Each face here represents a choice—a choice to fight for something bigger than ourselves. We are not just a band of mercenaries. We are humanity's last line of defense against Calico Jack Rackham's tyranny, greed, and oppression."

Inside the barracks, the loudspeaker crackled to life, and the Brigands rose to their feet as Brigid's words bounced off the walls. In the compound's brig, a guard hushed Reed and Cordial so he could hear the words of his leader.

"Jack believes he can hoard power, steal lives, and leave nothing but ashes in his wake. He thrives on chaos, on fear, and on division. But we are united. The Féth Fíada and the Brigands of the Compass Rose."

Back in the amphitheater, Brigid was in total command. Her gaze swept over the room, locking onto individuals—a nod to Wilder, a glance at Luz, a brief pause on Bonnie. As Brigid's eyes met hers, Bonnie swelled with pride.

"We are finally joined by our shared commitment to this just cause. And that is what makes us unstoppable. Rackham fights for himself, for his vanity, and for his own survival. We fight for each other, for the memory of those who went before us, and for the world that could be. A world without him."

She stepped closer to the edge of the platform, her intensity drawing the group forward, spellbound.

"This day, we strike not for revenge, but for justice. For every child he's orphaned. For every life he's stolen. For every dream he's crushed under his boots. This mission isn't just about dismantling his operation or cutting off his resources. It's about showing him that we will not bow, we will not break, and we will not disappear quietly into the night!"

APPLAUSE AND HOOTS OF APPROVAL!

Back in the barracks, Tanner looked at Barnaby as the sound rattled the speaker. "Damn, she's good."

Barnaby nodded tensely. "That's what's so scary."

"There will be danger," Brigid continued. "There will be sacrifice. Some of us may not come back, and that's the hard truth of what we do."

She pointed toward the exits, where the mission lay waiting, but her eyes were fixed on her daughter.

"So steel yourselves. Carry each other when the weight becomes too much. And let's remind Jack why the Féth Fíada is his living nightmare."

She paused, letting the room buzz with energy before delivering her final words:

"For freedom. For each other. For victory. Let's send Jack Rackham one step closer to Hell!"

The room erupted in cheers, cheers that reverberated in Bonnie's chest. With her mother at her side, she was about to strike a debilitating blow to the man who had destroyed her childhood and robbed her of her father.

She was finally going to do what she had been aching to do for months, what she had promised her father at his graveside.

She was going to make Calico Jack Rackham pay.

Chapter 41
The Malthus

The small "fishing" boat, the *Spridiúil*, cruised across the choppy waters of the North Atlantic, near the Moroccan coastline. The hum of the engines echoed in the cabin as FF members moved about, preparing for the mission ahead. In the galley of the boat, Brigid sat at a small table, scattered with maps and plans. Bonnie, Wilder, and Luz huddled around her. It had been a three-hour plane flight to the Portuguese port city of Albufeira. Then, a quick shuttle to the marina, where the *Spridiúil* was waiting.

Brigid reminded the team of the mission: the plan was to intercept the *Malthus* in international waters and sink it, crippling Jack's operation for months and costing him hundreds of millions in lost revenue. With help from FF operatives on the vessel, they would bypass night patrols, disable communications, and disorient the crew during the shift change. This coordinated strike would create enough chaos on board to get their sympathizers off the ship safely.

"Chaos is my middle name," Wilder said with a nervous grin. "Well, actually it's Anthony, but still..."

Brigid pointed to the map, her finger tracing the layout of the ship. "Just like we covered in the briefing, we'll split into two teams once we're inside. Bonnie, you, Wilder, and I will disable the bilge pumps. That'll prevent the ship from getting rid of any water it takes on once we breach the hull. Luz, you'll work with Donovan and Marcus to set the explosives."

"Still don't like it," Luz grumbled. "My job is to protect Bonnie."

"Your job has changed. You're FF now," Brigid said matter-of-factly.

"It's fine, Luz," Bonnie said, trying to reassure her fellow Brigand. "I'll be okay."

Luz clearly disagreed but nodded her assent.

Donovan joined them at the table, handing Bonnie and Wilder each a pistol and placing a semi-automatic rifle in front of Luz. "You know how to use this, right?"

Luz glared at him and picked up the rifle. "First, I remove the magazine by pressing the release right here. Then, I check the chamber like so. Next, I lock the bolt open using the catch on the left. Once I've loaded the magazine, I slide it in until it clicks, then give it a tug to make sure it's seated. Finally, I press the bolt catch to chamber a round. Close enough, champ?"

Donovan raised an eyebrow, impressed.

Luz gave a "what-else-did-you-expect" smile, eyeing the weapon. "The *cholos* back in East L.A. gonna be so jelly."

Brigid looked them over, her gaze sharp. "If anyone tries to stop us, take them out."

"What do you mean 'out'?" Wilder asked.

"I mean *out*," Brigid replied. "If Jack's mercenaries get wind we're on board, it'll be you or them. They won't hesitate. Neither should you."

The three Brigands exchanged glances. They could feel the mission's gravity settling in.

"As Wendell would say, I'm locked and loaded!" Luz's voice was full of resolve.

Brigid gave a curt nod.

Bonnie took a deep breath, her nerves tightening.

Brigid met her eyes. "Bonnie, we'll have to move fast. The bilge pumps are key to getting this ship down quick. It's a tight time window, but if we all stick to the plan, we can pull it off."

Donovan's eyes lingered on Brigid in a way that made Bonnie uncomfortable. She knew the Brigands were on the mission over his objection, and he wasn't exactly hiding his contempt for their presence.

"What about the crew?" Wilder asked. "What happens to them?"

Brigid's tone grew serious. "They're experienced seamen and there are plenty of lifeboats."

Brigid placed a hand on Bonnie's shoulder. "This is our shot. We take out Jack's source of funding, and we cripple him all across Europe. Just think of how you'll feel when that happens. Hitting Calico Jack Rackham where it *hurts*. I tell you Bonnie, it's a high like no other in the world."

In that moment, Bonnie wanted nothing more. She could almost taste it.

,   ,   ,   ,   ,

As the *Spridiúil* neared its target, the sounds of the engines blended into the night, leaving the crew alone with their thoughts and nerves. The vast darkness of the North Atlantic stretched endlessly around them, but the heavy silence in the boat was far from calm. The tension was palpable.

Once they were close, the engines were cut and Donovan flashed a light toward the *Malthus*. There was a beat, then from the inky darkness, a flash of light in response. Then two more quick flashes—a signal from the FF operatives on the ship.

"We're a go," Donovan said, securing his gear.

Brigid scanned her team. "Alright, you know your roles," she said. "We move quickly, we move quietly. On and off, like ghosts in the mist."

Bonnie's heart raced as they neared Calico Jack's vessel, a hulking mass barely visible against the night sky. But Bonnie felt no fear—only the adrenaline-fueled thrill of striking a blow against Jack's empire. Her finger twitched on the trigger of her pistol.

Silently, the *Spridiúil* sidled up next to the *Malthus*.

SKAT! SKAT! SKAT!

SKITTLE! SKITTLE! SKITTLE!

CHUNK! CHUNK! CHUNK!

On Brigid's call, pneumatically launched grappling hooks flew over the side of the *Malthus* and found purchase on the ship's outer railing. In a flash, the FF team scaled the ropes and boarded the cargo ship. One of their operatives helped them over the edge.

"Sloba," Brigid gave a quick hug to a large Serbian man who had the look of a guy who knew his way around a bar fight. "I knew we could count on you."

"Is not much time," Sloba replied, producing a map of the ship's interior. "You must to put charges below waterline here, here, and here. Before charges go off, we must to hurry for get off ship. Leave one man with me for to watch for guards."

Brayan Arenado stayed with Sloba as Brigid gathered the rest of her crew near the access point that led below deck.

"Follow Donovan's lead," Brigid said to Luz. "Once you're done, rendezvous with us on the second level."

Luz's eyes hardened. "Got it. But if anything goes wrong, you're gonna wish you had me at your side, *gringa*."

Brigid gave Luz a stern look. "If anything goes wrong, you're gonna wish you'd stayed home. Now, let's go!"

Chapter 42
In the Belly of the Beast

The teams moved swiftly, melting into the shadows as they descended deep inside the vessel. Even though they'd memorized the schematics beforehand, the narrow passageways felt claustrophobic. The scale of the ship turned every movement into a potential misstep. But at last, Bonnie's team arrived at its target: the bilge system's control room, nestled in the lowest recess of the hull.

The bilge pumps were the heart of the system, essential for preventing the ship from flooding. With Wilder keeping watch, Brigid and Bonnie got to work.

Bonnie crouched near the access panel, the vibrations from the ship's powerful engines thrumming beneath her feet. She thought of Clint Krokel, her foster father, and the lessons he'd drilled into her about hot-wiring cars. If he could see her now, he'd never believe it. Brigid was right. She would never be who she was if not for what she went through.

The first bilge pump stared at her, its metal casing marked with wear. She pulled out her toolkit and swiftly unscrewed the access panel. Beneath it, the pump's intricate wiring lay exposed— modern, cleanly routed, but vulnerable. Remembering the schematics from her briefing, she severed the main power cable with a pair of insulated wire cutters. A spark arced briefly, then died. She flipped the manual override switch, ensuring the pump couldn't be remotely reactivated. Satisfied, she moved on to the next pump.

She found a grim satisfaction in this act of defiance against the old defensive Brigand ways. She remembered the helplessness she'd felt back on the Cove brought on by Captain Ballister's intransigence, and later Reed's inability to mobilize. With each wire she cut, she felt a sense of liberation. Of power. *This* was how you got at Jack Rackham, not by feebly trying to protect marked ones. Bonnie smiled as she rose to her feet. Two pumps down, two to go. This ship's bilge system wouldn't save it tonight.

Down in the cargo compartment, Marcus and the Arenado brothers were busy setting explosives on several refrigerated fish containers that held the drugs.

Donovan was planting his devices on the interior hull.

Luz stood lookout, her gun at the ready.

Back in the bilge control room, Bonnie was working on the final bilge pump when—

Suddenly a noise! Heads whipped around to locate its source.

A man stumbled into the room, his greasy shirt clinging to his large belly. His wide eyes locked onto Bonnie, Brigid, and Wilder. He froze, clutching a wine bottle, his trembling hand barely able to hold it as three guns immediately trained on him.

He stammered something in Portuguese, his voice cracking in terror as his hands shot up. He dropped the wine bottle and took a shaky step backward, his boot squelching against the wine-soaked floor.

"Of all the damn places," Brigid hissed. "Wilder, zip-tie him."

"I dunno," Wilder said. "He looks like he's just one of the crew."

"—who will alert the entire ship if he gets the chance," Brigid snapped. "Take care of it now. Or I will." She pointed her gun at the man.

Wilder quickly stepped between the man and Brigid's weapon. He exchanged a quick look with Bonnie and set to work binding the man. The man whimpered as Wilder pulled his wrists together, the zip-ties locking with a harsh snap. Brigid tossed Wilder a grimy cloth she found nearby and Wilder reluctantly stuffed the rag into the man's mouth. A dark stain spread down the man's pants as Brigid's glare bore into him.

"Keep your eyes on him," Brigid barked at Wilder. "Bonnie, finish up so we can get the hell out of here."

The final bilge pump was in a particularly hard to reach location, and Bonnie struggled to remove the last screw on the access plate. *Just. One. More. Turn. And*—RATTLE!

The screwdriver fell from Bonnie's grasp, bouncing hard off the metal grating beneath it. Wilder's head turned at the noise, and that brief distraction was all the Portuguese sailor needed.

He suddenly sprang to his feet with surprising speed. Wilder lunged, but the man slipped past him, bolting down the corridor with desperate purpose.

"Goddammit! Stop him!" Brigid shouted, her voice cutting through the commotion.

Wilder trained his pistol on the man but just couldn't bring himself to pull the trigger. Brigid took several shots and one hit the man in the back just as he pulled a fire alarm. A DEAFENING BLARE erupted, the klaxon echoing throughout the ship.

Brigid's face twisted with fury as the noise drowned out her curses. The ship was alive with the sound of boots clanking on metal.

"Bloody Hell!" Brigid spat.

Bonnie rushed to the man's aid, but he was dead.

Brigid turned to Wilder. "Go back to the boat—you've done enough damage here!"

"Not without Bonnie."

"Did you not hear me? Get back to the *Spridiúil*. Now!"

"Go," Bonnie insisted. "I'll be right behind you."

He exchanged a concerned glance with Bonnie before turning to leave. He stumbled over his own feet as he went, the weight of his mistake hanging heavily on his mind.

"What's happening?" Donovan's voice crackled through their earpieces.

Brigid's tone was sharp. "Blow the charges and get out!"

Bonnie yanked at the final cables, severing the last pump's power. The bilge system sputtered, then fell silent.

Donovan's team finished their placements. "Move!" he barked.

At the waterline, Marcus detonated the first charge.

BOOM! Fire roared through the cargo hold. The ship lurched. Metal groaned. Chaos erupted!

"Time's up!" Luz shouted. "Let's go!"

Bonnie barely had time to brace as another explosion rocked the hull. Guards were swarming the decks.

Brigid grabbed Bonnie's arm. "Up top. *Now!*"

Fear gripped Bonnie as the ship's list deepened, and the cold reality of their mission hit her. The *Malthus* was sinking beneath them, and if they didn't get out of there fast, they'd be going down with it.

The murky ocean water poured through the breach in the hull. It became a living thing, a giant sea creature that devoured everything in its path. The hull began to buckle from the weight of the deluge. The sound was deafening, a cacophony of destruction that drowned out all else.

The FF teams raced up the stairs, engaging security patrols all along the way. The ship groaned even more loudly as water continued flooding the lower levels. They had to push harder now. The way the charges had been set, the stern of the ship would be the first to go underwater, lifting the bow into the air. And if all went according to plan, the ship would snap in two, sending the drugs to the bottom of the ocean and Jack Rackham back to the drawing board.

Both teams regrouped near the crew bunks, their breaths quickening.

"Bonnie, you okay?" Luz asked.

Bonnie nodded, out of breath.

"Where's Wilder?"

"Back at the boat," she said through gasps.

She hoped she was right.

The sounds of footsteps and shouted orders told them Rackham's mercenaries were closing in. The FF fighters were up to their knees in water now; it wouldn't be long before the ship went down. They reached a junction where the screams of trapped sailors pierced the air.

Bonnie stopped mid-stride, the cries cutting through the alarms, explosions, and rushing water.

"Wait! They need help!" she insisted, her voice filled with desperation.

"There's no time, Bonnie!" Brigid said.

"We can't just leave them!" Bonnie's heart ached at the sound of the sailors' cries. The idea of their drowning was literally taking her breath away.

Brigid grabbed her by the arm. "It's called collateral damage! You're not playing at pirates anymore. This is war. Now move!" Brigid continued up the stairs.

Bonnie looked back, uncertainly.

Luz, her eyes filled with determination, turned to Bonnie. "You go. I got this!" Luz took off running back toward the cries.

For a heartbeat, Bonnie hesitated, her compassion battling her commitment to the mission. Then, she broke the stalemate, turning and sprinting after Luz.

"Bonnie no!" Brigid yelled, quickly losing sight of Bonnie in the smoke and chaos.

"We should have never brought them along!" Donovan snapped at Brigid.

Bonnie caught up to Luz as she started down a metal ladder. "Luz! Wait!"

"I told you I got this!"

"*We* got this," Bonnie said.

The girls' bravery was unwavering. Luz knew Bonnie wouldn't leave the sailors to die, so she knew the best way to save *her* was to save them first. She fought through the rising water, determined to reach the trapped sailors.

Together, Luz and Bonnie managed to pry open cabin doors to free several sailors. None of them seemed to speak English, but they responded well enough to their hand signals as they showed them the way up to the deck and the lifeboats.

The air was thick with smoke, and the roar of oncoming water grew louder with each passing second. They fought through the debris toward the last group of sailors. They were almost there when a LURCH sent them crashing into the corridor walls. Sure enough, as expected, the bow was rising out of the ocean, creating a funhouse of impossible angles. It would be a matter of minutes before the ship snapped in half.

Suddenly, a loud CRASH echoed through the corridor. Bonnie turned just in time to see a section of the ceiling collapse, a steel beam hurtling toward her. She stopped, paralyzed with terror.

OOF! Luz slammed into her, knocking her clear. Bonnie hit the water hard, the impact jarring every bone in her body and completely submerging her in the oncoming torrent.

Flailing and disoriented, Bonnie finally gathered herself and got to her feet, emerging from the nearly chest-high water, coughing. And that's when she saw the horrible truth: Luz's selfless attempt to save her was successful, but in doing so, she'd become trapped along with several sailors—the huge metal beam creating a wall between them and Bonnie.

"Luz!" Bonnie tried to push through the power of the rushing water, but it kept forcing her back, a rising tide that churned with debris and chaos.

When she finally reached her friend, Bonnie struggled to move the debris between them.

"Hold on! I'll get you out!" she shouted, clawing at pieces of wood and furniture with desperate strength, her fingers bleeding as she tried to clear a path. The cold water stung her hands and surged around her abdomen.

"Bonnie, stop!" Luz's voice was firm, even as her face twisted with pain. "You can't do it. It's too much. The water—it's coming too fast!"

"No! I can do it!" Bonnie yelled, still fighting against the rising tide. Bonnie continued moving what she could until all that stood between them was the large beam. She picked up a hunk of twisted metal and used it as a crowbar. She pushed and pushed. She screamed with all that was in her as she tried to budge the beam. But nothing.

"Bonnie. Bonnie! Look at me. Look at me!" Luz said, her face illuminated by the flicker of the emergency lights. The water was up to their necks now.

"You can't do it!" Luz said. Bonnie started to object. "And I don't know if it would even matter. I-I can't feel my legs."

Bonnie's face flashed horror; she took a deep breath and went underwater. And that's when she saw the lower half of Luz's body pinned against the wall at a gut-wrenching angle.

She resurfaced and gasped.

"It's bad, huh?" Luz said.

"I'll go get help—" Bonnie started.

"There's no time. You gotta save yourself. Otherwise, what was all this for?"

"I'm not leaving you!"

"Yo *chica*. It was always gonna happen. It was here or the streets of L.A. Here's better."

"Luz—" Bonnie choked on the word.

For a moment, Bonnie looked past Luz to the faces of the sailors who were trapped behind her. In her desperation, she hadn't realized that they'd stopped screaming. They were huddled together, their faces stoic. They had accepted their fate. A few clutched rosaries and said a prayer as the water enveloped their bodies.

"Tell Daya I love her," Luz said as the water rose above her chin now.

"You tell her yourself." Bonnie took another deep breath and dove again. She continued her futile attempt to get Luz out, the water now rising so that Luz was completely submerged.

Bonnie felt a hand clutch her arm. It was Luz. The two young women looked at one another through the swirling water. Horror and devotion and friendship and love and all the moments of a lifetime they would never share passing between them in a matter of seconds. Luz smiled, proudly. As she did, bubbles escaped from her lips and then her nose and then... the life left her eyes. She stared into nothingness.

"Luz!" Bonnie screamed under water, her lungs taking in a rush of salty sea.

For a moment, Bonnie was back at the bottom in that high school swimming pool in Tucson again. And like then, she no longer felt the will to fight to find the surface. Or air. Or life. Her friend was gone, and the torment of it was too much to bear. If she stayed where she was, then the pain would be gone. The worrying, the constant fear, the unceasing burden of life's trials... all of it would be over. And she would be at peace. *Peace.* The word washed over her like one final rush of water.

And then, darkness consumed her.

Chapter 43
The Return

Bonnie VOMITED, ocean water forcing its way from her lungs. She coughed violently, her throat raw and burning. Her vision blurred as tiny pinpricks of light flickered in and out, slowly merging into the vast night sky that stretched over the Atlantic. The stars sharpened, taking shape—the familiar cluster of the Pleiades, the Seven Sisters. But something was wrong. She could only make out six stars. A surge of panic gripped her chest. *Where was the seventh? Why couldn't she see it?*

Then it hit her—Luz.

Her breath hitched, and the weight of realization settled over her like the tide. Slowly, she became aware of the rough wood beneath her, the rhythmic rocking of the *Spridiúil*. She was lying flat on the deck, her FF crewmates huddled around her. Hands pressed against her chest—her mother, desperate, administering CPR. But Bonnie was no longer fighting for air. She was fighting the hollow ache in her gut, the stark emptiness in the sky where a star—where Luz—should have been.

"You're alive!" Brigid said, immense relief in her voice.

Bonnie sat up and looked into her mother's concerned face. For all the horror of Luz's death, her mother was there for her. She cared that Bonnie was still alive. It moved Bonnie deeply. She reached out for her.

SLAP!

Brigid hit Bonnie hard across the face. Wilder rushed forward but was restrained by Donovan.

"You stupid little girl!" Brigid got to her feet, towering over her. "You know if you kill yourself, Jack automatically gets immortality!" She grabbed her roughly and shook her. "Don't you ever try that again or I'll kill you myself!"

She dropped Bonnie's limp body to the deck. Her head hit hard on the unyielding wood, and she cried out.

Brigid stormed away. Finally free from Donovan, Wilder went to Bonnie and helped her to her feet. She stumbled to the rail and vomited again into the churning waves. The tears poured from her eyes. Her face stinging as much from the humiliation as the pain. More so.

In the distance, explosions lit the horizon, not a lifeboat in sight. Bonnie saw what was left of the *Malthus* reach up to the sky, then slip beneath the murky depths—taking with it dozens of innocent souls—including one of the only friends she'd ever had.

’   ’   ’   ’   ’

In the hours that followed, Wilder did his best to console Bonnie, but his words of compassion trickled off her with no impact. Even the shared grief they bore brought her no solace.

As they boarded the plane back to Ireland, Bonnie thought of Luz, her body lost to the unfeeling depths of the sea. She had died far from home and everyone who loved her. There would be no Brigand burial for her, no final honors in the Field of the Fallen. Beautiful, devoted Luz, whose commitment to the cause had never wavered, was gone. Luz, the real hero, whose motives were always pure—unlike Bonnie's. She shuddered in shame.

She glanced at Wilder, whose pained expression mirrored her own, but even he could not share the depth of her torment. Gam

Gam's words about the weight of a soul echoed in Bonnie's mind. If Heaven indeed existed, Luz would surely be there by now, her soul light and unburdened. Not like hers. Or Brigid's.

She could see now that Brigid and the FF operated in a world where the ends justified the means, a world far removed from the ideals of Cormac's Cove. But maybe it had to be that way. Maybe the FF was just more honest about the way the world worked. Maybe the notions of good and evil needed to be left to the movies Gordon Prescott churned out every year, not meant for the harsh reality that Bonnie inhabited.

The thought sat with her, an indigestible truth, as she stared blankly at the dark waters below.

*   *   *   *   *

At that exact moment, the *Perdition*, cut through the Atlantic Ocean's surging waves with an eerie grace. The pirates on board moved with a nervous energy, their eyes fixed on the radar screen showing the plane on which Bonnie was now traveling.

A grizzled pirate leaned over the radar, scratching his beard. "Cap'n, we've got their coordinates."

Jack pounded on the console in elation. "The Féth Fíada has finally come out of the mist!"

"Their plane is heading west, straight over the Atlantic. Should we contact our friends in Morocco? We can force them to land."

Salifu stood close, but Jack remained apart, a dark silhouette against the dim glow of the screens. His sharp gaze never wavered from the tiny blip on the radar.

"No call to be so hasty," he murmured, shaking his head slowly. "We want to know where they're bound. Track them and see where they land."

Silence draped itself over the bridge. The crew kept their eyes locked on the shifting green glow of the radar, tension coiling in their spines. The ocean stretched endlessly beyond the glass, swallowing the night whole.

Jack exhaled and lifted his hand, watching as the hourglass ring pulsed with an otherworldly, liquid light. His eyes filled with tears. He was actually moved.

"My sins have bought my salvation."

*   *   *   *   *

Once the FF strike team landed at the secret airstrip outside Dungarry, it didn't take long to get back to the coastline. There, they boarded speedboats waiting to return them to Crag Inish. The sea air stung as Bonnie and Wilder took the ten-minute trip to the water cave on the far side of the island, where the boats would be moored. Bonnie's body still hurt and her eyelids hung heavy. She was so exhausted that she needed Wilder's support to get out of the boat and to the elevator that took them down to the underground compound.

With Reed and Cordial still under lock and key, the remaining Brigands were waiting anxiously when Bonnie and Wilder arrived at the barracks. As soon as Bonnie stepped into the room, they turned to her, eyes full of questions. Because of what happened with Cordial during the train heist, no one had been allowed to view the body cam footage for this mission. But word had already reached them that things had gotten dicey out on the water. It was Daya who broke the uneasy silence, craning her neck to look past them.

"Where's Luz?" she asked, her voice trembling. "Bonnie, where is Luz?"

Bonnie couldn't get the words out. A tear ran down her cheek.

Wilder delivered the news. "Luz didn't make it."

"Noooo!" Daya crumbled in sorrow into Malachi's arms.

Bonnie went to her. "She, she saved my life. If it wasn't for her, I'd be dead."

Daya lunged at Bonnie. It took both Maguires, Tanner, and Zion to restrain her.

"You *should* be dead! Luz should never have been on that mission! We all knew it. She only went because of you! You knew that, and you let her go... just to prove some goddamn point to Reed! All she wanted was to protect you. And all you could think about was yourself! And now she's dead because of you!"

Daya's wails echoed, slamming against the walls, cutting into Bonnie's chest like shards of glass. Fury and sorrow consumed the room, an unbearable weight pressing down on them all.

"Daya, come on," Micah said softly, his own voice trembling, though he tried to keep it steady. Zion nodded, his jaw tight as he helped guide her toward the door. She resisted, her body convulsing with sobs, but they managed to lead her out. The door slammed shut behind them, muffling her cries but not silencing them completely.

One by one, the other Brigands filed out, their faces etched with a mixture of grief and something else—disappointment? Fear? Bonnie couldn't bring herself to look too closely. Her eyes flicked to Barnaby for a moment, but he wouldn't meet her gaze. He shook his head almost imperceptibly and turned to leave.

Then there was Wilder. He lingered at the edge of the room, his hand gripping the doorframe so tightly his knuckles turned white. For a moment, Bonnie thought he might say something, anything, to fill the unbearable silence. But when his eyes finally lifted to hers, they were hollow, a storm of hurt swirling just beneath the surface.

"Wilder," Bonnie started, his name catching in her throat like a plea she didn't even know she was making.

He flinched as if the sound of her voice burned him.

"Don't," he said, his tone colder than she'd ever heard it. His eyes flicked down, then to the door, anywhere but her face. "This... this is too hard," he said, eyes fixed on the floor. "Maybe I'm *not* born for this." Then, he took a single step, then another, and before she could say anything more, he was gone.

The door closed behind him with a quiet finality, and Bonnie was left alone in the silence. She sank onto the nearest bunk, her legs refusing to hold her weight any longer. The room felt cavernous now, the emptiness pressing down on her from all sides. Daya's muffled cries still echoed faintly in the distance, a haunting reminder of what had just unraveled.

Bonnie pressed her hands to her temples, her mind racing but unable to focus. She'd seen the way they looked at her as they left— the hurt, the disbelief, the fracture in the trust she'd worked so hard to build. Even Wilder, in the end, had left her. She'd lost him. She'd lost Barnaby. She'd lost Reed. She'd lost them all.

In that moment, she felt split apart. The swirl of Read, Bonny, and Rackham blood roiling within her, each at odds with the others, battling for her soul. She knew it was time to choose, once and for all.

Chapter 44
Allegiance

Night had fallen by the time Bonnie approached Brigid's office. The compound was quiet, with only the occasional slap of boots from the night patrol. Bonnie hesitated at the door, steeling herself before she entered.

Inside, Brigid sat behind her desk, her posture as rigid as ever, but her face—paler and more drawn than Bonnie remembered—betrayed her weariness. Donovan was back at Brigid's right side, his expression angry and watchful. Aglain lingered in the shadows, his gaze flicking between mother and daughter. Bonnie had the sense they had been discussing her.

"I'm sorry to disturb you so late, but there's something I have to say to you," Bonnie began, then looking from Donovan to Aglain, "privately."

"What you have to say to me you can say in front of them," Brigid said.

Bonnie inhaled. "I need to apologize for what happened on the *Malthus*. You were right. I was being selfish. I was only thinking about myself."

"Do you really believe that, Bonnie? Or are you just telling me what you think I want to hear? Because we were just now discussing our concern for your safety. And what steps we may have to take to ensure it."

That sounded ominous to Bonnie.

She met her mother's eyes. "It won't happen again. I know now what's at stake."

Brigid glanced at Aglain and Bonnie saw him give her a slight nod.

Brigid leaned back, her expression unreadable. "And what brought about this epiphany?"

"What Luz said to me before she died. She said if I didn't save myself, her death would be for nothing. I can't let that be true... I just can't."

Brigid nodded. "Luz was a noble warrior, and her death is indeed a loss to the cause, but it's something you will have to reconcile. There is invariably a cost to what we do. Luz understood that, it seems, and if she made you come to the same conclusion, then we all owe her a debt of gratitude."

"I do understand," Bonnie said. "I have a greater responsibility. And I want to be part of that. But also..." She hesitated.

"What is it?"

"I also want to live to see Jack die," she said so fiercely that Brigid's eyes widened in surprise. But soon her shock gave way to a faint smile. She leaned back as Bonnie continued.

"He's the one who's to blame for everything. For Luz's death. And my father's. I want to be the one who's responsible for *his*."

"You're letting your rage guide you," Brigid said. "Good. Rage is far more useful than guilt. Guilt cripples. Rage propels."

Bonnie nodded, Brigid's words settling heavily in her chest. "Yes... I can see that now."

"And your fellow Brigands, your friends... what do they think?"

"I have no friends," Bonnie said. "Not anymore. Not after today."

Brigid absorbed this, nodding slowly. "Well. It's a shame they haven't come around to your way of thinking," she said. "A real waste of useful talent."

"They aren't like us," Bonnie said resolutely. "They don't know what it means to bear the mark. To carry the blood of Calico Jack. To feel the burden of the Stain of Musangu."

"We are unique," Brigid said, her voice softening into something resembling tenderness. "It's a terrible burden, yes. But also a precious gift. Few people are so clearly shown their purpose in life. Together, we'll ensure that purpose is fulfilled."

Bonnie looked at her mother. She saw the fierce conviction that etched her face beyond its years. For a fleeting moment, Bonnie wondered what kind of mother she might have been without the stain—without the curse. Would she have sung lullabies? Read bedtime stories? Would she have been warm, kind? Bonnie buried the thought. What-ifs were useless. This was her reality.

"So, are we agreed?" Bonnie said. "I'll stay. But I need you to promise me that the rest of the Brigands will be free to go and fight Jack in their way. I owe them that, at least."

Brigid and Donovan exchanged a look, and Aglain tensed visibly.

"Donovan," Brigid said. "Release Reed Ballister and the girl back to the barracks. Make arrangements for the children to be returned to their ship at first light."

"Yes, ma'am." Donovan nodded and left the room.

"You..." Brigid said to Aglain. "Leave us." She dismissed the priest, though his eyes lingered on Bonnie as he departed.

Once the men were gone, Brigid did something that left Bonnie stunned. She crossed the room and put her arms around her daughter, pulling her into a firm embrace. Bonnie hesitantly returned the gesture, her heart aching with a mix of longing and dread.

"Together, we'll be unstoppable," Brigid murmured.

In that moment, Bonnie couldn't help feeling a new kind of connection with her mother. A connection that, if she didn't know better, felt a little bit like love. It was what she had wanted. What she had craved. And to finally get a taste of it now... it made her heart ache.

Chapter 45
The Breakout

A BLUR OF IMAGES: Ocean waves crashing against a ship. Screams! Hands bound with rope. Figures on their knees on a ship's deck. A gun muzzle. FLASH! FLASH! FLASH! Lifeless bodies fall over, one by one. Gasoline pouring over a teak deck. The True North consumed in flames.

Cordial awakened with a start. She bolted out of bed to find Reed lying wide awake on his cot, as he had been since the news of Luz's death had reached him.

"Reed! Get up! They're coming!"

Reed blinked in slow motion, so deep in despair he barely registered her words.

"They're coming for *us*!" she repeated, banging on the bars of his cell.

The door to the holding area WHOOSHED open and footsteps approached. Reed finally jumped to his feet as Donovan appeared in the doorway.

"Step back from the cell door, Ballister—hands where I can see them," Donovan said.

"What's going on?" Reed asked. "What's this about?"

"Maybe fewer questions at this point," Donovan said, pulling out his sidearm. "You're being released. I said step back!"

They obeyed, though Cordial's glance in Reed's direction was full of warning. Donovan unlocked Cordial's cell, then Reed's with his key card.

"If we're free, what's with the gun?" Cordial asked obstinately.

"To discourage stupid questions!" He motioned for them to exit their cells. They hesitated. "I said move! Or—"

CLICK!

"Or what?" A woman's voice came from behind him, followed by the unmistakable press of a gun against his back. Donovan slowly put his hands up.

"Bonnie!" Reed said with astonishment.

It was indeed Bonnie, her pistol pressed firmly into Donovan's spine.

"I think the lady brings up a good question," she said. "What's with the hardware if you're just releasing them?"

Donovan stared straight ahead but remained silent.

"Drop the gun!" She shoved the gun harder into his back. "I said drop it!"

The weapon clattered to the floor, and Bonnie kicked it away. Cordial snatched it up and aimed it at Donovan. Bonnie stepped around to face him.

"Where were you taking them?"

"You know where. Back to their ship so they could leave, per your deal with Brigid."

"What deal?" Reed was confused.

Cordial interjected, "He's lying! He was going to take us back to the *North*, kill us all, and burn the ship!"

Donovan's eyes flickered in surprise.

"I saw it!" she said defiantly.

Bonnie's expression remained steely.

"Is that right?" Bonnie asked. "Answer me!"

"You're either with the Féth Fíada or against us," Donovan said, his tone unwavering.

Reed and Cordial exchanged a glance, realizing how narrowly they'd avoided their demise.

"So murdering kids is now part of the collateral damage?" Bonnie asked with cold contempt. "Is that the way you roll?"

"*Me*?" Donovan looked at her coldly. "You can't be that naive. Nothing happens here without Brigid's say-so."

Bonnie's lips tightened, but there was no shock, no denial.

"Yes, I believe that," she said quietly, more to herself than anyone else.

Her fingers flexed around the gun. She turned to Reed. "Pat him down."

Reed frisked Donovan, removing his communication device, key card, and anything else that could be used as a weapon.

"Get in the cell," Bonnie ordered.

Donovan went into the cell. Bonnie slammed the door shut.

"Uh, whatever your plan is here, Bonnie. I hope it includes more than three teenagers and a couple of guns," Reed said.

Just then the door WHOOSHED open. There stood Wilder, Barnaby, and Daya armed with their swords, recently liberated from the weapons cache.

"Oh, it includes a whole lot more," Bonnie said with a grin, then turned to the others. "About time, guys."

"Usually, a thank you would be appropriate at a moment like this," Wilder said.

Reed rolled his eyes. "Do you need a pat on the head and juice box too?"

"Nah, your eternal gratitude should cover it," he said, handing a sword to Reed. "I think this belongs to you."

Barnaby handed Bonnie her sword. "You know how you always say you can hear her? I coulda sworn I heard her calling your name."

The moment Siobhan was in her hands, Bonnie felt its surge of power and energizing hum. This was the second time Barnaby had rescued her blade. The last time was on the *Dark Star*, after she'd been kidnapped. She pulled Barnaby into a quick but fierce embrace. "I can always count on you."

Barnaby held on just as firmly. "Yeah. Maybe quit forgetting that."

"Okay, let's get out of here," Wilder said. "We got a boat to catch."

"You won't get off this island alive," Donovan said. "She won't let you."

"Shut up, bitch!" Cordial snapped, slamming Donovan's stolen gun so hard against the bars that the clang made him flinch.

The others exchanged glances, impressed by Cordial's outburst. As they stepped into the corridor, she smiled demurely. "Did I sell it? I really think I sold it!"

"I wouldn't want to meet you in a dark alley," Bonnie smiled.

Cordial beamed.

STATIC crackled from the comm device on Wilder's belt.

"I'm in!" Micah's voice came through.

"And we're out!" Wilder answered. "Lock it all down, my ginger amigo."

CLICK! The main door lock to the brig engaged, trapping Donovan inside. Then a series of CLICKS echoed throughout the compound as doors everywhere were remotely sealed by Micah.

Wilder handed comm devices to both Bonnie and Reed.

"C'mon," Bonnie urged, connecting herself to the comm device. "We're gonna rendezvous with the others."

"Can you just tell me what the hell is going on, Bonnie?" Reed asked.

"I'll explain as we go," she said, leading the group down the corridor.

Chapter 46
Putting the Wheels in Motion

What the hell was going on was that some truths had emerged in the aftermath of Luz's death on the *Malthus*. Cordial's vision about the group had been true. There could be no more illusions about Brigid and the FF. Not only could Bonnie never be one of them, but she also saw that the entire organization had to be destroyed. Knowing she couldn't do it alone, she had gone to the others.

"I am so sorry. I was wrong." Bonnie stood before them, full of contrition. "About all of it. About the FF. About my mother. I want to make it right. But I can't do it without you."

In the silence that followed, the Brigands exchanged glances, some uncertain, others resigned. They knew she was sincere—they didn't need Cordial to tell them that. But so much had happened. Their communal vow hung in the air like a thick mist. Finally, it was Daya whose voice broke through.

"I'll help," she said, her expression unreadable. "But I don't think I can forgive you."

One by one, the others murmured their agreement. They would stand with her. But forgiveness? That would take time. If it ever came at all.

Bonnie nodded, grateful. She could live with that.

Together, they crafted a daring plan: Bonnie would feign allegiance to the Féth Fíada in front of Brigid to gain her trust. As a condition of her staying, she would insist upon the Brigands' release. They expected Brigid to agree but knew she wouldn't be likely to honor her word, putting all of them in grave danger. Which meant they had to move quickly.

What she hadn't anticipated was Aglain's presence at the meeting. She was sure he'd see through her and recognize her motives. But the druid priest said nothing. Either she had put on the performance of her life, or he wasn't as powerful as he believed. Either way, it worked.

To better stack the odds in their favor, they decided to put the plan in motion late at night, when most of the FF were in their bunks, leaving only a skeleton crew on duty. It was a pattern they'd observed since they arrived. Micah would hack into the systems and lock the sleeping fighters inside their quarters, allowing the Brigands to escape—and destroy the place while they were at it—without interference.

Once explosives were planted by Wendell and his team, Micah would release the FF and give them ample time to flee before chaos reigned. It was exactly the kind of mercy that Brigid never bothered to extend to anyone who stood in her way—and exactly why her operation had to be toppled.

All of this was possible because Brigid, eager to recruit Bonnie, had granted the Brigands extensive access to the FF operation during her tours of the compound. She had severely underestimated her guests. And Bonnie had underestimated Reed.

From the moment they were forced into the compound, Reed had instructed Micah, Wendell, Tanner, Zion, and Yeun to discreetly gather intelligence—communications, weapons caches, transport, and security systems. He had been preparing for this moment all along.

It stung Bonnie to discover she had been left out of the loop. But she could see why. In fact, she had to admire Reed's practicality. If she had known, she wouldn't have taken it well.

It wasn't the first time Reed seemed to understand her better than she understood herself. Something she despised and found immensely attractive at the same time.

While Bonnie met with Brigid and then later trailed Donovan to the brig, the rest of the team focused on their roles. Wilder sneaked into the equipment center and gathered handheld transceivers, putting them on a private channel and distributing them so they could all stay in contact. Meanwhile, Barnaby retrieved their confiscated swords from the weapons cache and returned them to their rightful owners. He made a point to hand Luz's blade to Daya.

"She would have wanted you to have this," he said.

"Yeah, I think she would," she agreed, voice thick with emotion. Then she slid it into her belt.

By the time Bonnie freed Reed and Cordial, Micah Maguire had already been in the compound's main electronics hub for a couple of hours. Despite the importance of this "brain center" to the operation, it was surprisingly poorly guarded, with just a lone sentry passing by every three minutes.

Getting inside, however, was no easy task. Micah waited for the guard to turn the corner before dropping to the ground. To avoid the security camera, he performed a military crawl along the corridor, inching his way to the entry. A year ago, he wouldn't have had the strength to pull this off. And, though he imagined his new lifestyle had sent the stock price at Frito-Lay plummeting, he was glad to have left the unhealthy version of himself back on the Cove.

He reached the door without a moment to spare, slipping inside just as the guard returned. The door clicked shut behind him, and he held his breath, listening as the footsteps faded down the hall. No alarm. No shouts. He was in the clear.

Having already familiarized himself with the servers, networking equipment, and storage devices, Micah set to work. His fingers flew over the controls as he hacked the system, locking doors, disabling alarms, and switching camera feeds to earlier recordings so that prying eyes wouldn't see what was really happening.

The "empty" hallways on the monitors gave Wendell Noble cover to visit the armory—the one door Micah had unlocked remotely. And, with the help of Malachi and Tanner, he assembled enough remote-controlled IEDs to level the compound. Before slipping out, Wendell made sure to arm an explosive in the armory itself. If all went as planned, it would be quite the pyrotechnics show indeed.

"Lock it down," Wendell barked into his transceiver.

From the brain center, Micah worked his magic, re-locking and disabling the armory doors. Then, Wendell, Malachi and Tanner slung backpacks filled with improvised bombs over their shoulders and set out to plant them throughout the compound, which, Bonnie explained to Reed, was what they were at this very moment doing.

"Looks like you've got a future as a military strategist," Reed said, impressed.

"Maybe save that assessment till we're safe on the *North*," she smiled, leading the team from the lower level of the underground facility toward the designated rendezvous point—the boat dock in the water cave. There Yeun and Zion waited, having been dispatched to secure the area and prep their getaway boat. Everything was running smoothly—until it wasn't.

The echo of FOOTSTEPS filled the corridor!

Bonnie raised a hand, signaling for a halt. She peered around the corner. "Three guards. Armed," she whispered.

"Let's split up—take them from both sides," Reed suggested.

Bonnie nodded. "Wilder, you're with me. Reed, you, Barnaby, and Daya flank from the left. Cordial, cover our rear."

"I'm with Bonnie, too," Daya announced, drawing Luz's sword. Bonnie recognized the weight of the gesture. Daya was stepping into Luz's role as her protector.

She nodded. "Okay. Daya's with me.

"Remember. Fast and quiet," Bonnie said, her voice barely audible. "No gunfire unless absolutely necessary. And then only to disable." They had agreed at the outset—no unnecessary harm.

Wilder and Daya crept along the left side of the corridor behind Bonnie, while Reed and Barnaby approached from the right. Cordial guarded the rear with her pistol. The guards, rifles lazily slung over their shoulders, were oblivious to the impending attack, their focus elsewhere.

On Bonnie's signal, the Brigands struck! Wilder lunged first, slamming the hilt of his sword into a guard's skull. Daya finished him with a knee to the gut. Bonnie struck the second guard hard, sending him sprawling. On the right, Reed and Barnaby took down the last one. Reed delivered a gut punch. while Barnaby barrel rolled, sweeping the guard's legs out from under him. The man scrambled for his gun—only for Cordial to plant her shoe on his hand and aim her pistol at his face.

"Go ahead, player. I'm BEGGING you to give me a reason!"

The guard let go of the gun and Barnaby scooped it up.

Reed shook his head. "Okay. You're actually scaring me now."

Cordial gave him a wry smile. "That's the point."

"Nice teamwork," Bonnie whispered as they shoved the disarmed guards into a utility room. She patted Barnaby's shoulder—something small, but she could see it meant the world to him.

"Move out," Bonnie said, and the group continued quickly and silently down the corridor.

In another sector of the compound, Wendell lay flat on his stomach inside a narrow ceiling duct, covered with dust and cobwebs as he planted explosives.

"Okay, looks good up here. Hand the next one up," he whispered to Tanner, who balanced precariously on Malachi's broad shoulders to reach the open vent cover.

Tanner pulled an IED—C-4 plastic explosives rigged to lead wires and a remotely operated detonator—from his backpack and passed it up.

"I love the smell of cyclonite in the morning!" Wendell whispered, holding the putty-like bomb to his nose and inhaling dramatically.

Tanner rolled his eyes. "Enough with the panty-sniffing, you sick freak; just set it so we can get the hell out of here!"

"Philistine," Wendell scowled, muttering something about people not appreciating an artist at work. He crawled forward until he reached a vent overlooking CenCom. Wendell counted three FF manning the consoles. They were embroiled in a debate about some Gaelic football rivalry, most of which Wendell couldn't make out through their thick accents.

Wendell carefully placed the explosive. He then connected the IED to his Personal Mobile Radio that would remotely set it off when the time came. Green lights on both the bomb and the PMR blinked to life, signifying the sync was complete.

Wendell shimmied backward toward the vent opening.

"Stand by for re-entry!" he said, wriggling out feet first. Malachi caught him.

"So that's it then?" Tanner asked.

"All except the one for the computer hub," Wendell confirmed. As if on cue—

CRACKLE. STATIC.

"Tanner, where the hell are you guys?" Micah's voice hissed on the transceiver. "I'm done with everything, and there's a freakishly large dude that walks by every three minutes! Get me outta here!"

"Sorry, bro. On our way!" Tanner responded. "C'mon, Delta Force. Let's grab Micah so we can blow this freaking hunk of rock."

The trio started to run when suddenly—

KA-BOOM!

A distant explosion rocked the compound!

Wendell skidded to a halt, staring at the others in disbelief. "Uh. That... wasn't supposed to happen yet."

"No shit, you lunatic pyro!" Tanner yelled. "You set it off early!"

"Don't blame me!" Wendell shot back. "I didn't touch the PMR." He showed them the remote, still armed and ready to go.

RUMBLE! As Reed, Bonnie, Wilder, Cordial, Barnaby and Daya navigated the corridors, the shaking of the unexpected explosion reverberated through the fortress.

Suddenly, everything went dark, then emergency lights came on and klaxons blared! The group quickly ducked into an alcove.

"What's happening?!" Barnaby asked, looking to Cordial.

"Don't look at me. I read tarot cards, not temblors."

"I think it's one of Wendell's bombs," Daya said.

"Wendell! Wendell, come in!" Bonnie spoke into her comm device. "I didn't give the go ahead!"

"We know, Bonnie." It was Tanner who responded. "Wendell screwed something up!"

"Impossible! I set everything perfectly!" Wendell protested.

"Well, *something* set it off!" Reed growled through the comm.

Wendell hesitated, his face scrunching in thought. "Nothing could set it off early... except... I dunno. Maybe static. Or heat?"

Tanner pulled out the schematics he'd stolen and traced a finger along the compound's ductwork. "Oh, shit."

"What?" Bonnie asked, dreading the answer.

"Some of the ducts we rigged were heating ducts," Tanner said.

Wendell threw up his hands. "*Heating ducts?!* How was I supposed to know we were in heating ducts? I'm not a freakin' HVAC tech!"

"You didn't tell me we couldn't do heating ducts!" Tanner shot back.

"Wait a minute... Wendell, did you say *some*?" Bonnie asked. "Does that mean there are more that could—"

KABOOM!

Another explosion. Dust fell from the ceiling on Bonnie's group. The earth shook beneath their feet.

Wilder coughed out a mouthful of dust. "Wendell's clearly suffering from a case of premature detonation."

Just then, two armed FF ran past the alcove, not noticing the Brigands huddled inside.

"All hell's about to break loose. We need to double-time it!" Bonnie whispered into the transceiver. "Go get Micah. Everyone to the boat—ASAP!"

Both teams broke into a sprint, through corridors flashing with emergency lights as the fortress shook around them.

Up on the surface, at the monastery ruins, the angel mosaic buckled—an enormous crack moving jaggedly up across the middle and to the top. Nearby, a tall stone wall had completely collapsed, revealing the ocean beyond.

The angel seemed to gaze out over the turbulent waters of the Atlantic, where at that moment three speedboats laden with dozens of pirates headed toward the island from the south. On the horizon beyond hovered the cargo ship *Perdition*. At the bow of the largest of the speedboats with his coat billowing in the wind stood the leader of this expedition.

Calico Jack Rackham.

Chapter 47
The Response

The explosions that rocked the compound jarred Brigid awake. She sprang from her bed, snatched the gun she slept with, and ran to the door. She punched the control panel. Nothing. She pounded it. Still nothing. She was trapped.

"Goddammit!" she snarled, grabbing her comm device from the bedside table and activating it. "Donovan! Donovan, come in! What the hell is going on? Anyone?"

STATIC. Micah's hack of the system had blocked all FF communications.

Brigid rushed to her bed and pushed it aside, exposing a hidden floor panel. She yanked it open, revealing a ladder that descended into darkness. She flicked on a flashlight and climbed into the escape tunnel.

The tunnel took her directly to the Command Center, where she emerged moments later to find three FF staffers frantically typing at their terminals.

"What in the hell is happening?!" she bellowed.

"There's been a breach," one tech stammered.

"You don't say?!" Brigid snapped, her gaze whipping to the monitors, which all displayed empty hallways. "Who's behind it?"

"T-there's nobody... anywhere," he answered hesitantly. "Wait. Here's someone!"

He pointed to one monitor, which showed Brigid and Donovan in a hallway, walking and talking as if nothing were amiss.

"You idiots! That's old footage! They overrode the cameras!"

"On it, ma'am," a tech assured her, hammering keys to restore live feeds. One by one, the screens flickered to life, revealing the true state of the compound.

Visible for a moment on one screen, Tanner, Wendell, and Malachi sprinted down a corridor. Then just as quickly as the images appeared, they disappeared as Micah remotely seized control again.

"Those self-righteous little punks!" Brigid exclaimed. "Where is everyone? Where's Donovan?"

"Locked in chambers, probably," the FF tech answered, smashing down on a button as if the increased impact might have an effect. "They've locked the barracks doors, too."

Brigid grabbed the tech, shoving him back into his chair. "Well unlock them, or I swear, I'll serve your liver to the seagulls!"

The tech scrambled to work faster.

Brigid's hands tightened into fists. The Brigands of the Compass Rose had declared war on her, and it was a fight she intended to win.

In the water cave, Yeun and Zion steadied themselves as waves splashed onto the dock, their escape boat bucking wildly in the aftermath of the blasts. Around them, half a dozen FF watercraft rocked in the disturbed sea.

"What the hell are they doing?" Yeun asked. "I thought Wendell was gonna blow the joint *after* we were all together!"

VROOOM! The sound of engines reverberated through the cave.

"Speedboats!" Yeun and Zion said simultaneously.

They retreated into the shadows, just as two sleek vessels entered their view. Each teemed with pirates brandishing guns and swords. At the stern of each, Jolly Roger flags snapped in the damp sea air.

"Jack?" whispered Zion.

"That's his logo." Yeun indicated the skull and crossbones.

"Not much for subtlety, is he?" Zion said. Then he whispered into his comm. "Bonnie! Bonnie come in."

"Go for Bonnie," her voice crackled.

"Bonnie, we got us a big problem—"

"Don't I know it. Just make sure everything's set. We're on our way to you."

"No go. Abort!" Yeun whispered. "Water cave is compromised. Incoming. Jack's men."

"Calico Jack is here?" Reed's voice came through, sharp with concern.

"His men are," Yeun confirmed. "At least twenty. Heavily armed. They've blocked the exit."

"He must have tracked us from the *Malthus*," Bonnie said, her expression darkening.

Reed's mind raced. "Micah. Come in."

"I'm still here man, waiting for my ride," Micah said, his fingers flying across the keyboard. "The FF are hacking my hacks. I'm hacking back. Holding out so far. But don't know for how long."

"Micah, I need you to release the locks on the barracks doors!" Reed said.

Bonnie's eyes lit up. "Clever boy!"

Micah hesitated. "Uh... You know Wendell and them haven't gotten here yet."

"Doesn't matter," Reed explained. "Let Jack's men and the FF keep each other busy. We'll slip through the chaos."

Wilder clapped Reed on the back. "Wow, Cabin Boy! Keep this up and there might be a promotion in it for you to captain!"

"I'm already the captain."

Bonnie's voice crackled through the comm. "Attention all Brigands. New plan! Meet up top—by that mosaic. Then circle back to the boats from there. And watch out—halls are gonna be swarming with FF and Jack's crew."

"Aye, aye, Cap'n," Micah replied.

"Roger that," Tanner acknowledged, drawing his sword. Wendell and Malachi quickly did the same.

CLANK! WHOOSH!

With a single keystroke, Micah remotely unlocked all the doors at once. Within seconds, dozens of pent-up FF fighters surged into the corridors with weapons drawn, unaware that a new enemy had entered.

The compound was about to become a war zone.

"Doors are open!"

Back at Central Command, a tech watched as the monitors flickered back to the live feed, showing hallways teeming with FF.

"It took you long enough!" Brigid hissed.

"Wasn't us," he replied. "They did it themselves."

Brigid's brow furrowed. "Why would they do that?"

"That's why," came a familiar voice behind her.

Brigid's head whipped around. Free from his cell, Donovan strode into the center, Aglain on his heels.

Donovan pointed to one of the monitors. "There."

Brigid's face drained of color. Rackham's men were storming the compound. Firefights were breaking out all over!

"Jack found us!" Fear crackled in Brigid's voice. "Send guards to Bonnie's quarters immediately. Bring her to me right away!!"

"No can do," the tech said. "I can't get through. They still control comms."

"Then do it yourself!" Brigid screamed.

The tech started for the door.

"She's not there," Donovan announced.

"Where is she?" Brigid looked panicked.

Donovan leaned over the console and clicked through the security feeds until—on one monitor he found Bonnie, leading her team down a corridor, the recently liberated Reed and Cordial among them.

Brigid's fear turned to fury. Her daughter—her own daughter—had betrayed her.

She turned on Aglain, her eyes blazing. "*You!* Why didn't your so-called second sight foresee this?"

Aglain bowed slightly, his voice calm. "Just as you said, I'm useless, it seems." He threw her own words back at her.

Donovan circled Brigid with disdain. "All your talk about the cause. You're done in by this girl. Calico Jack didn't *find* us. He was led here... your daughter showed him the way." Donovan's anger boiled over. "And you let it happen."

"How do I know it wasn't you? It's *my* years he's after. Let Jack take me, and you've got the FF to yourself."

"Win the battle and lose the war? That's not the vow I took. That is your madness."

"You'd do anything to be in command!"

"No. Again, that's you! It's why you killed Keane, isn't it?"

A ripple of shock spread among the FF fighters.

"I did NOT kill him!"

"I think you did. I think he was starting to doubt his methods, and you didn't like it."

"I loved him!"

"Not more than you loved your cause."

"Lies! Arrest him!" Brigid commanded.

The fighters moved toward Donovan.

"No!" Aglain held up a hand, stepping forward. "He speaks the truth!"

All eyes locked on the priest.

"Long I have suspected it," he said. "But until the Gullah girl arrived, I could not see it." He shook his head, his voice full of sorrow. "So transformed has this holy place become, so consumed by bitterness, bastardized by hate. By *your* hate. No more. Enough. Enough."

"Mutiny! Seize them both!"

The fighters exchanged uneasy glances, their loyalty wavering.

JUST THEN A BLAST ROCKED THE ROOM! The bomb over Central Command sent chunks of the ceiling falling, crushing the computers. Everyone took cover, dust and debris raining down everywhere. Electricity arced and sparked. A fire flashed to life at one station. All the monitors flickered, then went BLACK.

In the distance, gunfire reverberated throughout the compound.

Brigid's empire was disappearing—as if it had never existed.

Chapter 48
The Chaos

When the CenCom blast occurred, Bonnie's team and a handful of FF fighters were in the midst of a battle against Calico Jack's men.

The Brigands had stumbled upon the group of FF being savagely beaten by the pirates. Without hesitation, they threw themselves into the fight, joining forces with their blood-bound allies in the battle against their mutual enemy.

They were well on their way to victory when the explosion sent a giant swath of the hallway tumbling inward. Two pirates were instantly buried. The others retreated, dragging their wounded compatriots with them.

"This whole place is coming down!" coughed Cordial as smoke from the fires filled the corridors.

"Micah!" Bonnie shouted into her comm. "Make the announcement!"

"Roger that." Then Micah's voice could be heard reverberating over loudspeakers everywhere:

"*Uh, yeah, this is a warning. In case you haven't already figured it out, explosives have been set all over the compound. She's gonna blow, folks! And soon. Abandon the island. Like now. Or the rest is on you.*"

As if on cue, ANOTHER MASSIVE BLAST!

Throughout the compound, gunfire ceased as FF and pirates alike stopped fighting. Chaos and confusion ensued as they all scrambled for exits.

Bonnie and her team stood before the passageway that had just collapsed, uncertain where to go next. The FF fighters who'd just been saved turned to the Brigands.

"This way!" one offered.

"Thank you," Reed nodded.

"No. Thank *you*!" the fighter said, leading the way to the surface.

Back at Central Command, fear, disgust, or maybe just plain old self-preservation took over. The moment Micah's warning came over the loudspeaker, the remaining FF fighters ran.

"Come back!" Brigid screamed after them. "That's an order!"

But they were gone, leaving only Brigid, Donovan, and Aglain amidst the ruins.

"You've lost them," Donovan said. "You've lost everything. All you have left that's worth anything is your years. Let's get you out of here before you lose those, too." Donovan opened the portal to the secret passageway where Brigid had entered, coaxing her, like one would a child.

Brigid backed away from him, a cornered animal in a cage.

Aglain watched the two warriors as they circled each other.

"I'm not going anywhere!" Brigid yelled. "Not without Bonnie."

"She's with the Brigands. They'll protect her. They've proved tonight they know what they're doing."

"I can't risk him getting her years."

"You're not the leader anymore. You're not even a Brigand. You're just another name on Jack's list. Now, let me do what I was born to do." Donovan grabbed her arm roughly, dragging her toward the secret entrance when—

A SHOT RANG OUT!

Donovan staggered back, then fell to the floor. In Brigid's hand, he saw a gun. Emotions pinballed in Donovan's eyes. Shock. Rage. And finally, stunned acceptance as blood bloomed across his shirt.

Aglain rushed to Donovan as he lay crumpled on the ground.

Stanching the flow of blood from Donovan's gaping wound, the priest looked up at Brigid. "This day will cost you your soul, Brigid Byrne."

Brigid stood amidst the burning wreckage around them. She looked deranged, almost... inhuman.

"That's a price I'm willing to pay." She chambered a bullet, stepped over the twisted steel that had once been CenCom's main door, and disappeared into the darkened compound.

As Bonnie and her team followed their FF guides through twisting, smoke-filled hallways, the going was slow. They kept encountering collapsed passages that forced them to continually change their route.

"Through here," one of the FF fighters indicated. He and the other FF soldiers disappeared into a stairwell.

They started to follow—but Cordial stopped in her tracks.

"What's wrong?" Reed asked.

Cordial could not answer. Her eyes were distant, unfocused, as a vision filled her mind's eye.

The crumbling monastery. The mosaic of the angel clinging to the wall for dear life. And strolling past it, Calico Jack Rackham.

"He's here," Cordial whispered.

"Who?" Bonnie asked, though she already knew the answer.

"Calico Jack! He's here on the island."

They all took in the awful news.

"Apparently, he has some business he needs to handle himself," Bonnie replied grimly.

With Micah's loudspeaker announcement having obviously done the trick, Wendell, Tanner, and Malachi encountered no further resistance the rest of the way to the computer center. Even the hallway sentry had abandoned his post.

"About damn time!" Micah snapped when they arrived. He slung his backpack over his shoulder. "Set those last devices and let's bug out before—"

RUMBLE! The whole place shook as a massive fireball raced through the heating ducts and flashed through the vents, nearly roasting them in the process.

"Dammit, Wendell!" Micah yelled. "Any bombs you *didn't* plant in heating ducts?"

"I'm sorry, okay?! Look. You guys go on ahead. I'll do my thing and meet up with you topside," Wendell said.

"We're not leaving you, bro," Tanner said firmly.

"Negative. This is gonna take me a little bit. And there's no telling how long we got 'til the next blast. It's not gonna do the cause any good if all of us end up pink mist!" Wendell said, referring to the grisly term for a human body blasted to smithereens. "I'll catch up. GO! GO!"

Tanner, Micah and Malachi looked at one another and then double-timed it out of there.

"I'm going back for Brigid," Bonnie announced in the wake of Cordial's vision. The thought of finally meeting Calico Jack face-to-face filled her with dread, but she started back the way they came.

Reed blocked her path. "Absolutely not."

"I have to."

Wilder's eyes narrowed. "Why? Because she's marked? Or because she's your mother? Cuz you ask me neither is worth risking *your* life for!" His tone was harsh. He had no sympathy for the woman who had abandoned Bonnie—and cost Luz her life. His loyalty to Bonnie far outweighed his oath to the Brigands.

"Both. Neither. I don't know. Because it's the right thing to do," Bonnie replied. "You all go on ahead. This one's on me."

"Then I'm going with you," Reed said.

"Me too," Wilder volunteered. "The three of us. Like the old days."

Bonnie allowed herself a fleeting smile.

"Count me in," Daya said.

"Us too," Barnaby added.

Cordial brandished the pistol she'd taken off Donovan. "As long as I get to use this."

Reed took control. "Here's what's happening. Daya, you and Barnaby take Cordial and get her up top. If something goes wrong, I need you to tell the others where we are."

Barnaby hesitated, then nodded. "Don't take too long."

Cordial went up to Reed.

"Stay safe, Reed Ballister," she said.

"You too, Cordial Grace."

Cordial impulsively threw her arms around him in a warm embrace. It took Reed aback, but he didn't exactly push her away. And for the first time, Bonnie did not feel a rush of jealousy. Simply acceptance.

"Hey, D'Artagnan!" Wilder yelled. "We're short a musketeer over here! You wanna speed it up a bit?"

"Go kick some pirate booty," Cordial said, and Reed joined Wilder and Bonnie.

"The band is back together, baby!" Wilder announced.

The trio exchanged faint smiles before turning and heading into the bowels of the complex.

Chapter 49
The Confrontation

Bonnie, Reed, and Wilder moved cautiously through the twisting tunnels of the FF headquarters. Their footsteps echoed off the damp stone walls, the sound unsettling amid the distant noises of crumbling rock and explosions.

They were now deep in an unfamiliar part of the underground fortress—far from the areas Brigid had shown them during her grand tour. The passageways were dotted with hidden chambers, more likely part of the original monastery than the compound. With the main corridors structurally compromised by the blasts, this was their only path to their destination—Central Command, where Brigid had last been seen according to the report of a fleeing FF fighter.

Bonnie knew she needed to get to her mother before Jack did and before Wendell's explosives turned the whole place into rubble.

"Kinda wishing I had my fingers crossed behind my back when I took that Brigand oath," Wilder joked.

No one laughed. Their nerves were too on edge. Each shadow seemed to move, each sound amplified in the cold, dark corridors.

And then, a voice—low and chilling—cut through the darkness.

"Hello, Bonnie."

She heard him before she saw him. But she knew who it was. She knew that voice from her dreams.

As they rounded a corner, the corridor opened into a wide, dimly lit chamber. And there he was.

Calico Jack Rackham.

He stood beneath a stone arch, flanked by several heavily armed pirates. His savage smile was as sharp as the blade he held in his hand. Impossibly tall and handsome, so much more modern, elegant, and cruel-looking than he had seemed in Bonnie's visions.

At long last, she was face to face with the author of all her pain. But she did not cower in fear of the man who'd taken so much from her. Instead, she felt a self-righteous rage surge within her.

Swords drawn, Reed and Wilder stepped into position beside Bonnie, their eyes locked on Jack's men. The chamber was thick with tension.

"Bonnie Hartwright," Jack said as if he were tasting each syllable in his mouth. His voice smooth, dripping with desire. "Fruit of my loins, a few times removed. Bearer of the Stain of Musangu. Long I have dreamt of finally acquiring you."

"Keep dreaming, because that's all it's ever going to be."

Jack laughed, a cold, mirthless sound. "You're rather bold for someone whose sole purpose is to provide me with time."

"Wow. You *are* full of yourself, aren't you?" Bonnie said, Siobhan buzzing with readiness. "I've known plenty of assholes like you. You're giving off heavy 'I'm a dick cuz I'm masking my fears' vibes. What are you afraid of, Jack? Maybe dying?"

A flicker of something dark crossed Jack's face, but he quickly masked it. Still, Bonnie noticed.

"You are! You're afraid!" The revelation gave Bonnie immense pleasure. It was her turn to laugh. "Deep down you're just a coward."

Reed and Wilder shifted nervously at Bonnie's antagonism.

"It would behoove *you* to be more afraid, little girl," Jack seethed. "Yet you ran right into the mouth of the lion. Perhaps you were in search of something—or someone?"

Jack signaled to one of his men, who pulled Brigid from a darkened recess. She was bound, bloodied, and barely able to stand, so badly beaten was she from the fight she'd obviously put up.

"Brigid!" Bonnie took an instinctive step forward.

The pirates trained their pistols on her.

"I said no guns, idiots!" Jack commanded, and the pirates lowered their firearms, brandishing swords instead.

The Brigands exchanged looks. They understood. In this small space, Jack couldn't risk Bonnie or Brigid getting killed in a firefight. The curse was specific—only drowning at Jack's hand would satisfy its requirements. No other death would do.

"You stupid child!" Brigid spat through bloody teeth. "You shouldn't have come back! Do you realize what you've done? He has both of us now! You've given him everything!"

For an instant, Bonnie flashed back to the moment on the beach when she had gone to save her father. Like Brigid, he'd warned her against coming. Her mother and father had both been concerned with her safety. But their motives couldn't be further apart. Bobby, because he loved her above all else. Brigid, because she loved her cause. A cause that now drove Bonnie to raise her sword in defiance.

"He gets nothing. She's coming with us!" Bonnie hissed, pointing the tip of Siobhan at Jack.

"I see you've inherited the delusion gene of the Mary Read bloodline. Well, I'm afraid I can't oblige you. Not after you were so kind as to go through all the trouble of leading me here... to her."

The realization hit Bonnie like a blow. "You were using me to find her?"

"See, Brigid? She gets the brains from *our* side of the family!" Jack stroked Brigid on the head, as if she were a pet. "For years, your mum here was so careful. But I knew the moment you got close, she'd drop her guard. That's the nature of mothers and children, isn't it? That eternal pull—like the moon and tides. My very, very late wife Anne suffered from it, too. Even went so far as to have me hung to protect the child."

Bonnie's eyes flicked to the rope burn on his throat. Jack saw this, quickly pulled up his collar and his expression went dark. "Didn't turn out well for her, though. Or him in the end, come to think of it. And it won't for you either. Get her!" He commanded.

With a roar, Calico Jack's pirates surged forward, blades ready to strike.

Bedlam broke out!

Steel clanged against steel, echoing loudly off the chamber walls. Bonnie met the charge head-on, Siobhan flashing as she parried the blade of a towering brute with braided hair and a cruel grin. To her left, Reed ducked a wild swing and countered with a tight, precise jab to the gut of one opponent—but another was on him before the first even fell. Wilder's blade danced in his hands as he fought two pirates at once, retreating toward a crumbled pillar for cover.

They fought with all the vigor of youth and the righteousness of their cause, but the truth became clear within moments—they were outnumbered and they were losing.

Bonnie ducked, rolled, slashed, and only missed a knife to the ribs because of the mandate not to kill her. These weren't just any pirates—they were Rackham's personal guard. Seasoned killers with no mercy and nothing to lose. And, if they captured Bonnie, it was over. Forever.

She risked a glance toward her mother. Brigid was staring at the fight through swollen eyes.

Watching the battle, Jack stood behind his pirates, arms crossed, savoring the carnage like a man enjoying a fine play.

"Such spirit," he murmured. "But even a fire dies, eventually."

So enraptured was he with the battle he didn't notice that behind her back, Brigid was working her bindings against a jagged piece of obsidian that jutted from the wall.

At that very moment, Bonnie was fighting for her life. Her blade met her opponent's—hard, fast—and then he twisted. Siobhan went spinning across the floor with a sickening scrape. Bonnie stumbled back, weaponless. The pirate had her cornered. The only thing that remained was for him to deliver the quarry to his captain.

"BONNIE!" Brigid let out a feral scream and her bindings SNAPPED. She surged forward, evading Calico Jack's reach, and went straight for Bonnie's attacker. She drove her head into his face, smashing his nose and stunning him. She snatched his dagger as he reeled backward. With one swift motion, she plunged the blade into his heart. He collapsed with a grunt.

Bonnie staggered, gasping. Brigid took her hand and helped her to her feet. Bonnie felt a rush of gratitude, but then—

SUDDENLY, Brigid locked her arm roughly around Bonnie's neck and pressed the dagger against her daughter's throat!

"Stand down! I said stand down!" Jack ordered his men. Everyone stopped in their tracks.

All fighting ceased mid-blow. Reed's face was bloodied, eyes wild. Wilder was limping, his shirt sliced through in two places. The Brigands were spent.

"Bonnie!" Wilder yelled when he saw what was happening. He started towards her.

"Don't take another step, any of you!" Brigid hissed.

"Wha-what are you doing?!" Bonnie's mind was reeling from the shock.

"I told you, I can't let him get your years."

"You wouldn't kill your own child," Jack scoffed, but there was a flicker of doubt in his voice. Brigid's grip tightened.

"You killed Seth for your reasons. You don't think I'd kill Bonnie for mine?"

A heavy silence fell, the tension unbearable. They all knew that she would. Even Bonnie.

"Please. Brigid. You can't do this," Reed pleaded.

"You and your ridiculous Brigands. You still refuse to understand what's at stake? What is her life worth compared to the world? To all of humanity?"

"To me, her life's worth everything." It was Wilder who spoke, and Bonnie could see the genuine love on his face. "Please, I beg you. Jack doesn't have to get her. Just don't hurt her."

"Jack will never let us leave here. He finally has us both. I'm already as good as dead. There's only one way to keep him from winning." She pressed the knife against Bonnie's skin, a thin line of blood trickling down her neck.

"Mom!"

The word was so foreign, so shocking to Brigid that it halted the blade for a moment. No one had ever called her that.

"Mom," Bonnie spoke soothingly. "You loved me once. I know it. I felt it. That night during the storm, when you first held me. When you had to leave me in that church. You cried. I felt your tears on my face. Remember?"

Brigid looked confused. *How could Bonnie know that?* It was impossible, yet... Tears welled in her eyes. Rolled down her face onto Bonnie's cheek.

Bonnie looked at her, looked in her eyes and in that instant, knew that she saw genuine love. The love of a mother for a child.

"You do love me. You do." It was what Bonnie had longed for for so long.

With that, Brigid's grip loosened and the knife started to move away from her daughter's throat. For a moment, Bonnie had gotten through.

THEN... A MASSIVE EXPLOSION followed by a ROCKING QUAKE!

Somewhere, not too far off, a part of the compound collapsed. The entire island shook and with it, Brigid was jarred from her hesitation. Her soft look turned hard.

"You're sentimental. Like your father. You'll only end up losing." She started to plunge the blade into Bonnie's neck.

Bonnie braced herself, but the strike never came. If she hadn't been overwhelmed by adrenaline, she might have sensed him, as she had every time before. But his scent mingled with the sweat, fear, and anxiety saturating the air, blurring the danger until she noticed him a split second before his dagger plunged into Brigid's back.

"Look out!" Bonnie yelled but it was too late.

Brigid's eyes went wide. She dropped her knife to the floor and a sharp gasp escaped her lips.

"She is for me!"

Behind Brigid stood the pirate Maks!

Chapter 50
The End

Maks's face twisted with unhinged rage as he yanked the bloodied knife from Brigid's back, eyes fixed on Bonnie.

For a moment, everyone stood in stunned silence. Even Calico Jack was caught off guard.

Brigid crumpled to the ground at Bonnie's feet.

"Mom!" Bonnie dropped to her knees, clutching her mother, who writhed in agony on the cold, rocky floor. Maks rushed to attack Bonnie.

Reed and Wilder intervened and pulled him off. They wrestled Maks back—straight into the path of an oncoming Calico Jack, who intercepted him and threw him hard against a stone wall.

"DAMN YOU!" Jack roared, the sound reverberating through the chamber. "You pathetic worm! You worthless piece of—" Jack was kicking Maks, who whimpered as he tried to shield himself from the blows and the barrage of hate.

"I'm sorry, Jack. Jack, please!" Maks cried. "I love you. I—"

Just when it seemed Jack would beat Maks to death, he caught sight of Bonnie dragging Brigid away.

"Don't just stand there! Stop them!" Jack screamed. Jack's remaining pirates turned to give chase. He gave Maks one last kick to the face and Maks lost consciousness.

Reed and Wilder dove into the fray, battling Jack's men to keep them from Bonnie and Brigid as Bonnie scrambled to help her mother toward cover.

Jack went after the two women, determined to claim what he believed was rightfully his.

He was almost upon them when Bonnie turned to face him, putting herself between her mother and Jack. She raised her sword. With a defiant cry, she swung Siobhan, the steel slicing through the dusty air. Jack met her sword with his.

Their swords collided with a deafening *clang*, sparks erupting from the clash of metal. Jack pressed forward with a relentless onslaught, his strikes precise and powerful. Bonnie parried with all her strength, each impact jarring her arms, but she refused to back down.

The chamber seemed to shrink around them as they fought, their movements a deadly dance of thrusts, parries, and counters. Bonnie's mind raced, calculating Jack's every move. Though she could tell he was avoiding any blows that could mortally wound her, he clearly had no issue maiming and disabling her long enough to drown her.

She sidestepped a vicious swing clearly aimed at slicing off her arm. She retaliated with a sharp jab toward his ribs, but Jack twisted away at the last second.

The battle grew more ferocious, each determined to prevail. Each battling their own flesh and blood. Jack's strikes were unrelenting, and his footwork was impeccable, forcing Bonnie to stay on the defensive. But she wasn't just defending; she was learning. She noted the slight hitch in his movement when he feinted left and the way his guard dropped slightly after a heavy swing.

Seizing an opening, Bonnie aimed a sweeping cut at his legs. Jack leapt back, narrowly avoiding the blade, but the move threw him off balance.

Recovering quickly, he countered with a flurry of strikes that pushed Bonnie back, her boots skidding on the rocky floor. One blow came dangerously close, grazing her cheek. The sting of pain only sharpened her focus. She had missed her chance once, but she knew if Jack tried that move again—

There it was! Jack feinted left again, leaving an opening on his sword hand. Bonnie swung her blade down toward Jack's exposed arm with all her might.

SCHLICKT!

Calico Jack stood stunned, staring down at the stump which had once been his hand. He watched the dismembered appendage fall to the ground with a sickening THWUMP! The severed hand clawed freakishly at the rocky floor, the hourglass ring on it

"YOU FILTHY SLAG!!!!" screamed Jack, stumbling backward to where the injured Brigid still lay in pain.

BOOM BOOM BOOM! Another series of explosions. Followed by a LOUD GROAN and DEAFENING CRACKING SOUND.

The shaking intensified. All battle stopped as everyone struggled to keep their balance amidst the quake. Bonnie saw a crack appear in the ground at her feet. It spread quickly, bisecting the rock until a massive chasm suddenly opened up. SCREAMS as Jack's remaining men were swallowed up by it.

Bonnie and Jack exchanged a look across the chasm—the realization dawning on them that the black bottomless pit stood between the Brigands on one side and Calico Jack and Brigid on the other. Jack shuddered in anger. Eternity so close and yet so far.

Furious and frustrated but unable to reach Bonnie, Jack grabbed Brigid with his one remaining hand and began dragging her into the blackness of the tunnel that led back into the monastery.

"NO!" Bonnie yelled, but she was powerless to give chase.

Bonnie, Reed, and Wilder stared into the dark tunnel. Brigid was gone.

WHIMPER. The sound of sobbing drew their attention. They turned to see Maks nearby, standing at the precipice of the chasm.

Reed and Bonnie both raised their swords ready to finish him, but Bonnie wavered and then held Reed back.

Maks' face was completely disfigured—from the beating, the slashes across his cheek and the zig zag scars over his mouth. The combined effect was that of something that was no longer human.

"Do it. I beg you. Show me mercy and end this pathetic, worthless existence," he whispered. "I am nothing. Nothing. Nothing." He sobbed. "I deserve nothing."

Bonnie just stared. And in that moment, she realized, the face before her wasn't just that of her father's murderer. Nor the face of the man that had made Reed an orphan. It was a face etched with profound suffering and abuse, another twisted product of Calico Jack's cruelty. Maks wasn't only a monster; he was a victim, too, one in a long, unbroken chain stretching back 300 years.

Tears blurred Bonnie's vision as she lowered her sword.

"I didn't think I could hate you more," Maks said. His eyes locked on Bonnie, clear and saner than she had ever seen them, and in one almost graceful motion, he threw himself into the void.

There was no sound from him. No cry. Only silence. And Bonnie just stood and stared into the abyss. A deep, personal understanding of its appeal.

BOOM! The earth cracked further, the gaping hole widened and Bonnie almost toppled in. Wilder yanked her back from the brink.

"We have to go!" he shouted over the thunderous sound of collapse, pulling her toward the only passage that was still unobstructed—a stairwell. "This way!"

Reed ran after them.

"Wait!" Bonnie yelled. She ripped herself away and returned to the battle zone. The still-moving hand of Jack Rackham lay before her. She quickly scooped up the severed hand, pocketed it, and ran to join her fellow Brigands as they escaped up the stairwell.

*   *   *   *   *

The passageway was dark and cramped and filled with smoke. Their eyes stung and they coughed as Wilder led the way upward through the various flights of metal steps. Earthquakes and falling debris continued, the compound crumbling in on itself around them. They suddenly stopped. The stairwell above them was nothing but twisted steel, hanging precariously.

A LOUD BANG and the SNAPPING Of METAL! Pieces of the blown-in stairwell began falling down toward them. No choice, they quickly jumped through the nearest doorway.

They emerged onto one of the floors of the compound just as the stairwell imploded behind them, a mountain of concrete blocking the doorway.

"So much for taking the stairs," Wilder said.

"What level are we even on?" Reed asked. Amid the mayhem, explosions and earthquakes, the trio had lost their bearings.

"Bonnie!"

It was Barnaby running toward them. And behind him were more Brigands—Daya, Malachi, Tanner and Micah. They were with Cordial.

"What are you all still doing here?" Reed was alarmed.

"This is as far as we got," Daya said. "The elevators are out and the stairs, well, you saw for yourself."

"Where's Wendell?" Bonnie asked.

"He stayed behind to set the last IEDs in the computer center," Tanner explained. "He said he'd meet us up top."

"Did he make it?" Reed asked.

"Don't know," Tanner answered. "Coms are out too. But *we* haven't made it, and we had a head start."

They all looked at one another somberly.

ANOTHER HUGE EXPLOSION rocked the compound! The hallway ahead buckled and collapsed, narrowly missing the group.

"There's got to be a way out of here!" Wilder shouted.

"We've been looking! No luck!" Daya yelled back, frustration etched across her face.

"I even checked the schematics!" Tanner added. "There's some kind of sewer system that empties to the water, but unless we can dig our way down—"

"There's another stairwell!" Cordial interjected, her voice cutting through the panic. "It's in the priest's chamber on the west side of this floor. It leads to the outside!"

"Lead the way!" Bonnie commanded.

Cordial hesitated. "But it only goes up—to the top of the island. And there's no way down from there."

They all looked at each other.

"I wouldn't mind seeing one last sunrise," Tanner said with a shrug.

The others nodded, their resolve hardening.

"Admit it. You really are a softie, Spray Tan," Bonnie said, putting an arm around him.

"I'll admit it. But only because you'll never be able to tell anyone." He winked.

And they all chuckled. It was dark, but funny.

If this was the end, they'd meet it like Brigands.

Chapter 51
Down... and Out!

Led by Cordial, the Brigands finally arrived at Aglain's chamber. The group was immediately struck by the primeval atmosphere of the place, as if the room were bathed in an ethereal glow.

"This is... so beautiful," Daya murmured.

"It feels like it's a thousand years old," Barnaby added.

"Older," Cordial said. "Over here!" She rushed toward the stone staircase at the far end, her pace quickened by the groaning sounds of the compound threatening to disintegrate.

The group crowded at the bottom, looking up into the night sky. The first rays of sunlight were piercing the darkness.

Dirt and pebbles were shaken loose up top, raining down over them.

"It's now or never, gang," Cordial urged.

Suddenly, a voice rang out. "Not that way!"

They spun around to see the priest Aglain standing in the doorway. There was a disturbing amount of Donovan's blood smeared on his Druidic robes, but he seemed uninjured.

"There's a passage through here," Aglain gestured toward his bedchamber. "It leads to the south shore. There's a boat waiting. It's mine. You can have it."

"It's a trap!" Tanner hissed, looking over his map. "It's not on here."

"It's known only to me. Built by the druids who inhabited this island millennia ago."

Cordial stepped forward, her gaze steady. "He's telling the truth."

The Brigands looked at each other, unsure. Then...

"If Cordial trusts him, so do I," Bonnie proclaimed.

"Lead the way, Father," Reed said, moving toward the bedchamber with the others close behind.

"Today," said the priest, "I am your brother."

Aglain approached a large tapestry on the wall, its woven image of Anu, the Celtic mother goddess, cradling the Earth tenderly. Bonnie couldn't help but shake her head at the irony of it.

The priest pulled the tapestry aside, revealing an ancient wooden door. It opened to a dark tunnel beyond.

Just then, the ceiling above Aglain's bed collapsed in a massive heap of rubble.

"Be swift!" Aglain urged, handing Bonnie a lantern.

The Brigands rushed into the tunnel, but as Cordial started in, Aglain reached out, clasping her hands. The moment their skin touched, Cordial felt a surge of power.

VISIONS OVERWHELMED HER: *Thousands of images flashing in seconds. Sword battles. A dagger. A disturbing story unfolding.*

 Cordial gasped as her own sight returned. She looked at Aglain, surprised by what he had just revealed to her.

"Oh, my God. Is it true? Do the others know?"

"It is up to you, now, to tell them."

Cordial suddenly saw Aglain through new eyes. "When I was in the jail, it was you who showed me the truth about Donovan—what he was going to do," she said, her voice heavy with emotion. "And you let Gam Gam see this place, too..." she continued, realization dawning. "It wasn't because our magic was stronger or yours weaker. You *wanted* us to come here."

"Balance is a tenet of our beliefs," Aglain replied, his expression somber. "The scales have tipped toward darkness for far too long. Now go! Hurry!"

"Wait... aren't you coming?"

"And miss sunrise from my altar on the day of Alban Eilir? The Spring Equinox? That would be unprecedented." He strode over to the alcove that led to the staircase, his robes flowing regally behind him. He paused and looked back at her. "Use your gift for good, Cordial Grace. Honor those who came before you. That is my wish for you." And with that, Aglain disappeared up the steps.

Cordial started after him when someone grabbed her arm.

It was Bonnie. She pulled Cordial back just as the entrance to the staircase collapsed, trapping Aglain on his sacred mound, for all of time.

A GROANING OF STEEL AND ROCK! The entire compound was buckling around them.

"Run!" Bonnie yelled. And she and Cordial sprinted into the tunnel. They ran with all that was in them through the ancient corridor.

Up ahead, they saw light. The surface!

They emerged on a ledge just above a rocky beach on the leeward side of the island. The sun was just rising.

Looking across in the distance at the ocean beyond, Bonnie was met with the sight of numerous boats, FF and pirate alike, fleeing the island. She felt immense relief.

"Over here!" Wilder yelled to them from below.

Bonnie and Cordial made their way down the steep and rocky hill to the water's edge where the Brigands had all regrouped. They had joined Yeun and Zion, who had also encountered Aglain. The old priest led them to safety and his sailboat, which they'd prepared for departure.

As Bonnie reached the beach, she was surprised to see Donovan propped up against a boulder, clutching his wounded chest, weak from loss of blood. Aglain had helped him to the surface as well. Donovan grabbed Bonnie's hand as she passed.

"Brigid?" he asked anxiously.

Bonnie shook her head. "There." She pointed to the horizon where the *Perdition* loomed. Pirate speedboats sped toward it, and Donovan understood Jack had Brigid among them.

He looked defeated. "I tried to save her."

"You can't save someone from themself," Bonnie said.

Another VIOLENT TREMOR crumbled one of the rock spires at the top of the island. Its remains barreled down the slope, some coming to rest in front of the tunnel entrance, some crashing down to the beach. The rockslide sent the Brigands scattering, barely missing them as the boulders rolled into the already turbulent ocean, creating even bigger waves.

If it wasn't clear before, it was clear now—the compound wasn't the only thing coming down. The island was going with it.

"Everyone! On board! Now!" Reed shouted.

"Come on!" Bonnie barked at Donovan, pulling him to his feet.

He looked at Bonnie, stunned. "Me?"

"Brigands don't leave Brigands behind," she said and helped Donovan toward the waiting boat.

They were finally all aboard and ready to go when—

"Wait! What about Wendell?" Tanner asked.

They all looked around. No Wendell. The harsh reality started to sink in when—

"Over there!" Barnaby pointed up to the entrance of the secret tunnel.

Every head swiveled and through the swirling dust, they could see a figure emerging, climbing over a large boulder. Scratched and filthy and with the biggest shit-eating grin imaginable plastered across his face.

"Wendell!" they all shouted.

"THAT. WAS. AWESOME!"

Wendell, his eyebrows singed off, yelled at the top of his lungs as he slid down the hillside on his rear end, spitting dirt with every syllable.

"You crazy torch head!" Tanner shouted, hugging him tightly. "I oughta kill you for scaring us like that!"

"Get us back to the *True North*, Yeun," Reed ordered.

"Aye, aye, Captain," Yeun replied, and cast off.

As they moved out into Dungarry Bay, a massive rumble deep within the earth rocked the boat. The Brigands felt it to their cores, more powerful than the crashing waves or gusting winds. Deep within the bowels of the compound, the fires had finally reached the armory, setting off millions of pounds of explosives and artillery all at once.

Set against the brilliant sunrise, they watched in horrified fascination as the island crumbled, collapsing in on itself. The towering spire of black rocks they had seen coming in—that Bonnie had seen in the vision—all toppled. *Like Jenga pieces,* Bonnie thought. Except this game had deadly consequences.

"The island that hate built, love has destroyed," Donovan murmured, equal parts regretful and relieved.

"I guess I won't need this," Wendell said. He was still holding the remote. The blinking green light flickered and died. "But I still get credit, right?" And he would indeed, in tales told around fires, for years to come.

So absorbed were the Brigands in witnessing the catastrophic destruction, only Bonnie noticed Cordial at the back of the boat. Cordial let out a startled gasp as she felt a jolt deep within.

Aglain. At his altar. Staring up at the sunrise, a beatific look on his face as the rock spires around him fell. Then BLACKNESS.

Cordial knew in that moment that the magic and force that was Aglain had been snuffed out, like a matchstick in a gale force wind. An emptiness crept in, and she knew that the world had just become a darker place.

"Aglain?" Bonnie asked. Cordial nodded, as a tear rolled down her cheek.

Bonnie looked over at the place where Crag Inish once stood, for centuries home to a beautiful monastery, and for millennia before that a druid temple. Both sites of reverence and love and peace, until the world changed and had no more use for such places. Now, all that remained was rubble. The mosaic—the angel, the scales, Heaven and Hell—that once adorned the walls lay shattered and scattered among the debris, its colorful tiles lost forever to the rising sea that was rushing in to consume it. A symbol of the battle of good versus evil buried with the past.

The mosaic was gone, but the fight it depicted was far from over. And in that fight, Bonnie Hartwright hoped she would find redemption.

Epilogue
The True North

Bonnie stood at the railing of the *True North* as it cut briskly through the waters of the Atlantic en route home. They had been at sea for three days now, and the sailing, as the saying went, had been smooth. Fair weather, calm seas, and prevailing winds that wouldn't quit.

With the arrival of the Spring Equinox, the days were getting longer. Light was finally triumphing over darkness. *At least for now*, Bonnie thought.

Bonnie marveled at how much had changed in mere weeks. She had started this journey feeling alone, burdened by a weight she thought was hers alone to carry. It had seeped into every corner of her being, darkening her vision and isolating her from her fellow Brigands—so that she had lost all sense of equilibrium.

She had become convinced that she needed to save her mother and avenge her father. That it was this family that was most important. She had lost sight of the fact that her true family, her Brigand family, was there the whole time... unconditionally... unwavering.

That's what family was, and it was a lesson she'd learned the hard way on Crag Inish.

That didn't mean she would give up on her mother. As a Brigand, it was her duty to rescue her from Jack Rackham.

Yes. Bonnie knew her mother was still alive—proof lay in her hands. In the burlap-wrapped object she now kept on her at all times in a small sling bag.

She unwrapped the rough cloth to reveal Calico Jack's twitching, undead hand and upon it, the ring which still glowed ominously. As long as the ring stayed on the hand, the revelatory power it possessed remained intact. Bonnie also knew that as long as the hourglass remained unfilled—the sands shifting imperceptibly but never diminishing—her mother still had time. And Bonnie had a dread suspicion as to why. For she knew that to get her mother back she would have to play into Jack's plan.

A BURST OF LAUGHTER startled Bonnie out of her thoughts. It had been so long since she'd heard it, it almost seemed foreign. She turned toward its source.

The Brigands were all gathered on deck, sailing and chattering, bathed in the light of the warm, setting sun. Wendell stood in the center of the group, animatedly recounting once again his narrow escape on Crag Inish.

"So there I was," Wendell's voice was full of dramatic flair, "walls crumbling, fire roaring down my neck! I'm dodging rocks, thinking, 'This is it, Wendell, you magnificent fool, you really bought the farm this time!' I mean, heating vents? What the hell? And then—BOOM!—the tunnel collapses, and I'm running for my life like I'm a freakin' Olympic sprinter!"

Wilder clutched his sides. "You're a lunatic, you know that?" he said, wiping away tears.

"That's Captain Lunatic to you!" Wendell shot back, bowing with a flourish.

MORE LAUGHTER filled the deck. It did Bonnie's heart good to hear it. Because in it, she thought she could hear the sound of healing.

"Bonnie! Come here!" It was Daya. "Check this out!"

Bonnie was surprised by the invitation. She had desperately wanted to rejoin her crew. But wasn't sure, after all her mistakes, they would have her back. That it was Daya who made the overture, made her heart squeeze with gratitude.

Bonnie went over and Reed scooched aside, making room for her at the railing between him and Wilder. A small gesture which told her he was also on the road to forgiving her. Cordial, who was on the other side of Reed, nodded to her. Bonnie nodded back.

Wendell continued, "So like I said, I'm running for my life! Which is something, cuz you know how I hate to run. Or sweat, which is weird since I love fire! Anyway! WHOOSH! The fireball completely takes off my eyebrows!"

"It's a good look for you!" Yeun said. "Maybe Tanner's dad can use you in his next movie!"

And everyone laughed. This time Bonnie laughed along with them, and found herself instinctively looking around for Luz, who used to relish moments like these. Then she remembered she wasn't there. Luz, whose belief in their mission had burned brighter than anyone's, who had given her life for it. And Bonnie's heart hurt all over again.

"Doubloon for your thoughts, Curls?" Wilder asked, his easy grin belying a hint of curiosity.

Bonnie leaned back against the railing, her expression thoughtful as she gazed at the white clouds. The sound of the waves seemed to mirror the tide of emotions swirling within her. After a pause, she began, her voice quiet but steady.

"Just thinking about the past," she said. "What we bring with us. What we leave behind. And what, if any of it, matters."

"I hear that. I don't have a clue about any of it myself," Cordial said from the other side of Reed. "But I do know when I get back, I probably owe my mom an apology."

"Just tell her you were out saving the world," Bonnie suggested. And Cordial lit up at the compliment.

They exchanged glances, each of them seeming to weigh Bonnie's words.

Saving the world. The battle was far from over. Bonnie tightened her grip on the ring and hand in her sling bag. Whether or not Brigid Byrne was her mother no longer mattered. Bonnie was a Brigand, her loyalty etched in stone in the caves of Cormac's Cove. Not as a Bonny. Not as a Rackham. But as a Read—a Brigand of the Compass Rose. Like her father. That was where her blood ran most true.

And now, the Brigands had something new in their battle against evil—something they thought had been lost forever.

Aglain had told them of it, just before his death, through Cordial's vision. A weapon.

A dirk.

And in that dirk, a way forward.

There was more laughter from the group as Daya drew eyebrows on Wendell. Bonnie watched the faces of her friends, happy.

No. It wasn't over. But for now, for this fleeting moment, there was peace—and hope.

And with that hope, a balance in her soul that hadn't been there for a long time. A feeling that things were finally starting to even out again. It would be quite a while before the weight of her actions would be lifted, if ever. But it was a beginning.

Just like spring.

About the Authors

Toni Runkle and Steve Webb have always loved telling stories. After becoming friends as students at the USC School of Cinema, they worked separately in movies and television before coming together to write novels for young readers. Their award-winning books have received wide acclaim.

When not writing, Toni loves scary movies, her garden, and the beach. Steve loves baseball, not-so-scary movies, and a good cheeseburger. Both writers are married (not to each other because that would get weird) and live in California with their respective families.

Don't miss Book One of
THE
PIRATE'S CURSE

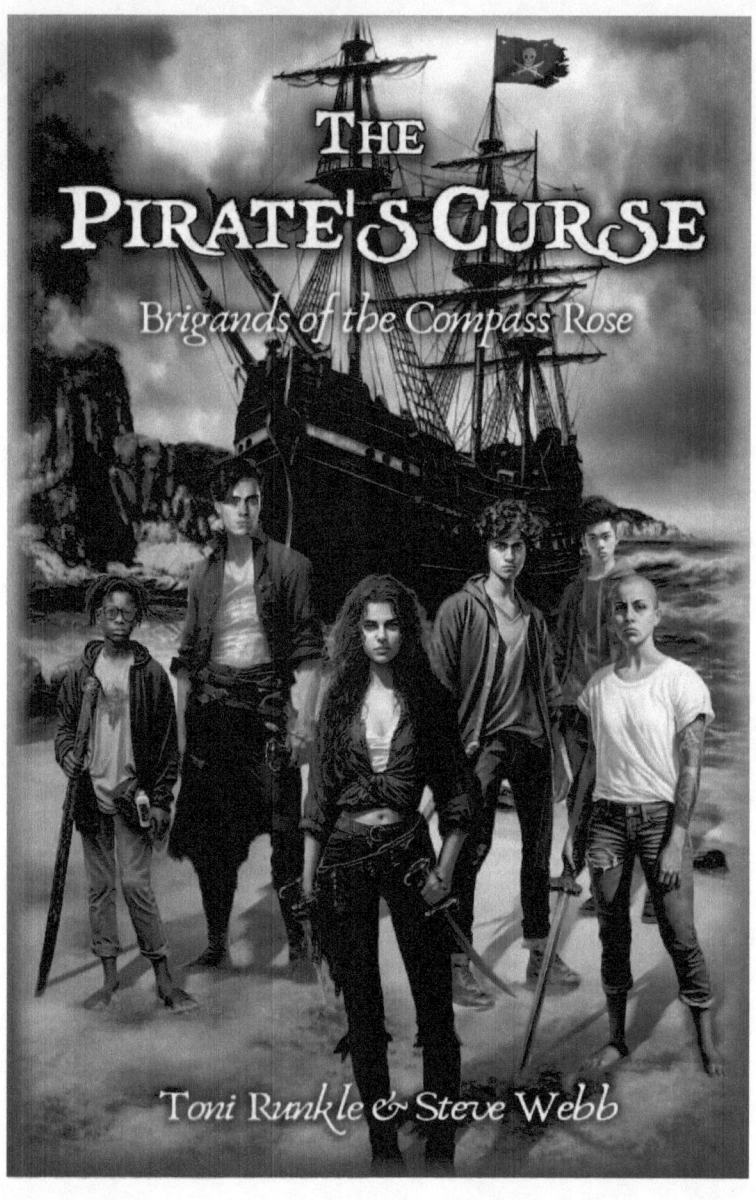

Note from Toni Runkle & Steve Webb

Word-of-mouth is crucial for any author to succeed. If you enjoyed *The Pirate's Curse: Weight of Souls*, please leave a review online—anywhere you are able. Even if it's just a sentence or two. It would make all the difference and would be very much appreciated.

Thanks!
Toni Runkle & Steve Webb

We hope you enjoyed reading this title from:

BLACK ROSE
writing™

www.blackrosewriting.com

Subscribe to our mailing list – *The Rosevine* – and receive FREE books, daily deals, and stay current with news about upcoming releases and our hottest authors.
Scan the QR code below to sign up.

Already a subscriber? Please accept a sincere thank you for being a fan of Black Rose Writing authors.

View other Black Rose Writing titles at www.blackrosewriting.com/books and use promo code PRINT to receive a 20% discount when purchasing.

www.ingramcontent.com/pod-product-compliance
Lightning Source LLC
Chambersburg PA
CBHW050615170726
48283CB00001B/250